The Alchemy Press Book Of
HORRORS

Anthologies from The Alchemy Press

Something Remains
Edited by Peter Coleborn & Pauline E Dungate

The Alchemy Press Book of Ancient Wonders
Edited by Jan Edwards & Jenny Barber

The Alchemy Press Book of Urban Mythic (volumes 1 and 2)
Edited by Jan Edwards & Jenny Barber

The Alchemy Press Book of Pulp Heroes (volumes 1, 2 and 3)
Edited by Mike Chinn

Swords Against the Millennium
Edited by Mike Chinn

Astrologica: Stories of the Zodiac
Edited by Allen Ashley

Kneeling in the Silver Light
Edited by Dean M Drinkel

Beneath the Ground
Edited by Joel Lane

The Alchemy Press Book Of
HORRORS

Edited by
Peter Coleborn
and Jan Edwards

Illustrated by Jim Pitts

The Alchemy Press

The Alchemy Press Book of Horrors
© Peter Coleborn and Jan Edwards 2018

Cover art © Peter Coleborn

Interior art © Jim Pitts 2018

The publication © The Alchemy Press 2018

Published by arrangement with the authors

First edition
ISBN 978-1-911034-05-6

All rights reserved. The moral rights of the authors and illustrators of this work have been asserted by them in accordance with the Copyright, Designs and Patents Act 1988

No part of this publication may be reproduced, stored in a retrieval system, or transmitted, in any form or by any means without permission of the publisher.

All characters in this book are fictitious and any resemblance to real persons is coincidental

Published by
The Alchemy Press, Staffordshire, UK

www.alchemypress.co.uk

CONTENTS

Ramsey Campbell: Some Kind of a Laugh	9
Storm Constantine: La Ténébreuse	27
Samantha Lee: The Worm	49
Stan Nicholls: Deadline	61
Marie O'Regan: Pretty Things	81
Gary McMahon: Guising	91
Peter Sutton: Masks	103
Debbie Bennett: The Fairest of them All	109
Mike Chinn: Her Favourite Place	129
Phil Sloman: The Girl with Three Eyes	145
Tina Rath: Little People	155
Madhvi Ramani: Teufelsberg	165
Jenny Barber: Down Along the Backroads	181
James Brogden: The Trade-up	191
Marion Pitman: The Apple Tree	203
Tony Richards: The Garbage Men	215
Stephen Laws: Get Worse Soon	235
Ralph Robert Moore: Peelers	261
Gail-Nina Anderson: An Eye for a Plastic Eye-ball	279
Keris McDonald: Remember	291
Adrian Cole: Broken Billy	303
Cate Gardner: The Fullness of Her Belly	323
Suzanne Barbieri: In the Rough	335
Ray Cluley: Bluey	347
John Grant: Too Late	367
Author Notes	383

ACKNOWLEDGEMENTS

"An Eye for a Plastic Eye-ball" © Gail-Nina Anderson 2018
"Down Along the Backroads" © Jenny Barber 2018
"In the Rough" © Suzanne Barbieri 2018
"The Fairest of them All" © Debbie Bennett 2018
"The Trade-up" © James Brogden 2018
"Some Kind of a Laugh" © Ramsey Campbell 2018
"Her Favourite Place" © Mike Chinn 2018
"Bluey" © Ray Cluley 2018
"Broken Billy" © Adrian Cole 2018
"La Ténébreuse " © Storm Constantine 2018
"The Fullness of Her Belly" © Cate Gardner 2018
"Too Late" © John Grant 2018
"Get Worse Soon" © Stephen Laws 2018
"The Worm" © Samantha Lee 2018
"Remember" © Keris McDonald 2018
"Guising" © Gary McMahon 2018
"Peelers" © Ralph Robert Moore 2018
"Deadline" © Stan Nicholls 2018
"Pretty Things" © Marie O'Regan 2018
"The Apple Tree" © Marion Pitman 2018
"Little People" © Tina Rath 2018
"Teufelsberg" © Madhvi Ramani 2018
"The Garbage Men" © Tony Richards 2018
"The Girl with Three Eyes" © Phil Sloman 2018
"Masks" © Peter Sutton 2018

Interior artwork © Jim Pitts 2018

"Why should not a writer be permitted to make use of the levers of fear, terror and horror because some feeble soul here and there finds it more than it can bear? Shall there be no strong meat at table because there happen to be some guests there whose stomachs are weak, or who have spoiled their own digestions?"

— E T A Hoffmann

SOME KIND OF A LAUGH

Ramsey Campbell

"Has anybody ever told you that you look just like—"

"Yes."

The diner frowned over the tasselled tome of a menu at Bernard. "Nothing wrong with looking like you're famous."

"I'd rather just look like myself. Have you all decided?"

"Have you got five minutes?" As everybody at the table laughed the man said "That's what your double always says."

"I'm sure nobody wants to hear it from me."

This earned a token laugh like a description of mirth. "I'll have the black pudding and marmalade to start," the man said.

His companions began with Thai cuisine and Cajun and Italian, and the main courses ranged even further. After all, the Bestrow Bistro's slogan was Tastes For Every Taste. As Bernard returned from conveying the order to the kitchen, Xavier beckoned to him. "So what was the issue there?" the manager said almost too low to be heard.

He was at the far end of the long black room, beside a mirror that belonged in a chateau. One hand was grasping his broad chin as if his plump ruthlessly jovial face were a carnival mask, and the mirror put on the same show. "I wouldn't say there was one," Bernard murmured. "Just a bit of banter."

"Not much of it from you, was there? We're here to welcome customers, Bernard. As the chappie said, it can't hurt if you remind them of someone they like."

"I never cared for him myself."

"A lot of people like Len Binn. You could be an attraction."

This left Bernard feeling less than himself, driven to enact someone else's script, but when the jokey diner asked for the bill Bernard attempted Binn's accent, a Lancashire twang as flat as a cap. "Have you got five minutes?"

"We haven't, no. We've a train to catch."

He had time to peer so hard at the service charge that Bernard came close to protesting it went to the manager. Once the party had departed Xavier watched Bernard clear the table. "Keep it up and you'll get it right," he said, which Bernard didn't immediately grasp meant his impersonation of Len Binn. At least none of the other diners drew attention to the resemblance, and when the last of them had gone he was able to feel some relief. He and his colleagues cleared up until Xavier betrayed some satisfaction, and then Bernard drove home.

He and Laura lived off the motorway, which had left half of their street standing. As he clambered out of the tilted Mini, having found a space among the cars with two wheels on the pavement, he saw the front room of the small thin house flickering like a film. He was letting himself in through the shallow plastic porch when he heard a voice he'd hoped was no longer part of his life. "Have you done?" Len Binn said.

It was another phrase the comedian had made his own. Bernard had the absurd notion that Laura was being somehow unfaithful to him. When he tramped into the front room she looked up as though her ready smile and eagerly raised eyebrows were lifting her roundish face. "I was only watching while you were out," she said, "but look, this might make you laugh."

She'd recorded an episode of *In the Binn*, and now she ran it back to the beginning of a sketch in which the comic played a waiter. "Have you done?" he asked a tableful of diners, a question apparently worth a burst of laughter and applause from the audience, unless the response was prompted by his lugubrious elongated face, where the nose and jaw appeared to be contending for prominence. When he set about clearing the table the diners insisted on helping him, piling dishes and utensils on top of the plate he'd picked up. Once the entire contents of the table were heaped under his chin he staggered through the crowded restaurant in an elaborate perilous ballet, executing desperate pirouettes that nearly sent him sprawling on his back while he struggled to balance his burden. Laura laughed almost as hard as the audience, glancing at Bernard to encourage him to join in. At last Binn managed to deliver the ungainly stack intact to the kitchen and returned to the table with the bill. "We haven't given you a tip," the recipient said, and when Binn looked gloomily expectant "Don't jump off a boat if you can't swim."

Having groaned with delight, Laura said wistfully "I thought you might like him being like you."

"That's nothing like me. Nothing whatsoever."

"I just meant playing a waiter. Why do you dislike him so much?"

"They used to say I looked like him at school when the shows were first on."

"I expect you must have even then."

"They didn't just say it, they imitated him around me. The more they saw it bothered me, the more they did it. I ended up dreaming about him. I thought I'd never get him out of my head, and it's all being brought back."

Laura had paused the recording, but now she switched the television off. "I didn't mean to."

"I wasn't saying you did it. I'm saying now the television is showing his old stuff more people are going to know him."

"It can't do you any harm at your age, can it?" When Bernard stayed as silent as the television she murmured "Come to bed."

This was often their way of resolving an argument or salvaging an unsatisfactory day, but tonight it didn't work for him. Well after Laura was asleep he lay with an arm around her soft waist, remembering a Len Binn sketch. The comedian had emitted at least a minute's worth of inventive snores before his wife elbowed him awake, and then his attempts to get comfortable contorted him into increasingly unlikely shapes, several of which tumbled him out of bed. When he dozed off hours later his wife immediately woke him to enquire how his night had been. "Have you got five minutes?" He said that whatever he was asked: for directions in the street, or if he wanted sugar in his coffee, or his name... As Bernard began to fear he might grow as restless as Binn had, the repeated question put him to sleep.

A kiss almost wakened him before Laura left for work. Sometimes her hours at the library coincided with his at the bistro, but not this week. At least they both had jobs. He arrived at the restaurant to find Xavier looking more resolutely jolly than ever. "You've a chance to see your friend in the flesh," the manager said.

Bernard had to hope he didn't know "Which friend?"

"The one you want to be more like. Len Binn. He's appearing live not far from here. Maybe you could pick some tips up."

"More than I do in here, you mean."

"That's the sort of thing he'd say. You're getting better at it."

Xavier produced his phone to demonstrate that Binn was starting his first tour for years at a theatre twenty miles away in Lancashire. Before Bernard could react to this or to Xavier's unwelcome remark, the first lunchtime customers came in. "I'm Bernard and I'll be looking after you today," he said.

"Not Len," one of the female couple said. "Not Len Binn."

"Very much not. Where did you get that idea?"

"Our friends told us we might find him in here," her companion said.

Bernard took their order, only to encounter Xavier outside the kitchen. "I'm not joking, Bernard. Whatever people want, it's your job to provide it if you're capable. You just heard why they came."

Bernard saw his colleagues avoid looking at him while making sure they overheard - temporary, both of them, and younger than him. The manager loitered within earshot when Bernard welcomed his next customers. "I'm Bernard and I'll be looking after you today," Bernard said and felt compelled to flatten his accent. "How've you bin?"

"Perfectly fine," a young businessman said and stared at him.

Presumably he didn't recognise Len Binn's invariable greeting to his audience, unless he found it inappropriate. "Sounds as if you haven't got it quite right yet," Xavier accosted him to mutter.

At home Bernard found Laura watching television - not Len Binn, though he wondered if she'd just switched off a recording. As she turned off a documentary about homelessness he said "Your favourite man's at large again."

"If you mean Len Binn he's not my favourite. You are."

"You knew who I meant, though. He's live in Mostyn on Saturday."

"I'm sure you won't be going even if it is your day off. I won't either."

In the hope she'd had enough of the comedian Bernard said "Why's that?"

"I mightn't like to see how he looks now. Those shows are thirty years old, remember."

That night in bed Bernard put himself to sleep by mutely counting all the seconds in five minutes, though he had to repeat it more than once. In the morning he used his phone to search for images of Len Binn. There were posters and photographs, quite a few almost illegibly autographed, but none more recent than the resurrected television shows. By the time the week was done with him Bernard felt desperate to resolve the situation - one diner asked him if he had five minutes, and he was sure that others expected him to ask as much as Xavier did. "Laura, are you sure you don't want to come and see Binn?"

"I'd rather see you. Don't say you're going."

"Xavier's decided I'm a draw. He's been trying to make me talk like the man."

Some Kind of a Laugh — - 13 -

"That's very committed of you, Bernard. If it helps you keep your job—"

"I won't be there to study him. I'll be snapping how he looks now, and thanks for making me think of it. Maybe when I've got pictures to show them, people won't be so eager to confuse me with him."

For longer than a moment Laura looked about to say a good deal more than "Come to bed."

Five minutes and five more and five again sent him to sleep, but it felt like delaying his encounter with Binn. All of Saturday did until he drove to Mostyn, a precipitous town on both sides of a valley. The Grand Theatre stood on a street like a giant stair, but had plainly once been grander. A cigarette butt sodden with at least one rainstorm protruded from a crack in the marble steps beneath a rusty stained-glass awning. Old posters adorned the faded lobby, and one showed Len Binn decades younger than Bernard. The manager, a perspiring fellow whose bow tie hung askew, was talking to a friend. "Don't expect too much," he said and looked away from Bernard, having blinked at him.

Bernard showed an usher the ticket on his phone, which felt close to anachronistic. The seats weren't numbered or reserved, and he tramped down a slope of stained frayed carpet to the front row. Soon nearly all the seats were occupied, and then the audience had a chance to talk - in fact, the blur of conversations carried on well past the time the show should have begun. Bernard thought the house lights were dimming more than once before they did. Eventually they flickered and expired, and the curtains stirred. A hand was fumbling the ponderous material apart, so tentatively that its owner might have lost his way, unless he was unequal to the task. At last a figure disentangled himself with a lurch, scowling at the curtains and then at the darkened auditorium. "Have you got five minutes?" he said.

This seemed not to be addressed to anyone in particular - it sounded like recalling what he used to ask - but it roused applause and laughter. Bernard felt as if he were looking at a waxwork of Len Binn rather than the man himself. The long face and large hands were unnaturally smooth and colourful, while the footlights lent them an oily shine. The extravagantly striped suit was at least a size too big, and made Binn look depleted by age. He waited for the last clap to carry off the final laugh before he said "How've you bin?"

This renewed the mirth, but Bernard thought the performer could have been referring to himself. He looked not so much waxy as embalmed, and Bernard sneaked his phone out to capture his appearance, having surreptitiously turned off the flash and the sound. Binn was telling jokes now, occasionally a new one – "Pontius Pilate says to Jesus, can you stop moving Easter about? We need to get you nailed down" – but mostly so familiar they felt like reminiscences, all too evocative of Bernard's childhood. He was glad when the curtains parted to reveal a double bed, which brought the routine to an end.

The lighting was so dim that he didn't immediately realise the figure lying in the bed was made of rubber. Once Binn joined it, the quilt couldn't hide how he had to manipulate its arm to make it interrupt his snoring. As he writhed in search of sleep he seemed bent on growing as bendy as his bedmate, but whenever he sprawled out of bed he looked hardly capable of clambering back. How much of this was an act? At last he returned to the footlights, meeting a wave of applause that Bernard thought could be acclaiming his stamina. The curtains faltered shut while he told more resuscitated jokes, and eventually dragged apart again. Four diners were seated at a table, and Binn shambled over to serve them.

Was this a new routine or one Bernard had forgotten watching? Binn tried to store all the orders in his head, only to plead repeatedly "Can we start again?" At last he fled towards an imaginary kitchen, plunging the stage into darkness that emitted a series of clatters and clanks. When the light faltered back it found the table full of the remains of dinner. "Have you done?" Binn enquired and set about clearing the table, relentlessly helped by the diners. He tottered back and forth across the stage in a dogged ballet, blinded by plates and utensils piled up to his forehead. The first knife he dropped Bernard took for a joke.

A plate and the utensils on it seemed less of one. Binn floundered about the stage, adopting a pronounced backwards tilt in a desperate attempt to balance his burden, but plate after plate toppled off the heap. The diners appeared to be paralysed by watching him. Long before the last dish shattered the laughter of the audience began to die away, not that Bernard had joined in. Binn flung the last plate down in a mime of resignation and lurched to the footlights. "Anybody out there?" he called. "All gone home?"

This dislodged a titter from the silence, though a nervous one. "Where am I?" Binn demanded. "Where's the nurse? Where's me medication?" Perhaps his increasingly flat accent was meant to identify all this as a joke. Bernard thought he should film the performance, and he was reaching for his phone when the movement caught Binn's eye. The comedian peered at him and reached a shaky hand across the footlights. "Is that me?"

As Bernard's neighbours glanced at him Bernard retorted "It absolutely isn't, no."

"By gum, if it's not it should be," Binn declared and leaned between the footlights as if to clear his vision. He was raising his hands beside his eyes when he lost his balance. "Hey," he protested, earning his biggest laugh for minutes. He appeared to be essaying a somersault, and a woman cried "Wow." However intentional they were, his acrobatics failed him. All his weight landed on the back of his head with a resounding thud and a snap that included a crunch.

Since his agonised grimace was upside down, he appeared to be grinning at Bernard. Quite a few of the spectators began to laugh and applaud until a woman on the front row added a scream. Someone else called "I'm a nurse" and hurried to examine Binn. She closed his outraged eyes before straightening up to say "I'm afraid that's the end."

This was surely everybody's cue to leave, and Bernard couldn't bear the sight any longer. Now that Binn's sagging eyelids hid his eyes the parody of a grin looked secretive, portending worse. As Bernard hurried to the exit, several people rather more than glanced at him. At the end of the aisle he came face to face with the theatre manager, whose stare looked resolved to halt him. "It was none of my doing," Bernard blurted. "It wasn't me."

The stare grew more accusing still. "Aren't you his son?"

"I should say not. Fenton's my name, Bernard Fenton. We aren't related in any way at all," Bernard said and dodged around the manager to struggle through the crowd.

The sight of Binn's dead face wasn't left behind so easily. As it lingered in Bernard's mind it twisted into a clown's contradictory grimace, threatening to blot out his route while he drove home. It was waiting for him in bed, where Laura lay asleep. He took care not to waken her as he turned in search of slumber. Whichever way he faced, the contorted features were in front of him. When at last he slept he had the impression that Laura nudged him more than once, almost waking him.

She was out when he came back to himself in the morning. At least Binn's face had gone too, and Bernard shared a grin at length in the bathroom mirror. He felt eager to be at the restaurant - to establish that they'd done with Binn. He was sitting in his car and had turned the key in the ignition when a voice said "How've you bin?"

It was on the radio, which he must have neglected to switch off, though he couldn't recall listening to it on the way home. A news bulletin was celebrating Len Binn's life with clips of him. Binn had been his stage name, but Bernard wanted to hear no more of him. He tuned the radio to a music station, which regaled him with "Send in the Clowns" as he drove to work.

Xavier was checking levels in the bottles that hung their heads behind the bar. "Ready for your routine?" he said.

"Which one is that?"

"The show you're putting on, Bernard, or can I call you Len? The one that's bringing customers."

"I take it you've not heard, but last night—"

"Your man lived up to himself right to the end with a bit of slapstick. He's all over the media, and that's publicity for us when we're offering our version of him."

"You don't think that would be tasteless."

"I think it's as tasteful as everything we do."

"I was there," Bernard said in desperation. "I know what he was like."

"Well, don't go showing anybody how he went. That really would be tasteless, but I'm glad you took the chance to study him."

"I mean I saw how decrepit he was." Bernard took out his phone and brought up the photographs. "I don't believe our customers would want to think anyone like this was serving them."

Xavier didn't speak until he'd finished skimming through the images. "No doubt of it, you're the comedian."

"I don't know what you mean."

"Except jokes aren't that good if you need to explain them. I'm not sure what you had in mind with this one."

Bernard made to speak as he retrieved the phone, and then his mouth stayed open. Somehow he'd reversed the camera last night, and every photograph he'd taken at the Grand was of himself. He bore a grin in all of them, though surely only because he'd thought he was photographing Binn unnoticed. "I never meant to do this," he protested.

"Let's hope you're more skilful at your job." As a party of diners came in Xavier muttered "Take them."

"I'm Bernard and I'll be looking after you today."

The four women scrutinised his face, and one of them apparently spoke for all. "Aren't you going to be Len Binn? Our friends you served the other day said you would."

"Forgive me, but you ought to know he died last night."

"We do," another woman said. "We thought you'd be putting on a tribute."

Xavier sent Bernard a look that urged him to comply, and Bernard gave in. "How've you bin?" he said, which gained him a surge of applause. Maintaining the flat voice was more of a distraction than he expected, so that halfway through taking the order he had to say "Can we start again?" This was appreciated too, and when he emerged from the kitchen Xavier detained him. "That's the ticket. Keep it up and I'll tell you what, we'll split your gratuities."

Bernard saw this didn't please the other waiters, who seemed unamused by his performance. He was doing more than them to earn the extra, and perhaps eventually he could take home as much as Laura did. "How've you bin?" he said to every diner he greeted, even those who appeared to find it odd. When anybody asked to order he said "Have you got five minutes?" This didn't always go down well, and before long Xavier took him aside. "Just do your routine for people who get it. It'd be a joke if it lost us any business."

How much direction would Len Binn have had to suffer? Bernard thought it might have been none at all. At least he had nearly eighty pounds in tips by the time he left the bistro. He would have given Laura the good news if she hadn't been waiting to say "Did you see him last night, Bernard?"

"I had the best seat. I was as close as I am to you."

"What did he turn out to be like?"

"Worn out, I'd say." Bernard reached for his phone but remembered just in time he would be showing Laura his own face. "Not up to putting on the show he was supposed to," he said.

"That should help you to forget about him, should it?" As if she'd been insensitive Laura said "Was it very bad, what happened?"

"A lot of people seemed to think it was his last joke. Let's go along with them."

Did she find him insensitive now? He was only trying to think as positively as she appeared to want if not to need. He wasn't going to be made to feel responsible for Binn's last pratfall. He was anticipating a good night's sleep, which he might have achieved if Laura hadn't kept waking him. He presumed he'd been snoring, and turned away from her, but his contortions failed to placate her. "Have you done?" he muttered on receiving yet another nudge, at which point she subsided, or his awareness did.

Perhaps lack of sleep left him unable to judge how long he spent at the bathroom mirror. There was no need to imagine he was in a dressing-room before a performance. Greeting Xavier was sufficient preparation, and Bernard said "How've you bin?"

"That's the spirit. The grin helps as well."

Bernard met all his diners with the phrase and had no

sense it was unwelcome. Some of them recognised it, and he concentrated his act on them. When they asked to order, what else could he say except "Have you got five minutes?" Most of them saw the joke. Of course he didn't keep them waiting that long, and he was pleased with his routine until he had to return to a table, having found the order less than legible. "Can we start again?" he said, which his accent did its best to turn into a joke.

At least he wasn't called upon to struggle with used plates and utensils, since nobody handed him any. Just the same, he headed home with some relief, which lasted until Laura greeted him by protesting "You didn't have to get rid of him."

"Who says I did? I was nowhere near him."

"His shows, Bernard."

"I didn't stop those either. He did by not looking where he was."

"The ones I recorded. They're all gone."

"That wasn't me." He was sure he hadn't been in the front room last night or this morning – in fact, he couldn't recollect doing anything at all. "You can't think I'd be that mean or that bothered either," he said. "It's a joke."

"Maybe I don't need them when I have the real thing."

He failed to notice her placatory tone until he'd demanded "What are you saying?"

"I don't need another man when I've got you."

Did she fancy he was jealous? That was a laugh, and he made a bid to come up with one before having recourse to their catch phrase in the hope that it would render dialogue superfluous. "Come to bed."

He waited to be certain Laura was asleep, and then continued lying absolutely still, even once his arm around her waist began to lose its circulation, making her body feel more like rubber. He mustn't start writhing in search of sleep, or he might end up adopting postures that no doubt anybody watching would find comical. Though he was unaware of snoring, he came to himself with his mouth open wide enough to let out several words. A poke in the ribs had roused him, and when Laura elbowed him once more he turned his back. As he clung with both hands to the edge of the mattress he felt he was preserving not just his posture but his sense of self.

His own words found him in a tortuous tangle of bedclothes. What had he said to rouse himself? Surely not a question about time. He couldn't ask Laura, who had already left for work. In the bathroom his reflection looked fiercely lit, as if the mirror was edged with lights. He mustn't feel compelled to rehearse, and he turned away before his grin could grow wide enough to hurt his face. How long did Xavier intend him to keep up the impression? The requirement had started to feel like a threat, and so did work.

Xavier was standing in the doorway of the bistro like a theatre manager waiting to welcome an audience. The first diners of the day gazed at Bernard with a version of delight, and the fattest man said "Have you got five minutes?"

"He's got those for you and more," Xavier said and told Bernard "There's your cue. You're on."

As Bernard ushered the party to a table he made himself ask "How've you bin?" and tried to feel complimented when the best-fed fellow said "Sounds just like he looks." The party even seemed amused when some of Bernard's scrawl on the pad forced him to say "Can we start again?" He delivered the order to the kitchen, only for the chef to emerge in search of Xavier. Once they'd finished muttering, the manager beckoned to Bernard. "No need to overdo your act. It's a good job chef remembered what you read out."

"I don't know what you're saying."

Xavier flourished the slip Bernard had taken to the kitchen. "No call to go this far. You needn't be this much like him."

Bernard stared at the scribbled chit. It wasn't merely hard to read; it wasn't in his handwriting. If it hadn't been the only order so far he might have accused someone of confusing his with another, but found himself saying "How much like?"

"Don't pretend. Damn well just like this."

Xavier brought images up on his phone – photographs and posters of Len Binn. Several were autographed, and there was no mistaking the resemblance to the writing on the slip. "Just do your voice and your words," Xavier said. "They're what your fans are here for."

Bernard felt desperate to be called by name. Of course he'd seen Binn's writing when he'd searched for images of him, but he would never have expected it to lodge so deep in his mind. He stayed clear of the diners until Xavier indicated they wanted him. "Have you done?" he couldn't avoid saying, and at once was afraid they meant to help him load the tray. "Al tek them," he said despite not knowing if Binn ever had.

Even loading the tray without anybody's help made him nervous, and he felt relieved not to be offered a tip in case it proved to be a prank. He needed a break from performing – an interval – and he held the door open to speed the diners onwards, only for another party to troop in. "Why, it's you," their leader said. "We discovered you the other day. We've been sending you our friends."

He was indeed the culprit – the diner who'd first drawn attention to Bernard's face. "You're very welcome," Xavier said as if they'd thanked him. "No prize for knowing who'll be serving you today."

As Bernard led the party to a table he felt as if he was trying to leave them behind. He passed out menus, realising too late that he'd failed to name himself. He refrained from asking for five minutes and strove to write legibly, but eventually had to plead "Can we start again?" He didn't simply read the order to the chef but ran his finger underneath the words in the hope that doing so would leave them comprehensible. All this was an uneasy preamble to having to ask at the end of the meal "Have you done?"

"All yours," the man responsible for his performance said.

This sounded like a threat posing as a joke. Bernard balanced the tray on his left hand and set about loading plates. His hands were fully occupied when the man passed him a plate strewn with utensils. "Don't," Bernard said in the flattest accent he could summon, which might simply have turned it into a joke. "Leave it," he cried so flatly that it sounded like an exhortation to live. He tried to fend off the plate before it could overbalance the tray, which he immediately dropped.

One corner struck the edge of a plate, flipping it over the tray to spill its contents into a woman's lap. Meanwhile Bernard dealt the man's plate such a shove that a fork flew off it, clawing the man's wrist. The plate fell out of his hand and knocked over a glass of red wine, splashing one of his companions as crimson as a murder victim. "I'm sorry," Bernard tried to say, but the last word disintegrated into laughter. "I'm," he said, "I'm," with diminishing success. He was close to howling before Xavier captured his attention. "That's it, Bernard. Get out and don't come back till you've heard from me."

Bernard stared into his face, which Xavier was clutching like a dramatic mask. The sight and the rebukes sobered him enough to let him say "At least you've remembered my name."

"Whatever it is, just take yourself home."

Surely there was a phrase to fit the situation - indeed, some phrases went with a variety of developments. Bernard turned back to the diners and had to struggle not to giggle at their bedraggled bids to clean themselves up. "Can we start again?" he said with a flatness meant to control his mirth.

"You're finished here, Bernard," Xavier said. "That's the end."

Of course every performance must have one. Bernard might have liked to find a better exit line, but his catch phrase would do. He drove home as best he could for laughing, and had to stop the car more than once to let his hilarity subside. It had by the time he heard Laura switch the television off. She looked taken aback, surely not because she'd been keeping company with anyone Bernard wouldn't welcome. "What are you doing home so early?" she said, and hastily "Not that I'm not glad to see you."

"Who are you glad to see?" Surely he needn't make her say his name, and he said "Don't worry, I know."

For some reason she had to decide what to say next. "So why are you back?"

"He had an accident at work."

"Who did?"

"Him." When she made to speak he said "I've already told you not to worry. It'll all be cleared up by tomorrow." This fell short of reassuring her, but he knew the phrase that always saved the situation. "Come to bed."

As he brushed his teeth the light that framed the mirror seemed to close around his face, squeezing out more of a grin. He kept that up while he climbed into bed but tried to reduce it, seeing that it disconcerted Laura. He caressed her as he always did, and couldn't help observing that it had become a routine, the physical equivalent of a catch phrase. He tried varying his posture, but the more he attempted to invent, the less appealing his wife seemed to find him. He'd begun to feel grotesque, more like a puppet than a performer, by the time Laura said "What are you trying to do? It isn't funny, Bernard."

At least it had made her say his name. He sprawled off her to lie on his back. "Have you done?" he didn't really need to ask. "Then we'll get some sleep."

"Don't you want dinner?"

"I've had enough of dining for one day. I need my sleep now. You could do with some as well. You seem on edge."

If she'd said she wanted to watch television, he didn't know how he might have reacted. He clasped her waist and imagined for a moment she was making to escape. "Can we start again?" he murmured, but since Laura didn't respond he presumed she had fallen asleep as readily as usual. He oughtn't to resent that even if he lacked the knack. "Keep quiet," he muttered, lowering his voice when Laura stirred uneasily. "Keep still."

At some point this allowed him to sleep. When he wakened it was daytime, and he was alone in a confusion of bedclothes. He'd contorted himself in the night after all. It made him feel robbed of control, and had it driven Laura out of the house? He was so grateful to find her in the kitchen that his grin brought an ache to his face. "How've you bin?"

Apparently she didn't recognise this as a question. "Will you have something?" she said.

"Why wouldn't I? I could eat for two, the way I feel." If he oughtn't to have said that, he would like to know why. He wished they had children as much as Laura did – they would be somebody for him to entertain – but he'd failed at that performance. A sense of his uselessness made him say "Let me help."

He regretted this at once. A loaf was waiting on the breadboard to be sliced, but Laura had to hand him the knife. He couldn't help wincing at the sight of the serrated blade resting on her palm – couldn't help remembering the dropped tray, the toppled glass, the explosion of red. "Don't give me that," he said, but perhaps it sounded like a catch phrase, especially in that voice. Repeating the words didn't stop him clutching at the handle of the knife. He drove to work determined to make up for whatever he'd done, but Xavier refused to unlock the door. "I'll send you what you're owed," the manager told him through the glass. "It won't be much."

Bernard couldn't go home with so little. He found he was uneasy about returning home at all. He'd seen enough street entertainers to know how to proceed. He retrieved an empty carton from a bin behind the bistro and stood beside it near the entrance. Whenever anybody glanced at him he said "How've you bin?" or "Have you got five minutes?" Even once he emptied all his change into the carton, nobody contributed. The occasional passer-by loitered to stare at him, and perhaps he shouldn't have responded "Have you done?" but calling after them "Can we start again?" didn't bring them back. At last a spectator lingered to address him. "Let him rest," she said. "You're nothing like him."

LA TÉNÉBREUSE

Storm Constantine

I DREAMED OF the house before we visited it, but dreams are rarely very accurate. I was sauntering up a red-pebbled driveway towards a yellow building which looked two-dimensional to me, like a cut-out. It reared backwards, so that the perspective narrowed its roofs, its peering upper windows. The bones of a dead clematis clutched the flaking paint and cowering within this fibrous frame was a pair of wooden doors that were also reddish in colour. As I approached, the doors swooned inwards and there was only blackness beyond. I felt wary yet not afraid. Perceiving a light within the darkness, I stepped onto the threshold, and realised that ahead of me was an open door through which poured molten daylight. Only a vast unseen chamber lay between me and the light. I could feel the space even if I could not see it. I extended one foot into the house and the darkness hugged my bare lower leg. I felt somehow ... *chewed*.

That was all, at first.

Vezi is one of my oldest friends. He annoys me greatly — always has — because of the puppy-like wincing he's given to and the mournful expressions. I told him he should be a poet, behaving like that, but he's not creative at all. Anyway, despite his flaws, I suppose I love him as one loves a sibling —

there's always an element of despising in such relationships I think.

A young man with the unlikely name of Nimrod Queneau had invited Vezi to spend some summer weeks at *Le Nid des Rêves*, his parents' country house in southwestern France. A nest of dreams: intriguing. Vezi asked me to go with him as he knows my tastes and felt I'd find artistic inspiration in the old place – perhaps commissions too. He insisted he'd pay for the trip. I thanked him for his thoughtfulness, aware there was no doubt an ulterior motive – as in he was scared of going alone. I'm frequently called upon as "muscle" for Vezi, a backup staring meaningfully over his shoulder at would-be trouble-makers, even if that's only his mulish cat-sitter. But ... free holiday. I'd be delighted to go. Of course.

We were both living in London at the time, in our late twenties and each – in our own particular way – eager for adventure. For Vezi, I was quite sure this would involve the finding of "true love". (He'd never accept my advice that this scabrous emotion was not real and all to do with chemicals, part of DNA's survival mechanism, with no morals or sense.) You see, poor pup, he had a poet's heart in an engineer's body. Cruel. As for me, all I wanted was to stumble upon things strange and unexpected. This only required being open to the possibility. If it frightened Vezi, all to the good as this might enhance the experience.

TRAVELLING ON A train through rural France and the bleaching light of what I call "the child's summer" (i.e. endless perfect sunlight in memory that rarely actually happened), I asked Vezi about the quirkily named Nimrod.

"We were at university together," he said. "Everyone loved him."

But particularly you, I thought.

"He was ... beautiful," Vezi continued, looking poetically pained.

Ah the thorns of unrequited love, desiccated into obscurity but now already reviving with the faintest drop of water; they scraped once more at his heart.

"Don't worry Vez," I said cheerily, "it was years ago. He's

probably started to get fat and lose his hair"

"You're not always right," Vezi snapped. "He might be the same – or better."

I sincerely hoped not. Another of Vezi's annoyances was that he aimed to find romance with people who would instinctively despise him – people like me I suppose, although not as tolerant and without the shared history. Inevitably, I was the sin-eater of his tragic romances and by now had automatic responses, which I knew would soothe him but meant I could be thinking about something else while he poured out his woes.

THE HOUSE STOOD on a hill at the apex of a long driveway lined by poplars. I was not surprised to find it painted yellow but that was where similarities with my dream ended. Many houses in the area were that colour. Also, there was no dead clematis clinging to the walls and the doors were painted a glossy black. There were turrets too, one to east and west, and the house in my dream had been square. This was not an immense chateau long abandoned by aristocrats who were now headless ghosts – it was rather more a glorified farmhouse, the abode of a successful land-owner.

Vezi and I were disgorged by our taxi – ancient, creaking, in keeping with the theme of our story – in the sweep of driveway before the house. But where I'd hoped for further eeriness in the edifice before me I found instead evidence of cosy domesticity. Windows were flung open on all of its storeys, and I saw vases of fresh flowers on the sills of several of them. The drive was well kept, and stunted bay trees in pots were arranged with apparently obsessive precision along the house's frontage. The place was neither creepy nor run-down. I found this rather disappointing, but the adventure was new so I wasn't ready to give up hope.

We approached the doors, at the head of three wide worn steps, and Vezi used the door-knocker. This furniture was of iron in the shape of a gargoyle, and I approved of it. We could hear the knock echo within the house quite ponderously.

"*That* will wake the dead," I whispered, grinning at Vezi.

He grinned back.

We heard no footsteps approach but presently one of the doors was opened by a beautifully peculiar creature. She stood well over six foot in height and wore a tailored black trouser suit with a startlingly white shirt. Her hair hung to her shoulders, thick, and cut severely straight, like an ancient Egyptian wig. Her milk-pale face was sculptured and bony – handsome you'd call it – and marred only by one thing: her nostrils. The nose was long, perhaps slightly too much, but well-shaped. The flared nostrils, however, were inordinately large, so much so the appendage didn't really look like a nose but more like some alien organ that served functions in addition to smelling. Such a deformity might make a person shy or awkward around others, or even hostile and defensive, but this individual appeared unaware of her difference. She smiled at us and said in English "You must be Vezi Torres and er ... Ms...?"

"Just Alex," I said and stepped past Vezi into the house.

The hall was panelled in wood the colour of dark honey, and sunlight fell in through a round stained-glass window high up over the door. The hall itself was the height of two storeys. A graceful oak stair swept seductively up to the second floor, like a beautiful woman in a ball gown with a train. The warmth in the chamber seemed to hum; this felt very welcoming. "What a lovely house," I said.

"Yes," said the woman. "I'm Posy Sala, the housekeeper for the family."

Posy? I had to stifle amusement. I had never met anyone less suited to such a name. I couldn't place her accent. Eastern European perhaps? But then ... maybe not. Certainly not French anyway.

"M Queneau sends his apologies he was unable to be here to greet you. So please spend some time settling in. I'll show you your rooms then perhaps you'd like refreshment." Posy indicated the stairs. We followed her up them.

Our rooms were situated next to one another on the first floor at the back of the house. Vezi bustled into his and shut the door on me, no doubt to undergo rituals of preparation before meeting again with Nimrod. I went into my room but left the door ajar. Through the open window, which reached down to the wainscot, I could see neat gardens that descended in terraces to woodland, and beyond that - it seemed - into primal landscape untouched by humanity. If only. My room was comfortable but disappointingly like one you'd find in a decent hotel - no brooding heavy furniture, no canopied bed, nor even a creepy ancestral portrait on the wall that would monitor my movements across the thickly carpeted floor.

I flopped onto the bed and lay on my back with arms outflung, staring at the cream-painted ceiling. Sounds from outside were few: birdsong and a kind of subliminal roar in the landscape itself.

After some minutes of daydreaming, followed by a visit to the bathroom to throw water on my face, I went back downstairs. The front door had been left open and summer light pooled on the warm wooden floor. I could hear someone singing in a far corner of the house, not a tune I knew - wistful yet repetitive, like a charm. It could have been the voice of a woman or a child. Now the ticking of a grandfather clock intruded; it stood beside the stairs. I went to stare up into its face, which was decorated with the sun, the moon, the stars. I heard the sound of soft shoes on tiles and then Posy Sala emerged from a corridor - this sumptuous gargoyle of a woman.

"Would you like tea?" she asked me. "Or something cold?"

"Tea please," I said.

"Outside or in ... to sit, I mean."

"I'd like to see the house."

"I'll show you to the sitting room."

This was a feminine chamber which I decided was - or had been - the province of Nimrod's mother. It was a museum of a room, all chintz and florid flower patterns, but was not uncomfortable. "Who lives in the house?" I asked Posy Sala.

"The Queneau family," she replied rather acidly then softened. "Nimrod, his sister, their aunt and their parents. He's alone while the rest of them are summer travelling."

I assumed the younger Queneaus did not work. What *did*

they do, out here in the middle of nowhere? Perhaps they only came home at certain times of year. I wondered then exactly why Nimrod wasn't here to greet us seeing as we'd come so far to stay with him, and thought I might as well ask where he was.

"He'll be back for dinner," Posy Sala said. "He had an unavoidable commitment today."

And then Vezi came into the room. When our gazes collided I saw a message in his eyes and interpreted it as: *What's going on?* He was mildly perturbed but that might not mean anything. Vezi is easily perturbed.

Posy went away to prepare our refreshment and we explored the room. There were several large paintings on the walls – intriguingly unusual. While the style was similar to that found in typical nineteenth century family portraits, the pictures were far from conventional. One resembled a photographic close-up of a woman's hands resting on a prayer book – her fingers curled loosely over the body of a dead dove. Another was of horses but not typical of its period. The picture depicted merely galloping hooves, the grey legs of the horses muddied and bloodied as if fleeing a massacre.

While Vezi examined ancient woodcuts around the fireplace I sauntered to a huge mahogany sideboard on the darkest side of the room where framed photographs were packed like tombstones in an over-crowded graveyard. I hoped to find historic photos of family corpses among the faces, as was the custom in centuries past, but no such luck. The people I assumed to be Nimrod and his sister – recent high-definition pictures near the front of the throng – were attenuated and elegant: thoroughbreds. They had a faint resemblance to Posy Sala I thought, but for the nose. They were very tanned in all the seasons of their recorded life so far, smiling ravenously at the camera through fringes of thick dark blonde hair with brown eyes glinting and sardonic eyebrows cocked. I could see at once that Vezi would have no chance with Nimrod, or with the sister either for that matter. Vezi came to join me, stared at the photograph in my hand, sighed deeply. I replaced it in the crowd.

After consuming cups of excellent Assam tea and divinely

sticky cakes that accompanied it, we went out to walk around the gardens, arm in arm, until it was time for dinner. There were elaborate follies in the Classical style, and an ornamental lake with a fabricated island in its centre where fake ruined arches crumbled into the moss. At the lake's edge, within a den of shifting willow withes, there was a boathouse, peeling and old, oozing memories of childhood I could almost see. We found a dilapidated rowing boat named *Pygmy* moored inside.

"What do you think Alex?" Vezi asked me.

"About what?"

He extended his arms to indicate the house and its grounds. "This place."

"I take it you don't want weird..."

"It's *not* though, is it? But there's something ... something..." He shook his head.

I suspected he was looking for ghosts, the tragic spirit of love, a mirror in time for his heart.

"It's a very nice house," I said aware this was a remark below my usual standard.

"I don't think he's away," Vezi said. "I think he's *in there*." He glanced up at the house on its hill above us.

"Nimrod? Really?"

"Yes. I don't know why I feel it but I do. Can't *you* have a ... feel about?"

I snorted. "I've never met Nimrod Queneau so despite my unparalleled occult talents it's unlikely I'd *feel* him. Perhaps he *is* here but simply wants time to finish up with something before he meets us." I grinned. "Perhaps he has to steel himself to see you again."

Vezi did not share my amusement. He frowned. "I know you'll laugh because what I'm about to say isn't typical of me, but I had a dream about this place before we came here..." He looked at me with the expression of a man about to be whipped.

"So did I," I said clearly surprising him. "How empathic of us. Mine was quite dull, but what was yours?"

"I dreamed we never met him but he was around us all the time. I can't explain."

"That's only your fears," I said taking his arm and shaking him mildly. "Really Vezi, you must stop investing so much energy into someone you've hardly seen for years. It's good to retain a youthful spirit and I applaud that in you, but it's also essential to grow up. From his photos I imagine Nimrod Queneau has a glut of casual lovers. Please be realistic for once."

He nodded, his expression glum. "I know you're right. It's just..." He shivered in the warmth of the day. "So what was your dream?"

"Oh, just that the only thing inside the house was a way out but it was through darkness."

That made him laugh. "I don't know why I asked."

We went back to the house.

POSY SALA HIT a gong in the hallway to call us to dinner from the sitting room. This was at 7:00 p.m., quite early by French standards. We wandered into the hall like tourists and saw Ms Sala standing by the entrance to another room holding a small mallet with a felt-covered head. The gong on the table beside her still hummed softly as its bloom died away. The housekeeper gestured with the mallet for us to cross the hall and enter the dining room.

I expected to see Nimrod already seated even though it was still odd he hadn't come down and introduced himself before the meal. But the dining room was empty. Two places had been set at a large glossy table, opposite each other at one end. No place was laid at the head.

"Is Nimrod not back?" Vezi asked.

Posy Sala inclined her head. "No. He sends his apologies and hopes you enjoy your meal."

"When *will* he be back?" Vezi insisted.

"Perhaps later but you might not see him until tomorrow."

Vezi sat down with his back to the door looking sullen. I sat opposite him and gave him a stern glance. He shrugged.

I had imagined the house empty but for Ms Sala, but now a brace of servants arrived carrying trays of covered dishes. They both wore black uniforms and white aprons. These individuals were young, in their teens, a boy and a girl, both ink-haired and beautiful. They were silent but had mysterious smiles. Natural tricksters. How delightful.

Posy Sala introduced them. "This is Ailie and Troyes, who run the house with me. If you should need anything and I'm not here you may ask them."

"Thank you," Vezi said coldly.

I smiled at Posy's familiars. They grinned back slyly.

The meal they brought was delicious; chicken cradled in an exquisite sauce, perfectly cooked vegetables. There was a cool greenish-white wine, so pure as to be almost without taste but for its fire. The dessert, when it came, was pears clad in spiced syrup and chocolate shavings.

I was wondering by now whether Vezi had been somewhat selective with the truth when inviting me on this trip. It seemed likely he'd bumped into Nimrod somewhere and with the cunning of the truly besotted had engineered an invitation to *Le Nid des Rêves*, perhaps a little against Nimrod's wishes. This to me seemed the explanation for our host's non-appearance. He must be making it clear to Vezi there was nothing to hope for in respect of dalliances. I felt some sympathy for Nimrod. Vezi can be truly terrifying in the grip of feverish desire.

BEHIND THE DINING room there was a chamber dedicated to the viewing of television and here a TV set only slightly smaller than a cinema screen stood waiting to open the doors of the world to us. Vezi and I spent the evening watching films we'd seen before and went to bed fairly early. I drifted to sleep quickly, tired by the earlier journey, and then began to dream.

It began as had my first dream of the house – me walking up the driveway – only now the building resembled reality more than the dilapidated edifice I had imagined. I was aware I was dreaming and was intrigued as to what I might discover. As before the doors of the house opened to me. I expected to find Nimrod inside so he could speak to me, tell me the truth, offer an excuse. But there was only darkness beyond the threshold and that distant light of another open door. I ran across the hallway down a corridor. Shadows clutched at my ankles but they were weak and insubstantial, couldn't stop me. I fell into the daylight and found myself on the drive to another house – the place of my previous dream. Was this collapse into ruin what lay behind the façade of domesticity and contentment?

BELLS WOKE ME – hundreds of bells. Surfacing from sleep I realised this was the ringing of telephones, all of them the old-fashioned kind rather than those equipped with modern bleeps and tunes. It seemed that every phone in the house clamoured for attention, and there must be a lot of them. "Answer it!" I snapped at the air. If there'd been a handset in my room I would've done so myself.

Then silence. Someone had got to a phone or whoever had called had given up.

The hush was too deep, as if the house held its breath, afraid to utter a sound in case it was *noticed*. I turned on the bedside lamp and peered at the compact alarm clock that stood beside it. The time was 3:00 a.m. Somewhat discomforted I got out of bed. The distance between me and the windows seemed vast. The curtains shivered but I knew this was only because one of the panes was open. I padded across the carpet and looked out.

My walk with Vezi hadn't taken me to this part of the garden. The trees looked unreal, like bizarre formations of coral or lichen. I knew I wasn't dreaming: my perception was skewed. I saw a large white object, which I realised was a bulky statue situated within a circular wall upon the lawn. This was around a hundred yards away from the house but I could perceive it clearly in the light of a half moon. What I couldn't make out was what the statue represented; it seemed ungainly, awkward, as if frozen in embarrassment. Was it a beast, an ancient god, or simply a rough-hewn block of stone?

Then I heard laughter and across the lawn ran two slender figures, hand in hand. Even from a distance I recognised them as Ailie and Troyes. She was dressed in a simple shift that fell to mid-calf; its fabric appeared to glimmer starlight blue. He was wearing only dark loose trousers. Both had bare feet which flickered pale against the shorn grass. I was sure these eldritch creatures would dance around the statue and they did so - pagan creatures from an earlier time. I wondered then if what I observed existed in real time and space. I was prone to glimpses into other-wheres.

I opened the window wider and yelled "Hello!".

The couple became still, turned to me as one then grinned and waved heartily. I waved back. Ailie blew me a kiss before the pair of them scampered off away from the lawn and into the grasping shadows of shrubs and trees.

THE NEXT MORNING there was still no Nimrod. Posy Sala served us breakfast and Vezi snapped "M Queneau's business must be serious. Did he get home very late last night?"

Posy smiled patiently. "He didn't come home last night. His *serious* business detained him. Perhaps he will be here today."

"This is all very ... odd," Vezi grumbled. "He knew we were coming. Is it all too inconvenient for him? Should we perhaps leave?"

Posy Sala raised her brows but her voice remained level. "M Queneau deeply regrets the inconvenience. He has stressed you should regard the house as your own. He asks that you enjoy your stay despite this setback. The countryside is beautiful. There is much to see."

"Did he call you last night?" I asked.

Posy flicked me a speculating glance. "Excuse me?"

"The phone rang in the middle of the night - many phones. The noise woke me."

"Yes," the housekeeper said then added briskly. "I'll bring you more coffee." She glided out.

Vezi was staring at me.

"What?" I asked.

"I didn't hear any phones," he said.

I shrugged. "Well it's hardly surprising. You sleep like a drunk."

"This is all so peculiar."

I sighed. "We have a simple choice my dear. We take advantage of the facilities and have a holiday - Nimrod or no

La Ténébreuse

Nimrod - or we waste your money and go home, you in a grump, me bitterly resigned to your stupidity."

I could see Vezi's lower lip was on the brink of trembling. "He'll have to show up eventually - won't he?"

I wasn't sure about that.

The day passed uneventfully. Vezi and I took bicycles from the stable yard and cycled into a nearby village where we ate lunch at the bar. The locals nodded and smiled at us but were not moved to make conversation. After lunch we strolled along lanes, gazing out over the vineyards and the swatches of sunflower fields placed between them. We drifted through clots of shadowy woodland which appeared supernaturally dumped between the viniculture and flowers. I hoped grotesque fairy-tale creatures might lurk among the trees. If they did they hid from me. I was aware of the antiquity of the countryside, the weight of its fecundity, the intoxicating witchery of its perfumes. As we walked Vezi and I discussed the house and its mysteries. I told Vezi about the statue in the garden and how I saw the servants gambolling round it.

"We might be seeing mystery because we want it to be there," Vezi said trying hard to be sensible but sounding only prim.

"Perhaps," I said, "but if we plaster mundane explanations over everything we shut the mystery out. We should simply remain neutral on the matter, our minds wide open to anything."

WHEN WE RETURNED to *Le Nid des Rêves* we went into the garden to look at the statue. By day, it was unremarkable, a roughly-hewn lump of stone with some strange scorings on it, like engraved claw marks. It didn't resemble a creature of any kind.

Posy Sala later enlightened us after we asked her about it. "It's a very old boulder believed to be from the Ice Age. It was found somewhere in the grounds and Nimrod's great grandfather had it moved to the lawn. It's said he had the marks sculpted into it then to make it look like an ancient sacred object."

I was disappointed by the relatively mundane explanation but perhaps Posy Sala warped the truth. I could only hope so.

And yet from that moment it was as if the mystery of *Le Nid des Rêves* reined itself in - perhaps suspicious of us. Vezi and I passed the evening watching more TV. We went to bed and slept peacefully. In the morning still no Nimrod. This continued for three days. Despite the lack of bizarre events however, I did have a faint sense of being observed. It was not unpleasant but kept me alert.

On the fourth morning I awoke unusually early, full of energy. I was in no mood to try and go back to sleep so got up and dressed. It wasn't yet time for breakfast. I decided to stroll around the garden for an hour or so, soak up the atmosphere of the morning.

Outside, a frill of mist hugged the lawns and spilled into the valleys beyond the grounds. It seethed and rippled as if alive. The air smelled rich, full of promise. Soon the sun would burn through the mist and retake the land. Summer would reclaim its territory.

I'd wandered over to the lumpen statue hoping I'd feel something unusual about it. Beneath my hand the stone thrummed with faint energy but had nothing to say to me. Then I became aware of the sounds of hoof-beats - a horse galloping towards me. The thunder drew nearer and nearer until I could hear the animal's snorting breath. It loomed out of the clotted air, black and immense, appearing slightly later than it should have done - but sound might warp in the mist. Its rider pulled the beast to a dramatic halt although I'd been in no danger of being trampled. It would've had to smash through the statue to achieve that.

The horse pranced towards me and its rider took off a wide-brimmed hat in a strangely formal manner of greeting. This revealed the sculptured face of Nimrod Queneau. I was grudgingly impressed by the flamboyance of his arrival and almost clapped my hands to him but realised this might appear rude.

"Hello," I said before he tried to speak to me in French. "You must be Nimrod. I'm Alex, Vezi's friend."

"Good morning," he said in a rich musical voice. "You're

an early riser."

"Sometimes." I wanted to appear aloof and mysterious but found myself smiling.

"I'm sorry I haven't been here," Nimrod said. "Business ... you know."

"Not really but I've heard of people doing such things." My smile widened unstoppably into a grin. "There's no need to apologise. Vezi and I have been exploring. This is a beautiful place."

Nimrod dismounted and offered me his arm. "Let's walk to the house. I shall order Posy to conjure us an immense breakfast."

We walked for some seconds in silence, the horse plodding dozily beside us, then I asked "Have you travelled over night?"

He laughed at the idea. "No. I've ridden from a friend's place nearby. I stayed the night there."

"How disappointing. I hoped I'd wandered into a pleasing fantasy where the master of the domain thunders through the dark on horseback."

He patted my hand that was linked through his arm. "Then by all means believe so if you'd prefer it."

"Thank you."

By the time we reached the house I knew that I had in my hands a weapon to inflict a mortal wound on Vezi. How annoying that I was too fond of him to use it. Nimrod, I felt, *knew* me as most people didn't or couldn't. He wanted to know more too; that was clear.

Over breakfast we had much to say to one another. Nimrod talked about the history of the house, claiming he could tell I'd be interested.

"I have an ancestor who used to speak to heads that hung hidden in the ivy outside her bedroom window," he said. "The legend goes they told her the deepest secrets of everyone in the house."

"Whose heads were they?"

"She didn't know. Eventually she married and moved away and no one saw or heard the heads thereafter. Then the ivy was taken down from the house. No heads were found."

"What a shame."

"We have several ghosts though. My favourite is that of a woman dressed in gauzy black robes and a veil who rides a grey lion along the edge of the forest, just inside the tree line." He grimaced sweetly. "Well maybe she's more of a local goddess than a ghost. We call her *La Ténébreuse*."

"Have you ever seen her?"

He grinned. "I'm not sure. I wanted to so badly as a boy I might've dreamed her up now and again. I once saw a dour female face staring at me from the rhododendrons but she turned into leaves and flowers."

By this point I could almost have fallen in love with him but I was no Vezi. It takes a very strong magic to work on me and I'm always cautious. He fascinated me though - the way he identified my preferences and wove these into a clever seduction.

We were still sitting at the table talking when Vezi came down to breakfast. He greeted Nimrod in a reserved manner. Nimrod stood up and embraced him briefly. "You must've thought I was dead!" he exclaimed with glee.

That day Nimrod took us out in his car - a black vintage Mercedes convertible - to visit a local vineyard which the Queneaus owned. Vezi and I got mildly drunk over lunch in the restaurant there. Then we drove on to a ruined chateau which clung to a cliffside above a serene lake where Nimrod told us many people had killed themselves by drowning. "This land is drenched in history," he said, "some of it deliciously dark."

I asked about the Ice Age boulder.

"You mean the lion?" he said.

"It doesn't look much like a lion, more like a lump."

He laughed. "Perhaps. But that's the mount of *La Ténébreuse* the dark lady who rides in the forest."

"I think you made that up!" I said. "The fantasies of a little boy."

Nimrod held my gaze. "They might be. I can't remember."

When we got home Vezi went to the bathroom and wasting no time Nimrod slid close to me in the sitting room and murmured "May I come to your room tonight?"

I regarded him steadily. "I was hoping you'd take me outside once everyone's gone to sleep – to see ghosts, to see a boulder turn into a lion."

He returned my gaze unflinchingly. "If those are your conditions."

"They are not conditions, merely requests."

"As your host I shall fulfil your requests."

AT 2:00 A.M. I got out of bed, where I'd lain sleepless, and went to the window. The bright moon burned the lawns and the ugly statue glowed white. Nimrod and I had made no specific arrangements so it must all be part of an adventure. I put on a long white linen dress and went barefoot down into the garden.

I was drawn to the boulder but, try as I might, perceived no lion in its awkward lines. I reached out to touch it and then a hand was laid over mine. A chill threshed through me. Turning quickly, I found Nimrod close behind me. "You walk like a ghost," I said.

He said nothing, but jumped up onto the plinth of the boulder, reaching down to pull me up beside him. The boulder seemed larger now, and more potent. Effortlessly Nimrod put his hands around my waist and somehow threw me onto the boulder so I was astride it, riding it. I felt slightly disorientated; the world shifted.

"Will you lead me to the tree-line of the forest?" I asked aware of the high tone of my voice. I didn't want to be afraid, fought it.

"If you want to ride that beast you must become *La Ténébreuse*, and she is without ambivalence. Could you sacrifice that Alex?"

"Not funny," I said.

"It's not meant to be. Can you feel the power of the land?" He opened his arms wide. "Smell it, breathe it in."

My head had begun to ache. The air was fractured. I didn't know what I was dealing with but sensed it was powerful. Shadows clustered and writhed at the edge of the trees. I felt eyes upon me but realised it was simply one enormous eye. The land watched.

What did Nimrod want from me? It couldn't be the obvious, could it? I wanted to get down from the boulder because I felt exposed and vulnerable up there, yet when I tried to move, my body froze. "Help me down, Nimrod."

He stared at me, his mouthed curved into a lunar smile that had no feeling, his white teeth glowing. His hair was a nimbus of moonlight. He neither moved nor spoke.

The ground seemed so far away. My brain seemed to lurch in my skull. I knew I must take back control, be brave enough to make the jump and trust I'd not be badly hurt. I closed my eyes and half threw myself, half clambered, from the back of the lion. I fell to the lawn and sprawled there.

Nimrod looked down at me his smile never wavering, but now he spoke. "Oh, how disappointing as *you* might say. You're not prepared to ride?"

I stood up. My dress was streaked with grass stains and the scent of turned earth was strong in my nose. "Perhaps not with you," I snapped. I brushed with futility at the marks on my clothes and noticed my hands were covered in soil, as if they'd been plunged in damp earth to the wrists.

"You know," Nimrod said in a casual tone, "I didn't intend to meet with you and Vezi at all while you were staying in the house."

"But...?"

He shrugged. "Vezi seemed desperate to come here. I allowed it. It's a place of dreams after all, and I'm generous with them. But then ... *you*. I like unusual things."

"No," I said flatly, "whatever you're thinking, no."

There was a brief moment of staring, like hostile cats sizing each other up.

Then he said "I'm sorry. I've been inappropriate." He offered me a hand which I took; his so clean, mine a golem paw. "Come. We'll walk."

We went down through the flowing landscape into the patchwork of vines and then into crowds of giant sunflowers, some of which were already withered and left to rot in the fields. Alive or dead, these flowers were huge and oppressive; I could sense their awareness, and a kind of lunacy. But of course - they feared the moon.

Tufts of boscage littered the land, within them teeming herds of deer whose eyes glowed green even if their motionless bodies could not be seen. Here were trees infested with mistletoe, species I could not identify but which were not oak. The woods seemed tiny somehow despite their swarming population of deer, mere islands in an endless sea of vines and flowers. Primal landscape – ordered, yet not.

Nimrod and I did not speak, merely walked or drifted. Eventually I heard someone singing, as I had on my first day in the house. We came to a field where the flowers lay slaughtered on the ground. These were not spent rotten blooms but recently vibrant, at their peak. I smelled their blood, the rich sap; it smelled yellow.

A crowd was gathered there, dressed in dark clothes, yet they were blurry figures. I couldn't see them clearly. The only ones who were distinct were Ailie and Troyes who stood facing us. And then Posy Sala appeared behind them as if in a photograph developing. She loomed tall like a guard. Her face wasn't remotely human. Why had I ever thought otherwise?

The strangely shifting crowd surrounded a small shrine which was fashioned of slender white columns and had no roof. And in the centre of the shrine piled upon the floor, *She* reclined. She was comprised of shadow, buzzing lines of darkness which made my eyes ache. She appeared to be naked, lissom as a panther and three times as big. Her face, what I could see of it, was a gargoyle mask from which a long tongue lolled. She writhed about like a restless hungry serpent yet had the tenuous shape of a woman. Her hair was smoke upon the air, tangling around her worshippers.

La Ténébreuse.

I knew her kind, fashioned of what lies within the earth; that which hides in the light and shadow of forests, which slumbers beneath the crop fields – and can be conjured forth by need.

"Now you see," Nimrod murmured to me clearly proud of revealing his great secret. "Isn't this what you wanted, what you've *always* wanted, grubbing through little mysteries but never finding the source?"

"Oh," I said, "I've seen the source before. This is but one rendition, like the song you sing to her." I looked into his eyes. "You've shaped her well."

He paused for a moment then said smoothly "I'm glad you've surprised me. I thought you would be shocked."

"No... Perhaps in some curious way, by some accident of formation, I was born of the same stuff as entities such as this. I don't fear them. *Your* creature however, is ravenous. Perhaps this is her special night."

"It is..."

I sighed, resigned. "And now I suppose the climax comes. It's the moment when my life could end, or I could be transformed in mind or body and the land will go on for ever. Which version of the story is it?"

He laughed. "Neither of them. You've already said no, Alex. This ... is simply a gift. An invitation to our party as a guest, that's all."

I frowned. "Am I seeing what you're seeing?"

"I have no idea. How can I?"

Ailie came to me with a goblet which I took but offered to Nimrod first. He drank from it without hesitation then I did also. The dark wine within this vessel affected me but did not take away my senses, merely muddled them a little.

I remember a bonfire was lit and there was singing and dancing. Shadows flickered against the flames, sometimes looking like people but most often not. Dreams of the slumbering earth that had taken on flesh. I felt the attention of *La Ténébreuse* upon me and knew that she could see me and where I'd been, what I'd done. I had to make her feel we already knew one another because I was not wholly safe.

After some hours, while I drank and occasionally danced, Nimrod took me into the trees at the edge of the field and there kissed me. It was as if he were a shadow. I felt nothing.

"I know who you are, *La Ténébreuse*," he said. "A walker in shadows."

He wasn't entirely wrong but it was irrelevant. He was a phantom, nothing more than the suggestion of a man.

I thought then *The first image of the house was true.*

I left a memory of myself to make love to him, then

walked back to the sunflower shrine. There was no one there and only a few sullen embers remained of the bonfire. I didn't pause but ran through the fields of vines and flowers, all the way to the nest of dreams where the plinth of the boulder lay empty, and the eyes of the house were open in the dark.

I CLIMBED THE stair to Vezi's room and crawled into bed beside him. "Tomorrow we leave," I said.

His arm went about me. "Yes."

"We must leave before it all changes and dreams become true."

"Yes..."

I knew for now it was safe to sleep, and did so.

We rose early just after dawn. Barely speaking we each packed a few things into a small bag and left everything else behind. We scurried out through the open door of the house like robbers. I glanced at the door knocker: the sleeping face of Posy Sala. The whole house slept now, didn't even open an eye. I was concerned there would be some impediment to our departure because now, by daylight, it seemed we'd escaped too easily – and on waking I was sure it *was* an escape no matter how Nimrod had attempted to reassure me. I'd pacified this landscape once perhaps but didn't want to risk it twice.

Vezi and I stole bikes from the stables and pedalled fast into the village and beyond it. We would go to a town. We mustn't think of anything behind us, anything that might pursue. Also, we mustn't yet talk of what had occurred. In silence we were invisible.

By 6:00 a.m. we came to a larger village, not quite a town, and it had a station. All the time we'd been in the house we'd never been that far from civilisation.

Once we were on a train heading to an even larger town, from where we could travel further to an airport, Vezi broke the silence with which we'd sealed the topic of Nimrod. "It was never him Alex. It was ... something else."

I reached across to take his hands in mine. "I think it *was* him Vezi, just ... not how you remembered. *That* perhaps was never him."

Vezi shook his head. "No, you're wrong. We never saw Nimrod in that house."

There are two pictures. In one of them Nimrod Queneau awakes to a house empty of guests and realises he went too far with his games. Or ... we were seduced and glamorised and if Vezi and I should ever go back to that nest of dreams all we'd find is the ruin I'd visited in sleep, dead leaves scratching along the driveway. I'd raise my eyes to the windows and feel someone staring back. We wouldn't stay there long.

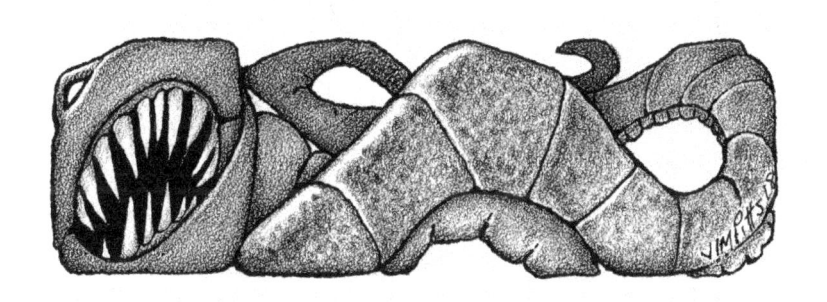

THE WORM

Samantha Lee

I WAS SITTING by the window reading, waiting for Ms Fenchurch to put in an appearance, when the worm turned up again. Only this time the worm had teeth. I don't mind telling you that I was out of that chair like a rocket, overturning the mug on the armrest, drenching my jeans in scalding coffee. And swearing.

Ms Fenchurch was late. She'd been conspicuous by her absence for a while now. Nobody seemed to know her whereabouts. I'd made a couple of phone calls in that regard but the powers that be had been "unable to assist me with my enquiries". Typical. Social workers. Never there when you needed them. Like now, for instance, when you were being stalked by a worm with teeth.

The damn thing had been appearing on and off for days, sneaking round corners, slithering out of hidey holes, sliding over the windowsill, swinging upside down from the lampshade. And now it had teeth. No eyes mind. But teeth aplenty. Long serrated *needley* spikes in a mouth that opened and closed like a sucker on the top of its bilious green head. A luminous mist rose up from it's insides every time it breathed out, poisoning the air with the scent of rotting garbage as it undulated across the carpet in my direction. Sniffing. Questing.

I tried to consider the situation logically. As if. What the hell was it? Where the hell had it come from? Was I hallucinating again? It couldn't be the DTs this time. I'd been off the sauce for yonks. Then again maybe it was a throwback to the kind of nightmare some people got from dropping too much acid or popping too many Es? Rumour had it that the horrors could keep coming back like a song for months, years even, after you stopped using. The drug lodged in the brain. Twisted it out of shape. They didn't call them mind-altering drugs for nothing. Could booze be as potent as that? Face it, I'd had a skin full in my time.

Then again maybe it was association of ideas? I'd been reading a book called *Salar the Salmon* and there was a bit in there about a sea slug that attached itself to fish and sucked out their innards, eating them alive. A long slow agonising death and no way to shake off the invader. Gross.

I flung the book at the worm but my eye was right out so I missed it by a mile. *Salar* hit the dining table scattering pizza boxes thither and yon. As for the worm, it just kept on coming at an even pace, body rising and falling in little humps like a mini Loch Ness Monster. It looked suspiciously as though it might be growing. Either that or I was shrinking. Like Alice.

That's something else I'd been reading. Do a lot of reading since they repossessed the telly. No more watching old re-runs of *The Sweeny* (you're nicked) of an afternoon. Got the book out of the library for free, cash money being in short supply. Oh yes, and a load of so called "self-development books", courtesy of Ms Fenchurch, thank you very much, I don't think. Some of them were practical ("always make your bed as soon as you get up – a tidy house, a tidy mind"); some mystical ("we are all one, you are the Universe" – yeah, right); some were just plain shite. The idea of creating your own reality was a laugh for starters. You'd need to be nuts to create the sort of life I've had. And who in their right mind would conjure up a worm with teeth?

A thought occurred. Something had conjured up the damn thing. Just supposing it *was* me? Then maybe I could *unconjure* it? At this point anything was worth a try. The damn thing was far too close for comfort. I backed up against the bookcase and fixed it with what I hoped was a disintegrating stare. An optical death ray. But the worm just laughed. Laughed and kept on coming. A laughing worm. With teeth. You couldn't make it up.

Wait. Wait. Wait. Maybe I'd nodded off while I was reading? That's what happens in stories with a cop-out ending, when the author can't think of a better way to rescue his characters from the mess he's put them into in the first instance? Of course. It was all a dream. So I tried to shake myself awake. Gave myself a pinch. Ouch. That hurt. So, no. No joy. No dream. The worm kept on coming. It was starting to give me the heebies now. I admit it. I had a notion what it was aiming to do. It was going to slither up my leg and enter the nearest available orifice and suck out my insides.

So now I started to feel distinctly sorry for myself. Not to mention pissed off. Why was this happening to me? What had I done to deserve it? All my life I've been told things were my fault. Spent most of my childhood apologising for sins that I hadn't committed. Confessed. Just for a quiet life. Just to stop from getting a hiding. I figured that if I could find out what I was supposed to have done this time, then maybe I could make the worm go away. Go away? How? Beg forgiveness? Ask for mercy? Who from? God? Don't make me laugh. The worm was the one laughing.

By this time it had reached my feet and I could hear it sniggering to itself. Then a tongue, long and thin, like a piece of suppurating string, snaked out from between the teeth and gave my big toe an exploratory lick. I closed my eyes. I couldn't bear to watch. Hairs rose on the back of my neck. I could just imagine myself after the thing had done its worst, crumpled on the floor like an airless sex doll. Ms Fenchurch, horrible, interfering, perpetually cheery busybody that she was, would get the fright of her life when she came upon the empty parcel of skin that was all that remained of me. Like something a snake had sloughed. She would have a conniption fit.

I started to laugh and the worm reared up in surprise as I fought back a moment of hysteria. Always an upside then.

Miss Fenchurch with the heebie jeebies and me going viral all over social media. Conspiracy theories galore. Nobody would be able to work out what had happened. Because the rest of me, my interior workings, blood, sweat and tears, would have disappeared inside the soon to be bloated body of the nasty little green excrescence that had mysteriously appeared out of the woodwork. Downside? I wouldn't be there to enjoy it.

The worm gave my ankle a little nip and I let out a yelp, standing up on my tip-toes to try to get away from the teeth. My skin started to crawl with goose bumps. And like an idiot I started to hum. A rhyme I remembered from when I was little. A very appropriate rhyme.

"Nobody loves me. Everybody hates me. I'm going into the garden to eat worms."

A revolting idea and no mistake. On the other hand, it might be the get-out clause I was looking for. Eat me. Alice again. Maybe I could get the first bite in? That would teach it to terrorise solitary females down on their luck. I peered down at it through hooded lids. The thought of its slimy body wriggling down my throat made my gorge rise. Could I pretend it was an oyster? Not that I'd ever eaten an oyster but I'd been force fed worse in my time. Other people were always the excuse. The "starving millions in China" my gran used to go on about when she was shovelling tripe and onions into my face. Horrendous old fart, her false teeth clacking, a constant teardrop of snot always hanging from her nose. The teardrop fascinated me as a child. I used to watch it when I was being "baby sat". It defied the laws of gravity. It never seemed to fall. After my mum went away my gran took me in permanently. "Out of the goodness of her heart," her cronies said. Though the old biddy hadn't had a heart. The kids at my school used to say she was a witch. Called me "spawn of the devil" in the playground. Maybe she *was* a witch? She was wicked enough. Wicked enough to be burned at the stake. Instead, she fell down the stairs and broke her back. Nobody questioned it at the time. Everybody very solicitous in fact. Happy days.

Much cheered by the memory, I reached down to pick up the worm. Nothing ventured. But then, would you credit it, when I was just about to pop it in my mouth the damn thing did a disappearing act? The teeth hovered for a moment like the Cheshire cat's smile before it vanished into thin air with a soft plop. A pantomime villain. Now you see it.

My shoulders, which had crept practically up to my ears without my realising it, relaxed. I found I was shaking all over and covered in sweat. I'd wet myself as well. The acrid smell of urine mingled with the spilled coffee from my earlier mishap. I peeled off my soaked jeans, staggered into the bathroom, flung them and my saturated knickers in the bath and sat down on the loo to finish the job. While I was running my hands under the warm water afterwards I caught a glimpse of myself in the mirror over the sink. I looked like the wrath of God. My face was all sunk in, skin whiter than a whiter shade of pale. I looked as though I hadn't had a decent meal in a week. I could have murdered a large scotch.

How long since I'd had one? Must have been a while. Signed the pledge after the old man died. Not being hammered helped me through the initial stages. Glad to be shot of the bastard. Nobody would have blamed me if I'd stuck a knife in him. Too big. Scared me witless. Dropped dead with a heart attack while he was bending over to get the red-hot poker out of the fire. To give me what he called "a good scorching". Hit his head on the fender. Landed face down on the coals. Blessed relief. Nobody questioned it. Black and blue as I was. Authorities were very helpful for once. Got me into detox. Sent me to Alcoholics Anonymous. Assigned me Ms Fenchurch to keep me on the straight and narrow. No more pink elephants. Never looked back. Until now.

There was the goddamn worm again. I could see it reflected in the mirror. This time it was crawling along the ceiling above my head. Gave me the shivers. Last thing I needed was for it to fall into my hair. Like Goldie Hawn in that movie, what was it, *Bird On A Wire*, trapped in the shower with the "cockroach from hell"? My hair looked lank and greasy. Ran my fingers through it. Started coming out in clumps. Yikes.

I grabbed a towel and swiped at the worm, catching the

tail end and sending it down to the floor in a luminous green spiral. Then I tried to stamp on it. But the thing was faster than me. Faster than the speed of light. Is it a bird? Is it a plane? No, it's the *toothworm*, out to chomp your liver and lights. Given half a chance.

If anyone had seen me then, they'd have thought I was stark staring mad. Doing a flamenco dance in the bathroom, in my bare feet, using the towel as a "red rag to a worm". Olé.

I aimed a kick at it and it scuttled under the sink, chortling to itself. Can a worm chortle? Apparently this one could. And snigger. Teeth. Laughter. Triggering memories I'd rather forget. My gran that time I came out of the bedroom to show off the party dress they'd given me at the Salvation Army, cackling with glee, telling me I looked like the "back end of a bus", false gnashers falling out of her mouth as she tumbled down the stairs. My man's hoarse chuckling when I used to scream for him to stop, leaving his teeth marks in my bare flesh. Still got the scars. The Reverend Tomlinson's pious tittering as he straightened his cassock, reminding me not to say anything to my religious fanatic foster mother. Who would have believed me anyway? Giving me a shilling before I ran out to throw up in the graveyard. My teeth almost falling out with the force of the retching. Not that I did a lot of laughing myself.

Worms. Some people were worse than worms. Though a green one with teeth would give them a run for their money.

I was suddenly overcome by a raging thirst but since the sink was full of hair, mine, I wrapped the towel round my waist, pootled through to the kitchen, turned on the tap, poured myself a glass of water and glugged it down. But there was no escape. As I put the glass back on the draining board, out of the corner of my eye I caught a glimpse of something green emerging from behind the garbage can. The worm again. Dogging my footsteps. Can a worm dog? Woof, woof.

A horrible thought assailed me. Was this a new worm? Was it the same one that had attacked me in the lounge? The same one that I'd just knocked off the bathroom ceiling? Or was there a posse of them, hidden in the cracks and crevices of the building, secreted in night-dark corners, waiting to pounce when my guard was down, to insinuate themselves into my sleeping persona? I whirled around trying to catch this new one off-guard. But the kitchen was empty. At least it's not a spider I thought, my brain taking a lateral turn. If there's one thing I cannot abide its spiders. I'll flush them down the loo without a moment's hesitation. I know it's not logical. I know they don't do any harm, not unless you live in Australia, anyway. In fact, they're a positive benefit to mankind if you believe the spider marketing press. Eating flies and all that. Still. I cannot stand them. Not at any cost. Don't mind the occasional Daddy Long Legs. But not spiders. Nasty *scuttly* things. Give me worms any day. Although preferably without teeth.

The worm in question must have read my thoughts. Was there no end to its abilities? Because there it was again. Lurking behind the fridge this time. I picked up a carving knife and it retreated, skittering along the skirting board and out of the kitchen, heading for the far end of the hall. The bedroom door was shut but it wormed its way (see what I did there?) through the gap underneath, the end of its tail giving a derisory little flick before it disappeared.

That did it. I don't lose my temper very often but you can only push me so far. I flung open the door and lunged in after it, shouting "gotcha" and waving the carving knife about in a menacing manner. I could see it was heading for the bed. Then a swarm of bluebottles erupted from something on the floor and started buzzing around my head in a noxious cloud. And after them came a stench strong enough to turn your stomach.

On further observation, the something turned out to be Ms Fenchurch. She was lying on her back halfway between the bed and the window. The curtains had been drawn but even in the half-light it was clear that she wasn't having an afternoon nap. Her body was heaving with white wriggly things and her insides were strewn all over the carpet.

The worm made a beeline for the corpse, presumably to have a chat with the maggots. I shuffled after it, holding my nose to stop herself from puking, leaning over the remains to get a better view of the deceased. I couldn't for the life of me work out what Ms Fenchurch, (not Mrs, not Miss, Ms if you please) was doing in my bedroom, and in such an obvious state of disrepair.

Stepping back, more to get away from the smell than anything else, I stubbed my toe on something cold and hard. It was a whiskey bottle. Empty.

Disjointed images started to float into my head. I tried to piece them together. Put them in some sort of sequence. Make some sense out of them. Finally, they all came back in a rush. Ms Fenchurch, fat frowsy Ms Fenchurch, self-appointed saviour of the damned, so out of touch with reality that she thought there was good in everyone and it was her duty to extract it whatever the cost, had come in and caught me with a large scotch in my hand. I'd been sitting quietly on the couch, minding my own business, getting nicely sozzled, when the blasted woman had let herself in without so much as a by your leave. No bleeding privacy. It was my birthday, I did remember that, July first, and I hadn't had a card from anybody. Not even one of those email ones, which in my opinion don't really count. Well, you can't put them on the mantelpiece, can you? No telly so I even went to the library to check. No phone calls either. Nothing. Nada. Zilch. It was as if I didn't exist. Long and the short of it, totally brought down, I decided to troll along to the off licence, give myself to a bijou *treatette*. To mark the occasion. I could go back on the wagon tomorrow. The tomorrow that never comes.

Anyway, Ms Fenchurch had started into one of her holier-than-thou lectures. Said she was disappointed in me, that I'd let her down, that although "delinquent" was a word she didn't often use in this case it seemed to fill the bill. Said I was ungrateful. Weak. A waste of space. That I'd never amount to anything. Same garbage my pious foster mother had spouted to the good Reverend Tomlinson when she asked him to "take me in hand". Imagine her face when she found him with his head bashed in. Death put down to drug addicts rifling the poor box. A robbery gone wrong. Last time he'd put his hand up my skirt, dirty old sod. And me only nine.

This time I was older and loaded. Ms Fenchurch hadn't a

clue what she was dealing with, shouldn't have tempted providence. Serve her right. Up to my eyebrows in scotch, full of false bravado, I just laughed in the woman's face. Could have left it at that. Should have. But then she'd waved one of her pudding fingers under my nose and started to prod me in the chest and I simply lost the plot. Lifted the closest thing to me. The scissors. Cut off the offending finger and when Ms F started to scream followed her down the hall and into the bedroom, tearing and rending and stabbing and chopping. Quite enjoyed it. Didn't feel an ounce of remorse that I can remember. Don't feel any now. Just sat down beside the remains and polished off the rest of the bottle of scotch.

Must have had a blackout after the event. A long one. Looked like Ms Fenchurch had been lying in the bedroom for quite a while considering the state of her.

So what about now, was my immediate response, after I'd given the scene of the crime the once over? How the hell was I going to clear up this mess? Nobody was going to sympathise this time, like when my gran died or give me the benefit of the doubt like when my old man kicked the bucket. They'd probably cart me off to the funny farm. The same one they took my mother too all those years ago, screeching that she didn't do it, blaming her daughter. Imagine. Such wickedness. As if a child could do such a thing.

At this juncture somebody started banging on the door. Gave me the fright of my life. When I peered through the curtains I could see a police car parked in the street down below the flats. Some busy body must have complained about the smell. I have to admit Ms Fenchurch was a bit ripe. Too late to hide the evidence now. I'd have to think of something pretty impressive to talk my way out of this one. Better just give in gracefully. Fess up. Then again with a good lawyer, mitigating circumstances, abusive childhood, morbid addiction. "I was drunk your honour, and I promise I'll never ever do it again." I might get a reduced sentence. People are so stupid. You never can tell.

The worm sidled out from under the bed where it had shot when the banging started and winked at me. Somewhere along the line it seemed to have grown eyes. Eyes and teeth and a mouth on the top of its head and hair all over its revolting wriggling pulsating body. By now I'd ceased to be amazed. It didn't even scare me anymore. When I sat down on the blood-stained duvet and it crawled up my bare shin, settling itself on my knee, making itself comfortable, I didn't even flinch. I just gave it a little pat and told it to prepare for the worst. They'd probably put me away for good I told it. But not to worry. Free bed and board anyway. At least we wouldn't have to worry about where the next penny was coming from.

Since we were chatting, or at least I was, I enquired after its immediate plans. Was it a case of "For lo I am with you always," as the Reverend Tomlinson used say, closing the vestry door, "even unto the end of the world." If so, what was the story? Had it been sent to punish me? The worm of conscience? In which case it was wasting its time. Then I reminded it that it might not be exactly an accomplice but it was certainly an accessory after the fact. Because I'd finally remembered now where I'd seen it before. It had been there to share the startled expression on my granny's face when I gave her the push that tumbled her downstairs. Ditto the look of astonished disbelief registered by the Reverend Tomlinson just before I hit him over the head with the votive candlestick. And it had also been a witness to my mother's reaction, that picture of horrified disbelief when she'd woken up and found her five-year old standing by the bed in her nightie with the latest fancy man's eyeball stuck on the end of a knitting needle. That man had never liked me.

I told the worm that with all that behind us, so many memories in common, I thought a truce would be a good idea. I said I would be prepared to think of it as my own personal "familiar". Made a change from a toad or a black cat. But if so, I hoped I could trust it to play its part? I didn't want to spend the rest of my time on this earth worrying about it sneaking inside me every time I closed my eyes or turned my back. The worm seemed amenable. Nodded the end where the eyes were anyway. I'm just not sure whether I can trust it. I mean would you trust a worm with teeth? I have a sinking feeling it may renege on the deal one day and devour me wholesale. My nemesis. I just hope it's quick. Better that than a bit at a time. Like Salar.

The nemesis in question beat a hasty retreat when the authorities finally broke down the door. I did my best to explain about my invisible friend. Even tried to whistle it back so that I could introduce it. But what was the point? As usual they thought I was making it up. Like when I told them about my granny putting me into scalding baths on purpose. Like when I tried to shop the good Reverend Tomlinson and got thoroughly walloped for my pains. Like when my old man dragged me out of the church by my hair when I'd gone in seeking sanctuary. Give me my due, I did try. But all they said was that I must have done something to deserve it. Lies, lies and more lies. In the end the Lord helps those as helps themselves.

So, despite the fact that I screamed loud enough to bring the house down and managed to kick one of the paramedics in the balls, they eventually got me into the straight jacket and winched me out of the apartment. The worm wriggled behind like a pet poodle and hoisted itself onto my shoulder as they closed the van doors. Nobody objected. Nobody seemed to even notice. It's still here with me keeping me company in the padded cell. It hides in a corner when anybody comes in. It's my one consolation. At least someone knows the truth apart from me. Otherwise what would be the point?

It may be a while before I get out of here but meanwhile the worm and I have a wealth of memories to sustain us. The recollection of my mother's horrified shrieks as she pulled out the knitting needle, covering it in her own fingerprints in the process, sealing her fate. Of my granny's sunken toothless face as she hurtled from tread to tread ending up like a broken marionette at the bottom of the stairs. Of the Reverend Tomlinson's hairpiece falling off as he collapsed on the vestry floor in a hail of silver from the evening collection. All that gold there to be relived in moments of boredom. I especially like the sound of the solidly satisfying crunch my old man's skull made when his head caved in. He lost his balance when I put my boot on his backside and shoved him into the embers. He'd lit up like a firework as his hair caught alight. That image is enough to warm the cockles of your heart.

Sadly, Ms Fenchurch's death is an open book. They've got me bang to rights on that one. But I'm damned if I'm going to confess to anything else. Why guild the lily?

The rest will be my little secret.

Mine and the worm's.

Tomorrow it's going to do a little errand for me. I've recently discovered that one of the warders here, Big Stan, is the son of my old foster mother. Didn't recognise me of course. I was long gone before he was born. Still lives at home too. Can you credit it? And him a grown man. Co-incidence? Or the hand of fate?

The worm's going to wriggle off and have a surreptitious listen. See if we can find out where she lives. An earworm. Chortle. Might even be the same place? She always said I'd come to a bad end.

It's a long shot I know. They may never let me out of this place.

But I can dream, can't I?

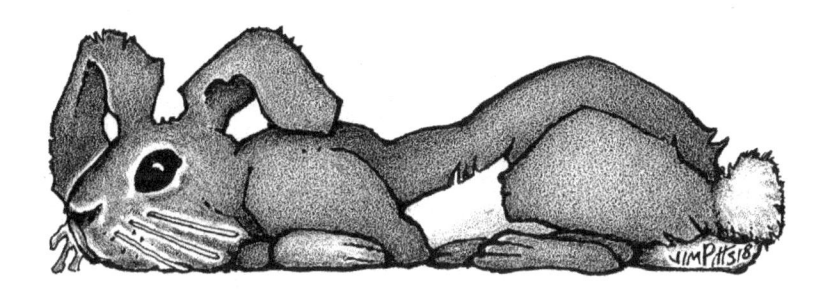

DEADLINE

Stan Nicholls

April hated getting up when it was still dark. But when you had a toddler and no help there was little choice. And she had a full day ahead. Very full.

Sighing, she killed the alarm and crawled out of bed.

Ethan was already awake of course, and unhappy. She could hear him griping and noisily tossing things around in his room. When she padded in he was upending a crate of plastic bricks, adding to the shambles.

"What's the matter?" she asked.

He turned pleading tear-filled eyes on her. "Can't find Bobbin."

"Let's see if we can find him together, shall we?'

Her son resumed the hunt for his favourite soft toy with all of a four-year old's haphazardness. April, still blinking away sleep, tried searching more methodically. She was sure the blessed thing had been on Ethan's cot the night before, as usual, but it wasn't there or underneath. Drawing the blue patterned curtains – she made a mental note that she really ought to wash them – revealed a cluttered windowsill but no Bobbin. Nor was there any sign of it in the open wardrobe or among the jumble on the tiny corner table.

There was no time for this. Bobbin would probably turn up crammed behind a radiator or buried in the clothes basket if past experience was anything to go by.

She grabbed another toy at random, a threadbare rabbit, and delivered with a hug it saw Ethan grudgingly placated. Then it was downstairs for the messy battle of a quickly prepared breakfast. After what seemed an age they were ready to leave. She glanced in the hall mirror. The face staring back was reasonably creditable for a thirty-something, she thought, flicking away a stray lock of auburn hair. But it was a pity she looked so damned tired. Then they were out of the door.

Most of the houses in the street were in darkness with just the occasional light indicating another early riser.

She got Ethan into his place in the back of the car. Sliding into the driver's seat she clipped on her belt and turned the ignition. There was a grinding noise, and it died. Several more attempts brought the same. Could it be the cold? It was quite chilly this morning but hardly cold enough to freeze the engine. She looked at the fuel gauge. Zero. She was sure she'd filled it the day before yesterday. How could that amount of fuel disappear in two days? She'd have to borrow a can of petrol from one of her neighbours later to get to the garage. *Damn it.*

She looked at her watch. Nothing for it but to catch the bus. She wrestled a complaining Ethan out of his child seat and grabbed her bulging shoulder bag. They made for the bus stop, the rabbit dangling by one leg in Ethan's sticky grasp.

When they got to the stop she saw that the bus she needed wasn't listed on the sign or on the digital screen in the shelter. All the other routes were there but none of those helped her. April thought it must be a mistake. After ten long minutes she began to wonder. She collared a passing elderly woman and asked her. The woman seemed confounded and said she didn't recall that particular bus number, let alone it stopping there. April looked for someone else to ask. Ethan fidgeted.

A bus arrived, though not hers. She called to the driver as its doors opened.

"No, doesn't stop here, luv," he said.

"Where then?"

The driver shrugged. "Nowhere I know of. Maybe one of

those routes on the other side of town, by the new estates? Where do you want to go?"

She told him.

"You'll need two buses for that. The one behind me to the shopping mall, then change." He closed the doors and moved off.

April reckoned they must have discontinued the bus she wanted since she last used it, which admittedly was quite a while ago. She thought of getting a taxi, though there seemed to be fewer of those about than usual this morning. A couple of minutes later the bus for the mall arrived and she bundled Ethan onto it.

The journey wasn't as fraught as she feared as there weren't that many people travelling despite being the rush hour. Nearing their destination on the second bus, she noticed that a sweet shop popular with local kids was no longer there. But Ethan looked blank when she pointed it out.

They got to school just in time. The substituted toy that Ethan held so tightly was now given up without protest with school a more alluring prospect. Child safely delivered, April was about to start the return journey when a middle-aged woman approached her. She recognised her as one of the school secretaries, although she couldn't recall her name.

"Mrs Barker?" the woman said.

"Yes," April replied. "Well, I suppose it's Miss now. And I prefer my maiden name: Morris."

"Miss Morris," the woman corrected. "I'm Valerie Simpson, admin staff."

"Is anything wrong?" She had visions of Ethan having done something terrible.

"No. Well, it's a little embarrassing really. You'll remember the questionnaire we sent home with the children a few weeks ago."

April didn't but nodded anyway.

"There's been a bit of a problem," the woman went on. "The returned questionnaires have been ... mislaid."

"Really?"

"'fraid so." She looked embarrassed, and added hurriedly,

"I'm sure they'll turn up. But in the meantime, we're having to ask all the parents to fill them in again." She handed over several stapled sheets of paper.

Forms, April thought wearily as she stuffed them into her bag. Always forms to fill in these days. She added it to that growing mental list of things to do.

Ethan could be seen inside the entrance's glass doors, queuing with the other children. She blew him a kiss and left.

Having to ride the almost empty buses home was a nuisance but at least it gave April some precious time to herself. Her mind was on the writing assignment she had to turn in tomorrow, and whether she could make the deadline. The piece was for a prestigious women's title she'd recently managed to break into. Good paying too, which was rare these days, what with the 'net hollowing everything out. Freelancing brought in much needed money, as well as realising her long-held ambition to write, and she was grateful for it. But her real passion was *the book*.

Her attention was drawn to a man on the pavement. Scruffily dressed, with long unkempt hair and beard, he seemed to be shouting. In typical English fashion such people as were about gave him a wide berth. He held a makeshift sign. It was difficult to see what it said from the moving bus but she made out the words *God*, *Judgement* and *Repent*. April recognised it as one of those fortuitous writerly moments and saw how the scene would fit nicely into her novel. She reached into her bag for her notebook. It wasn't there. She rummaged, finally turning out the bag's content onto the empty seat beside her. No notebook. She patted her pockets. Nothing. *Hell!* Sourly, she checked her watch. She was feeling pressured, even this early, and losing her notes didn't help.

Trying to relax, she gazed out at the streets they were passing through. The shoe shop in the high street had gone. So had the hardware store, and that had been there for years. Shame.

That's one thing to be said for using the bus, she reflected. You get to see how things are changing.

*

ONCE SHE WAS home she rang the bus company to see if anyone had handed in her notebook. She got a recorded message saying the number wasn't recognised, despite several tries. That seemed odd for a national company. Or maybe the phone people had got it wrong. She had no trouble getting through to the school, though whoever answered didn't seem to know who she was. After an infuriatingly long wait she was told a notebook hadn't been handed in. She decided to try to forget about it until later, probably tomorrow. The important thing was her deadline.

But first she had some household chores. Chores always pressed when you had a young child, but these pressed more than most. The next hour was spent loading the washing machine, ironing and mopping. Tasks made no easier, or her mood any lighter, by not being able to find half the cleaning materials she was sure she had.

A cup of coffee to hand – fresh, never instant, one of her few indulgences – she sat down with her laptop and brought up the file with the article she was writing. It was empty. The back-up was the same. *Shit!*

A thought struck. Near panicking, she checked her novel. It was there, and the thirty thousand words or so she'd written seemed to be complete. April had that backed-up too, several times, but she found a flash-drive and copied it again. She placed the drive in her pocket and felt a shred of comfort.

But the article. The bloody article!

She glared at the laptop and would have happily smashed the thing to pieces if that wouldn't make the situation more disastrous. Taking a breath, she decided she'd just have to start again, from memory, though she despaired at getting a publishable eight-thousand-word piece ready by tomorrow's deadline. She knew that a "proper" journalist would have no problem with that. And she was a professional, wasn't she? Sort of, her little inner voice came back. Because she wasn't the fastest writer in the world. Not slow exactly, just a little … fastidious. Well, she'd have to get over that. She tried to remember what she'd already written and began tapping on the keyboard.

It was still morning, just, when April surfaced. She had the opening of the piece okay, about a thousand words, but not a lot else, and Ethan would be home in a few hours. This was impossible!

Inevitably her mind turned to Matt, her ex. The manipulative, controlling bastard.

Think what she could be doing if he hadn't left her in this position. Like finding enough time to meet deadlines, for instance. There was no help from him with Ethan, and little in the way of money, and that had to be squeezed out of him. Not to mention the snide remarks and occasional verbal abuse. But she was taking all that *shit* and pouring it into her novel. They say write what you know, don't they? She was doing just that. It made up in a small way for everything she took from that arse-for-brains she'd made the mistake of marrying.

This doesn't help, she told herself. Focus.

She made another cup of coffee.

How about ringing her editor to ask for an extension? After all, it wasn't the first time she'd worked for that particular magazine. Actually, it was the second. But she turned that piece in bang on deadline and the editor had complimented it. She'd understand about the laptop losing her copy, surely?

She rang the magazine's office and again got the number-not-recognised message. After a couple more attempts she gave up. It had to be the miserable phone company. She rang *them*.

After the obligatory message saying how much they appreciated her call, and that it would be recorded for security and training purposes, she got a human.

"Hello. My name's Denise, how can I help you?"

"I keep getting number unobtainable when I ring people."

"Are you sure you dialled correctly?"

"*Yes*," April replied through clenched teeth.

"Who were you trying to call?"

She gave her the magazine's number.

A moment later Denise came back with "That seems to be a non-existent number, caller."

"It can't be, it's a huge publishing company."

"No record of it here, I'm afraid."

April expelled a breath. "All right. How about this one?" She read out the bus company's number, and waited.

"That isn't listed either, caller," Denise said.

"*What?* They're another big company."

"Sorry. I've nothing here on them."

"That's *ridiculous*. Don't you have any kind of a number for them?"

"Nothing listed, I'm afraid." A note of perplexity crept in. "What number are *you* ringing from, caller?"

April told her.

"I don't have a listing for that number either. Would you mind repeating it?"

It was repeated, slowly.

"You're not on the system," Denise announced, tone hardening.

"What does that mean?"

"We've no record of the number you say you're calling from."

It was the *you say* that did it for April. She bit back the torrent of invective that was building and hung up. They were obviously incompetent or refusing to admit to a fault in their precious system. Sod 'em. There was too much on her mind to worry about it now.

She hadn't eaten, unless she counted the hurried meagre mouthfuls at breakfast. She headed for the kitchen thinking food might even her temper. But delving into the fridge and larder showed that eatables she would have sworn she had weren't there. For a moment she considered the chilling possibility that Matt had somehow got hold of a key, had a copy of hers made perhaps, and was playing his tedious mind games. Then she decided that a tin-foil hat didn't suit her and got a grip.

She managed to put together a sandwich, then weakened and tried ringing the magazine again, hoping the phone company had fixed whatever was wrong. The number was still not recognised. All that would have to wait; she needed to buy some groceries before the boy got home. It was a nuisance but the supermarket was a short walk and she didn't need *that* much.

Outside, she glanced at the fuchsia dominating the front garden. It was terribly overgrown and untidy, and she really should prune it. Yeah, in my abundant free time, she thought wryly. And now she had to waste more of it with unscheduled shopping.

As she set off she cursed not owning a car.

THE ROAD LEADING to the shopping precinct looked different in some way. At first, April couldn't put her finger on why before remembering it should have been lined with rows of mature ash trees. There was no sign of them now. Bloody council! Mind you, her not noticing it before showed how cut off you got from the world when you were imprisoned with a toddler.

She found the supermarket less well stocked than usual. There were gaps on the shelves, and in places some were completely empty. She had to pick substitutes for several things she needed. One item she couldn't swap, unless she wanted to deal with a tantrum, was Ethan's favourite cereal. But the shop had none, or any other brands of cereal as far as she could see. She spotted a sales assistant, wearing a badge announcing that she was called Claire. April asked her about the cereal.

"I don't think we've got any," the young woman told her.

April was doubtful. "Are you sure? Come to that, where *are* the cereals these days? I couldn't find any."

"Just a minute. *Daisy!*" Claire shouted to an older woman at one of the tills. "We got any cereal?"

"If it's not on the shelves we haven't got it!" came the brusque reply.

April thought a supermarket not having a staple like that was pretty strange. Ethan would just have to go without and she'd weather the storm. This was turning out to be one of her less sunny days. She took her basket to the older woman's till.

"Are you short-staffed?" April asked, thinking that must explain the barren shelves.

Daisy looked as though she didn't understand the question. "No."

To break the uncomfortable silence that descended while the woman scanned her purchases, April said "Where's Alice today?"

"Who?"

"You know, she works on the checkout. Been here for years. *Alice*," she repeated for emphasis.

The woman looked blank and shrugged. "Don't know her."

April didn't have the will to argue, particularly with someone taciturn and grumpy.

Only when she was leaving did she recall that the woman she'd just spoken to had also been there for years. She'd seen her many times. Yet she denied knowing a colleague she worked alongside. Maybe they'd had some kind of falling out, April reasoned, and Alice's existence was not to be admitted to.

As she was carrying shopping she decided to take the short bus journey home, and she was one of the few passengers. She saw further shops standing empty. Times were hard, she knew, but seeing that kind of thing brought it home. Not far from her turning she noticed that some demolition had apparently been going on as well. Two or possibly three nice Edwardian terraced houses were gone. And it was a very clean demolition job, as though the houses had been lifted out like slices of cake, leaving none of the detritus you usually got when buildings were knocked down.

Arriving home, she surveyed her empty drive and the completely bare front garden. It looked a bit of a sight, she had to admit. Perhaps she should plant it up. Maybe with a shrub of some sort, like an azalea or fuchsia. Assuming she ever found the time.

Putting the shopping away she was irritated to find that she hadn't done as thorough a job of checking what she needed as she thought. Several things, including quite basic items, weren't there. And her purse, when she happened to look in it, contained none of the cash she was sure she had. Too much on her mind, she supposed, and another item for that ever-growing mental list.

In the living room she noticed the light flashing on the house line answer phone. She hit play.

The message began minus niceties. "Returning your call." It was Matt, her ex, finally returning a number of her calls in fact. "How many times do I have to tell you I can't afford more than you're getting? If you can't make ends meet that's your problem. But you never were much good at housekeeping, were you, April? Anything else you want to whine about, call my lawyer." A sharp click.

The *fucker*. He didn't even mention Ethan. Avoiding his responsibilities. Bloody typical. April was minded to call him back, but knew it was better to do that when she felt calmer. She allowed herself an instant coffee and a brief sit down.

Only then, glancing at the calendar, did it strike her that her period hadn't come on. It was nice not to have that particular complication on a day like today, but strange. She was uncannily regular and it wasn't like her for it not to turn up. One thing was sure: she could rule out being pregnant. With a kid, occasional part-time jobs, running the house, deadlines, and a still possessive ex-partner in the background, she should be so lucky.

She rang her editor again. Number not recognised. Although certain she had the number right, she thought to check their website. The screen displayed *Not Found*. Out of curiosity she tried six or seven other sites unrelated to the magazine. Four of them, including the bus company, returned not found. The bloody phone company again, no doubt. Surely the publishers couldn't have gone out of business in one day? An organisation that size, she would have heard about it on the news. She realised that she hadn't actually seen or heard the news today and reached for the remote.

The first channel she tried showed nothing but buzzing grey static. So did the second and third. The fourth did come on and was running a news bulletin. A few minutes in had her noting the absence of certain things. Where was coverage of the latest murky political crisis, that celeb who died, or this evening's big match? Not that she had any interest in football; that had been one of Matt's addictions. She couldn't see how what was on the news, or rather what wasn't, had anything to do with the phone company. Could it be sunspots or something? So why nothing about that on the TV? She considered another call to the phone company but decided against it. Ethan would be home before she knew it and she had to plough on with her article. Assuming she could recall enough of what she'd originally written.

It occurred to her that she really ought to keep a notebook. It was a wonder that she didn't. It's what writers do, isn't it?

The article occupied the next hour or so. Taking a break, eye on the clock, she remembered her ex's call and decided, with some apprehension, to get back to him.

"Hello." It was a man's voice she didn't recognise.

"Can I talk to Matt, please?"

"Who?"

"*Matt.*"

"Nobody here with that name."

"Matthew Barker," April emphasised.

"Like I said, there's no Matt here."

"Is that 781616?"

"Yeah."

"That's his number."

"You must have got it wrong."

"Are you *sure* Matt isn't there?"

"I told you so, didn't I?" He was irritated now. "Make sure you've got the right number next time." The line went dead.

Probably one of Matt's dimwit friends he got to answer the phone when her name displayed. A typical windup. Well, he can go to hell.

Turning back to her laptop she looked at the clock again, and it dawned on her that the hands hadn't moved. It had stopped! She checked her wristwatch and it showed the same time. Shaking her wrist, as though that would make any difference, confirmed the watch had stopped too. How in fuck had that happened?

Her laptop seemed to show a more accurate time, and it was later than she thought.

Shit, *Ethan!* There was just enough time to get to the school to collect him.

She dashed for the door.

THE JOURNEY WAS tense. Not being there when her child came out of school was something every mother was desperate to avoid. But there was nothing April could do to speed up the bus, which she occupied almost alone, though hardly anyone getting on at any of the stops helped a little. Watching the world go by was her only distraction.

She was surprised to see that they'd knocked down one of the local churches, and another swathe of shops had apparently vanished overnight. The empty library was especially shocking and a sad reflection on the times. As she observed earlier, there seemed to be quite a lot of property development going on. The demolition side of it anyway.

Finally arriving at the school, she saw a change there too. The hedge, taller than her, which ran along just inside the railings had gone since this morning. Whoever did that made a swift job of it. Neat, too. You wouldn't know it had ever been there. But what was the point of removing it? Some sort of health and safety thing, she guessed.

A few kids were starting to trickle out to be greeted by a gaggle of waiting mums and the odd dad. A much thinner crowd than usual. Maybe there was a bug going around and the little darlings were housebound. She'd have to remember to take Ethan's temperature when they got home, just in case.

She fell into chatting with a couple of the parents she vaguely knew. None were aware of any kind of infection doing the rounds. To break the awkward gaps in conversation that tended to arise when the only connection was that they all had children, April asked if anyone had seen one of the mums she knew well enough to call a friend of sorts. That brought shrugs and vacant expressions.

"June," she repeated. "You know, Brandon's mother."

Neither mother or son registered with any of them. What is it with people today? she thought.

Children kept exiting in dribs and drabs and left with a parent. Soon the playground was empty except for April.

Concerned, she headed inside. A woman she didn't recognise was sitting behind the counter in reception. She gave April a professional smile. "Can I help you?"

"I've been waiting for my son but he hasn't come out."

"What's his name?"

"Ethan. Ethan Morris."

"Ethan? I'm not familiar with him." She turned to her screen and tapped at the keyboard. "I can't see his name here."

"You can't? Maybe it's under my old name, though it shouldn't be. My married name, that is. Barker."

The woman checked. "No, not that either."

April had an alarming thought. "No one else has collected him, have they?" She could too easily imagine Matt being up to his old tricks.

"As I say, we don't have a record of a child with that name."

"I don't understand. What are you saying?"

"Well, are you sure you're at the right school?"

"*Of course I am!* I brought him in this morning."

"Did you?" A hint of disbelief had crept into her voice.

"*Yes*. In fact, I spoke to one of the admin staff. A Miss Simpson."

"Who?"

"Simpson. Er... Valerie Simpson, I think."

"You think."

"Look, she gave me a questionnaire." April delved into her bag. The form wasn't there. "I know I had it..."

"We don't have a Miss Simpson working here."

"What?"

"There's nobody on the staff with that name."

"I've had enough of this." April pointed at the inner door leading into the building proper. "Let me through."

"I can't allow that, I'm afraid."

"This is ridiculous! Ethan's been coming here for almost a year!"

"Not according to our records."

"Bugger your records!"

"Calm down please."

Deadline — 73 —

"*Don't you tell me to calm down!* This is my four-year old we're talking about! Where is he?"

"You're obviously distraught. Why don't you—"

"I want to speak to your superior. Someone in authority."

"I can assure you—"

"I don't want your fucking assurances. I want my son!"

"There's no need for that sort of language."

"I want to talk to whoever's in charge," April repeated. "This is my boy's school and I want to know where he is!" She felt hot tears running down her cheeks.

The receptionist was about to say something, checked herself, picked up an internal phone and whispered into it. "Just bear with me," she told April. "I'm sure we can sort this out."

"You'd better," April managed between sobs. She felt bad for crying, as though it somehow undermined her credibility. But she didn't care how it looked when it came to Ethan.

A couple of minutes later a balding man in a suit arrived.

"What's going on?" he wanted to know.

"Who are you?" April asked.

"Robert West, head teacher.'

"What happened to Mrs Reynolds?"

The head seemed puzzled.

April waved a dismissive hand. "That doesn't matter. Where's my son?"

"And you are?"

"For God's sake! *April Morris*, and my son's *Ethan*. Now can we forget the bureaucratic bullshit and *do something?*"

"You son's name doesn't ring a bell." He asked the receptionist for confirmation while April fumed, then added "There's obviously been some kind of error. But I don't think it's on our part."

"What are you saying? That I'm lying? Or deluded?" She was shaking now.

"No, no, of course not. Only that there's been ... some sort of mistake."

"Not by me. I just want my child!"

Several members of the teaching staff had gathered in the reception area, dressed for home, and were exchanging looks as they eavesdropped. The head teacher noticed. "Look, I think it might be best if you stepped into one of the offices."

"I'll not be fobbed off."

"Not at all. Just while we sort this out."

Reluctantly, she nodded and followed. He punched a code on the keypad by the inner door and led her along a corridor, its scuffed beige walls bearing cork noticeboards and askew posters. The office they came to housed a cheap wooden desk, a couple of chairs, a grey filing cabinet and shelves packed with textbooks and files. He invited her to take a seat.

"Can I offer you tea, or a coffee?" He saw her expression and swiftly retracted, looking sheepish. "Er, no. Perhaps not. Please wait here and I'll check on the situation."

"What's to check? I've come for my child. Why is that so hard for you to understand?"

"I promise we'll do our best to rectify whatever might have happened."

"Just find my boy," she replied, her voice almost breaking.

He left.

April was still trembling, still tearful. She felt sick. What the hell had happened? Where was Ethan? Why were these people so disbelieving, so unhelpful?

After a while she began to gather her thoughts. The suspicion grew that the school had failed in their responsibility to care for her child and were hiding the truth from her. But what could she do? Of course! The police. They'd know what to do. Why hadn't that occurred to her before? Or to that head teacher, more to the point.

She found her mobile and tapped at it unsteadily. What she got was the engaged tone. Sure that she'd hit the wrong keys she tried again. And again, and again. Since when were the emergency services *engaged*? It was insane!

Waves of despair swept over her and her mind lapsed into a sort of miasma. Bowed head in her hands, tears trickling, she lost track of time.

A sound roused her. Opening her eyes, she felt confused and uncertain of where she was for a moment. She took in the room, which was entirely empty of furniture or anything else, save for the chair she was sitting in. The sound came again and she realised someone was knocking softly on the door. It opened and a youngish woman came in. Her starched white blouse with one of those upside-down watches hanging from its breast pocket indicated that she was a school nurse.

"How are you feeling?" she asked.

"Oh, okay, I suppose."

"Some of my colleagues were a little worried about you."

"I'm ... I don't know. I'm a bit muddled about what I'm doing here."

"That's to be expected. You had something of a turn."

"Did I?"

"No one's really told me what happened, to be honest. I reckon you felt unwell on the street, maybe even fainted, and you were brought in here to recover."

"Oh."

"That's the likeliest thing. I mean, you don't have a child at this school, do you?"

"Uhm, no. No, I don't."

"There you are then."

"I can't quite remember..."

"It'll probably take a few minutes for you to feel yourself again. Any medical condition that might account for it?" She placed a palm on April's forehead, checking her temperature. Her hand felt cool.

"No, nothing," April told her. "Not that I know of."

"Might be best to see your doctor, just to be sure. Or should I call an ambulance?"

"No, I don't think you need to do that."

The nurse looked relieved, probably glad to avoid having to deal with it, and the inevitable paperwork. "Can I get you anything? A glass of water?"

"I'm fine. I should be getting home."

"I might be able to find somebody to take you, if you don't mind waiting a while."

April shook her head. "That's very kind, but I'll be all right."

"Well, if you're sure. The fresh air will do you good, I expect."

April thanked her.

Leaving the empty room, she made her way along the corridor with its totally bare walls and was let out of the building.

APRIL WALKED THE deserted streets, eyeing what her parents' generation would have called bombsites, and there were plenty of them. Great yawning gaps where houses, shops and blocks of flats had been. She needed a cash machine although for the moment she couldn't quite remember why, as she had a nagging feeling that she had sufficient at home. Still, best to be on the safe side. But when she arrived at her bank she found that it had gone too, leaving a cavity as precise and sterile as all the other voids she'd seen. She couldn't summon the energy to seek out another ATM and, as it was getting dark, decided to go home.

The bus was a long time coming and she was the only one on it. Nobody else got on at any of the stops, and in fact the bus simply swept past most of them when it was obvious no one was waiting. Soon they were clear of town and in open countryside.

Her stop was a fair walk from where she lived. After she got off she glanced back. The bus hadn't moved. Its doors were still open and there was no sign of the driver. Nipped out for a pee in the bushes, she assumed.

Night had fallen. The lights of the bus and the few lights in the town well behind her began to dim the further she trudged. But the moon was full and a canopy of stars dusted the sky.

Reaching her isolated house at last, she felt hungry. But there was nothing in the fridge or cupboards. April regretted not having any neighbours; maybe she could have cadged something to eat. She lightly berated herself for her poor housekeeping, thinking how different it would be if she ever had children, or a husband around. Couldn't be so sloppy then.

Having no TV, she flipped on the portable radio in the kitchen. All she got was a scratchy hissing, wherever she turned the dial. Reception was bad out here in the back of beyond, it seemed. She switched it off.

Where had her energy gone? Unusually for her she felt tired enough to take a nap. Climbing the stairs, she idly wondered why she lived in so large a house. On the top landing she glanced into the room next to her bedroom, thinking that she really ought to wash the blue curtains in there. The empty room could probably do with a lick of paint too. Maybe she should turn it into a study, a place to write. But April didn't want to think about that now. Going to her room she fell asleep as soon as her head touched the pillow.

She woke up hours later, in the middle of the night. Something was tickling the back of her mind. Of course. That damn article. She got off her bed, the sole piece of furniture in the room, and walked the naked floorboards to the uncarpeted stairs.

In the living room, with its single couch, a coffee table with her laptop and nothing else, she opened the file. Before starting to re-read what she'd written she fancied a drink, which was uncharacteristic as she rarely favoured alcohol. But there were no bottles on the table that was the only fixture in the kitchen. Perhaps one of her friends had finished it when they were last here. Though she couldn't remember when, or who that could have been.

Returning to the laptop she gazed at the open blank file and tried to remember what she meant to do. She allowed herself to imagine how nice it would be to have a commission, perhaps from one of those high paying women's magazines. Then, of course, there was her novel. She really ought to start it. Or at least make some notes.

Maybe she'd begin tomorrow. New day, new start, right?

April looked through the uncurtained window. Still muzzy from her nap she felt the need for a breath of fresh air. She went to the front door and stepped out.

The sky was pitch black, lacking moon or stars. There were no lights anywhere or planes passing overhead. Nor were than any other houses. Walking a little distance, she turned around and found that to be literally true. She stood alone on a desolate terrain, unbroken in every direction by trees, hills or structures of any kind.

She realised that she was barefoot, and her clothes were in tatters. Crumbling and falling from her, in fact. It was rapidly growing difficult to remember very much, including her own name. Everything was ... evaporating. Not least her self-awareness.

Yet when all else was gone, when the very atoms of her being departed and the gloom deepened, she retained one thing until the end. Something she couldn't comprehend. A sense of loss.

Then even the darkness went away.

PRETTY THINGS

Marie O'Regan

THE CLUB WAS so full of die-hard dancers jumping around it was practically vibrating. John looked around at its occupants as they writhed on the dance floor, comfortable with his hard-won spot at the crowded bar – he couldn't believe the place was this full on a Sunday night, let alone that he was actually in it. He took a swig of his beer and leaned back against the counter trying to ignore the slight damp feeling that signalled he'd leant against a spill which was now trickling over the bar's edge – reminded all over again of why he'd given up on clubbing years ago.

He was getting a headache, the pulse at his temple thumping in time to the music. Christ! He hadn't even wanted to come, really; it was Sunday after all, work in the morning, and clubs weren't really his thing anymore – but Adam from work had insisted he turn up, promising he wouldn't regret it as he scribbled the address on a scrap of paper. "The women," he'd said, his tone almost reverent. "I've never seen so many babes."

The fact he'd used the term "babes" said to John that Adam didn't often go out to clubs or indeed anywhere anymore; and yet... John's interest had been piqued. Single for almost six months now, he was bored. It was time for a new diversion. And Adam had been right, in a way: there were a lot of women here – although he wasn't sure he'd call any of them "babes", even if that had been a word he was prone to using. He kept his gaze casual, trying to avoid the stares he was garnering in return from women hoping to hook up. No one had caught his eye so far; his taste ran to the slightly more unusual.

The music changed, the beat ramping up in volume until John thought his fillings were coming loose, and he sighed as he looked around in vain for Adam. The lighting didn't make it easy to spot anyone in particular; the strobing almost manic in its intensity. No use. Adam obviously hadn't been able to make it out tonight. A routine cheat, his wife must have sensed something in the offing and put the kibosh on nights out for a while. It had happened before and would no doubt happen again in the not too-distant future. Adam just couldn't help himself.

John smiled at the memory of the last girl his workmate had conned, a twenty-three-year-old secretary from work, just moved to London from her parents' place in Devon. Shy and slightly overweight, slow to make friends, she'd been easy prey.

His smile fell as he remembered the outcome. Annie – that's right, Annie – had left work abruptly. Rumour around the office was of a failed suicide attempt – wrists cut, found by a flatmate returning early. Annie was back in Devon, heartbroken, safe in the bosom of her family, while Adam went back to wifey without a care in the world. Or maybe Adam had just set him up for a laugh; who knew?

Still. John wasn't like that. He went out with a lot of women, that was true, but he was strictly a one at a time guy. They just didn't tend to work out, that's all, he always got bored – and if a woman got clingy that sounded the death knell on their relationship immediately. He frowned as he tried to remember the last time a girlfriend had been around for more than a month, then smiled as a new prospect caught his eye. What did that matter? Plenty more fish and all that...

The woman dancing in front of him stood out. She was tall, maybe five-ten or so, with dark hair that looked as if it fell to shoulder-length normally; now it was sweat-soaked, whipping around her face as she whirled and swayed to the beat. She was so pale she could have been mistaken for a ghost – with scarlet lips and dark, dark eyes, heavily made up to accentuate that fact. She was oblivious to everyone around her, and those surrounding the woman seemed to edge back to leave a space almost unconsciously, leaving her a clear area to dance and be observed.

John smiled. She'd do. He stood straighter, puffing his chest out slightly and sucking in what little gut there was – he was slightly embarrassed as he spotted a few fellow drinkers noticing his actions but that soon faded when he turned back to the girl.

She was staring right at him.

She started to walk towards John, a corner of her mouth starting to tilt upwards into a semblance of a smile at the shocked expression on his face as he watched. It was a matter of a few seconds before she was standing beside him, leaning into him as she whispered "Want to dance?"

It seemed an answer wasn't required. She grabbed his free hand and started to pull, forcing him to follow even as he slammed his beer back on the bar, spilling half of it. She led him back into the crowd, which parted silently as they passed. Several men seemed eager to turn away, hiding their faces as John and his partner passed by.

He frowned and tried to look closer, but they were gone before he could see more, and he found himself alone in the centre of the dance floor with the beauty who'd grabbed him. She was dancing once more, rubbing against him every now and then as she did so, whirling in time to the ever-pounding beat, staying close and filling his senses with her perfume. He tried to dance, tried to move in time with her, but was painfully aware of his shortcomings as a dancer and felt himself flushing with embarrassment. He never had been good with music.

She didn't seem to care.

Then she was in front of him, standing still, staring directly into his eyes. Was that blood? A single red drop was welling in the corner of her right eye, brilliant against her impossibly white skin, but it didn't fall. He could smell her perfume again; it was intoxicating this close to her and he swayed as dizziness rushed at him. He forgot about the tear, forgot about everything. She leaned into him and brushed the corner of his mouth with her lips; they were soft, tender. She cupped his chin in her hand and tilted his head a little so that her lips met his directly when she kissed him again. He offered no resistance. His lips parted, and he could taste her – so sweet. So intense. This was all there was.

"COME ON."

"What?" He shook his head, looked around. Miraculously, the lights were up – couples blinking and scowling in the sudden onslaught of bright light as they broke apart, headed to the sides of the dance floor. Singletons were scattered around the room's edges, looking sheepish as they finished their drinks and headed towards the exit.

When did it get so late? Dimly, he felt her grasp his hand and exert pressure. He followed her outside without a word; the sight of someone turning away from him even as they put up a hand to hide their face serving as a reminder that certain members of the club's clientele didn't look right, somehow. Most ignored him, and he wasn't worried about them – they were the usual crowd, nothing out of place, more interested in closing the deal and getting their partner home than what others were doing. But some ... some shifted aside as he passed, shielding their faces from view just as the first had. He couldn't see anything specific that was bothering him but the very act of hiding was enough. They stood slightly stooped over, shoulders rounded, faces turned away. They weren't together; they were dotted around the club, watching those surrounding them, apparently trying to remain hidden.

John managed to catch one of them in the act of turning, and glimpsed the side of his face, quickly concealed as he completed his manoeuvre. The man's skin wasn't just pale, it was white – and shiny as if it were a plastic mask. Could it be one of those Kabuki things? Or white pancake make-up, like they wore on stage; the skin had that flat sheen to it. Then his companion was pulling him forward, leading him towards the exit. He was seeing things in flashes; disjointed images that made no sense, didn't even appear connected: a face; eyes bleeding; a flash of sharp teeth; the bar; the bouncer ushering him forward; the doors ... and then he was outside, standing on the street taking huge breaths of the night air, wondering why he felt so drunk. The ground was shifting beneath his feet, his stomach roiling in response. He could taste vomit, sour and hot, at the back of his throat, and he couldn't seem to stand straight without swaying. He'd only had a couple of beers – this shouldn't be happening!

"This way."

She pulled him towards a limousine that was waiting, sleek and black, by the kerb outside the club. Various club-goers were casting surreptitious glances at it, no doubt wondering who'd booked the posh car. The door swung open, held by a tall slender individual in a black overcoat. Another of the pale-faced tribe he'd been noticing all night; this one was no different, eyes downcast so that John couldn't get a good look at him. He was so *pale*. John wondered if it they were related – could it be a family trait? Or was it an illness they shared? Hell, maybe it was a lifestyle choice – they could all be nocturnal, for all he knew.

She laughed as if she'd heard him, the sound grating against his ears, and he flinched. Then he was being pulled, headfirst, into the dark interior of the car, dimly aware of other car doors slamming shut; they had company, it seemed. He sank down into the well-cushioned seat and tried not to throw up as he was overpowered by the scent of freshly polished leather and something sweeter, more cloying. He closed his eyes, and then she was kissing him again. He felt his stomach rise and dip and then he knew nothing.

HE WAS IN a room. What kind of room he couldn't say; it was dark and it was big, but he couldn't see more than that. He shifted his head slightly, realising he was half-sitting, half-lying on some kind of reclining chair – a dentist's chair, maybe? No, that was stupid – and yet he was more lying than sitting, that had to be said. The air smelled of ... something. It was sweet, pervasive and had a ... an almost metallic tang?

He swallowed as he realised what it was. He could smell blood. By the strength of the odour quite a lot of it had been spilt somewhere nearby. Shadows loomed and ducked on the wall nearest to him as John tried to focus. There were figures lining the walls, people standing just out of his range of vision, watching him. One looked up, and he saw a flash of white. So, more of the masked.

"What's the matter?"

He knew that voice. He turned his head to the left and there she was, magnificent as ever. Tall, dark hair falling sleekly to her shoulders, as he'd known it would, and that bloody tear was in the corner of her eye again. Or was it the same one? He hadn't seen any tears fall, no tracks on her face, so maybe it was a piercing of some kind? Something jewelled?

"It's blood," she said as if he'd asked her that question, and he shook his head again, trying to clear it, to focus. "It remains there to remind me of what is, what was."

"I don't understand," he said and swallowed sickness back once more. He tried to raise an arm and was shocked to discover he couldn't - it was bound to the arm of the chair by a thick leather strap.

"We don't want you hurting yourself, do we," she whispered, fumbling at his other side, and then one of his arms was free.

He reached for her but she was gone, dancing back out of reach as if knowing that was his intention. John groaned and knuckled his eyes in an attempt to clear his vision. No use. It was barely lit at all, this place, and yet somewhere something was glinting on the walls and floor, sending up what looked like wet sparks from the...

His eyes narrowed, and he stared harder at the floor. It was wet and the liquid was dark - but was that because of the lack of a light source, or...?

It was blood. Of course, how had he forgotten so quickly? That explained the strength of the metallic odour; it was all around him. He cried out, tried to wrench his other hand free but it didn't work - the straps were very tight, cutting into the puffy flesh of his wrist. How long had he been trying to get free, he wondered? What else didn't he remember?

One of the crowd moved forward, hunched over his free arm and tried to grab it, force it down.

John hit out and was pleased to hear a low grunt in response. He wasn't powerless after all. He clenched his fist and aimed again but this time the blow glanced off the man's cheek. Something shifted. John reached out and grabbed, wondering if he'd been right.

The thing that had shifted had been a mask.

His fingers scrabbled for the edge of the mask and he pulled hard, even as the other man tried to step back out of reach. The mask came away with a ripping sound – and the man screamed.

John stared at the thing in his hand. It *was* a mask, white, but not plastic as he'd thought. He wasn't sure what it was made of. It had a shine to it, like marble, but it didn't feel like stone. It was warm, felt like flesh, and the inside of it was slick with blood. He looked up into what was left of the other's face, and groaned. The man was whimpering, holding his hands in front of the ruin that was underneath, but seemingly afraid to touch the flesh.

His face was gone. The skull underneath was a yellowy-white, with gobbets of bloody flesh adhering to it here and there. He was sobbing, the ruins of his tongue clearly visible as he swallowed through the gap between his upper and lower sets of teeth. The teeth, unencumbered by any soft tissue at all, appeared large and sharp – as if all he possessed were canines. The creature was moaning softly now, swaying from side to side even as John offered back the mask, eager to cover up the mess of its face and ease its pain. He glanced at John, just once, as he took the mask back and his eyes were full of fire. He let the hand holding the remains of his face hang at his side and walked off. John could hear him sobbing as he went.

"That wasn't very nice."

Her voice was harsher now, as she swung a leg across him and sat in his lap. She traced a nail down the side of his cheek – and he felt the skin separate beneath it. A trickle of blood started to trace a path down his neck.

"Don't," he said.

She laughed. "Don't what?" She leaned forward and forced her tongue into his mouth, tasted him. She ground into his lap and he was uncomfortably aware that he was growing hard. It didn't seem to make any difference that he was terrified.

She stroked his face again and this time he couldn't feel it – there was a weird feeling of pressure, like touching something through a glove, but he couldn't actually feel her skin against his.

"What did you do?"

She smiled. "Nothing you should worry about, beautiful."

"What?"

She sighed and gestured to her companions, clustered now at the far end of the room, around the poor unfortunate he'd unwittingly maimed. The creature had his mask back on but his eyes were burning and he stared back at John as if he wanted him dead. A bloody trail etched one cheek, and as John watched he wiped it away, examining his hand and holding up the evidence so John could see what he'd done.

The light was brighter now. As John looked around he realised this was nothing as simple as a room; it was a kind of chamber, with high, vaulted ceilings and rough-hewn walls – a cave? If so it was enormous. The flickering was constant and there was a sound like wind in a bellows, and moaning. Someone was definitely moaning, somewhere just out of sight.

"Where are we?" he asked.

"We're home," she answered. "Where all the pretty things go. And you're definitely pretty, John." She set to with her nail again and he felt the bleeding increase – he could feel wetness but no pain, just the feeling of his shirt growing sodden as liquid trickled down.

She leaned close and whispered into his ear. He felt a nip as she bit his earlobe. "Where do you think we are, pretty? Any idea?"

He shook his head and moaned as a bright spark of pain lit up the side of his face like a neon sign. Whatever she'd used to numb his face was wearing off – he could feel it all.

She sat back, stared at him. The woman was clearly bored now. Her face too was like the others – this was the first time he'd noticed it was a mask. Shiny and white, just like theirs – the light down here lent it an almost greasy sheen. Her eyes were dark, flames flickered in their depths, and the red tear was ever-present, only now it was wet. As he watched it dripped down her cheek and was replaced by another perfect teardrop in the corner of her eye. It glittered like glass. Her lips too were scarlet – he couldn't work out how she made a mask smile. He wasn't even sure he wanted to know. She smiled wider, and her lips parted to show teeth, tiny and perfect and extremely sharp. She leaned forward and bit his lip. And pulled. He screamed and then all was dark once more.

TIME PASSED. HOW much, he wasn't sure. He was still in that dank underground chamber, still watched by the creatures with the white faces and tear-marked eyes, still in the chair. He tried to move a hand and was shocked to find it worked.

Tentatively he reached up to touch his face but couldn't feel anything. His face felt cold, smooth to the touch. Someone giggled and he whirled around to see who was finding this funny.

There she was.

"Oh lover," she said, and came closer. "Don't you get it?"

John saw she was holding a mirror and now he didn't want to know; didn't want to see. He closed his eyes and twisted his head, trying to avoid her.

Someone caught his jaw and forced him to face forward. The woman was standing directly in front of him, her expression sad. "Don't you want to see?" she asked.

He shook his head or tried to, but couldn't shake free of his captor's grasp.

She sighed. "Too late now, John. You have to."

The glass rose and he started to cry. There in front of him, in the looking glass, was another of the masked creatures, a red tear forming even now in the corner of his eye. He could feel it forcing its way out, like trying to pass a stone. He groaned and as he did so he saw his eyes flicker. They were on fire and now he could feel the heat. It was under his skin, in his eyes, it was everywhere. He was fire. And he was lost.

"You're one of us now," she said. "You'll always be one of the pretty things, a creature of blood and bone, of flesh and desire."

"The what? Where are we?"

Now she laughed and the sound was cruel, echoed by his companions. "Oh lover," she whispered, "we are where all the pretty things go."

GUISING

Gary McMahon

WHEN JUDITH HEARD the sound a second time she went to the window and tilted a single wooden slat in the horizontal blinds so that she could see the road outside her house. The television volume was turned down low from the last time, when she'd thought she heard a loud clatter from outside, and the only light in the room came from a low lamp on a corner table.

She thought in that moment how vulnerable she suddenly felt in her own home. All it took to break the illusion of security was a sound she could not identify - a knocking sound from somewhere along the street.

Her small front garden was more attractive than most of the others on her road. She prided herself on keeping it neat and tidy. The borders were well tended. The black and green wheelie bins stood guard, one at each side of the gate. The footpath and the roadway beyond were deserted. Halloween lanterns glowed in a few windows, but not many. They tended not to celebrate things like that on this street - Halloween, Easter, even Christmas was a muted affair. The cost of having middle-aged and elderly neighbours, she supposed. There was not even the sound of distant traffic to disturb the peace.

"Nope," she said. "I must be hearing things." She'd taken up talking to herself not long after Trevor died. She found herself unable to cope with the silence he'd left behind, the lack of background noise, so she filled it with the sound of her own voice.

Turning away from the window she walked across the room and sat back down in her armchair. She picked up her cup from the antique table and sipped her tea. The honey tasted sweet behind the bitterness of the cheap blend.

Judith grabbed the remote control from the arm of the chair and switched off the television. She picked up a paperback book from the floor and opened it at the page she'd been reading last night, before falling asleep in the seat. It was a collection of poetry. Rilke was becoming her favourite. She enjoyed the rhythms, the way that the words failed to mask a yearning that echoed with her own sense of longing for the return of her the things she had lost.

Even as she read, Judith listened out for another sound. She was spooked. Something had caused her to bristle, like a cat challenged in an alley.

When her eyes began to close she did not fight it. In fact, she welcomed the slowly encroaching darkness. Sleep was her ally, it was her friend. When she slept the pain faded and the loss of Trevor seemed to diminish, a figure on a distant shore, waving, moving even farther away.

The sound woke her. It felt like only minutes had passed but glancing at the clock flanked by old school photos of Trevor smiling shyly in his uniform, she realised that she had been asleep for more than an hour. Licking dry lips, she struggled to her feet. That was another thing about getting older – even standing out of a chair made things ache.

"Stupid cats," she said, thinking about the neighbourhood strays. "Always messing around in the bins."

At the window she paused before adjusting the blind. She

couldn't fathom why she was delaying the action, but something felt wrong - or, if not wrong entirely, it felt strange, as if a shadow had crossed her face.

There was nothing out there.

She closed the blind.

Feeling brave she went to the front door and stared at the patterned glass panel set into the woodwork at head-height. There was nobody out there, standing silently on the step. To prove it beyond doubt, she stepped forward and opened the door, surprising herself with her forcefulness.

The cold crept inside. The streetlights did not flicker. The dark did not grow darker. Everything was normal, all was well. Rubbing her arms more out of habit than against the chill, Judith felt emboldened enough to walk along the narrow path to the gate. Leaning out over the waist-high painted metal barrier, she looked up and then down the street.

Right at the far end, on the corner, past the parked cars and the white van that was always left with one of its front wheels on the curb and the pothole outside number four, stood a figure.

Judith wasn't afraid. Why would she be?

The figure was motionless. It was draped in what at first looked to be a dirty sheet.

"Tomorrow," Judith whispered. "Halloween is tomorrow. You're a day early."

The grubby ghost could not hear her, it was too far away. The figure simply stood there facing away from her - she could tell by the feet; the sheet, or whatever it was, only came down to the knees.

Judith turned away and went back inside, walking just a little bit faster than usual. She hated herself for rushing, but she couldn't quite shake the feeling that the figure had slowly turned and began to scamper down the street toward her.

She looked back quickly before shutting the door.

The figure had not followed her. The street was empty. The garden remained neat and tidy. The night was still and quiet, as always in this part of town.

Disturbed and unable to settle back into her book or watch any more television, Judith switched off the lights, shut the downstairs doors, and went up to bed. Undressing before the mirror she recalled stripping off her clothes for Bill, her late husband, too many years before. They'd shared a passionate relationship and Trevor, their son, had been an offshoot of that passion. But now her arms were thin, her back was brittle, and where once she'd had generous curves the shape of her ribs showed through her skin.

Slipping her nightgown on over her head, she moved to the window. Opened the blinds. The figure was no longer at the end of the street.

It was closer, now. Standing in the road beside the white van with its front wheel on the curb. From this distance Judith could see that it was not draped in a dirty bed-sheet after all. The figure was wearing a costume that consisted of a sheet of bubble wrap. The same stuff in which she'd packed her china plates when they'd moved to this house. It had come on a roll, and every time she turned her back Trevor would tear off a piece and start popping the little plastic bubbles between his finger and thumb. It was cute at first but soon the repetitive sound – *pop, pop* – became irritating and she shouted at him to stop.

If he were here now she wouldn't shout at him. She would sit down and join him, popping the bubbles, laughing and crying at the same time.

Out on the street, the figure did not move. This time it was facing her, but of course she could not see its features beneath the bubble wrap. It looked like a boy – short, stocky, lacking any sense of the feminine.

"Tomorrow," she said again. "Come back tomorrow."

She shut the blinds and went to her bed, feeling

unaccountably sad. She wasn't afraid. She knew she should be at least a little unnerved by the figure outside, but for reasons she could not examine right now fear was superseded by an ache of melancholy.

It did not take Judith long to drift off to sleep. She felt that a soft-blistered hand was holding hers, and even though that hand was her own it offered comfort.

The ringing brought her up out of sleep. Reaching for the phone she sat up in bed, blinking into the darkness. "Hello," she said, putting the phone to her ear.

Nothing. Just the sound of static, like a wind.

"Hello ... who is it?"

Pop. Pop.

"No..."

Pop. Pop. Pop.

"Trevor? Is it you, darling?"

The plastic bubbles kept popping, small fingers squeezing them.

Pop. Pop.

When she awoke again she was unable to grasp whether the phone call had been real or just part of a dream. She rummaged around for her phone and checked the call history. Nothing. It had been a dream after all. Of course it had. Trevor was gone. He was never coming back. They'd found his body on a rubbish dump a mile away from home, with twenty-seven stab wounds in his torso and face.

A local gang, the police had said. A case of mistaken identity, because everybody knew that her son was a good boy and kept away from the street gangs. He wanted to be a doctor when he grew up. Or a policeman. Someone who did good.

Had there been sheets of bubble wrap on the site where he'd been found? Discarded packing material from decaying cardboard boxes scattered across the ground? Had his body been partially encased in a bubble wrap shroud?

Pushing aside these thoughts she got out of bed and put on her robe. Moving through the house like a ghost, as she often did, she went downstairs and put on the kettle. It was still dark outside. She did not sleep much these days. The clock on the wall told her it was 4:00 a.m.

The knock on the door made it seem so much later – too late, in fact.

Judith turned slowly to face the kitchen door, and the hallway beyond. Through the glass panel in the front door she glimpsed an inchoate shape – a mass that might have been a face, but covered in something.

"Tomorrow ... please."

The sound of the kettle behind her, building up a head of steam. Soon it would boil and the clicking sound as it switched itself off would break the spell.

The glass panel in the door was clear now. There was nobody outside. Had she imagined the knock at the door? Things were slipping ... reality was fragmenting, but only partially. Everything was normal except for the times when it wasn't. How long ago had her husband died of cancer? How many years after that had her teenage son been murdered? Was she forty-five or fifty-five years old? When was her sixtieth birthday? Had she missed it, in the way she had ignored so many other milestones since being left behind by the ones she loved?

"Are you out there?" She had no idea to whom she was speaking, she didn't know who she meant. Moving slowly, as if she were still dreaming, Judith drifted along the hallway and opened the front door. The sky had lightened, the day was coming. She walked to the garden gate and looked both ways along the street. A figure was turning the far corner, moving away, trailing behind it on the ground a sheet of bubbled plastic, the other end of which was clasped in its concealed hand.

"Come back." She knew it would. It was only a question

of when.

Back inside, she drank black coffee and craved the cigarettes she'd given up before Trevor was even born. That seemed like only yesterday, and it seemed like a hundred years ago. Everything was now – now was never. Time was unravelling before her, like a ball of yarn sent spinning down an incline. Today was yesterday was two or three decades ago.

The morning slowed down and passed without incident. She wished she had a dog or a cat – some kind of pet to at least fill a corner of the house with life. But Bill had not been an animal lover, and Trevor was always too selfish too look after anything other than himself. It would have come down to her. It always came down to her, in the end.

She put on her shoes and her coat and left the house, needing to be involved in the world, even if it only meant a trip to the corner shop to pick up something she really didn't need. A couple of neighbours waved at her from their gardens. A man she didn't know was pruning the hedge of number seventeen. He wore a woollen hat and a pair of workmen's overalls. His eyes were narrow. She didn't like the look of him, so hurried on towards the shop. There was a grubby scrap of bubble wrap in the gutter.

Tariq, the young Pakistani man who ran the shop for his parents, was sticking prices on Halloween masks when she walked in.

"Morning missus," he said smiling. He was always smiling, such a happy boy.

"Good morning, Tariq. How are your folks?"

"Fine thanks. They're down south visiting family."

She nodded, smiled, had nothing else to say. Browsing the aisles of the small shop, she looked for something to buy. The red-top newspapers all looked like the comic books of her childhood; she had plenty of milk in the fridge at home; she'd stopped eating bread a couple of years ago after some trouble with her stomach. Eventually, on impulse, she picked up a four-pack of beer. It was the kind Trevor had liked to drink. She knew he was too young but she'd rather he told her about it than sneaking cans out of the house when she wasn't around.

"Taking up ale drinking?" Tariq laughed as he rang up her purchase.

"Just fancied a couple, that's all."

"So, these aren't for the trick-or-treaters later on tonight?"

"I'd better get some sweets for them," she said. "Give me a couple of those big bags there. Can't have them going away empty-handed..."

"Or playing a trick, eh? Last year we had eggs chucked at our windows."

She left the shop feeling better, more included in her own life. If people were speaking to her it meant she still existed. They could see her. She was still there. Sometimes, when she was shut away inside that house for days, she began to doubt the truth of her own existence. It wasn't unpleasant, it was simply lonely, and loneliness never hurt as much as you thought, not when you became accustomed to its slow quiet music.

Back home, she opened one of the cans and poured beer into a glass. She remembered the empties she'd always had to pick up from the floor of Trevor's room, and how he'd yelled at her whenever she went in there while he was out. The things she'd found in his drawers – the knives, the little plastic baggies filled with white powder.

But he'd been a good boy. The best.

His death had been a terrible mistake; he had nothing to do with the gangs that had taken over the old housing estates a few miles east of here.

A good boy. They were all good boys, until they turned bad.

Fighting back tears, she drank the beer. It was horrible but she forced it down, gagging once or twice as she finished off the entire glass in one breathless swig. It didn't make her feel any better. The edges of her world were frayed, flapping like torn rags in a silent wind.

Time compressed again and it was dusk. She went around the house turning on the lights, trying to hold back the darkness. It always came down to her. Part of her job was to stave off the night.

Her life was leaking away. It was as if she were a plastic bottle in which there was a tiny, unseen hole. A pinprick. The liquid within was escaping slowly - you couldn't see the level go down unless you stood and stared for hours. The next thing you knew, the container was empty.

She wished that she'd bought one of those Halloween masks from the shop, to hide behind. Or at least a couple of spooky decorations that she could have placed in the window to welcome the ghosts and the ghouls and the figures that drifted through the shadows. Instead, she poured the sweets she'd bought into a large bowl and set it down on the shelf near the front door. She didn't expect any visitors. They'd stopped coming a long time ago. They all stopped coming in the end, staying away rather than straying too close to the cold embers of a lightless fire.

When she looked out the window the figure was standing at the gate. The gate was open but the figure had not stepped through. The bubble wrap was dirty, streaked with what looked like mud and greenish patches of decay. The plastic was torn in places; through the flaps she could see bulges of pale bloated matter, like pulped paper.

"Have you come for me?"

The figure moved. Its hands, beneath the plastic, twitched, and even though she was unable to hear she knew that the fingers were at work popping the tiny plastic bubbles.

"I'm not sure if I'm ready, Trevor."

The figure stopped moving.

It wasn't Trevor. She knew that. Nothing in life was so

neat and ordered: your ghosts did not return to save you, the love you shared withered and died, good boys all went bad in the end.

But it would suffice, this figure. In the absence of her imperfect family this rotting image would serve a purpose she didn't quite understand. She wasn't sure if it had come to guide her to another place or to imprison her here, in this mausoleum of a home.

In the end, it didn't matter. Nothing mattered. Not anymore.

She turned away from the window, put on her coat, and went to the door, grabbing a handful of sweets from the bowl on impulse. She stared at the glass panel and a blurred shape appeared there, on the other side. When she opened the door, it was waiting for her.

She could hear the popping sound as what passed for fingers crushed the plastic, and she smiled as it reached out for her, the plastic-wrapped hand slipping softly into her own. It felt too soft ... spongy, perhaps even boneless. The way the fingers moved was all wrong, as if they had too many joints, or no joints at all.

The figure led her out of the garden, into the road, and along the silent street. On the corner several more bubble-wrapped figures waited, each of them small and silent and inscrutable. Wherever she was going there would be more of them there. This world was not theirs but they had crossed over on this night to fetch her. She would not be missed and she would miss nothing that she was leaving behind. Her memories were all broken; the life she had clung to for so long was nothing but a sham, a string of bitter images she had moulded into something more palatable.

The people she thought she had loved had not loved her as much in return, and when they were gone she had nothing to fill the gaps they left behind.

Around her, the figures began to move. She dropped the

sweets on the ground at her feet. As the small, almost shapeless hand tightened its grip on her fingers, more bubbles popped. For some reason, the small, inconsequential sounds made her heart ache. One of the other figures stepped forward to drape a stained sheet of bubble wrap over her head – the ragged hem reached to a few inches below her knees.

For what felt like the first time in her life Judith closed her eyes. And finally, she could see.

MASKS

Peter Sutton

THE MORNING FOG soaked him to the core, like always. He had spent too long here and now night touched day. He shivered. The wood-and-bone mask he turned over and over in his hands, made slippery with dew. No one remembered whose idea the masks were. No one wanted to remember. The masks were idealised animals. They had made birds, reptiles, cats. Predators made from flotsam and jetsam, and the bones of unfortunates: animals, and men, washed ashore. He sighed, time to return. He span the likeness of a hare between his fingers.

He clambered to his feet and contemplated the sea. The booming rolling breakers, one wall of their prison on the beach, sounded ethereal in the fog. Their constant susurrus accompanied all waking and sleeping hours. He remembered his nightmares, the long tolling of alarm bells, the screams, the battering force of the water.

The cold wet clothes made him shiver again as the first intimation of the morning sun started to burn off the fog. A fogbow arched over the waves as they smashed into the coast. A dim ship's outline, ghostly black in the white of the fog, became perceptible. Seabird shapes on all its surfaces shook themselves in preparation. The fog wisped away as if it had never existed. In a short amount of time he wished that the cold had remained: the sun blazed as it rose. Having watched the uncovering of the grave of many of his friends a fierce need to survive gripped him.

All he could focus on was the wreck – stark against the fathomless sea, covered in guano, nothing more than a nest for birds. Merely one example of the rapine sea's harsh legacy upon the beach.

They'd explored many miles in both directions, until the cliffs to the north stopped them and the unknown vastness of desert dunes to the south. Wrecks and bones littered the landscape. Hundreds of years of failed seamanship; death from thirst, from hunger, from worse. Hyenas roamed at night cracking the bones and sucking the marrow from them. Not the first to wash up here; they wouldn't be the last. The vast salt pan to the east, a featureless plain that stretched for countless miles of waterless waste, their last barrier to escape.

The sun, the enervating sun – their captor.

The black, somehow vulpine, seabirds sprang aloft as one, their voices raised like mocking laughter. The six-storey wicker man will appear to burst into flames. He hurried his step.

The mask, face up with sightless eyes judging him. He already knew who would celebrate and who would be worried. Shana would have woken by now. The box of masks open, his absence – signs and portents. She'd wait for him to announce it but by the time he returned – his nonappearance, her being alone – would alert some of them. His coming into camp from the direction of the sea, the mask in his hands, the bright red ribbons fluttering in the rising breeze, would be all the signs needed. His reluctant steps brought him closer to the camp.

As ever, after a still night, after a drowning fog, the sun burned the sand. He steamed in the sunlight. He narrowed his eyes in what had become an instinctive gesture. The sun burnt all and everyone, young and old alike, displayed white crow's feet from the eternal scrunching. A breeze sprang up that would build throughout the day. The finest particles of sand, ancient ground bones, tiny particles of quartz, mica, feldspar, scoured the camp.

Driftwood and whalebone huts rose from the sand haphazardly. His path brought him to one slightly larger than most, a little lopsided, once green tarpaulin, much-mended, billowing in the swell of the breeze. It reminded him of the sea; another of their captors. He paused at the entrance. A few men had watched him return to camp. They had planned for fishing, were up early to put it into play. He knew that they'd fail. Like all the others had failed. He turned away from their eyes, sighed deeply, squared his shoulders then swished the material aside and entered his dwelling.

The contrast between blinding sun and blinding dark confounded his eyes for a few seconds. His partner Shana sat very still by the box of masks, the red velvet bag – a recovery from the wreck that had once held something of monetary worth – a splash of colour upon the grey and white.

"So soon?" she asked.

He nodded. The silence stretched. He sighed again. "The children…"

She closed her eyes, turned her head. He yearned to offer comfort but knew she would take none. Their own child a memory sharp and painful; nothing grew here. His hands opened and closed. In two strides he was at the box and let slip the mask he carried which landed with a soft sound onto the piles of its siblings.

"We have to."

Only silence greeted his words.

"I'll let the council know."

Today the *council*, a collection of former ship's crew and a couple of representatives of its former passengers, met, ostensibly to hear the report from the cliff committee and the fishing committee. But they'd know by now that he'd raise the issue, that a new hunt would be soon. He stalked out of the hut casting a last glance over his shoulder at Shana, sat forlornly. It had to be now. He marched over to where the committee, former ship's officers, squatted talking about lost rope, lack of projectile weapons to reach the birds, the hyenas and other such trivia.

"It's time for another hunt," he said dropping the words into the uncomfortable silence. He watched their reaction:

sideways glances, a smirk from the purser swiftly hidden, a deckhand closing his eyes, a woman's hitched breathing and blush. No one argued; the necessity was beyond doubt – they needed to eat. "We must think of the children," he said.

The nurse spoke: "About the children. The baby is likely permanently blind..." When they'd first arrived, before they'd created shelters, before squinting became second nature, many had suffered eye complaints. The baby had been exposed, helpless. Its mother was one of those that had been buried shortly after they arrived. She'd survived to see her baby to the beach then her heart had given out. The swim had tested each of them to their limits.

He thought about Shana and their lost child. "Do what you can."

The nurse looked as if she might say more but then gave a swift shallow nod.

THE DRIFTWOOD BURNED with an eerie green flame that cast a lambent glow upon the castaways gathered like penitents around the box of masks. He lifted the velvet bag and shook it, the clack of disks of bone sounded loud in the hushed assembly. Eager hands plunged towards the bag. He watched with some detachment. Different people had different strategies. If you chose early the odds were in your favour of choosing a white bone disk rather than the blackened one. Others hung back, wanting to defer the knowledge of which they'd be until the very last minute, hoping that someone would pull the fire-blackened disk before they had to make a choice.

Those that pulled from the bag first trooped across to where Shana handed out the masks.

"No! no-no-no." The man who'd pulled the black disk stared at it in horror. The grabbing hands disappeared and people, without glancing at the prey, clamoured for the rest of the masks. Unlike some of the others the man, one of the passengers, didn't beg. He skipped directly to running. One by one the people putting on the masks changed – their stances, the way they moved, became baser, regressed. Arms dangled, backs slouched, hunched. Figures cavorted around the campfires. A bacchanalian vortex ready to explode into the hunt, awaiting his signal.

He turned the mask over in his hands and glanced at Shana. He wondered if people just used the masks as an excuse, a communal shucking of responsibility to be more than animal; a shared hallucination of devolution. Some of them expressed excesses of guilt afterwards, the taste still in their mouths, dirty fingernails. But the masks gave them a convenient willed illusion. He could never bring himself to share in that illusion. He had to retain more control than the rank and file. He retained the "honour" to give the signal.

The fire leapt as a log burnt through and crashed into pieces spitting sparks high. He lifted the bone whistle to his mouth and gave three sharp blasts. With a great roar the congregation sped off in pursuit of its prey. He ran to catch up.

As they rushed across the sand the sudden tolling of a great bell rang out. Pursued and pursuer froze. The tones came from the sea. An alarm. Without pausing to take off their masks the crowd moved as one towards the waves. Still shambling and shuffling like degenerates.

He lifted his mask so it rode on his head like a hat. He wondered, was it a rescue, a summons? He sprinted past the horde of animal-headed figures. But once he got to the ocean he could see a ship in trouble. Some way off but clearly struggling. Its lights swung crazily and the bell tolled deep, a sound he remembered in his nightmares. The treacherous coast boasted swift currents and riptides, hidden sandbanks and rocks, deep fogs. It was too easy to become lost and run aground. That looked to be the problem. The sea smashed the ship against a hidden obstacle like a thrush knocking a snail against a stone again and again with a deep thumping crack.

Then vague shouts and cries split the night air in the distance. The gloom of the evening obscured events, with just the light of a half-moon granting half-glimpses. The sound of lifeboats being put to sea was unmistakable though. He strained his eyes searching the darkness; what was happening?

He remembered their own efforts at rowing to shore. The

lifeboat turned into a plaything of the ocean, smashed against the sea floor within the monumental and insurmountable breakers. Each of the boats having to contend with walls of water. Many didn't make it. Some did but lay like shattered dolls on the beach afterwards, their brains shaken, their limbs broken, ruined.

He spotted the prey hanging some distance away, observing the spectacle of another wreck in progress, unable to stay away.

He watched the masked flock strung out across the beach, waiting expectantly. He swallowed and tasted salt; the spindrift a fine spray even so far from the waves. The long black birds swirled above the new ship, their squawks mixing with the screeches of the men and women in torment upon the sea.

The lifeboat approached, figures gesticulated, called out. The gathering on the beach had been spotted. Surely the people in the boat thought rescuers stood ready. They expected help. The boat reached the swell, then climbed atop a wave, then spun side-on and flipped. He could clearly see the round holes of mouths in pale faces as the boat's complement screamed into the breaking waves. If anyone had watched when his ship had been wrecked they would have seen the same thing. The boat's human cargo was regurgitated at random, some swallowed by the sea, some never to be seen again – just as some of his ship's crew and passengers had disappeared. Some would be washed up on the beach, days later.

He watched the breakers carefully and the first body was thrown clear to land unmoving. The collected crowd took a step closer. Masked figures squatted to haunches like cheetahs ready to sprint. The waves spat forth another body, some crawled, some dragged by shipmates. He pulled the mask back over his face. The cries of the newly castaway became nonsensical. He raised the whistle to his mouth and gave three sharp blasts. With a howl the pack surged forward. Fresh screams rent the night air.

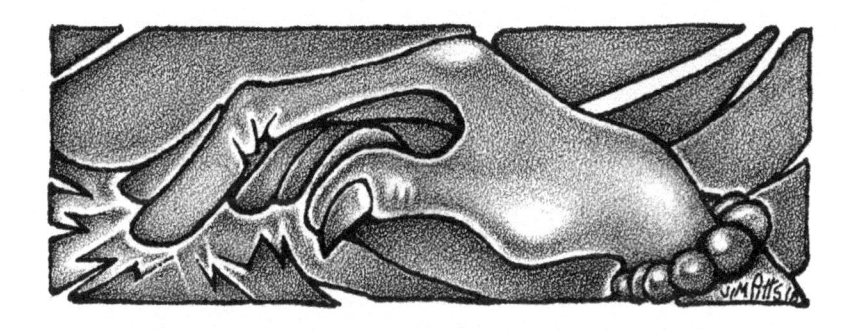

THE FAIREST OF THEM ALL

Debbie Bennett

Day 1

THERE'S A POT of very expensive moisturiser on the dresser. She borrowed it from her mother last week and so far the theft hasn't been noticed - or at least if it has Mum's said nothing. She's too tied up with the solicitors to notice much of anything these days. Who knew that arranging access visits for her little brother could be so time-consuming? Or expensive. She wonders if Jack has any idea how much he is costing the family, how much they are going without to ensure that his no-good dad can get to spend every other weekend in some naff cinema, sucking the face off his girlfriend while Jack watches some crappy film Mum wouldn't approve of. Sometimes she thinks he only does to piss their mother off, and that really he couldn't give a shit about Jack. And Jack - he doesn't care if it means he gets to eat pizza and stay up until midnight on alternate Saturdays. He's just a child.

Whereas *she* is a woman. She smooths the rich cream across her face, in a world of her own. A world where step-parents and family courts don't exist. Where the universe remakes itself around her. And she - at its centre - controls it all from her throne of power.

Does it show?

She examines her reflection. Does it show the passage of her life? Yesterday she was a child too, but today she is a woman with a woman's needs.

Yesterday – last night, somewhere between eight and eight thirty – on Mum's bed underneath the lilac-flowered duvet, and again on the cabinet in the en suite, in the dark because she's still shy about her body ... yesterday she lost her virginity. Liam sneaked in the back door while Mum was out doing a late-night supermarket shop, and as Jack watched some stupid cartoon on the television she and Liam made love for the first time.

Does it show now that she's a real woman?

She tucks her shirt in, then pulls blonde hair up with one hand, tilts her head and pouts at the mirror. Her reflection gazes back, sultry, seductive; Liam calls her his princess. She remembers wanting to be a princess for her fifth birthday – a princess in an ivory tower. A semi in Warrington has never quite matched her dreams. Maybe Liam will take her away from all this. Perhaps they'll get married and have a family of their own. Liam will get a job in an office and wear a smart suit; he'll kiss her goodbye each morning and she'll get their children ready for school. One day.

The moisturiser has made her face shiny. She rubs the excess off with a tissue, staring into the mirror intently. Something shifts, changes, and a shadow passes behind her reflection. She spins – but it's nothing, a shadow over the sun or Jack darting into her room to steal the gel pens she guards so fiercely. He's always pinching her stuff but Mum won't let her have a lock on her bedroom door. She knows her mother will freak if she finds out what happened last night but there's no reason why she should. They were careful – she made the bed exactly as it had been and by the time her mother came home she'd had a bath and was getting Jack ready for bed. Sometimes she resents being the unpaid babysitter but she loves her brother really and he's just a child.

An alarm rings somewhere downstairs. The timer on the cooker. Her mother always sets it each morning, so they all know exactly when they have to leave the house; Mum drives Jack to primary school but she insists they all leave together so nobody will be late. She does it in the evenings too - at mealtimes and sometimes at bedtime. Nobody else lives their life to the beat of the cooker timer, do they? It's just weird.

"Caitlin?" Yelling.

She scowls in the mirror. The face looking back at her is ugly now, more wicked witch than princess. But she's too old for fairy tales now that she's a woman.

Does it show? She doesn't think so. But she remembers the way he kissed her last night, the way his hand caressed her breasts, and now she's blushing, her cheeks rosy in the mirror as she recalls how he grunted when he came. It wasn't how she'd imagined it would be at all. How it ought to be. The earth hadn't moved and she hadn't felt much at all really, other than faintly silly at the noises Liam was making. It wasn't very different the second time either, except the cabinet was slippery-shiny and she'd ripped the edge of the wallpaper with a toenail. She wonders if it will get better with time or whether it's all just a giant conspiracy thought up by boys.

She runs hands up and down her body cupping her breasts through the white shirt. Does it show? Hah. She really is a woman now, isn't she?

"Caitlin!" Louder now. "Hurry up!"

She sighs and takes one last look in the mirror. It's darker in there and she turns to go, grabbing her sweater from the bed. If it's going to rain she'll need an umbrella otherwise her hair will be a mass of frizz by lunchtime and Liam won't fancy her then, will he?

"Caitlin - I'm not going to call you again!"

Well, thank God for that, Mum. She runs from the room and down the stairs. Who on earth cares if she misses the bus, anyway? Liam doesn't go to school every day, so why should she?

Day 2

SAME OLD, SAME old. Jack's dawdling in the bathroom and she can't clean her teeth. And Mum's repossessed the moisturiser ... no wait – there it is in the mirror ... and she turns and it's where it was before on the dresser. She dips a finger in the pot and dabs it on the end of her nose, makes a face in the mirror and takes a selfie. She goes to add ears and a tongue in Snapchat, but the picture isn't there and then Jack's jumping on her bed screaming that he's parachuting from a helicopter and she stuffs the phone in her bra and runs for the bathroom before he can get there first.

She cleans her teeth. The mirror in here is dirty; there are toothpaste splatters across the tiles and she wonders if mum ever cleans anything anymore. The pinger goes on the cooker downstairs and now she's got only minutes before her mother will be calling her, but time to have a quick wee and another look at her phone. The photo is there and she adds bunny ears and sends it to Liam. *Snapback.* He probably won't reply – he never does. It's not cool to talk to girls. She wonders whether he'd reply if she sent him a picture of her naked boobs. Her best friend Hayley did that to her boyfriend and now she wishes she hadn't as half of year eleven has seen it – and the other half probably want to. But then Hayley has big boobs and she's always showing them off.

Her own much smaller boobs are quite sore today. Maybe her period is due. Mum says she should keep a note of when she gets her period but she can't see the point and she always forgets anyway.

"Caitlin?"

Here we go again. She washes her hands and runs downstairs.

On the school bus Liam's already sitting on the back row with four of his mates and there's no room for her. He looks up as she approaches but doesn't move, so she slides into the row in front and stares out of the window. The boys are looking at their phones and laughing and she wonders if he's seen her bunny ears or whether they're all still obsessed with Hayley.

Liam doesn't speak to her at all. When they troop off the bus in the school car park, he's still with his mates, looking edgy in his jeans and beanie hat. She knows he'll be sent home to change – jeans aren't allowed even in the lower sixth

– and she knows he knows this already and is just looking for a reason to get out of school so he can go down the skate park and practise. That's all he ever does, practise, and she has no idea when he thinks he'll ever be good enough to do whatever it is he wants to do. Liam's not interested in school or exams and he's only in the sixth form because his parents won't let him get an apprenticeship.

She waits for him in the corridor by the hall but he barges past her without stopping – he doesn't even notice her. One of his mates catches her eye and smirks and she blushes, although she doesn't quite know why. What has Liam been telling them?

But Hayley's here now, grabbing her hand and pulling her into the toilets. Hayley's shirt is way too tight, buttons threatening to pop any second. She's still got her nose stud in and her black eyeliner is over-done. Caitlin thinks she looks like a tart but Hayley's her best friend and she shouldn't think bad thoughts about her friends, should she?

"What's up?" Hayley is straight to the point.

"Liam's ignoring me."

"Liam's a prick."

She knows this deep down. But they made love and that must count for something. Doesn't it? Caitlin tries not to cry. She runs a finger under each eye, catching any mascara smudges and checks her appearance in the mirror. She's putting on weight; her shirt looks almost as tight as Hayley's.

But Hayley sticks her chest out further and pouts at the mirror as she reapplies pink lipstick. "Don't get hung up on him, girl. He's, like, so bad news." She hesitates. "And he's a crappy kisser."

"You kissed him?" Caitlin doesn't know why she is surprised. Hayley's kissed most of the lower *and* upper sixth, and probably all of year eleven too – the boys anyway, and maybe even some of the girls. Hayley's *been around*, as her mum would say. Caitlin sometimes thinks going around has got to be better than going nowhere at all. "When?" she asks although she doesn't really want to know.

"Last year. At Abby Fisher's sixteenth." Hayley wrinkles her nose. "Hands like an octopus and mouth like a fish." She makes popping noises with her mouth. "He wanted to *do it* but I said I wasn't doing it with just *anybody* and not in his mum's car in like about minus-twenty!"

"I did it," Caitlin blurts out. She's been desperate to tell somebody and Hayley is her best friend, even if she wasn't in school yesterday, and it wasn't something Caitlin was going to commit to her phone. Not ever. She and Liam were better than that.

"You did what?" It takes Hayley a minute to connect up the dots. Then her eyes widen. "You did *it*? With *Liam*? When? Where?"

"Night before last at home." It's a relief that Hayley knows.

"Caits!" But then her best friend pouts. "Well that explains why he's avoiding you."

It does? "Why?"

"Because he's done it. Why would he want to stick around now?" Hayley's not being intentionally cruel – she's just saying it how she sees it. Some people think she's a bitch but Caitlin can see through the mask.

But the tears are coming now and she can't stop them. Hayley grabs her in a bear hug and you wouldn't think that Caitlin was the elder by six months.

Day 3

CAITLIN DOESN'T WANT to go to school. She lies in bed until the last possible moment, wondering what Liam is doing, if he's talking about her. She texted him twice last night and sent two photos on Snapchat – both fully-clothed – but he's not replied.

It's not fair. Why does it have to be this way? She still loves him and she knows he'd love her too if he just stood still long enough to realise it, got away from those sad mates of his with their childish jokes. If he was enough of a man to see her as a woman.

She rolls over in bed and sits up, looks in the mirror. Her hair is standing on end in places and she forgot to take off her make-up last night; panda-eyes stare back at her and she belches suddenly, retches and runs for the bathroom. She's sick, twice, and her eyes water making yesterday's mascara streak further down her cheeks. She looks like an extra from a cheap zombie movie. Liam won't fancy her now.

The pinger goes downstairs – "Caitlin are you ready?" – and she's not even dressed yet. She grabs cotton-wool and make-up remover and cleans up her face; there's a zit building in the crease of her nose and her stomach is heaving. She feels like shit.

"Mum? I don't feel well," she calls and she hears an exasperated sigh as her mother comes up the stairs. In the mirror her mum's face looks different as she stands in the doorway and it isn't even Mum at all, it's some weird trick of the light and she swings round and nearly throws up again as her mother catches her shoulder with a look of concern.

"Caitlin? Were you drinking last night?"

"No." Caitlin doesn't know why Mum thinks she would be drinking. She doesn't drink – well not much, anyway. And last night she was too busy worrying over Liam to do anything else.

"Well somebody's finished the bottle of Pinot that was in the fridge and I don't think it was Jack."

So that makes it me does it? Then she recalls Liam the other night and realises the empty bottle is probably under Mum's bed. She'll have to sneak it out later.

Her red face proves her guilt and Mum sighs. "I don't know what to say to you these days, sweetheart. You'd better stay home today and we'll talk later." Mum kisses her forehead. "I'll be back as early as I can."

She crawls back under the duvet and falls asleep. When she wakes the room is darker and it's raining outside. She wonders if Liam has noticed her absence. She checks her phone but there are no messages, not even from Hayley.

Maybe she's invisible. She sits up and looks in the mirror. Is she even here at all? The room is cold and the house eerily quiet now the central heating is off and the neighbours all out at work. She reaches out with her hand. Her reflection copies her – mirrors her – and their index fingers touch, separated only by glass. She is real, solid, here. Her image says so.

She presses her hand against the mirror then removes it and sees the imprint on the glass, sweat and grease from her skin leaving a residue. Her reflection isn't quite so quick and she wonders whether there is a matching mark on the *other* side of the mirror too.

And then there's an almost imperceptible *snick*. A tiny noise, almost a scratch and there's a hairline crack on the mirror right where her finger first touched the surface. The mark is fading already but the crack is still there.

Caitlin frowns, licks her finger and rubs at the mirror. The crack disappears – *just a hair* – and she lies back on the bed again—

—and wakes up. The house seems even stiller somehow, like it's waiting for her to say something, do something. Anything. Was she asleep? Did she dream waking up before?

Her mobile rings, a tinny tune she doesn't remember. She reaches for it, but it's not ringing and there's a bead of blood on the end of her finger.

Did I cut myself?

The mirror in her dream.

Her phone is still ringing. In the mirror her phone is jumping around on the bedside table, but when she picks it up again it's silent and still. And the crack is still there.

Caitlin wonders if she's still asleep. Is it possible to dream within a dream? Or else she really is ill. Perhaps if she has a shower she'll wake up properly. Maybe the mirror-phone will stop ringing then.

The sound stops abruptly and hush descends again. She doesn't like it so she switches on her television and listens to Jeremy Kyle shouting at some guy who has six children by six different mothers and doesn't want to pay for any of them. She focuses on the screen and tries not to look at the mirror at all, scared it might show her something she doesn't want to see.

The adverts come on. Somebody's talking about real coffee and Caitlin feels her stomach flip over again and she leaps out of bed and runs for the bathroom. She retches but nothing comes up and she sits on the floor and cries, wishing Mum had the day off work.

Is it possible to be pregnant when she only had sex two days ago?

Day 4

SATURDAY. THE ONE day she can have a lie-in and Caitlin's awake by seven, thoughts racing through her mind so fast she can't keep up. She can't possibly be pregnant and yet she can't keep any food down and even water makes her want to heave. And her boobs hurt and she thinks her period might be late.

They'd been careful; Liam used a condom and she remembers being both impressed by how easily he'd rolled it on with the air of being an expert in these things, and annoyed by the fact that he was clearly far more experienced than she was.

Now she thinks about it, it hadn't been *making love* at all. Just sex. And not even very good sex at that – not that she has anything with which to compare it.

But she might be pregnant.

Liam will make a good dad. *No, he won't.* Yes, he will, she argues with herself. They'll have a boy first and he'll play football with his dad. Then they'll have a little sister in a year or two, and they'll be a family of four and...

Shit, Caits. He'll dump you as soon as he finds out! Of course he will. If they are even a proper couple in the first place. It's not like they've ever been out together anywhere, is it?

Her mobile rings, the noise deafening in the sleeping house. Caitlin's heart thumps and she grabs the phone but it's lifeless in her hand. She can still hear the ringing and it's freaking her out now. Yesterday was too weird but she'd put it down to stress and maybe hormones? Now she isn't sure.

Mum and Jack will be in here in a minute if she can't shut the mobile up. But the house is still quiet and she wonders if maybe only she can hear it. As she thinks that thought it stops and in the darkness of the bedroom she sees a flash in the mirror. A text. Leaning forwards, she can see the illuminated screen reflection – and yet the phone in her hand is dark and silent.

She stabs a button and there *is* a text. From a number she

doesn't recognise.
You're beautiful.
And her insides turn to water. All the hurt and the doubt and Hayley's harsh words are drowned in a sudden rush of emotion. Liam does love her. He hasn't replied to her messages because he's lost his phone and now he's got a new one. Everything will be all right if Liam loves her. She falls back to sleep, cuddling her mobile and the message close to her heart.

Day 5

IT'S BEEN A long day. Jack's bouncing up and down on her bed and wants to know all about her weekend away with her dad. Jack's been off to see his own father too, and Caitlin suspects he's probably been bored shitless again. Staying up late when you are only nine may be fun for a while but if you are alone with only Netflix for company it must be pretty dire.

Caitlin's had a good couple of days if truth be told. Her dad's new girlfriend is probably closer to Caitlin's age than his, and the two of them had a girly shop in town yesterday. In fact, Caitlin's dad looked a bit pissed off when they went to get their nails done and came out giggling and refusing to tell him what they'd been chatting about. Sarah let her drink wine too, although she only had a few sips and poured it into the plant pot when they were both away from the table in the pub where they'd had dinner last night.

But now she's home the doubts are back again. There's been no word from Liam since the text early on Saturday. She texted him back on the new number but she's heard nothing.

She takes her make-up off carefully. The zit is still there – she wrinkles her nose and can feel it sulking under her skin. In the mirror her bedroom looks gloomy and even Jack's reflection seems slightly off-key.

"You look fat!"

"What?" Caitlin turns around and he's sitting on the edge of the bed looking into the mirror.

"In the mirror. You look fat."

"Cheers Jack. Isn't it past your bedtime?" She shoves him and he runs out of the room, yelling for Mum. He's over-tired – he always is when he comes back from his dad's – and he'll be grumpy for days.

But he's right. She looks in the mirror. She does look fatter. She looks down at her stomach clad in T-shirt and leggings and runs a hand over herself. In the mirror there's a definite bump. Panic spikes suddenly and her heart catches. Maybe she *is* pregnant?

The mirror is still cracked from Friday. She touches the crack and sees it fracture further – tiny feathery lines like ice-crystals on a January window. The glass darkens and she pushes further, watches the surface of the mirror soften as her finger pushes *through* the surface. It doesn't hurt.

In the mirror her reflection – *her other self* – pushes back and she sees something coming out of the glass. A finger. *Her* finger.

Caitlin snatches her hand away and pulls it to her chest, eyes wide as she meets the gaze of her image. And there's a text message on her mobile.

Still beautiful.

Day 6

SHE HASN'T SLEPT much. Her bedroom is hot and airless and she woke several times in the night, too scared to turn over in case her reflection was doing something totally different. But somehow not-seeing is worse and eventually she switches on puts the bedside light and lies on her back staring at the ceiling and wondering if she is going mad.

On the way to school she gets off the bus early. Liam is still ignoring her and she wonders what he'll say when she tells him she's pregnant. If she's pregnant. Her reflection this morning looked even fatter, her boobs swollen and her face looked flushed and hot. And yet her school skirt doesn't *feel* any tighter and neither Jack nor her mother seemed to notice she looked any different.

There's a parade of small shops on the road before the school. In the chemist she buys a pregnancy test. The pharmacist looks at her with an expression that says exactly what he is thinking and Caitlin doesn't say it's for her mum or her friend or make any excuses. She just glares at the man and shoves the box to the bottom of her schoolbag and doesn't think about again it until lunchtime when the smell of food in the cafeteria makes her feel like throwing up again. She hides in a cubicle and wees on the stick while Hayley stuffs chips into her mouth and keeps the seat free next to her. Caitlin hasn't told her, as it's the fastest way of the whole school finding out – they already know about her and Liam now and maybe that's why he's avoiding her. Maybe he's embarrassed to be seen with her – after all she's not Hayley with her big boobs, overdone make-up and attitude, is she? Caitlin's never been an in-your-face kind of girl and maybe that's what Liam likes.

It's supposed to be morning wee but she needs to know now – and really will it make any difference? Either she's pregnant or she isn't. It can't be that hard to tell. If it's positive she doesn't know what she'll do. Hayley would march straight up to the father-to-be and shove the stick in his face still wet with wee and demand he did the right thing. But then Hayley would never be dumb enough to be in this situation, would she?

The first line appears straight away and Caitlin finishes her wee and sits on the loo waiting. Girls come in and out of the toilets, year seven by the sounds of them and chattering innocently about puppies and sports and the latest episode of *Hollyoaks*. Caitlin feels too old and wise as she looks at the stick and waits patiently for the second line to appear. She studies the graffiti on the cubicle wall and wonders if Mr Phillips really does have sex with Miss Griffiths. She can't imagine either of them *doing it* and the thought makes her want to giggle.

After fifteen minutes she wraps the stick in loo paper, chucking it in the bin by the row of sinks. She's not pregnant.

The relief is overwhelming as she takes the seat next to Hayley and eats pasta in a chilli sauce. She's starving and Hayley's talking for both of them, so she concentrates on her lunch and thinks about Liam. Fuck Liam. Except that she's already done that and there's nowhere else to go now, is there?

Day 7

THIS MORNING SHE feels much better. The nausea is gone and she's wide awake when the alarm goes off, and ready to restart her life and forget the last week ever happened. Forget Liam and concentrate on her GCSEs. She needs to decide what A levels to take and think about where she sees her future. And what about uni? She loves science at school but she's also good at English and quite fancies the life of a journalist; working on a newspaper or on television news sounds glamorous and fun and a world away from rainy Warrington. Her dad took her on a tour of Media City last year and she'd imagined she was a celebrity arriving in a taxi for an interview.

Caitlin jumps out of bed. The house is still quiet and she might get a shower in peace before Jack is awake. She checks her mobile and there's nothing much happening. Hayley's snapchatted a picture of her and Mark Abbott - they look like they're in the cinema and Caitlin remembers her friend talking about it yesterday. She sends a smiley face and a thumbs-up back and then decides a selfie is what she needs so she poses in front of the mirror in her Winnie-the-Pooh pyjamas—

—and drops the mobile on the floor in shock. The girl in the mirror is straining at the waist of *her* Winnie-the-Pooh pyjamas with a recognisable pregnancy bump and full breasts. Her hair is shiny and thick and her face is - and Caitlin hates the cliché - *glowing* with health.

She looks down at her body and can't see any change at all. Slipping a hand inside her pyjama bottoms they feel loose and comfortable and no different. So why is the mirror-Caitlin so huge and the real-Caitlin not? Why is mirror-Caitlin pregnant when real-Caitlin isn't? She did the test yesterday and even if it was faulty - even if it really did need morning wee - even if she *was* pregnant, she wouldn't be that fat already. Not in just a few days.

In the mirror she can see her mobile vibrating on the

floor. She can hear it ringing and yet her real phone is still and silent.

And mirror-Caitlin reaches down and answers it.

Real-Caitlin stares, a hand in front of her mouth and watches her reflection move independently and answer the phone. Then real-Caitlin does the same and for a minute she's not sure who is who. She touches the mirror again, hesitantly. Mirror-Caitlin copies her and now they're playing tag, one leading and the other one copying and neither knowing who is following who. Time slows down. The glass is thick and syrupy on her fingers and who knows what might happen if it melts altogether, if she pushes through and reaches the other side?

"Caitlin? Are you up yet?"

She snaps back into reality, pulling her hand away, and her reflection is just that – an image. But she's still fat, still pregnant.

"Which one am I?" She whispers but there's nobody to hear, nobody except the girl in the mirror.

Day 8

MUM KNOWS.

Last night she couldn't stop crying. Mum kept asking her what was wrong and she was hiccupping so badly she could barely speak. Jack was hanging around in the doorway, not sure whether to be concerned or entertained by his sister's outburst but as soon as he'd gone for a bath she blurted out that she might be pregnant – even though she knew she wasn't, that she'd done a test, but the girl-in-the-mirror was pregnant and that must mean that she *is*, but she can't feel it and can't see it and Liam still isn't talking to her apart from the strange text messages and why won't he answer her when she calls him?

This morning her mother has kept her off school and is making her do another test. Who knew Mum kept these things in the drawer in her bedroom? *Does Mum have a boyfriend?* Caitlin realises she doesn't know much about her mother's life these days.

Morning wee this time. Now she'll know for sure, won't

she? Last night she slept in Mum's bed. Sometimes you need a cuddle even when you're fifteen, and last night she slept all night with no dreams she can remember.

Her mobile pings and for a second she's too scared to look but it's only Hayley: *Where R U?*

Sick, she sends back.

Is Liam there?

What? Why would he be here? It's barely nine o'clock. *No. Not in school. Didn't go home last nite.*

Where is Liam? Where was he last night? Caitlin needs to be in school, needs to find out, but Mum's calling and she's desperate to wee, so she stuffs her mobile into the pocket of her dressing gown and runs upstairs.

She wees on the stick again and gives it straight to Mum without even looking. Her phone pings again while she's washing her hands.

Police want to talk to you.

She has no idea why. She hasn't even spoken to Liam since *that* evening – only seen him in passing and on the bus. Surely they know that? The last thing she needs is the police turning up on the doorstep. She's in enough trouble already.

Her mother comes back into the bathroom and hands her the stick. She's still not pregnant. Caitlin wonders what is happening to her life. She thinks about telling her mum about the mirror, but it's too crazy and nobody will believe her. Maybe she has a brain tumour or something? What else could cause hallucinations? Mum says she can stay off school today but she needs to catch up on her homework and stay away from Liam. Well, that won't be too difficult if he's gone missing, will it?

Mum promises they'll have some girly time at the weekend – just the two of them – and she goes off to work and Caitlin makes a mug of tea. Liam must be okay because he was still sending her messages last night, still telling her she was beautiful. Perhaps he just can't talk to her in front of his mates. She snapchatted another selfie last night but he didn't reply.

She drags her schoolbag up to her bedroom and empties it out on the bed. Several notebooks, a clear plastic pencil case and a tampon land on top of her collection of stuffed animals; she shoves them to one side and flips up the top of her laptop. Sitting cross-legged on the bed she's got her back to the mirror, but the screen is a reflection too and she can see herself, see her the back of her dressing-gown and a million other Caitlins vanishing into infinity.

And mirror-Caitlin turns around, up onto her knees on the duvet, belly huge with baby. In the dead screen of her laptop Caitlin watches the mirror-girl lean forward and pick up her mobile phone. Real-Caitlin's mobile pings with a text message and she reaches out carefully with one hand, her eyes not leaving the reflection.

Soon.

One word. What does that mean? By the look of her mirror-Caitlin is due to give birth very soon. What will happen then?

Real-Caitlin spins suddenly catching her reflection by surprise. The girl in the mirror is crying, both hands on her tummy and real-Caitlin wonders if perhaps there's a whole other world on the other side of the glass and she is Alice or Snow White or maybe even Coraline. But it's a darker world over there where nothing is what it seems – her reflection shows her that – and she's read the books and she *knows*. Mirror-Caitlin is older or is it just that real-Caitlin is younger, more innocent? *Naïve.*

She touches her face and feels tears; her image does the same and now the baby is kicking too, this new life inside her that is ready to be born into the world.

Which world?

The mirror is bulging outwards, as the other girl pushes with the flat of her hand. Caitlin can't help but do the same and they are touching now, hand-to-hand and small fingers grasp her own. The girl's expression changes then and she's holding on tight. Real-Caitlin struggles as she's being pulled closer to the mirror.

Her mobile is ringing, that stupid pop-song ringtone she once thought was cool. Caitlin grabs it with her free hand and it's Hayley.

"Why are you at home? Where's Liam?"

"Hayley? I can't—"

But she can. As Hayley's shrill voice shatters the silent bedroom the mirror snaps back into place and mirror-Caitlin stares back at her angrily.

And behind her in the gloom of her reflected bedroom, is mirror-Liam.

Day 9

THE PAIN WAKES her, a knife slicing through her stomach like nothing she's ever felt before. She screams but the bedroom absorbs the sound, cocooning her in a womb of duvet. She fights free of bedding, drenched in sweat and panting as another wave of pain hits her deep down inside and she's doubled over, holding her belly in agony.

It passes and she flicks the switch on the bedside light. Instinctively she looks to the mirror, and the other her, the image of her, has given up the pretence of mere reflection – she's standing with both hands flat on the glass as if she could step through at any moment and be real. She's still huge but she looks tired, weary with the sheer effort of pregnancy.

Her expression is one of concern now as she watches Caitlin. There's something approaching sympathy in her eyes as Caitlin doubles over again when another wave hits her. The girl in the mirror opens her mouth as if she's trying to speak, trying to offer words of support – of help maybe – or perhaps she is just waiting for this to be over, whatever it is.

"I'm not pregnant. I'm not pregnant." Caitlin says the words over and over. Is this what giving birth feels like? This deep intense pain as if her insides are splitting open? She thinks of that scene from *Alien* when the creature bursts from the guy's stomach and that's how she feels right now – as if something is exploding inside her. It doesn't feel right but then none of this is right. *I'm not pregnant.* And she *isn't* pregnant. She did two tests. It's only her reflection that argues anything different.

Up on all fours on the bed she wonders why Mum and Jack haven't come running in. They must be able to hear her screaming. She yells out for her mother, for anyone to come and stop this pain, but the bedroom swallows her voice, sucks it into the night. She grabs her mobile; the screen says it's three o'clock and she stabs Hayley's number but there's no signal, no connection with the rest of the world. Just Caitlin alone in her bedroom with only the girl in the mirror for company.

She screams again, a long low animal howl. In the mirror the girl looks startled, as if she has no idea what is going on. In between the waves of pain – the contractions. They're contractions – she's giving birth! *I'm not pregnant!* In between the *contractions* Caitlin's gulping in air and looking at the mirror-girl and she's not alone. Behind her is mirror-Liam, his arms around her waist and both hands flat on her extended belly. Is it his child too? Has mirror-Caitlin been having sex with mirror-Liam in the mirror-house? It's all too surreal, too *un*real.

And yet it's happening. There's no doubt about that. However impossible it is Caitlin is giving birth, right now on the bed. She's watched enough films to know what is going on, sat through enough episodes of *Call the Midwife* and *One Born Every Minute*. She knows about panting and pushing but that doesn't make it any easier when she has no idea which she's supposed to do when, and it doesn't look like it hurts so much on television even though they're only acting. She knows that if they showed the pain, the literal blood, sweat and tears involved, that no woman would ever have sex again.

Another wave of pain and now she feels tighter *down there*, as if she really needs to go. A bit of wee escapes and she realises she's supposed to have broken her waters or something like that before she can actually give birth. *I'm not pregnant!* She looks at the mirror again and her reflection is watching expectantly.

Mum said she was in labour for two whole days with Jack. Caitlin feels like she's been here – been watched – for just as long but she knows it's maybe ten minutes at most. It can't be time to push and yet her body is taking over, great shuddering waves focussing on her abdomen and pelvis and she's out of control now, giving in and going with the flow. From the corner of her eye she can see mirror-Caitlin-and-

Liam with their backs to her watching the bed as if they are themselves reflections from her bedroom. She takes a deep breath in a moment of calm and then her whole body is straining and she's sitting in a mess of blood and fluid and there's something else there too.

A baby?

There can't possibly be a baby. She's not pregnant. This is all just some weird dream and she'll wake up soon. When she tells Hayley they'll laugh and Hayley will say it's a guilt thing and she needs to go on the pill. Hayley's been on the pill since she was fifteen. Her mother has no idea but Hayley doesn't want children. Not ever, she says. Caitlin does – but not for at least another ten years. And not like this.

In the mirror the couple run towards the bed. Caitlin falls back exhausted and can't even look at what may or may not be between her legs. But there's a high-pitched cry. Mirror-Caitlin picks something up and holds it aloft, triumphant, as if offering up a sacrifice. Instinctively Caitlin looks down at the bed – and there is nothing there. Nothing at all. The bedding is twisted, sweat-damp, but nothing more than that.

I wasn't pregnant.

Caitlin sits up. The girl in the mirror is stepping towards her holding something out. It's swaddled in her old cot blanket – the one that's normally draped over the chair by the window – and Caitlin can't see what's wrapped within its folds. She swings her legs over the bed, wincing as her stomach muscles complain and leans forwards.

Her reflection has one hand on the glass again. There's a connection between them – mirror-girl is after all Caitlin's own reflection – and she reaches out too, palm to palm. The tiny fracture is still there, physical evidence of what has happened and is still happening.

Caitlin stands up facing herself, and now she can see the tiny bundle in the blanket. She reaches out her other hand trying to touch the reflection of the baby that never existed at all.

And mirror-Liam grabs it and holds on tight.

Caitlin yelps, a tiny sound. She is part of the circle now with the baby at the centre, and Liam pulls them tighter. The baby mewls and Caitlin feels her body respond to the cry – a mother's instinctive reaction to be with her child. Instead of pulling away she pushes forwards and the mirror moves, softens and flows around her like molten metal. The baby is real, mirror-Caitlin and mirror-Liam are real, and she is ... what? An image, a reflection?

No! There's a popping sound, a shifting of reality and now she has a baby in her arms. Her baby. The one that doesn't exist in the real world because she was never pregnant.

The baby is a strange one. It's hers and yet not-hers. A reflection with no source. There's a flatness in its eyes and she realises she doesn't even know if it's a boy or a girl. She hugs it to herself but it's not real. Which means she's not real either.

She looks around herself and everything is the same – yet different. Darker, less-solid and not quite there. *Reflected.* Unreal. She turns back still holding the not-quite-baby tightly to her chest and there's a scream building from deep within her.

And in the mirror, the now-real-Caitlin and real-Liam hold hands and smile at her – before turning away.

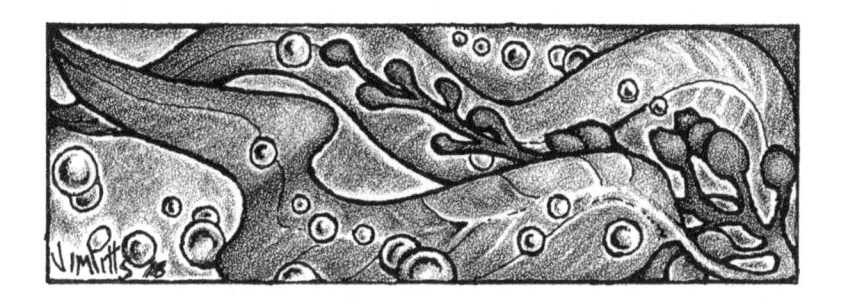

HER FAVOURITE PLACE

Mike Chinn

CLARRIE STEPS OUT into the garden. Behind her voices are raised, almost drowning a woman's plaintive song. The party's getting out of control. Time to leave.

It is still out among the plants and flowers, cool and fragrant. A dying breeze rattles the leaves all around her carrying the scent of roses. Their movement fragments light into pale dancing shafts. Clarrie ducks under an arch of leaves, not quite avoiding the hard points. They scratch at her hair, trying to tug it loose.

She's not alone. In the distance, luminous against the dark leaves, is another woman. She's holding something, cradling it like a baby. She rocks it gently, her face lowered. Trying to get it to sleep, Clarrie thinks. The woman would certainly stand no chance back in the house.

Clarrie steps closer, trying to be quiet, not wanting to disturb mother or baby. The woman turns anyway, raising her face. Her grin is huge...

CLARRIE AWOKE WITH a shudder, momentarily disorientated. She's standing by the floor to ceiling observation windows, left hand resting on the frigid armoured glass. The ocean beyond was a deep, bruised purple. There must have been a bright full moon up top as a few ghostly strands of light had made it down this far. They danced against the dark water, reflecting off the glass. The giant kelp forest was too far away to be visible, the artificial lighting quenched for the night. Clarrie couldn't see any fish: they probably had the sense to be fast asleep. Hugging herself against a purely subjective cold – the interior of Sea Farm Three never dipped below 22° Celsius – she returned to bed.

"You sleep walking again last night?" Lois asked during breakfast.

Clarrie swallowed her coffee. "No. Why?"

Lois shrugged half-heartedly. "Thought you got up."

"Bathroom."

"You were gone a long time."

"So now you're timing how long it takes me to pee?"

Lois raised her own coffee mug and stared over the rim. She said nothing as Clarrie buttered a slice of toast and began to nibble at it, trying to ignore her wife's stare. The toast just went round and round her dry mouth. Eventually she tossed the slice down and met Lois's pale eyes.

"What?"

Lois carefully placed her coffee on the table. "I think it's time we went back up."

And there it was, out in the open at last. Lois had been tiptoeing around something for days: never quite saying what she so clearly wanted to. Conversations abruptly stilled or their directions not so subtly changed.

"Why?" Clarrie poured herself more coffee and took a gulp; her mouth still felt like a desert.

"They told us to look out for the signs: irritability, odd behaviour—"

"Such as?"

"Like sleep walking every night for the last two weeks. You know you have."

Clarrie took a deep breath. She couldn't argue. "So?"

"So we're getting cabin fever – or whatever fancy name they're giving it this year. You know it was inevitable, cooped up down here with no one except each other—"

"You'd've said that was romantic, once…"

"This isn't our honeymoon, Clarrie. We're two hundred metres under the ocean – not on Lake Tahoe. Even though every couple they selected was in a long-term relationship of some kind – used to each other – none of them managed more than four months before the isolation got to them. We've been down here fifteen weeks."

"Don't you want to break the record?" Even to her own ears Clarrie sounded petulant.

"No." Lois was quiet, almost apologetic. "I want to look outside and see something other than artificial light and seaweed for once."

"And if I don't?" Clarrie stared at the mug she was rotating on the table top. She wondered at her reluctance to leave; after all, she was the one dreaming about gardens up top most nights.

Lois's voice was softer than ever. "Then ... we have a problem."

"A few more days – a week." Clarrie was aware she was pleading. "I have a few more correlations to do on the seventh and ninth quadrats. After that, if you still want to go..."

Lois leaned back in her chair, staring hard. Her mouth started to open, closed without a word. Whatever she'd meant to say died in silence. "Okay. Get the correlations done and we're out of here."

Clarrie reached across and squeezed her hand. "Thanks."

"I won't change my mind, Clarrie. We're both getting stir crazy. We have to go. Sooner rather than later." She pulled her hand away and stood.

"Sure." Clarrie wrapped fingers around her mug again. "I'll get suited up."

SHE FINISHED CHECKING all of the drysuit seals before slipping the clear bubble helmet over her head and clipping it in place. Flipping open the comms circuit she pinged Lois. "How'm I coming over?" Her voice sounded at once both enclosed and echoey.

"Five by five. Telemetry reads your tanks are full..."

Clarrie glanced at her wrist readouts. "Confirmed." She

stepped up to the raised lip around the airlock's floor hatch. A little water was running over the top despite external and internal pressures being equal: a persistent circular waterfall. Dragging herself onto the rim by means of the hoist dangling over the drop, she paused a moment. "Be back in no time." All she got back was the hiss of an open circuit. Was Lois sulking? That wasn't like her at all.

Clarrie let go, falling into the cold water.

Buoyed up, her drop slowed to a graceful descent. The only sound was the rapid gurgle of the rebreathing apparatus. Reaching the bottom of the lower access shaft she held onto a grab-rod with one hand, unmooring a metre-wide yellow diver propulsion vehicle with the other. Attaching a safety line, she grabbed both handles and opened up the vaguely manta-shaped DPV. It hauled her away from under Farm Three, its twin engines a high muffled buzz.

"Still reading me?" she called.

"*Loud and clear. All telemetry shows green.*"

At least Lois responded that time. Last thing Clarrie wanted was to be out among the kelp while her wife was having a colossal snit.

"I'll be at the ninth quadrat in—" she checked her watch "—four minutes."

"*Roger that.*"

The water was clear and well-lit. The artificial light towers ringing the kelp forest were full on. Two hundred metres down, between the sunlight and twilight zones, not even GM kelp could find enough natural light to thrive. She slipped into the forest, the DPV giving her something close to the grace and agility of a seal. Weaving around the towering stands of weed Clarrie tried to imagine what it would be like to be a natural denizen of the sea: perfectly evolved for the medium. Not barricaded in a drysuit and rebreathing apparatus. Humanity might have permanently manned habitations like the Sea Farm Three kelp-research facility dotted around the oceans but they were artificial environments: hyperbaric bubbles fixed to the seabed. Clarrie and Lois were the figurative opposites of fish out of water.

Her wrist readout began to flash. She'd arrived at Quadrat

Nine. Shutting off the DPV she withdrew a palm-sized tablet from a small compartment in the back of the stubby port wing. "Okay. I've arrived," she said.

"*Acknowledged. How's it looking?*"

Clarrie pulled herself deeper into the designated area of kelp, the tethered DPV bobbing in her wake, holding onto the thick upright stems and broad waving fronds. She didn't feel whatever current they were responding to. With the tablet she took a series of high-resolution pictures to be studied in detail later.

"Everything appears healthy. No sign of sea urchin activity."

Three weeks ago Quadrat Twelve had been devastated by purple sea urchins. Something in that kelp's particular genetic modification had really appealed to the spiny little bastards.

"*Good. Other wildlife?*"

Clarrie turned her head. One thing about the bubble helmets, they gave good all-round visibility. "Seems pretty quiet. Was last time I checked too. Kelp's healthy as hell but not a fish to be seen."

"*Maybe whatever they've done to that kelp is having the opposite effect to Quadrat Twelve.*"

Clarrie looked around at the closely packed stems. Maybe there was a hint of the kelp growing wild and unrestrained. Sea urchins were known to have a role in keeping the forests healthy and controlled. She took a few more pictures – some just to capture the effect of the towers' light rippling through the swaying weed. "Yeah. I'll log it. On to Quadrat Seven."

She slipped the tablet back into the DPV, firing up the engines. As she angled the tug to draw her out of the stand of kelp something a couple of metres down caught her eye. Something pale. "Stand by."

"*What is it–?*"

"Give me a moment…" Clarrie dropped the DPV's nose; it drew her smoothly towards the pale object. She cut the engines once she was alongside and just floated, looking carefully.

It was a little bigger than her fist, almost white,

constructed in a complex spiral that reminded her of petals. It nestled against the stem, at the base of three fronds.

"*Clarrie – what is it?*" There was a rising note of concern in Lois's voice.

"Must be some kind of coral…" She reached out a gloved hand brushing her fingers lightly against the shape. It gave, the complex folds parting as though it was no more rigid than the kelp fronds. "Actually, it's more like a flower."

"*Kelp isn't a plant.*" The worry had been replaced by cold annoyance. "*It doesn't have flowers–*"

"I know!" Clarrie choked back her own irritation. Did Lois always have to state the blindingly obvious? She took a deep, hollow breath. "Could be a new form of soft coral. But who knows what they've spliced into these test subjects? It's always such a big fucking secret! There could be flowering plant genes in here for all you and I know…"

"*I seriously doubt it.*"

"Yeah? When did you get to be an expert? We're observers – not techies." And you don't want to be down here anyway, she added silently.

She closed her hand around the pale object and tugged. For a moment it resisted then broke free of the stem. Opening another compartment – this time in the starboard wing – she fed the pale mass inside and shut its door.

"I've removed it. We'll send images to the experts when I get back." Let them worry about it.

"*Copy that. Can you give me an air reading?*"

Clarrie glanced at her wrist instruments. "Seventy percent. The CO_2 filters still at optimum. Confirm?" At this depth even with rebreathers air was consumed something like twenty times faster than at the surface. Her suit might have been fitted with all the latest monitors but by the time the alarms sounded it would likely be too late.

There was a moment while Lois double checked telemetry. "*Confirmed. Better get to the next quadrat.*"

"On my way."

It was a short hop to Seven. Quadrat Eight had already been declared a failure. The stems had grown at a rate phenomenal even for kelp, changing colour as they did so.

Now it was a thick overgrown plot of choked weed, shot through with bloody reds and bruised purples. The strong artificial sunlight no longer seemed to penetrate. Like Nine, it was devoid of life. Clarrie always skirted the place – preferring to go round through more healthy stands of kelp. It gave her the creeps. Why no one had come down from Surface Control and eradicated the failed quadrat was a mystery. They weren't normally so slow to clear up their mistakes.

Even before she'd finished her diversion she saw Seven had been blighted. Stems were covered with the white flower-like encrustations. They gathered in clumps, usually around the base of fronds, accentuating the resemblance to flowers. Clarrie was reminded of the roses her parents grew back in Oxford: tall thick bushes covered in tightly-furled blossoms. Floribundas they were called. It was the only thing her parents never seemed to argue about. As a small girl Clarrie had often gone out into the garden and hidden among the leaves.

"Problem," she muttered.

"*What's up?*"

"More of those white growths. Seven's covered in them. Looks like–" She stopped herself saying *a rose garden*. "Don't know what it looks like. Not healthy though."

Lois sighed. "*Surface is not going to be happy.*"

"Tell me about it." Clarrie aimed the DPV at one broad stem that seemed to be more blighted than the rest. "I'll take another sample – see if it's the same as the one from Nine."

"*You think it won't be?*"

"Gotta be sure. It's what the techies'll want."

"*I guess.*" Lois didn't sound happy. Maybe she thought this new development would delay their return to the surface.

Clarrie pulled a white bloom off, picking it at random. It was just as soft as the first. She slipped in into the starboard compartment before taking out her tablet and taking plenty more photographs. Surface would want to see this. She took another air reading: half of her air was left. "I'm coming back. No point staying any longer."

"*Agreed. I'll turn on the porch light.*" That sounded more like

Lois; Clarrie was glad to have her back.

"See you in five."

THEY BOTH STARED at the screen. Lois's expression was a perfect mirror of Clarrie's thoughts: what the actual hell?

The moment Clarrie returned Lois had lowered the hoist and pulled her up into the airlock - DPV and all. While Clarrie removed her helmet, Lois had placed two clear trays on the floor and emptied the DPV's starboard compartment into them. One white blob in each. Unsupported by water both sagged like defrosting ice cream. Any resemblance to flower blooms was long gone.

They hurried up to Sea Farm Three's so-called lab, a white room containing a few simple instruments. Nothing fancy. Anything worth real analysis was hermetically sealed in bags and floated to the surface on marker buoys. Clarrie didn't think that was going to happen in this case.

Both specimens were slipped under a dissecting microscope. Clarrie focused on each as Lois pinged Surface Control sending the images in real time. There wasn't a lot to see: the blobs rapidly dried and collapsed. By the time Lois had raised Surface the images on the microscope screens could just have been small mounds of fine white sand. Clarrie downloaded the images she'd taken, comparing the complex radiating structures from the forest to the piles of moist dust.

"What's your guess?" asked Lois.

Surface was silent for a moment. *"No guesses, Farm Three. Whatever those are is completely new to us. Coral, some kind of infection or disease... There's nothing like it on record."*

"Why'd they collapse like that?" Clarrie wondered out loud.

"At this point we're surmising the whole thing is essentially a water-filled bladder," came a second voice. *"A thin membrane covered in calcium carbonate. That would explain the movement when you touched them."*

"Once removed from the ocean it couldn't sustain its own weight," added the first voice. *"The membrane collapsed and punctured, the internal watery medium draining away. In Farm*

Three's atmosphere it would dry out very quickly."
Clarrie already knew the answer even as she asked "So what do we do?"
"Bring in more specimens," replied the first voice. *"Sealed in hydrostatic boxes. Then send them to the surface unopened for examination."*

"I AM NOT going out again until tomorrow!" Clarrie stripped off her drysuit, trying to ignore Lois's furious expression.

"You're just trying to delay returning to the surface!"

"No – I'm trying to not get killed. I'm tired and cold, Lois. You know how much diving in these pressures takes it out of you even with a DPV. I'll go out again, no problem – but not until tomorrow after I'm rested. You want those specimens today you go get them yourself!"

Lois fell silent. She let her expression do the talking. She was by far the weaker diver, more than happy to let Clarrie do as much of the underwater work as possible.

After tense moments she spat "Fine!" and stamped from the lab.

Clarrie finished removing her drysuit, carefully hanging it up before slipping into her coveralls. Taking her time, letting her emotions cool as her body slowly warmed.

"That's a no, then," she whispered when she finally trusted herself to speak.

THE SOUND OF the piano ebbs and flows with the cool breeze, sometimes rising above the loud voices, sometimes drowned by them. There are words accompanying it but Clarrie can only catch stray ones. She wants to hear the song clearly – it feels important – but she's afraid to go back inside. Instead she goes deeper into the garden away from the noisy party, ducking under the swaying branches. There's a familiar scent on the breeze: roses. She hurries, stepping around dark-leaved bushes, top heavy with pale blooms. They sag under their weight. The complex blooms nod at her as she passes, giving their approval.

She's looking for her favourite place, deep within the shadows. Hidden from the fingers of moonlight plucking at the fragrant darkness. It's a secret; not even her parents know about it. They musn't.

There's someone waiting for her: green and grey among the ivy. She turns for Clarrie to see what she's cradling in her long thin arms. The pale bundle quivers. Clarrie reaches out a gloved hand. The bundle bursts—

CLARRIE JERKED AWAKED. She was sitting in the lab in the darkness. In front of her, still under the switched-off microscopes, were the trays of desiccated white growths. She had a hand planted in each pile.

The lights flickered on. Clarrie flinched, turning her seat. Lois was at the doorway, hand still over the light switch.

"You were talking about roses." Lois's voice was flat, neutral.

Clarrie wiped her hands down her pyjamas. The powder was sharp and clinging; most of it stayed on her palms. "Was I? I - I think I was dreaming about them..."

"I thought you hated roses."

Clarrie stood, still scrubbing her palms against her PJs. The grit didn't want to come off. "That's dreams for you." She walked towards the doorway. Lois didn't move, blocking her exit.

"We're leaving, Clarrie."

"I have to get the specimens—"

"Soon as you're back we're going. I've already informed Surface. They're sending down a shuttle. We can take the sealed specimens up with us."

"But—"

Lois placed a hand against Clarrie's mouth, cutting her off. Clarrie wasn't sure what she was going to say anyway; the protest was just a token.

"We're out of here." Lois stepped aside allowing Clarrie to leave. As she stepped past, Clarrie realised her bare feet were also coated in the desiccated grit. She needed a shower.

ACCORDING TO CLARRIE'S instruments the water was no colder than yesterday but she still felt an extra chill through her drysuit. Beyond the lighting towers the water looked grey, slatey.

"*You okay?*" It didn't sound as though Lois was even pretending to care anymore. The words were just routine, said without thought.

"I'm fine." Clarrie told herself her teeth were gritted against the cold. "Kind of nippy out here."

"*Telemetry says—*"

"Fuck telemetry!" Clarrie sucked in a deep breath, concentrating on the rebreather's gurgle. "It's cold. I feel cold. All right?"

For a while the line went dead except for a distant barely audible hiss that sounded like interference from a radio station. Except that was impossible. Clarrie wondered if Lois had shut down their link.

When she finally responded Lois sounded tired, defeated. "*Sure, whatever.*"

"I'm nearly at Seven." Clarrie had taken a detour making sure she didn't get within so much as eyeshot of Quadrat Eight. A minute later she'd crossed Seven's perimeter. It was worse than yesterday.

The white mounds were bigger; there may even have been more of them. Most were the size and shape of a soccer ball, no longer looking anything like flower blooms. Their spiral structure looked swollen, engorged. Clarrie carefully touched one with a forefinger: it gave reluctantly, a taut inflated bladder. She pulled her finger back, reluctant to prod any harder, fearful of what might spew out if it burst.

There were four hydrostatic boxes clipped to the dorsal surface of her DPV's stubby wings. She unsealed all four, allowing the lids to bob open. Gingerly, yesterday's wonder turned to faint revulsion, she twisted one of the growths free. It was heavy, far heavier than something that should be no denser than the supporting seawater. She lowered it into the nearest box, shut and sealed the lid. A digital readout flickered to life detailing the internal water pressure and density. Until the seal was broken they'd remain steady.

Clarrie had to stop herself wiping hands down her drysuit. She was being ridiculous.

Methodically she filled the remaining boxes, shutting and

sealing each. She wanted to hurry – get it done and return to Farm Three – but she held herself in check, monitoring the box readouts, her own suit telemetry, moving slowly and deliberately. Rushing cost air that was already being rapidly exhausted, and it might damage the growths. She was sure she really didn't want to do that.

"I'm on my way back," she finally announced. Then, not sure what she wanted to hear, asked "Any sign of the shuttle?"

"It's being prepped. It'll be ready when we want it." Lois paused. "*You don't need to rush.*"

Bit too late to be conciliatory, thought Clarrie. "Okay. See you in five."

She opened up the DPV, turning away from the overrun quadrat. She took another leisurely route back – no need to rush, after all – drifting through the kelp forest. Everywhere felt gloomy, erupting into vivid green only where stems parted and the towers' light cut through. Kelp strands waved like huge snakes, fronds beating at the dull water. There was a strong current building. Clarrie wondered if it was choppy on the surface. Would it delay the shuttle? She realised she was smiling at the thought.

"Getting a little lively here."

"*Surface just advised me there's a storm approaching. Not enough to affect our leaving though. Don't worry.*"

Who's worried? "Whatever."

"*Clarrie ... I–*"

The link broke up. That faint buzz was back again. Clarrie thought it sounded like a woman's high voice: indistinct, barely audible. Something about it was naggingly familiar.

"Lois?" She checked her wrist instruments: everything read green, though over half her air was gone. "Lois, are you there...?" She cut the DPV's engines, hanging in the water as she ran a quick diagnostic. Everything checked out – but that distant not-quite melody was still all she could pick up.

Clarrie thought she caught movement off to her left. She turned her head on reflex imagining a shark moving silently through the forest. There was nothing except waving kelp, a few fish, a giant spider crab clinging to a nodding frond.

The background noise swelled; for a moment it made sense. Abruptly it silenced.

"–hello? Clarrie...?"

"I'm here. Signal broke up a moment."

"Yes." A pause when Clarrie thought the line had died again. "Has it done that before?"

Hell of a time to ask. "On my way out. Just for a few moments."

"I'll let Surface know. You'd better bring the suit up with you when we go."

"Yeah." She could see Farm Three's exterior lights through the forest, the habitat itself a pale luminous yellow against the grey background. "Coming in."

"Roger that."

Clarrie slipped clear of the forest, aiming the DPV towards the seabed. Skimming rocks and sand she rode in between Farm Three's support struts heading for the lower access airlock. Hanging onto a grab-rod she summoned the hoist and clipped all four boxes securely in place. As they disappeared inside the shaft Clarrie secured the DPV. A minute later the hoist dropped back into view and she rode it up into the airlock.

Lois had packed all four boxes into a skeleton crate by the time Clarrie pulled herself out of the water. She unclipped her helmet.

"We good to go?" she asked, trying to force as much enthusiasm into the question as possible.

Lois shook her head. "Shuttle's not left yet. Time to put together all the stuff you want to take topside. I'll get this upstairs." She slid the crate across the damp floor, opening the service elevator and pushing the packed boxes into its snug interior. Punching the button for the upper access airlock she glanced in Clarrie's direction. "And don't forget to bring that suit with you."

Clarrie bit down on her sharp reply. She hadn't forgotten. Why did Lois insist on repeating everything? "I'll get changed. Meet you upstairs."

She changed into her coveralls, packing the drysuit and helmet into one of the cases they'd been delivered in - way back when Sea Farm Three had been commissioned. She wheeled the case towards the observation window to take a last look. Outside, the kelp was beating slowly back and forth, agitated. She pressed up against the cool glass craning her head to see if she could make out the surface. She could see nothing; the kelp and glare of the lighting towers blocked her view.

Time to go.

In the circular anteroom for the upper access airlock, next to a short ladder leading to a ceiling hatch, Lois was leaning on the wall. Her back was to Clarrie. An LED on the room's external comm link was flashing green. Lois must have just received a message from Surface Control and left the channel open.

Clarrie stood her case upright. "They're not coming, are they?"

Lois spun around. She was furious. "Weather up top has changed – caught them by surprise apparently. A real hurricane. So much for the billions spent on meteorological super computers! Support vessel's re-stowed the shuttle and headed back to port until it blows over."

"How long?"

"A day. Maybe two."

"I'm sorry, Lois, I know—"

"Don't you *dare* say you're sorry!" Lois pushed herself away from the wall lurching towards Clarrie. "Looks like you got what you wanted. A few more days—"

Clarrie flinched. She'd never seen her wife so furious. "No Lois, honest..."

Lois stooped and grabbed at the case of hydrostatic boxes. With a scream she slammed it across the smooth floor. It smacked into a wall cracking open. One of the boxes split, the pressurised contents foaming out. The white growth inside spewed like geysering mud, spreading across the floor, thick and pallid. Clarrie thought she saw small shapes twitching and thrashing inside it.

"What have you done?" she whispered.

Lois laughed, her face ugly. "So what? You've got time to go fetch more!"

Clarrie took a step back. "Lois. Take a breath. This isn't you. This is—" what had she called it? "—cabin fever. Stress. I'll get on to Surface tell them what's happening. Maybe they can send a long-range mini-sub from port? Go under the storm?"

"We could have gone a day ago." Lois stalked closer. "But you had to wait. To delay. Be the good little farmer. 'Oh yes sir— I'll go fetch you more specimens'!"

Clarrie stumbled against something. Losing balance, she fell back hitting the floor. For a moment she couldn't breathe. Lois dropped to her hands and knees; her enraged face inches away from Clarrie's. Her mouth gaped in a wordless scream. Clarrie clenched her eyes waiting for the first slap.

There was something resting across Clarrie's right hand. On reflex she grabbed it, batting out blindly. She heard her wife grunt and she dared open her eyes. Lois was kneeling back her face sagging in a puzzled frown. After a moment she pitched to one side, flopping to the polished floor.

Clarrie struggled to her feet. Her case lay on its side, contents spilling open. In her hand was a smeared bubble helmet. Lois stared blindly up towards the ceiling hatch, a large puddle of blood under her head. It was spreading.

CLARRIE DIDN'T SHUT off the DPV until she was deep inside the kelp. The screaming, the raised voices, were far away at last. Despite the undulating stems, deep in the forest it felt still. It was cool; she imagined she smelled the fragrance of roses.

All around her fronds beat the water, green against the grey ocean. Their movement fragmented a peculiar light – an opalescent glow – into pale dancing shafts. Clarrie ducked under a stem bent double under the weight of the growths encrusting it. They squeaked against her suit. Tattered fronds scratched at her helmet trying to tug it loose.

Clarrie knew where she was. In the end it hadn't taken her long to find it. Every night she'd been told where to meet, after all. The little girl inside her, forever retreating to her favourite place. Her safe quiet place. The place she'd always gone when the shouting started. The hitting.

The woman was luminous against the dark kelp, wreathed by wriggling pulsing growths that glowed as much as she did. She was holding something, cradling it like a baby, her face lowered.

Clarrie unhooked herself from the DPV and drew closer, holding onto the kelp stems. The sea rocked her gently. As she neared the woman raised her face. Her bundle erupted into a confusion of tiny white spidery crabs - scattering across the kelp fronds and down the stems. The white growths split, their pale contents joining the exodus.

The woman smiled a vast grin, hauling herself up through the weed on multiple armoured legs. She gestured, beckoned.

Clarrie smiled back. Ignoring the alarms, she reached for her helmet seals. As she unclipped them she smelled roses again - thick and heady.

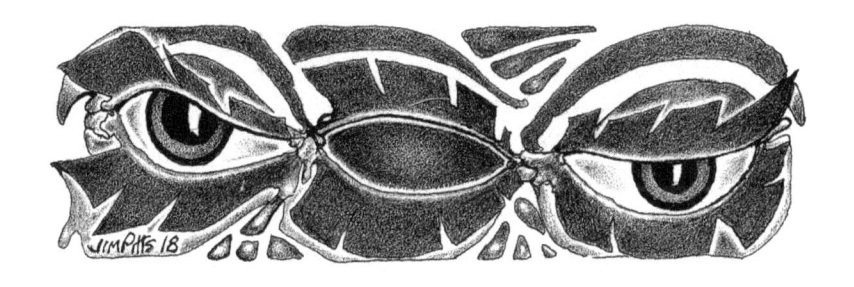

THE GIRL WITH THREE EYES

Phil Sloman

NO ONE EVER truly sees the world around them. No one. We're all head down, scurry, scurry, scurry from one point to the next. Pause to check in on social media. Note the likes, note the comments, note the anger, note the hate, comment back, screenshot, share, wait, wait, wait, then on to something else. Scurry. Scurry. Scurry. Eat, sleep, repeat. And in this world where no one truly sees, no one notices the monsters walking among us until it is too late to stop their barbarities. Not until it has become a feature on the six o'clock news with platitudes for the victims and disbelief about the killer, the rapist, the thug who was such a loving caring person, a pillar of the community or someone who kept themselves to themselves but would always say please and thank you in the grocery store and undoubtedly loved their mother. And then that monster is forgotten over time as we wait until the next abomination rears its ugly head amidst a sea of finger pointing acceptance that someone was at fault and something should have been done by someone. But that someone is always someone else; never us. And so, the monsters continue to strut around in plain sight with no one spotting them until it is too late. No one raising the alarm or trying to stop them. No one, that is, except me.

*

THERE IS AN unspoken social hierarchy within any educational institution. The kind of structure which results in the formation of cliques of one kind or another. You have the jocks, the geeks, the fashionistas, the middle-of-the-roaders, the gamers, the shamers, the parental blamers, the petrol-heads, the hippies, the goths, the stoners, the ones who want to save the planet, the music freaks, the film buffs, the wannabe YouTubers and then you have me. Me all out on my own. Watching. Seeing. Understanding.

And that is what I am doing today. Watching

Amy is sitting in the college canteen three tables to my left and two rows forward. She is one of the fashionistas. One of the clique who always look immaculate, who looks as if they have stepped straight from the latest glossy edition of *Vogue* or *Cosmopolitan*. Never seen without a "to die for" clutch bag monogramed with the initials of the label du jour and always sporting a hundred-dollar haircut from the high-end salons.

Amy is also one of the shamers. Part of that clique who like to point and mock and jeer, though she would deny this.

My lunch sits unopened before me in a brown-paper bag. It consists of a cheese sandwich, crusts trimmed and thrown out for the birds; a carton of orange juice, the synthetic kind filled with a host of E numbers; and dessert is an Oreo biscuit wrapped in cellophane which prevents the creamy centre from oozing everywhere when the biscuit is invariably crushed within my bag. Everything is packed precisely, as it always is, waiting to be opened while the universe waxes and wanes to the whim of Amy Myers.

Amy's friends are sitting beside her. Their elbows form a supporting structure on the table, their faces bathed in a pale glow as they send messages on their phones. They start taking selfies, laughing at the pictures as they are passed between each other. Amy doesn't take a selfie – she never does.

I wonder what would appear on screen if she did. Would her secret be revealed? Would everything be warped and twisted, a rain-washed picture with her at the heart of a pulsating storm? Would that be the moment she is finally outed?

Amy is normal in many ways. Average height, petite figure

and off-brown hair which kisses her shoulders. Everything as lovely as homemade apple pie. You would walk past her on the sidewalk and think nothing of her other than perhaps to think how pretty she is. It is certain you would not notice her middle eye. The eye which only I can see.

Of course she has two others. Cornflower-blue irises set against pure white sclera all surrounding the blackest of pupils. Each eye is positioned exactly where you would expect. One to the left of her perfect nose and one to the right. Both eyes look out at the world as the world looks back and adores her, but it is the middle one which fixates me.

There is something desperate about that eye though perhaps in reality it is more of a void. A void that wants to feed. It is eager to suck you in to sustain itself. A black hole hungry for matter, leeching light from the surrounding world; a kaleidoscope of colours pulled and stretched as she feasts unnoticed. Amy's immediate world resembles Munch's masterpiece, everything swirling as it fights to escape an inexplicable gravitational pull. People should be screaming as their essence is dragged into the gapping maw. Except no one else seems to notice; each person drifting by in their mundane lives barely glancing in her direction other than to offer a friendly smile.

Amy truly is queen of her domain.

I lift the sandwich from my bag, setting it on the table before removing its tin foil wrapping. The foil rustles as I smooth out its crumpled form on the table top. Crumbs scatter left to right before plummeting over the lip of the table and skittering across the floor.

I have been studying Amy for weeks, ever since she arrived from out of state. She ingratiated herself into our systems with a nonchalant ease. Solid grades and dyed-in-the-wool friendships all fell into place. Welcoming faces greeted her across the campus with the world bending over backwards to accommodate her. They don't understand or recognise the danger they are in.

I have hypothesised that her third eye collects thoughts as well as light. It reaches out to wrench our memories and innermost feelings from us. I wonder what she does with those thoughts. Are they hers? Does she own them? Would she own you?

Glancing in Amy's direction, I remove my beanie hat and place it on the table. It casts a lopsided shadow across the laminated surface as I gather the foil between my fingers. Knowing looks swing my way. Banal conversations mutate into barely disguised laughter. People are pointing. Staring. Laughing. People I thought were my friends. The words "weirdo" and "freak" echo in the air but none of them come from Amy so it doesn't matter.

My fingers work quickly and efficiently, creating the millimetre thin protection that will keep me safe. The foil feels peculiar as I place it on my head, the unusual sensation of metal in contact with the fine strands of my hair. I use both hands to sculpt it further, working the foil until it clings tightly to my head. When I am satisfied I retrieve my hat, using it as an additional layer over my foil skullcap. I pull the wool down, feeling with my fingertips for any aluminium poking from beneath, tucking any stray pieces away and out of sight. Always use protection, that's what the sex education teachers told us and I can't see how this is any different. After all, if Amy can hear thoughts through her third eye then what will happen if she hears mine?

The bell for class rings, jerking me alert, displacing me from the world of Amy Myers. Trays clatter as they are piled high in the collection racks ready to be cleared. Lunch bags and exercise books are thrown into rucksacks. People leave the canteen with open reluctance, phones held before them, eyes fixated on the screens as they trudge towards class little knowing what will pass before the week is out.

The group at Amy's table rises as one. Two of them look my way, Emma and Helen, giggling behind their hands while the others continue their conversations. The group weaves between the tables heading for the exit, Amy leading the way. Sweat pricks up across my palms as she edges nearer. I watch with fascination and fear as the eye edges closer to my table. Salt cellars tremble as Amy saunters past, napkins twirling up from their square silver dispensers to flourish in the air. All the time her friends ignore the disturbances which surround them: Mary and Alice engrossed in their phones; Hayley and Rachel chatting; Emma and Helen still giggling; each acting as if the explosion of chaos were the most natural thing in the world.

The gap between us closes, metres becoming centimetres, the distance dwindling by the second. I cannot flee. Amy would know I was different, for sure. She would know that she unnerves me, here in college where everyone else adores her, where they all accept her without question. I am not ready for this. I thought I was but I now realise I have made a grave error, one that is too late to change. And then Amy is here, beside me, her arm brushing my back, ruffling the fabric of my black t-shirt, the sleeves cut to the shoulder exposing my thin pale upper arms. I grip the edges of the table to prevent myself from being dragged away in her vortex, knuckles whitening as my fingernails dig into the cheap, laminated surface.

And then I am alone, Amy and her friends a memory as the canteen doors swing closed behind them.

MY NOSTRILS TWITCH at the hint of oil which scents the surrounding air. The aroma is sweet and heady and reminds me of afternoons spent at the rifle range with my father. The gun itself feels solid in my hands. I have borrowed it from my mother's safe. A nine-millimetre pistol with fixed front and rear sights, bought second-hand from Bud's Guns: *Home for all your hunting and personal defence needs.* I don't think she realised I knew it was there or that I had guessed the code to the safe: my birthday in reverse. The gun appeared in the house not long after they took Dad away, his fists a little too unforgiving one evening. He said it was the alcohol talking but all it looked to me was the booze acting as interpreter, translating his bitterness into words of hatred scrawled across Mom's face in cuts and bruises.

The temptation to take the gun to court when they sentenced him had repeatedly played over and over in my mind in the days preceding his trial. A nagging urge with a devil and angel fighting over each shoulder. That day the angel won and I was glad because it left me free with the means to dispose of Amy Myers resting coldly in my hands.

The walk to college took little more than ten minutes. Eyes of neighbours and passers-by, normally cast anywhere except towards me, seemed to be honed in my direction, assessing the additional bulge in my rucksack where the gun nestled in amongst my college books.

I had gone straight to class, attending a lecture on the science of atoms. Professor Byrne delivered his usual rambunctious exploration of the world of physics. I often contemplated speaking with Professor Byrne about Amy, seeking his interpretation of her state of being. If anyone could understand, it would have been him. Perhaps if I had done that then the next four hours would have turned out differently. But it wasn't to be.

I HAD EXPECTED my hand to waver by this point, agitated by a sense of nervousness and anticipation, yet it remains steady as the proverbial rock.

Screams sound around me. So many screams. All coming from her friends; Emma and Helen leading the chorus. Have you ever heard the scream of someone who thinks they are about to die? There is an unequivocal uniqueness which lives with the listener long after the event. The sound launches itself from the forgotten depths of the soul, a defence mechanism rearing up to its fullest height, teeth bared and claws sharpened, in an attempt to scare Death back into the veil. But they don't need to worry. It is only Amy I care about. Amy, the only other person in the room who is not screaming.

Her head tilts the way a cat looks to its owners for food, quizzical yet with an air of authority. Around us the canteen quickly empties. Courageous jocks running for the exit, pushing past the smaller, less athletic students. Canteen staff downing serving spoons, fleeing in panic through the kitchen. Someone hits the fire alarm, the incessant dinging escalating throughout the campus, mingling with the screams of students and the scrape of furniture being thrown aside amidst panicked escapes.

All of it is a distraction, background noise to the main

event. Amy Myers has to die.

She is standing there before me, her cohort in attendance, challenging me. Daring me. Encouraging me to act. And all the while her third eye feeds on the fear emanating from the two-bit players on the periphery.

I pull the trigger.

Amy raises an eyebrow, shrugging indifferently as the first bullet kisses Emma's neck. A fine spray plumes forth, peppering the white of Amy's blouse. Emma's face blanches with shock before the second bullet finds her heart.

I now know the tin foil doesn't work. It likely hadn't the first time when Amy brushed past me. I watch helplessly; my arm twitches to the left, squeezing off two more shots, Helen and Rachel crumple like rag dolls, falling to the ground next to Emma. They lie still. Unmoving. Three rag dolls all limp and wide eyed. Helen and Rachel to the left, Emma to the right, crimson spreading on the grey linoleum beneath their bodies. I half expect them to stand up, to brush themselves down like this is all an ill-thought out children's game. But they don't.

None of the others run. Why do none of them run? They could break away and be free but they stay rooted, immobile, waiting for the bullets to end whatever energy sparks within their flesh.

Sirens sound beyond the canteen as my arm jerks back to the right, three more bullets picking off the remainder of Amy's friends: Mary, Alice and Hayley, all now dead.

And then there are only two bullets left. One for Amy and one for me. No one else remains. The canteen robbed of the living, with six young innocents ready to be presented on the evening news, carried out on hospital gurneys their faces hidden inside black body bags, the ambulances which take them away running without sirens.

I stare at Amy. My arm is held out straight, the gun rock steady in my grip (*her grip*) with its barrel pointing directly at her face. The world rages all around her, crackling with electricity, pulling energy into her eye. Do human souls exist? I honestly don't know. But whatever mortal ties were broken, she is feasting on the release of energy. Amy devours the carnage around her, gorging on her dead friends, a smorgasbord of delicacies for her to savour.

I can hear a commotion from outside the door, barked orders telling someone to "shut that goddamned alarm off" and to "get something to break these fucking doors down". Doors which have never been locked but something, someone, is keeping them closed.

Amy focuses on me. A fox fixating on a chicken. Victory is etched across her face. I can feel her inside my head. I am fighting her, seeking to maintain control. I lose. I feel my finger tighten around the trigger, gradually squeezing the curve of the metal until I am watching the bullet flying towards her. And as it flies she mouths one word to me.

"Run."

The image of the bullet burying itself in Amy loops within my mind as I run; a wounded queen to be adored by the all-conquering media. At the rear of the canteen are doors which lead to dead ends. Each door marked with the silhouette of a person, the words *His* and *Hers* printed above them.

Bodies invade the room behind me as Amy slumps to the ground, that smile undoubtedly still welded in position. Except they will only see tears and anguish and a single pair of eyes. The same face every household in America will come to love as news of the tragedy spreads.

There is nowhere for me to go inside the toilets. The door to the girl's bathroom is wedged shut. Someone had found their way in before me and barricaded themselves in. I go to the left instead. The door opens. My heart sinks. There is no spacious window for me to crawl through, no secret door to another dimension where I can claim residency or immunity or whatever would appease the natives. Only a piss-stained room, four urinals and three cubicles with graffiti inked across the walls.

I fling myself into the nearest cubicle, collapsing to the floor, legs apart, gun resting between them.

She has saved me one bullet. A way out. A way to bury her secrets.

There is only one avenue for me. No one will believe me.

There will be the chair, or lethal injection if I am lucky, all preceded by years of beatings and sexual assaults while I protest my innocence. She is still breathing out there in the canteen. The shot was not fatal. All is as she has intended. She will be hailed a heroine, a survivor of a lunatic, everyone oblivious to the truth.

My arm moves north, the muzzle of the gun wrinkling the skin of my forehead as the police hammer against the door. The trigger clicks beneath my fingers...

HERE I AM in the institution, although we are not allowed to call it that. A "mental wellbeing facility" are the words they use. The bullet bounced off my skull, entering through my forehead and veering off at an angle. The wound is healing, my own third eye formed of reconstructed skin and scar tissue. They would have called it a miracle if they all didn't want to see me dead. Miracles are the preserve of the righteous and the good. Only the heroes and heroines get those accolades. None of them seem to understand I was doing it for the greater good. Maybe they will in time.

There is a nurse here who reminds me of Amy. Thick dark hair, that all-American smile, and a third eye sitting smack dab in the middle of her forehead, the universe ebbing around her. She dresses in a long white uniform and her shoes squeak as she walks down the corridor. Everyone loves her. None of them can see what I see. I understand that now. I realise I am the only one cursed to witness the truth.

It's okay this time. This time I know where I went wrong. The gun was a bad idea. You have to get close. You have to disguise your thoughts, deny everything until you are close enough to touch her. And then...

Not long now. They'll thank me in the long run. She'll be here soon with my medication. And when she comes I'll smile sweetly, so incredibly sweetly, as I beckon her towards me. And I'll watch that third eye blink. Once, twice, three times. And then close forever as my fingers nestle around her throat.

But for now I have to think happy thoughts, peaceful

thoughts, otherwise she will be on to me and then who knows what will happen.

LITTLE PEOPLE

Tina Rath

"Mummy. Can I ask you something?"

Allegra looked up warily. "What is it, love?"

Not, please, not another Cake-Bake. She had provided a tray of little cakes last time to be sold for the Headmistress's Gin Fund, or whatever Good Cause the school had in mind. They had been prettily iced, playfully decorated with coloured sweets, and she got the whole lot back, intact. Because E-numbers, apparently. She and Bel-Bel had eaten them all that evening without noticeable ill effects, but it had not been a happy experience.

"Mummy..." The child hesitated again. Allegra stopped trying to unload the washing machine while keeping an eye on the potatoes and turned her full attention to her daughter.

"What is it, love?"

"Mummy, when are we going home?"

Allegra sat down abruptly on a kitchen chair. For a moment she literally could not reply. Then she managed to stammer "But darling ... we talked about this. You know ... we live here now. Because..."

Because your daddy is such a devious bastard.

One evening Paul had announced they were going out to dinner. His mother, the Wicked Witch of West Hampstead was coming round to babysit Bel-Bel and they were going to have a special evening on their own. Even while they were finishing the main course Allegra had still thought he was celebrating a major deal, especially when he started talking about how much he wanted Bel-Bel to grow up in the country. She'd decided he was about to suggest they bought a weekend cottage and thinking of ways to veto this nicely. It was only halfway through dessert, a serviceable sticky toffee pudding ruined by a pretentious glob of gritty lavender ice-cream, tasting like old lady's cologne, that he said casually "I know you realise it hasn't been working for us for quite a while," that she understood she was going to be divorced, that *she* was going to buy a house in the country with the money he would give her for her half of their London home.

Too numb to argue she had allowed Paul to erase her and Bel-Bel from his life. Even her mother, the most laid-back woman in the world (her own description – Allegra rather preferred "terminally selfish") had remarked that if she couldn't stand up for herself she might at least have done it for Bel-Bel, before departing for the Spanish Riviera with a girlfriend and reducing her communications to the odd post-card.

As soon as Allegra was out of the way, London house prices escalated (had he *known?* Probably, it was his job) and he was a bricks-and-mortar millionaire, married to a gangster's daughter (who was possibly the reason why "it hadn't been working for them") who almost immediately after the ceremony transformed from slapper to domestic goddess, and presented the Devious Bastard of an ex-husband, the Wicked Witch now Besotted Gran, and her Gangster Father with the boy baby he had always wanted. Apparently. Paul had certainly known about *that*. Allegra, working out dates, could tell that he must have seen the scans... No wonder he wanted everything to go smoothly. And quickly.

So here she was, trapped in dormitory village that didn't have a shop, or even a bus, no friends, no support network, a daughter who wanted to go home, to a home that would never be her home again. And a house full of mice.

The mice were not Paul's fault of course, or hers, in spite of her mother-in-law's acid remarks about no really *clean* house attracting vermin. Sometimes she fantasised about capturing a few, hopefully including a breeding pair, in a humane trap, and taking them to London by night, with Bel-Bel safely asleep on the back seat, of course, to post them through Baba Yaga's letter-box. Instead she had spent a day contacting Pest Controllers. None of whom had answered her initial emails and several of whom cut her off as soon as she gave her address. Finally, one man agreed to come out, but left her feeling she had better jolly well understand he was doing her a major favour. All this ran through her mind, like the glimpses of the past that are supposed to flash before to the eyes of a drowning man.

"You did know it was permanent, darling," she said as soon as she could speak coherently, but looking at the child's face she realised only too well that she had not.

"I thought – I thought you said that if we didn't like it we could go home."

Had she? She might have done. (*She'd probably said something about a pony too, but thankfully that hadn't come back to bite her. Bel-Bel, it turned out, didn't want one.*)

"Don't you like your new school?"

She *could* do something about the school. In fact, she must. Mother Grendel was paying the astronomical fees for the first year (and was that actually a loan? Had she told the old besom she'd pay her back just as she had, apparently, told Bel-Bel this was only temporary?) by which time Allegra was supposed to have re-established her business and be able to go on paying herself. *That* wasn't going to happen.

"Oh. School," Bel-Bel said with ineffable contempt. Obviously she didn't like it, but then who *did* like school?

"What is it then, darling?" (*And please let it be something I can deal with.*)

Bel-Bel was looking down at her school shoes. Still looking down she muttered "I don't like my bedroom."

A sudden billow of black smoke from the saucepan reminded Allegra she should never have taken her eyes off the potatoes. By the time the minor panic was over, and she had opened a tin of soup instead of the dinner that no one wanted to eat, Bel-Bel had retreated into silence again.

Next day the man from Pest Control arrived. He was, unexpectedly, a very nice man. He scouted the mother-in-law's hints about dirt.

"These are country mice, madam," he assured her. "Fresh as little furry daisies. But out of place in the domestic environment and we can't have that, can we?"

She almost had the impression that he was going to round them up, give them a good talking to, and send them back to the woods and fields. But he was very professional and searched the house, starting with the kitchen, for signs of infestation.

And found none.

"There's nothing down here, madam. I wonder if it was a little harvest mouse you saw."

"I haven't *seen* anything. But my daughter's heard them. Running about. She woke me in the night once to tell me..."

"Could it have been a nasty dream, madam? Perhaps brought on by a bit of indigestion?"

Or E-numbers? had it happened on the night of the cakes?

"But – but I've *smelt* them." Argue with *that*.

The man sniffed rather pointedly. The kitchen still smelt faintly of nothing worse than burned potatoes.

"Upstairs."

He followed her up the white painted staircase and, suddenly shy, she opened the door of her daughter's bedroom, not hers. There really was no chance of his becoming either embarrassed or – or unnecessary at the sight of a double bed, but still... They both sniffed the air. And there it was, a faint mustiness... She opened the window to let in the fresh rain-scented air.

"Well, there's something ... but it could be damp ... no, I'd be taking your money under false pretences if I put poison down."

Just as well, perhaps, considering what he charged solely for his visit. And now should she worry about the damp? She went back and sniffed again. Not damp. Possibly not mice either but something more familiar ... an old memory from being a student, and going to a party in a shared house where the room she left her coat in smelt of sheets that had not been changed often enough. Bodies that had not showered regularly. And ... sex. Only that was impossible. Yet ... it felt downright perverse to sniff her daughter's bedclothes but she did. And they, washed every three days just as her own were, smelt only of biological detergent. So where was that odour coming from?

And then her mobile chirruped. Reception here wavered between very bad and non-existent but she heard the words "school nurse" and "nothing to worry about but..." enough to send her flying down the stairs and into her car. She was not even sure she had shut the front door after her, never mind locked it, and she didn't care. She had to force herself to drive at a reasonable speed. An accident would not help either of them but by the time she arrived at the school she was frantic. A class lined up in the school playground stared at her as she ran past, someone's mother, wild-haired and weeping. One or two giggled. Once inside she realised she didn't know where to go and ran wildly down the corridors, coming at last to the Headmistress's office, throwing open the door without knocking.

Bel-Bel sat stiff and miserable but alive and unbandaged on a hard-backed chair, flanked by Nurse and Headmistress. The Headmistress turned and spoke as if to a delinquent pupil.

"Ah. Mrs Billington. Please come in and close the door."

Allegra did neither. "Tell me what's wrong with my daughter."

"Now there's no need for dramatics. I asked my secretary to make that quite clear when she called you."

The Nurse ran a professional eye over Allegra and came to take her by the elbow and steer her to a chair. "Really, there's nothing to worry about. It's just – would you like a cup of tea?"

Control, Allegra told herself. Control. Or perhaps they won't let you take her home. She sat down and said "Yes, please."

The Headmistress, who had clearly not been envisaging a

tea-drinking situation looked sour but nodded. "Perhaps we could all do with a cup."

"I'll see to it." The Nurse seemed too eager to get out of the room but perhaps while she was gone and there was only the Headmistress to deal with, Allegra could push her aside and snatch Bel-Bel...

"Now. All that has happened is that our gym-lady noticed some – some marks on Mehitabel's arm when she changed for games this afternoon. And quite rightly..."

"Marks? Show me, Bel-Bel."

The child rolled back the sleeve of her school jersey. There were half-a-dozen thin cuts on her inner arm, running from her elbow to her wrist. They could only have been made with a very fine sharp blade which had divided but not torn the skin. Allegra thought numbly *She must have hardly felt them at first, but they would spread open afterwards and begin to smart...*

"But how..." she began helplessly.

"She has been unable – or unwilling – to explain."

Bel-Bel suddenly hurled herself into her mother's arms and screamed with all her strength. "They did it! They did it!"

"Who? Girls here at the school? Do you know their names?"

"*No*, the little people, the ones I told you about but you said they were mice. They cut me with their swords and they laughed. They come out at night and do horrible things and I want to go home!"

"Oh, Bel..." She wrapped her arms round her daughter and rocked her while they both sobbed.

And then they went – not home but back to the house they lived in now. Bel-Bel was on indefinite leave from school, by common consent. Both School Nurse and Headmistress had been reluctantly convinced that Allegra had not harmed her daughter, but this meant that the child must have been "self-harming". She was very young, the Nurse confided to Allegra, but there *were* cases amongst even younger children and she should, of course, see a psychiatrist. Indeed, she would be put on a waiting list but apparently it was a very long one.

"Quite honestly by the time they get someone to see her it

will probably all have cleared up," the Nurse had added cheerfully. "Just be patient with her and let her regress as much as she likes." (Her stories of "little people" were a symptom of regression. With any luck she would have forgotten all about them in a year or so.)

Allegra nodded and made the occasional noises of assent – and never told anyone that when they got home they found Mr Bear, Bel-Bel's old teddy, lying on her bed his furry belly ripped open and the stuffing pulled out. He had been gralloched.

Bel-Bel, beyond crying now, said stonily "It was because I told. They don't like being talked about."

Allegra picked up Mr Bear and pressed the stuffing back inside. It was almost a joke, in its way. Black humour. And Bel-Bel could have done it herself before she went to school, just as she could have cut her arm. *(But with what? And why?)* The Nurse had an explanation for that, of course. "She told you. She wants to go home. I'm sure this sort of thing never happened when you and your husband were living together."

"He's not my husband now," Allegra had said.

The Nurse ignored her. "She's 'acting out'. Perhaps she feels that her little brother pushed her out of her house where she felt safe. She identifies him with the little people."

"Perhaps."

She made up a bed for Bel-Bel in her own room and locked her daughter's bedroom door. Somehow the child felt this would help. They, whatever they were, she believed could not operate outside certain parameters. Allegra supposed that if she was imagining them then she could control them, so the rest of the house was safe. If not... She sat down that evening and mended the re-stuffed Mr Bear with tiny almost invisible stitches, and set him up defiantly on her own pillow. Once or twice, late at night when neither of them could sleep, Bel-Bel, perhaps feeling that they were safe behind a locked door, talked about what the little people did. They fought and wounded each other. Some were dragged off, dead she thought. And there were ladies too, and the men *hurt* them. It was as if they were enacting the more unsuitable scenes from *Game of Thrones* on Bel-Bel's bedroom carpet.

And how could she have invented that? She had never watched anything scarier than *Frozen*.

If they were real what were they? Allegra wondered if they could be a kind of fairy. A nasty kind, of course, but why not?

She knew that somehow she must get Bel-Bel out of the house, sell it for next to nothing, if necessary, even if they had to live in a B&B with their worldly goods in carrier bags piled round them. But she could not find the energy to even begin.

And then, unbelievably, help came from where she least expected it. Paul's mother. She plucked a picture of the village from the web and sent it with the house-agent's rather flattering photograph of the house to Paul's new wife. Random mischief was probably her motive and it worked, probably beyond her wildest dreams. Both the girl and her gangster father fell in love with it.

So English. So quaint. Just like *Midsomer Murders*. Much too good for poor Paul's cast-off wife and useless daughter. And, really, for them it wasn't far enough away. Couldn't they be shipped out to Spain to live with the Other Grandmother? Wouldn't that be much the best? Especially as the little girl was – or so the school had told her – *peculiar*. Peculiar and no doubt dangerous ... suppose she came into contact with her little brother in spite of all their care. No it wasn't to be thought of. He – the father – would take care of everything.

Money can do so much. Money would buy the house from Allegra at twice the price she had paid, if that were necessary. Money would buy, if not a castle, then a villa in Spain and persuade the Other Granny to take responsibility for her strange offspring. Allegra was probably as peculiar as her daughter. But in Spain they would be harmless. Perhaps even happy...

Allegra, faced with these suggestions, acquiesced as she had acquiesced to the divorce and her exile to the country. Spain was just that bit further away. But far enough. The little people would not follow them there and if they did she would know they were imaginary, and get treatment for her daughter. And for herself because she had begun to hear them scratching at the other side of Bel-Bel's bedroom door, trying to get out...

It was surprising how little luggage they had to take with them. The furniture had been included in the sale price. She packed their clothes, some books and Mr Bear, and her laptop, and they were ready to go. She vaguely hoped her mother would *be* there when they arrived, but that hardly mattered so long as nothing else was.

When the driver arrived to take them to the airport Allegra asked him to come upstairs while she made sure she had left nothing behind. If he was surprised by this he did not say, but accompanied her as she requested. She looked round her own bedroom casually and Bel-Bel's more carefully. The young man picked something up from the carpet and gave a sharp exclamation.

"What's that? A bit of one of those anatomical toys they do nowadays?"

Allegra looked at the thing he held between his fingers. It was a tiny skull.

"Well. He came to a nasty end by the look of it."

Something like a sword – or an axe – had nearly split that little head in half.

"He didn't walk away from that."

Allegra spoke at last. "Yes," she said. "A toy."

He stared at it whitely then threw it down. "Gawd. You'd swear it was real."

Allegra put her heel on it grinding it to powder. "It's wonderful what they can do," she agreed. "There's nothing up here. Let's be on our way."

If she told Paul he would take it as confirmation that she was mad and had passed her madness on to Bel-Bel. He would probably remember incidents, jokes, eccentricities, unnoticed at the time, that proved it. His mother would chime in. "What sort of woman calls her daughter after a cockroach?" and there would be no one to point out that *Mehitabel* had been a *cat*. The famous poetic cockroach was Archie.

Paul probably wouldn't have accepted the skull as evidence. Even if she hadn't destroyed it.

She wondered if they would put the baby in Bel-Bel's room and what would happen. Nothing good, she thought. Sad, of course, because he was certainly innocent. But it couldn't be helped.

She followed the driver downstairs. To the long black limousine that was to take them away.

TEUFELSBERG

Madhvi Ramani

As soon as I got off the train I knew I was right about the story. The station was small. One platform. One waiting room. One sign held up by two twisted iron posts: Teufelsberg.

Herr Koch climbed off after me with his bags of knives. He was long and thin, all angular features and crisp shirt lapels. I had heard of people resembling their pets, but their jobs? Then again, here I was in a frayed trench coat looking as shabby as a thumbed tabloid. Your typical disgraced hack. We wished each other *Aufwiedersehen* and agreed to have a beer together if our paths crossed again.

"You always meet a person two times in life," he said in accented English and I vaguely recalled my German grandmother saying something similar.

He wasn't the type I normally drank with. There was something old-fashioned about him even though he couldn't have been more than forty. Still, we had made small talk upon boarding the train together in Berlin.

"Then to Nurnberg, down to Munich and into Austria..." he had said outlining his schedule.

"Must be difficult being away from home so much," I replied.

"Yes, it is. Although sometimes I think it is better being

on the road where I have the comfort of warm thoughts of home. It is never so satisfying when I get there. Sebastian locks himself away with his computer. Anna is so bossy even though she is only seven and my wife does not even..."

He chuckled realising he had overstepped the boundaries of polite train conversation. I smiled and nodded to help him out, then he looked out of the window while I browsed the day's stories on my laptop. He had proven the perfect travelling companion. My old journalism professor's words echoed in my head: *Don't burn your bridges; you never know when you might need a contact.* It was unlikely I'd ever need a quote from a German knives salesman but I took his card anyway.

"Be sure to catch your train," I said.

His grey eyes flashed with amusement. *Facetious American.* He had almost an hour before his connecting train to Erfurt but I knew something he didn't: an uncanny number of people had gone missing from this station. People just passing through or waiting for their connecting trains, like Herr Koch. A couple of cast iron cauldrons overflowing with marigolds stood at either side of the entrance to the station. Bright red. Flourishing oddly out of season. They glowed as if pulsing with heat, like a wound against the bleak sky.

A cello's mournful melody drifted out of a window and accompanied me down the main road. I stopped at the first *Pension* I saw, lingering at the door to hear the rest of the tune but it abruptly stopped. I sighed and entered a dark lobby making a bell tinkle. The room smelt of warm wood. A goth with black hair and dark eyes, wearing clinking silver bracelets, appeared. She didn't exactly fit in with her quaint German surroundings. I deposited my bag in the single room – it was standard fare, flowery bed sheets, dinky bathroom – and went down for an early dinner of goulash and *semmel knoedel*. I sat at the table and opened my folder of notes. A newspaper clipping fluttered out. I picked it up.

It was the short article that had started this whole escapade. A fluff piece by Maria Weimann about a man who had gone missing, last seen getting off at Teufelsberg even though it wasn't his stop. His wife had followed in an attempt to find him but she too had disappeared. I didn't think of it again until a few weeks later; the same paper noted the death of the journalist who had written the story - Maria Weimann. That's when I got that feeling, that tingling at the back of my neck, that alerts me to a story.

I looked into it. You can't trust everything you read, I knew better than most. I got in touch with an old Berlin correspondent under the pretence of looking to get back into the game and he grudgingly put me in touch with someone at the same newspaper group. When I called her, she told me there were no jobs and she couldn't help me, but you don't spend over ten years being a journalist without learning how to push. We met for a coffee. Her lips were so pursed her face creased. My reputation had preceded me.

I asked her banal questions about company structures, editors and freelancers until about thirty-five minutes in when we were almost done - because that's when you hit them with the real question - I said I was sorry to hear about the recent death of her colleague. Her lips loosened at that. She revealed that Weimann had collapsed in a bar in Teufelsberg from alcohol poisoning. That tingle again. How many deaths were caused by alcohol poisoning? Afterwards, because we journos are terrible gossips - if we weren't we wouldn't be in this business - people talked about how they sometimes caught a rancid whiff on her breath. Sometimes her eyes were a little red. Her lipstick smudged. Yes, Maria Wiemann was an alcoholic.

On the way back, I thought about it. I'm no stranger to drink - especially in these last three months of my ... sabbatical. The more you do it the better you get at it. From what I had heard Weimann was a high-functioning alcoholic. A pro. So how could she just get smashed like that?

I confirmed the disappearance of the man and the woman but there was no big conspiracy there. According to the daughter he had a wandering eye and was probably shacked up with a new woman. Her mother had an envious nature and refused to let him go. I was beginning to think the whole thing was nothing more than a coincidence - just one misfit following another into the void - but a few days at the archives confirmed I was on to something. Yes, this unremarkable little town was Germany's very own Bermuda Triangle.

After dinner I went out to find Atopia, the bar where Weimann had her last drink. "Turn right out of the *Pension* and take the second left. It's a few hundred metres down," said the goth. Her eyes were like dark pools in the dim light.

I stepped out into sharp evening air and set off at a brisk pace. The cello was playing again, its tempo faster now, more urgent. I was back on the trail of a story. The street lamps cast everything in a greyish light. People scuttled by, ducking in and out of shops like ghosts. I passed one left turn and kept walking. The cello strokes faded behind me. Ahead, there was a major curve to the right before the road ended in darkness. A dead end marked by a looming dark mass. Had I come too far? Missed the second left? I walked on, pulled towards the blackness. It was a massive unlit building. Probably the *Rathaus* - the town hall - a staple of every small German town. Still, there was something unnatural about its shadowiness, the way light vanished at that point. As I got closer I fancied I could make out a thorny forest rising like a mysterious mountain in front of the building. The name of the town, *Teufelsberg* - Devil's Mountain in German - popped into my head. I stopped. There was an alley to my left. Was this the second turning? I ducked down it, escaping the terrible shadow vision forming in front of me.

The alley widened into a road of row houses. There was no bar in sight. I took the next left, following the rule that *left, left, and left* gets you back to where you started. That was in the US though, where we had the grid system. It didn't work in these old European towns. I turned and turned getting further entangled in a web of little streets. Typical. This was what had landed me in trouble in the first place. Not knowing when to stop. What had led me from being Christian Finkel of *The New York Times*, reporting from Nigeria, Somalia and Afghanistan, to Christian Finkel whom no one would publish, lost and alone in a random German town.

My descent had started with a made-up quote here and

there. You don't know what it's like in those places where people speak a hundred different dialects and even the translators get tongue-tied, where no one wants to talk and if they do it's to lead you on wild goose chases based on rumours, tales and fables, where you spend two days bumping along the desert to meet someone who doesn't turn up, or turns up three hours late looking to get paid. What was I supposed to do? Admit I couldn't file a story? The quotes had to be massaged. There was no other way. Plus, it *worked*. For a while anyway. I shouldn't have taken it further but I was enjoying my success, and the pressure to continue breaking stories grew. People recognised my name. At bars my gleaming image was reflected in the eyes of women, enchanted by my tales. Towards the end I was fabricating everything. The truth was elusive, impossible to get, didn't make any sense – and people wanted a story. It was only a matter of time before I got caught. *The Times* issued a full-page apology. *Your credibility is all you have as a journalist. Lose that and you're out of the game.* And I was out. My name smudged. Women turned away, repelled. I ignored calls from family and friends and decamped to Berlin, city of losers and wannabe artists. How was I going to get out of this mess? Was this how people disappeared here? They just got lost? My heart started to pound. I didn't want to die, to disappear into the oblivion in some small German town.

A deep low moan pierced my thoughts. Was it me? No, it was ... the cello. Rogue notes carried on the wind. I followed their direction, navigating my way through the crooked streets and piecing together the tune, until I emerged on the main road once more. I tramped back to the *Pension*, exhausted. The bar would have to wait until tomorrow.

The next morning everything seemed brighter. I peeled hardboiled eggs – their smooth white exteriors revealing wicked yellow insides – as I read the papers. I read the news every day. It was a habit I had kept up even in Berlin, where I was living off my savings drinking cheap beer, going to sex parties and nursing hangovers in my self-imposed exile. It stung seeing the names of my colleagues in print but reading the paper was the only thing that kept the days from blending into one another. It was a little bit of hope, proof that fresh stories and new developments emerged every day. That the world was still spinning and anything was possible.

I decided to give last night's directions another try. I turned right out of the *Pension*, passed the first left and there it was, a second left not soon after. I must have missed it in my excitement. The door of the bar was propped open by a couple of crates of beer. Inside it was dark and cigarette-smelling. A slot machine whirred and clinked in the corner fed by a thin sallow man.

"We're closed," came a voice from my left – a man loading beers into a fridge behind the bar.

"Hi. I just wanted to ask a few questions about my colleague Maria Weimann."

The bartender paused and turned. The slot machine whirred.

"You remember her?"

He nodded, once.

"What happened?"

"Drank too much, collapsed. They took her to hospital."

The slot machine emitted a jangle.

"Was she alone? Did she talk to anyone?"

"Just me."

"What did she talk to you about?"

"She told me what she wanted to drink."

I sighed as the slot machine fell silent. It was a typical German answer. Literal, direct. Despite being half-German myself it was a quality I loathed. Truth lay in the grey areas.

"And what was that?" I asked as the gambler dropped more coins into the machine.

"Vodka, gin, a few Jägermeisters – a mix."

The machine whirred.

"You kept serving her? Didn't think she'd had enough?"

"It's a bar. People order drinks. They get what they order."

Jangle. Jangle. Jangle.

"Yes, but an exceptionally high number of people have died of alcohol poisoning in this town and since this is one of only three bars—"

"Maybe it's time you left," said the man. It sounded like a

warning. His eyes were like deep wells. Were he and the goth related? It wouldn't be unusual in a small town like this, then again he was fair-haired and it was probably just the lighting in this dingy place that made his eyes resemble hers. I left, the sound of coins clinking behind me.

At the main road I turned left instead of heading back to the *Pension*. I needed to think, and to think I needed to walk. Plus, I wanted to see the *Rathaus*, or whatever it was, in daylight to banish the queasiness from last night. There was the curve to the right and straight ahead a redbrick building with a clock tower. Definitely the *Rathaus*. Behind it a mountain – or rather a hill – rose up. That accounted for the unusual shadowiness of the spot. In front of the building was a statue. I circled it: seven demons dancing atop a hill. Yes, all those horns and swinging tails could seem like thorny branches in the dark.

Each demon represented a deadly sin. Sloth was sprawled lazily on the slope of the hill, with Gluttony emptying a bottle into his mouth nearby. I thought of Weimann and shuddered. Greed's fingers reached grabbingly into thin air. The figure of Lust was dominated by a grotesque erection. The man Weimann had written about in that first report had, according to his daughter, been lustful. Envy glanced at her companions through narrowed eyes. That was his wife. Wrath's eyes were made of copper, as was her raised sword. Vanity gazed into a black glass mirror and, rising above them all in the very centre, was Pride. My very own sin. What was such a strange statue doing here in front of the town hall? *Teufelsberg.* Of course. It was a representation of the town's name. Devil's Mountain. For the first time, I wondered about the history of that name. I strolled on towards the *Rathaus*. Maybe someone there could tell me. It would be a colourful fact to throw into the article.

Inside, the *Rathaus* was disappointingly stale compared to its rich exterior. All signs for administrative buildings and long grey corridors. I turned down one at random, passing ticket-number dispensers and people milling in waiting areas, when I saw a sign saying *Bibliothek am Rathaus*. A library. Perfect. I followed the sign pushing through two sets of double doors before stepping into a dim space with towering bookcases. I paused and breathed in the musty air. It was disorienting, the way things morphed in this town.

I walked along a row of dusty books ... Goethe, Schiller, Mann.

"The immortals," came a voice behind me. It was an old man with pale skin, red hair and a wispy beard.

"Hi. I'm looking for information about the town's name ... Teufelsberg. It's unusual."

"Yes, yes," said the man. His eyes were like sunken black pebbles in the lined landscape of his face. I waited. Normally if you wait people will talk to fill the silence.

"It's a long story," he said finally and turned, his shoes tapping the stone floor as he walked further into the library. Did he expect me to follow? *Words, old man, use your words*, I thought as I trailed down the maze of aisles after him. He stopped and pulled a big leather-bound book from its shelf. *Das Komplette Geschiste vom Teufelsberg*. A Complete History of Teufelsberg. I took it. Its weight pressed my fingertips. The old man was right: it was a long story.

Tap, tap, tap.

"Wait, isn't there a short answer? I'm just visiting..." I said as the man disappeared around the end of a bookcase. I followed.

"I can't check this out – I'm not a member."

He turned down another aisle.

"I just need a few details for a story..."

The old man stopped and turned.

"To write a proper story you need to research. How else will you end up here with the immortals," said the man waving at the German greats on the shelf next to him. Somehow we had ended up back at the entrance. He was right of course. Rigorous research and fact-checking were exactly what I needed for my comeback.

"Take it. You can bring it back when you're finished," he said.

"What?"

The man's eyes were hard and determined. I shrugged and left with the book. What kind of a librarian was he? It was a wonder there were still any books left in there if that was how he ran the place. Must be losing his marbles.

I went back to the *Pension* to drop off the book. When I got there I sat in the armchair by the window. The cellist was playing again. Repeating that same tune with slight variations each time. I picked up the book; now was as good a time as any to do some background research. It wasn't as if there was anything further to be achieved today. Tomorrow I had an appointment with the local police station chief which would probably generate some new leads. I turned to the first page.

The hill, and surrounding lands – the area currently named Teufelsberg – is notable for its rich fertile soil. The Goths considered it a place of extraordinary natural power where they made human and animal sacrifices.

Talk about complete history. I skimmed over the next few pages detailing various excavations, belief systems and rituals until—

During the Christian era the area was named Teufelsberg being, as it was, a place associated with pagans and devil worshippers. Christians from the villages on the periphery of Teufelsberg were warned to stay away from the wild wooded area. Despite this an uncanny number of children and adults were recorded missing...

My neck prickled. Church records dating from the sixteenth century listed, with the same regularity as births, deaths and marriages, details of persons disappeared. The cellist switched to a higher register. I kept reading.

...resulting in the 1636-42 witch trials in which fifty-eight individuals were found guilty of luring people into the woods as offerings to the devil. Evidence included eyewitness accounts of bodies hanging from trees...

I thought about how, just yesterday, I had made that statue in front of the *Rathaus* out to be some kind of shadowy forest. Yes, it would be easy to do - imagine bodies hanging among the branches in a dark woodland. After all, people are prone to making up all sorts of things.

Other "evidence" from the witch trials included testimony from a farmer who claimed that the darker richer soil of Teufelsberg, compared to that of the surrounding farms, was a result of human blood and putrefaction. He obviously had an axe to grind over some nutrient deficit which caused his crops to fail in 1603, 1605, 1611, et. al. - but never affected the vegetation of Teufelsberg. I skipped forward.

> *It was only after the Second World War displaced millions, causing the biggest migration of people across Europe, that Teufelsberg became settled. Much of the woodland beneath the hill had been destroyed by fires caused by bombing, and the town was built on this wasteland, from the rubble of the war. The original settlers were said to have made a pact with the devil in order to live on his land. Upon making this deal the colour of their eyes turned the colour of the Teufelsberg soil to which they belonged. Their descendants are to this day still recognisable by their dark eyes...*

I paused. The cellist was inserting extra phrases to his tune, making it longer, more complex. I had been pulled in. Suckered. This was no history book. It was folklore, presented as fact. I flipped to the cover. The author was Henri Faust. Was this a joke? I turned back to where I had left off. The book might have been a curious mix of fact and fiction, but it was a compelling read. Besides, something about the muted sunlight diffusing through the room and the cello's increasing momentum as it travelled further away from its original tune was hypnotic. I turned the page.

> *...and are said to continue to operate as tools of the devil by luring people to their deaths on this land. The native populations from the villages surrounding Teufelsberg always viewed the new town's inhabitants with suspicion, being, as they were, outsiders who arrived dark-eyed from the East with no clear history, place or...*

Snap! I opened my eyes. I could still sense the vibration of the string, taut and high-pitched, before it snapped and silence descended. The clock glowed 02:38. Had the cellist been playing until now? Or had it been a dream? My ears pulsed in the stillness. I stood ~ the book slid to the floor with a thud - and crawled into bed, my eyelids heavy with sleep.

THE POLICE CHIEF looked bewildered. His eyes and hair were

the colour of mud, flecked with gold. The files on his desk were piled high like heaps of dead leaves that he had to wade through.

"What can I say? It's an anomaly. A coincidence." He shrugged. He had been repeating the same phrase in different ways throughout the interview. I got the feeling it was an explanation he repeated a lot, not just to me. I almost felt sorry for him. Almost. Another part of me wanted to punch him. He had given me nothing. Not a hint of a serial killer, a sect, or something sinister in the water. Just a shrug and a nod to the chaos of the universe.

As I walked back into town my eye caught a tall sharp figure hurrying down the street. I paused. Herr Koch! I hurried after him, turning down one street then another until I found myself on an empty road of row houses. There was nowhere he could have gone unless ... had he entered one of the houses? Was he selling knives in this neighbourhood? No, he was due to be in Nuremberg right now. It might not have been him but that figure, so distinct. I dug out my wallet and shuffled through a bunch of receipts and cards until I found his. I dialled his number and held my breath. This was ridiculous. What did I expect? Was he ducking behind a car, waiting to spring out like a Jack-in-the-Box? It rang and rang... Voicemail. I hung around for a bit waiting for him to come out of one of the houses. My fingers and toes started to turn numb. No one could discuss knives for this long. It was time to give up.

On my way back, I came across Atopia. Now was as good a time as any for a drink. The bartender raised his eyebrows at me when I walked in. I sat down and ordered a beer and a shot. Fuck him. Robert Johnson crackled through the speakers.

Standin' at the crossroad,
I tried to flag a ride,

Apart from me there was just one other guy nursing a beer and the gambler from yesterday, feeding coins into the machine.

Didn't nobody seem to know me,
Everybody pass me by

The story was dead. My Woodward and Bernstein moment gone. But... The machine whirred. If that was Herr Koch and he hadn't caught his train to Erfurt it was proof something odd was up. He could tell me why, what happened. He was the key to breaking this story. I tried calling him again.

Mmm, the sun goin' down, boy
Dark gon' catch me here

Voicemail again. The gambler dropped more coins into the machine. Idiot. I wanted to shake him. Didn't he know he was never going to win? He needed to do something else. Jangle. Jangle. Jangle. Shit. *I* needed to do something else. I was just like that guy. Delusional. I probably even imagined seeing Herr Koch. No, I wasn't about to become another lost soul in this small town. I needed to stop thinking I could win back my former glory and just get a nine-to-five. I didn't need to be Christian Finkel, journalist extraordinaire. I could be Average Joe. Normal. Anonymous. I downed the beer, threw down some coins and left.

I went straight to the train station. The cellist was playing again, frantic and demented. Last night wasn't a dream. One of his strings really had snapped leaving his tune a little off. I walked past the blood-red marigolds as I entered the station – and remembered the book. All those fairy tales about the special Teufelsberg soil fertile with human putrefaction. I'd have to return it to the library before I left. I bought a ticket to Berlin for that very evening then went back to the *Pension* to fetch the book.

The *Rathaus* corridors were shushed with only the shuffle of papers and a few murmuring voices. People were leaving for the day. I wandered around searching for *Bibliothek am Rathaus*. Somehow, I couldn't find it. It was like a sign. I was going to disappear into the great blob of humanity, never to be remembered. I'd never make it into the library. How come I always lost my way in this damned town? I recalled a passage I had read last night.

The phenomenon of objects and buildings shifting and subsiding in Teufelsberg has been subject to much theorising. Architects and geologists are in agreement that the soil and rubble upon which the town was hastily built is still settling, accounting for a degree of movement and disorientation. Occultists argue that the town occupies a supernatural space which transmogrifies to tempt people into its net...

The fluorescent lights overhead started to flicker. Fuck this. I wasn't about to get trapped in some administrative building and miss my train. I'd leave the book at the *Pension*. I followed the *Ausgang* signs and made my way back.

I got to the station an hour early and paced up and down the platform thinking. That book. The way it described things shifting in this town felt true. And all that stuff about inhabitants having eyes as dark as the Teufelsberg soil? The goth at the *Pension*, the guy at the bar - even the librarian - had dark eyes. I strode over to the marigolds and peered between their petals: glistening black soil. My heartbeat quickened. No. Just because certain things in the book were on point didn't mean all that stuff about witches and the devil was. It was ludicrous. The book was just joining certain dots of reality, fabricating the space between. I couldn't do that. Not again. I was a journalist, I dealt in facts. It would be different if I had an actual source...

I tried Herr Koch again. It rang and rang. Voicemail. I tried him again and again. I was acting like a crazed stalker but I couldn't let go of the feeling I was onto something. The chance of the big break I needed to get out of this rut. The railroad started to rumble and the train to my new life of mediocrity approached. The phone rang. The train glided to a stop. The doors slid open. Shit. Answer your fucking phone. People got off. Voicemail. I hit redial. It rang. The doors started to close. He was going to pick up this time. This was going to work. I was too good for anything else. All those stories. Paedophilia in the Afghan Army. The Somalian Weapons Black Market. Corruption in the Nigerian Cabinet. The doors shuddered shut and the train chugged away. Voicemail. Fuck. I dropped the phone. What was I doing? It was over. My ears started ringing. I tried to breathe. Calm down. It wasn't a big deal. What difference did it make if I was down and out in Berlin or here? I would just get another ticket for tomorrow. That's when I noticed it. The phone flashing. The ringing wasn't in my head - someone was calling. Herr Koch. I answered.

"Herr Koch. Christian Finkel here. I'm sorry, I just realised my phone mistakenly dialled—"

"Actually, I thought you might still be in Teufelsberg and were calling about that drink," said Herr Koch.

"What? You're here?"

HERR KOCH LOOKED different. His cheeks were fuller, flushed. He welcomed me into a row house on the road where I had lost him the other day. It smelt of warm bread and cakes. My stomach rumbled. When had I last eaten? I smiled as Herr Koch introduced me to Marta, a plump woman in a white apron embroidered with purple flowers, Katrin, a doll-like girl, and Kilian, a polite serious boy - trying to make sense of this picture.

In the living room Marta poured tea into porcelain cups and served cake on doily napkins. This wasn't my idea of a drink but I was glad for the food. In all this obsessing over the story I had neglected to eat. Had Herr Koch moved to Teufelsberg with his family? But didn't his children have different names? I wracked my brain trying to remember.

Katrin sang a song then curtsied. Kilian recited a Goethe poem. I pretended to be charmed. They weren't acting like normal children. They had dark eyes like their mother. Herr Koch's grey eyes, or any of his features, were nowhere to be seen. They were not his children. Marta brought in some cookies then slices of freshly baked bread with butter and honey. I watched Herr Koch eat. No wonder he seemed fuller. Finally the kids went off to play and Marta brought us two *Weissen* beers along with some pretzels and "left us men to it".

"So, the last time I saw you, at the station..." I started.

"Oh yes, that's where I met Marta. It started as a chat but by the time the train came I knew I wasn't ready to leave."

"But what about your job? Your—" I lowered my voice to a whisper "—wife, children."

Herr Koch crammed some pretzels into his mouth.

"All of that just wasn't working out. With Marta I feel like

I've finally found what I have been looking for..."

By the time I stepped out into the cold evening air I was reeling. My stomach churned with cake and pretzels. Thank God I had managed to get out of the roast dinner Marta had been insisting I stay for. I needed to gather my thoughts. I started walking.

The facts, Finkel. Stick to the facts. Herr Koch, who was supposed catch a train to Erfurt, had been tempted to stay in Teufelsberg by Marta, a well-off widow. Her eyes were the same colour as the soil beneath the marigolds. Teufelsberg soil. Herr Koch was now engulfed in perfect family bliss. I recalled the brief conversation we had had on the train here. It was as if he had been tempted by his deepest need: his desire for a comfortable home and family life. Was this all a coincidence or proof that Teufelsberg's inhabitants really were operating as tools of the...? I stopped myself. Facts. Right. I recalled a passage from the book.

In 1961 the US National Security Agency (NSA) built a field station atop the hill to listen in on Soviet and East German military communications. The station closed after just one year due to an exceptional level of false alarms causing high levels of anxiety and panic among the soldiers stationed there. Many of them had breakdowns or went AWOL. The few available documents from the station do indeed support the theory that the soldiers were suffering from stress. Many of them claimed that they were not in fact picking up military signals but tuning into the thoughts of the people who lived below the hill...

Was this land and the folk who belonged to it able to pick up on people's thoughts, morphing in order to feed their desires and lure them into darkness? The ground felt as if it was pulsing, undulating beneath my feet – or maybe it was my own pulse, my excitement at finally piecing together a story. The problem was I needed proof. Facts. Not only because I needed to re-establish my integrity as a journalist but because a story like this, that involved supernatural elements, would need to be substantiated. But that very word – *supernatural* – meant something that went beyond the natural world, beyond what could be touched, seen, proven.

I walked around town getting lost in its labyrinthine streets, turning the problem round in my head. There had to be a way. I needed to verify. Investigate. I was a great journalist. I was Christian Finkel of the *NYT*. If anyone could do it, it was me.

I stopped at Atopia to talk to the gambler. His bones jutted beneath his saggy pale skin. He reeked of piss. How long had he been sitting here?

"Excuse me, could I ask you a few questions?"

He didn't blink. His eyes were fixated on the machine. If he wasn't careful he was going to die on that stool. I moved on.

The more I walked the more I saw it. This town was filled with crazed people, spiralling in a *Teufelskreis* – a devil's cycle, unable to escape. I took notes. Peered into people's eyes to see what colour they were, stopped them on the street to get interviews, quotes. I banged on the cellist's door. His tune was becoming desperate, obsessed. His silhouette, like a deranged puppet in the window, never paused. He never stopped to answer the door. One by one the rest of his strings snapped. Then silence. The gambler disappeared. This town was eating up people. Somebody had to do something about it. Somebody had to save them. Herr Koch was getting fatter. We met sometimes. I told him he needed to leave. He told me I needed to leave. We stayed. He couldn't get up from his armchair. I couldn't stop walking, thinking.

The heels of my shoes were wearing out, my clothes became looser. I was going to make it into that library. I was going to go down in history. Once I was done with this story everyone would want it. *The Guardian, The Times...* There would be a bidding war, a book deal, a Pulitzer. I was going to cause a sensation, rock the foundations of modern thought, smash rationalism.

DOWN ALONG THE BACKROADS

Jenny Barber

WE HEARD THE travellers approach long before the open-top jeep spluttered off the slipway in lurches and coughs, shuddering into silence not a few feet from the entrance to Marie's. There were three in the car: two up-front, with a dazed otherworldly look to their eyes that would blink away once their feet hit solid ground, and the one in back, clearer eyed and faster moving, and if her skin looked a little green in the fading light we were too polite to mention. We watched as she leant over to talk to the driver, quiet, calm, a hand on the boy's shoulder while her other hand pointed at the gas station, to Marie's, and the sanctuary of the rest stop.

"Who's got space to put them up?" Lizbeth asked, soft as worn cotton. "We're full, what with the Graham clan and all."

Stephie spoke up then, worried eyes never leaving the young woman. "We've got space round back of Pete's. At least for two. Someone else will have to take the hitchhiker."

"Oh aye," said young Andi, "reckon we could squeeze yon gal in. Jess won't mind. That's if the new un's fixin' for a bed and not hoofin' it onwards."

The gal in question had shouldered her pack and made a beeline for us, not looking up to meet our eyes till she was right close. "Excuse me ladies," she began, her voice a smoky rasp, "but would you know anyone who can fix automobiles?"

It was Stephie who answered first, words measured with care. "Know a grease-gal. Late for it now. Where you headin'?"

"Haven't decided," the visitor replied, meeting Stephie's eyes with such a fixed look that even young Andi felt something pass between them, and stepped back to half hide herself behind my chair.

"Just so long as you're not intending trouble," Stephie said, careful not to flick her gaze to the growing shadows of the Wilds beyond the slipway.

"I came from trouble," the visitor assured coolly, "got no need to raise it." She held herself like an ancient statue that had survived long centuries, and she too spared not a twitch of a glance to where she'd driven in from.

To my mind any with a decent set of eyes could see our new visitors were not the kind of trouble worth the worry that night, so while they wasted good eating time with staring at each other I dared a look where they would not. The gateway of twisted trees that arched over the slipway was shifting just a little, branches dancing despite the lack of a breeze to call them on, and a deep silence was reaching out from the darkness beyond. I knew the taste of that: that damn gateway was setting to crawl a little closer to us again, trying to claim a little more space for the Wilds and hoping we wouldn't notice in time to burn the advance guard back.

"Well enough," Stephie was saying to our visitor, their staring done for the while, "then you'll be welcome. You got a name."

"Rose," she said, curling her fingers to try and hide the thorns in them.

"Well now Ramblin' Rose," says I, "why don't you help your friends out the car and we'll see if Marie's got any grub going."

With a moment's confusion Rose glanced over, her travel-companions gone out of her mind, then with a nod she was back off to the car to attend to the two.

"Gonna need to clean the Wilds off the motor," Stephie

murmured. "Too much muck hanging tight to it."

And she was right at that. That little rust-bucket had been through the wars and then some. Mud was thick to the base of the windows, deep scrapes arced the sides for all like some clawed beast had made a grab as they drove past. But worse, and more troublesome, were the browny-green creepers caught up under the wheel arches, creepers that reached out when Rose passed and stretched further when she steered the other two travellers around the danger zone. We'd all seen plants like that before. Seen what happened when they caught hold of the unwary. No one wanted that again.

"I'll get Lou," Stephie said, "get it sorted."

"Atta girl," I said.

WE GET A lot of travellers passing through, like our current crop: the vehicles just a little bit wrong, the bugs splattered on the front grills just that little bit nastier than any caught when we travel the lanes between Marie's and the huddle of vans that make up our encampment. Most travellers are gone before they can see the colour of the sky or gape at the ruins of a world that's moved on from the worlds they knew.

They leave maps behind sometimes. Garish things they spread out on tables or car hoods or the oak stump picnic table out front of Marie's. They plot their routes and plan destinations, then lose their focus as the road calls them onwards, and leave in a belch of smoke and a blast of tinny music.

We'd tidy up behind them and later, when there's a gap between visitors, we'd go into the back room and split up the treasures stolen from cars left unguarded while comfort was sought. Small treasures. Treasures unlikely to be missed for a time. A book. A brush. A sweater. Loose change from the floor. Abandoned tickets for far-away places. Forgotten candy. Salvage we'd make use of somewhere.

Sometimes we get hikers though they are rarer. Speed gets you safest through the Wild zones where the flora is as dangerous as the fauna, and a wrong turn can get you stuck in a mire that will never release its grip.

The hikers stay longer with us. Sometimes hours,

sometimes days, sometimes even months. Settling in to our camp for a time until the itch in their feet draws them onwards and their shadow meets the horizon and walks out of our minds.

Rarer still are the ones that stick. Like young Andi, who is not so young now as when she came toddling out of the trees one evening as we changed over to the night shift. The child has grown here, and so home it is for her without question, and not the slightest wistful look did she spare for the latest traveller to speed up the slipway and along the roads we never travel.

Our Stephie, though, I'd always thought she'd be one to move on soon as the chance arose. She arrived a summer or ten ago in a bust-up Beetle, traded it to old Pete Kole for a pair of walking boots and a long coat, and promptly talked her way into a job at the trading post up-road. Has an eye for a good deal, that one, and none's so sharp at haggling with the river traders as she, yet for all her bravado there was always fear in her when it came to what lay beyond the slipway.

WE SHUFFLED THE new folks in – the driver a scrawny ghost of a lad name of Jamie, with Dan his bulkier driving buddy – and settled them down, backs to the window. Not looking would be healthier for them, for a time, and while we distracted them with hot drinks and calm conversation, Stephie and Lou set to with long-handled pliers, picking off the roadkill and trapped foliage, hauling the twitching things into the fire pit kept out back. The whole time Rose seemed there but not there. A living ghost watching the hustle of the rest of us. Something about her that made you want to move on quick, though you couldn't have said why.

Then Lou and Stephie came back from their errands, singed and smoky. They headed straight for Lou's stash of hoarded beer, staying away from the new visitors. More specifically, they stayed away from Rose and it didn't take too much to guess that it was at Stephie's instigation. Not that Rose seemed to mind. That one was huddled so deep into herself that evening, even a couple of Marie's blueberry-cherry turnovers weren't sweet enough to loosen her tongue.

The boys though, once they'd calmed down from the journey, told a tale that any one of us could have ticked the main points of. They'd picked Rose up in the Wilds, though that we'd known from near the first. She'd been walking along the track, thumb out, so of course they'd stopped. They couldn't remember exactly how long they'd been driving before that. They'd taken a wrong turn and lost signal to their little navigation device, but it had been long enough for them to not consider turning back, and long enough again to believe that any they encountered would be just as in need of help as they. Good hearts, those young'uns. Not many travellers coming through the Wilds would have been so kind. Most would have sped right on by.

But these boys had stopped and let her in, had heard her plea for them to start up fast and be gone from that place, and been just a fraction too slow in hitting the gas pedal. There'd been something grabbed them, Jamie said. His fella, who had seen more, wasn't talking much about that. Jamie, eyes to the road and foot to the pedal, had only heard the crunch of something scraping his car, had felt the drag as the rear end held for a tick or two, had seen a large shape in the rear-view as he glanced over before the car had lurched out of grip and they'd hurtled onwards.

A second more and they'd not have made it, by my reckoning. Especially in a tin can like that, all open to the elements as it was. I've seen the results of the caught, a time or two, and it never made for a pretty sight.

But made it they had, and safe they were for now. Though a touch reluctant to go back through the Wilds with memories so fresh. Given time that would fade. Given time they'd pass off what fragments remained as sun dreams, and when their feet started twitching towards the sunset they'd be back in their patched-up jeep and daring the Wilds to go on to the next place and resume what lives they'd had on the other side.

TRAVELLERS LODGED A safe distance away, we survived the night unscathed, and next morning found us yarning out front of Marie's when Stephie wandered down the slipway with the look of someone who had been up and working far too early.

"Change your mind?" asked Lizbeth, nodding towards the Wilds.

Stephie swallowed, steadfastly refusing to look back before answering "Wildlife is twitchy. Wanted to check there weren't any unwanted visitors on the horizon." She quickly took her leave and hied on down the town road to the trading post and its solid walls.

"Getting braver, that one," Lizbeth said, watching until Stephie became a distant dot.

"Aye," I allowed. "Takes more than brave though."

"Aye," Lizbeth agreed.

We both turned to gaze on the gateway for a spell – its waving branches still taunted us but the air had settled some. It was waiting for us as much we waited for it, waiting to see how Stephie would turn out too, I reckon – new blood was always of interest. New blood that had once been part of its own even more so, and no matter how long you've been gone from it, the song of the Wilds stays a-thrumming in your veins.

I'd come down the slipway myself once upon a lifetime ago. Come down and had no desire to ever go back to those wicked wild depths, where the edges of a hundred worlds shivered and the cracks between gave passage to any that could find them. There were things that lived in its shadows that no one wanted to see this side of the border. Things that only came out at night, for the light of the sun burned them deep and sent them running back to the dark.

But their kind rarely came this way now, not unless something particular stirred them up. Not since the fall of everything. The eating was not so easy and the world not so welcoming to them and their ways; and if they ever got to thinking otherwise, why, there were those of us ready to make sure their minds soon got changed back again.

Thing was, Rose and her fellas had stirred up trouble in the Wilds, trouble that would try and follow them out. Of that much I was certain, but it could take a day or three for trouble to stir itself this-a-way. Till then, we'd keep our watch and be ready as we'd done these many years past.

WHILE THE SUN was at my back I ventured to the edges of the Wilds. Not by the slipway, no. That was too obvious a place to enter and the folks at Marie's would be watching that way while there was still light, weapons in reach just in case.

No, my way was a meander sidewards. Angled from the back of Marie's to the brush that touched the edges of the waste ground there, and in the shallows of the Wilds I could slide along the edge of the day and work my way to one of my view posts near the slipway exit.

The plants weren't so fidgety there and not a one tried to grab onto my swinging trench coat. Not that the plants would have had any luck had I been deep enough in for them to be so inclined, as the worn leather had been treated with a few oil mixes of my own invention and the local flora weren't so keen on the taste. Nor most of the fauna, for that matter, though a few had made a good try at it as the bite dents told.

And I could hide all manner of things beneath its folds.

It didn't take much effort to see where someone had rigged wires and nets along the sides of the track. That and the shimmer of a recent oil spill told much about what business Stephie had been up to. It was not a bad try on her part, but the only way to be sure of these things was to see to 'em personally. My gut said she'd be coming back with hardware later, and if so then she'd go up in my estimation, as one like her coming back here was a task akin to old Jason of legend going after that snake with all the heads. No small thing and definitely not to be done lightly, and I should know. I'd done it often enough, and like as not, be doing it many a time to come. All that was left was to settle in the crook of a tree and wait for the night creatures to wake.

TWILIGHT CAME FAST that time of year, and at twilight it was when the Wilds truly woke up. The distant chittering grew louder and closer, things shuffled in the undergrowth, big and heavy and moving with steady purpose. Pin-prick lights in all manner of colours blinked on, some moving in flitting zig-zags in the air, some holding steady in pairs in the shadows. The air thickened, a rising heatwave with the phantom of a thunderstorm not quite breaking and a depth to it that made it harder to breathe as it pressed on your lungs. Lethal for most, in the long term. It'll slow you down if nothing else did, leave you trapped in its glue until something found you. Been quite a few caught like that. The Wilds were not a place to be standing still and survival meant always moving onwards and never looking back.

Wasn't long until Stephie put in her appearance. Rifle in hands, hunting knife at her belt. I favoured an axe and machete combo myself, but if it worked for her I'd not complain. She stepped off the slipway and took a few steps along the track, planting herself right in the middle to challenge the things that were working their way towards our little piece of the world. She'd always had a steel to her, that one, and after batting off the raiders last summer I knew she had grit enough to put up a fight. Though whether it would be good enough in the Wilds was yet to be seen.

Something moved nearby, and searching vines reached their way out towards her as advance guard. She stood there, picture of calm, waiting for them to come closer. Good. Wouldn't do to waste her fight on the testers. Leave her with nothing else when the main deal put in its appearance.

She ducked out of reach, flicking her knife to slice the ends off when they got near enough to touch skin. The vines retreated quickly, green fingers stung by the cut. Stephie held her ground and waited. Soon and soon bigger things emerged. Things of thorn and poison, things that might've been human once a long time ago, before time and the Wilds had changed them - such changes rippling down through generations until only the slightest fragments remained of who they might once have been. There were other things too. Great lumbering beasts that bumped the trees as they passed, things that slithered in the bushes, skittering things that scrambled in the branches overhead. In the twilight gloom they all gathered.

Stephie snapped the rifle to and pointed it at the lead wildling. "I won't warn you twice," she said cold as stone.

"Leave and let it go."

There was a rasping screech of a laugh. The wildling stepped forward and Stephie didn't hesitate. She shot once, twice, with enough impact the wildling was pushed back. Small things swarmed up its legs, prowling things that were too twisted-up to call cat or dog, slunk out to the track, all growl and hiss. Stephie calmly reloaded, set her stance and pointed again. She'd need more than bullets to take out the wildlings. They were made of stranger stuff, and I know she knew it.

They advanced on her, the moss-green hoard, and she stepped back then shot at the ground to the edge of the track. Something pinged. Something thumped. Something left her hand in an arc of light, then a whoomph and something ignited, fire lazily crawling a line between her and the wildlings as a wire snicked up from the other side of the track and sliced across and through all in its way.

Elsewhere, nets triggered, weighted and wicked sharp, they covered and cut into the things they caught, held them still for the flames to catch.

Not bad at all for a young 'un, but still not enough to catch 'em all.

The first to break free of her collection of traps was a slithering thing with a spider head and a tongue that whipped the two feet out to her ankle, only missing contact because she thought to step back. She was fast with her knife, I'll give her that. A quick bend and flick and the tongue was short a few inches, the hissing screech going up a pitch or two as the slitherer hesitated.

Which was when the monkey thing dropped out of a tree and landed on her head. She put up a good fight, but it had too good a grip and she was bumped to the ground in no short measure. I decided it was time to join the fray.

I shucked the coat, dropping it on a branch as I passed. My other arms curled free – tensile and thorny – tentacle like, if you were from the world outside the Wilds, but in the Wilds we'd never thought much either way about the things we had and the things we didn't.

I hummed a line of song that the old woman before me

had sung when she was about her business. It could charm even the most uppity invader, for a time at least, and as I hummed I swung my axe. First at the monkey creature, knocking it clean off Stephie, then at the next to advance. When I'd got the rhythm up, I could swing the axe one handed and let the momentum do the heavy work while my spare hand went for the machete and filled the space left at my other side. It was a killing dance and my bones weren't so old that I couldn't keep its steps going. Not yet anyways.

As I danced, my other arms scraped their thorns against the smaller wildlings, poison pumping through into creatures whose venom was lesser until by and by, there were none left to meet me. The track clear, the woods quiet, the moon high and bright and pushing through the gaps between the trees.

They'd be gone awhile but the next day and the day after and the day after that they'd be back, until enough time had gone by that Rose's escape - like those of us who'd escaped before her - was a lesser memory than the pain of coming too near the world we walked in, and the message to stay away from the bright lands was sent from leaf to branch to hot-blooded beastie in the song that connected them all.

I helped Stephie up and for a moment her eyes flared deep green and she nodded. "Kept that quiet," she said, nodding at my other arms.

"Always the best," said I. "You back tomorrow for the rematch?" Could go either way with that one, too soon escaped from the Wilds herself.

"Might as well," she said after a long moment that had her staring down the track to where the deeper darkness waited.

"Good girl," said I. "Lemme get some kip and in the morning I'll teach you a few new tricks."

She nodded again, a faint smile flashing quick over her lips. "I'd like that."

I furled myself back into my coat and we walked down along the road back to the world we'd come to call home.

THE TRADE-UP

James Brogden

"SNAP," SAID CHARLIE even though there was nobody to hear except the car overtaking him. It was a dead ringer for the one he was currently driving.

Not that it was *that* easy to tell at one in the morning, in the rain, on a deserted stretch of the M54 without lampposts, but several things at least were clear: it was a VW Golf just like his, it was metallic silver just like his - insofar as it was possible to judge colour under his headlights and the drizzle which smudged the outlines of everything - and it had a roof rack just like his.

And when it passed him he saw that it even had the registration number BP35 PDE, just like his. He sat bolt upright behind the wheel and stared as it cruised by with a kind of lazy insolence. It wasn't going all that much faster than him - overtaking slowly enough in the middle lane so that he could get a good, long look.

He experienced a fleeting moment of dizzying disorientation in which he wasn't entirely sure which car he was actually driving. Maybe he'd forgotten that he'd borrowed Ruth's little purple Ka - that he had, in fact, been using it all weekend on this stupid bloody training course and only assumed that he was in his Golf because that was what he usually drove. He was so rattled that he actually looked around himself to be sure. Yes, he was in the Golf. His paperwork was stacked neatly on the passenger seat and his bottle of water was in its little holder. He breathed a deep sigh of relief.

Yes, there he went, cruising gently, tail-lights crimson in the dark, rear wiper wagging. He watched it pull ahead, dumbfounded.

Then the answer came to him: they'd cloned his car.

He'd read about it in the *Daily Mail*: organised criminals from Bulgaria or Syria or *Whateverthefuckistan* sticking fake number plates on identical models of the owners' vehicles to commit robberies or worse. If they could do it with phones and credit cards they could definitely do it with cars.

He glared at it. "Really? I don't think so mate." He checked that his dashboard camera was on - a little excited that he'd get to use it for something more interesting than trolling cyclists and middle-lane hogs on YouTube - and accelerated, pulling into the overtaking lane behind the fake.

The fake accelerated too, continuing to pull ahead insistently. He pushed it, the speedo creeping up to the eighty mark, as fast as he would normally dare go though not at night. Yes, the speed limit was seventy, and yes everybody knew that the cops would turn a blind eye to eighty, but he liked to think of himself as a prudent and careful man not given to taking risks.

Something about this fake, though. The cool arrogance of it. It got his blood up.

He took her up to eighty-five. So did the fake.

Ninety. Something in his car was vibrating and making a high-pitched hum, and his heart was thumping in sympathy as he gripped the wheel with slick hands; this was as fast as he had ever dared go.

He was making ground on the fake. It was getting closer. Possibly it was letting him but he preferred to believe that he was actually winning this weird game of chicken. With surprise he found himself growing hard in his trousers. If Ruth had been there she'd have been yelling at him long before now and clutching the dash in panic. She'd have been asking him was he *crazy*? Did he actually *want* to draw the attention of these people? He felt his hard-on wilt just as suddenly.

He drew parallel with the fake so that he could get a better look at the driver's side. There was one thing he wanted to check.

Damn, but they'd done their homework well: there was even a dent in the wing panel just like on his. Hardly able to believe how reckless he was being he glanced up at the driver's window to see what an actual organised criminal car cloner looked like.

And behind the steering wheel of the car that was not his and yet was, a face identical to his own looked back.

The other driver had the same shining forehead and receding hairline as his own, the same little goatee to give definition to the same uninspiring little chin. But the shit-eating grin which sprang from the other man's teeth was an expression which Charlie's face had never worn. Charlie thought he could see every tooth the other man owned in that grin.

He came within a shade's spit of stamping on the brakes which – even though there was no-one behind to plough into him – would still have caused a fatal flip and roll. As it was, in the dark and the drizzle, he still had to fight to stop from fish-tailing all over the fast lane, and managed to pull over clumsily onto the hard shoulder where he sat, shivering and panting, watching the tail-lights of the other (his) car smearing away into the night like blood down a drain.

He sat that way for a very long time.

It was an urgent need to pee and the shuddering of his limbs which brought him to his senses. God knew how long he'd been sitting there with the engine off, misting up the windows with condensation as his body lost heat.

It had been...

A mistake. Poor visibility. Fatigue. He needed a break and a cup of tea or seeing things was likely to be the least of his problems. He liked to joke to the other reps that if he ever had a crash he'd be better off saving time by making it a fatal one because Ruth would kill him anyway. He'd stop at the next services he came to, or get off at the next junction and find a twenty-four-hour garage. He dismissed the idea of taking a quick whizz off the hard shoulder; sod's law being what it was, the police would choose that moment to come along while he stood there with his willy in his hand. He started the car, his satnav came to life in a homely glow, and he indicated as he pulled into the slow lane even though there was nobody around for him to indicate to.

Nobody except...

Yes, a nice safe digital road on the satnav screen telling him that the next services were eighteen miles away, and containing nothing but the clean pixelated icons of junctions and mileages and absolutely no rapacious grinning doubles of himself.

He turned on the radio. Absolute Eighties. "Stop Me if You've Heard This One Before" by the Smiths.

"Fine," he told it. "But if you play 'Highway to Hell' or any of that shit you're out the window, got it?"

The services off-ramp slid out of the drizzling gloom without any kind of sign and he'd have missed it completely if he hadn't been concentrating on driving slowly and carefully. There was nothing on the satnav either, but that wasn't especially unusual; the bloody thing had once tried to tell him to take a left turn onto the Worcester-to-Birmingham canal. It definitely hadn't been eighteen miles though. In the end the pressure on his bladder won the argument and he pulled off the motorway and into the nearly deserted car park.

There was only one other vehicle parked there. Only one, but it was very familiar.

He crawled past, heart pounding. There was nobody behind the wheel so he stopped a few spaces along, got out and wandered back, pulling his hood up against the rain. The number plate was still his but now that he had the luxury for a long close look under better lighting he could see that it wasn't an exact replica of his own car after all. It was slightly larger, and a lot cleaner, with a more impressive dash including an iPod dock. If the registration was to be believed it was the same age as his ten-year old banger but it looked like it was fresh off the production line and at least a few grand more expensive. Even the dent was gone. He felt a sudden absurd desire to take his car keys and gouge it all along its shining length, but instead he turned around and headed for the main doors in search of caffeine, sugar and the toilets.

As he walked in he thought that this must have been what the Titanic looked like as it was sinking: brightly lit up and deserted, aquarium-like, chairs and tables and polished chrome and all human life fled as it plunged towards the depths, only drowning in the sub-zero time of two in the morning rather than Atlantic sea water.

Almost deserted.

At a table in the restaurant area surrounded by lifeless fast-food concessions was a man dressed exactly as he was, head down over some paperwork, a pot of tea-for-one to the side plus a plate with a franchise-standard chocolate brownie and a knife. The other man looked up with a polite smile of welcome as he pushed out the chair opposite with one foot and gestured for Charlie to take a seat.

Charlie approached, but remained standing.

"I suppose you're wondering..."

"What the bloody hell is..."

"...going on here?" they finished together.

"Snap!" The seated man laughed. "Well, I suppose that was inevitable."

Just like with the car, Charlie saw that on closer inspection he wasn't dressed identically – not even close, really – why had he thought that? Charlie rubbed his aching eyes. The watch on the other man's wrist was flashier, he wore a jacket instead of a hoodie, brogues where Charlie wore trainers, and was probably few pounds lighter around the love-handles. Facially though, they could have been twins.

"Who are you?"

The man signed off one last document, clicked the shining ballpoint and tucked it neatly away. He cut a piece of brownie and popped it in his mouth as he sat back and spread his hands wide as if explaining the simplest thing in the world.

"I'm your trade-up, of course. Charles. Pleased to meet

you." There was that grin again, flecked with brown crumbs. Jesus, did *he* smile like that? Charles extended a hand.

Charlie ignored it. "My...?"

"See, the thing is this, and please forgive me for being blunt, but there really is no other way to put it: you're a waste of life."

"What do you mean a waste of life? What kind of bullshit practical joke is this?"

"Life, yes. Absolute waste. You've fucked it up from beginning to end, I'm afraid and it really has now got to the point where something has got to be done about you. Hence me."

Charlie was finding it increasingly difficult to follow the thread of this conversation. He looked for someone else in the restaurant area – anyone, not necessarily to talk to, just a simple human presence which would tell him that this was not some kind of bizarre dream. But the room was deserted. There were no staff behind the takeaway counters and no cleaners. The only sign of life came from outside, beyond the large plate-glass windows; he stared through the reflection of his own gaping face at where a car-clamping truck was in the process of hoisting his Golf away.

Charlie didn't know what any of this "trade-up" business was but he had no trouble understanding that his car was being towed.

"Hey!" he yelled. "*Hey!*" And ran for the doors.

By the time he got outside the tow-truck was already starting to move off. As it picked up speed he chased it yelling and swearing, hammering with the flats of his hands on the side of the cab where a dark human shape lit by the dim poisonous green of dashboard instruments ignored him completely. The truck outpaced him down the exit ramp to the deserted motorway and was lost in the drizzle.

Hands on his knees. Gasping. Sick and light-headed. Lower belly cramping.

He lurched inside, found the gents, did what needed to be done.

At some point he became aware, as he stood with his head resting on his arm propped against the wall above the urinal, that Charles was standing at the one next to him. He looked down at Charlie's penis and nodded at it. "Yeah, I'm a trade-up on that too," he smirked zipping up. The smirk disappeared. "Tidy yourself up, man. We have business to settle." And left.

The first thing Charlie did was take out his phone and dial 999 to report that his car had been stolen. The call rang out and eventually disconnected which should have been impossible. He hesitated before calling Ruth, not wanting to be on the receiving end of her temper for phoning her at two in the morning but needn't have worried because that rang out too. So did half-a-dozen numbers picked at random from his contacts before he gave in.

He freshened up as best he could and went back out to where Charles was still working his way through his paperwork, humming to himself as he filled in forms and ticked boxes. There were bank statements, utilities bills, a driving licence, a passport.

All familiar.

All his.

A slow, greasy spiral of terror uncoiled itself in his guts as he recognised the tune Charles was humming: "Stop Me if You've Heard This One Before". The brownie was completely gone. Just crumbs left.

"What's going on?" he demanded. "Who are you really? Why did those men just take my car?"

"They took your car Charlie ... sorry, *my* car. Pronouns get sticky in these situations. Because I'm not going to be needing it any more. I'm trading up remember? Car gets an upgrade. So do the clothes, career, house. So does Ruth for that matter. Hey, you want to see a picture?" He took out his phone.

"This isn't funny."

The phone went away. "It's no joke, Charlie. This is deadly serious. You've been given every privilege, every opportunity, and every chance to make something interesting of yourself and you've just pissed them all away time after time."

"Listen, I don't know who you are but you don't know a

bloody thing about me, all right?"

"Please don't make me go through it all," Charles sighed and laid one hand on the paperwork stacked in front of him. "The audit's already been done you know, and these people are very thorough. The situation's still a bit, shall we say *in flux*, but basically all here. And here." He tapped the side of his head. "Things you've never told a living soul – that only I can know. Because I'm you."

"Bullshit!" laughed Charlie but there was a shrill sound to it that he didn't like the sound of at all.

"Oh no?" Charles arched an eyebrow. "Nineteen eighty-nine. Dudley Zoo. That thing with the meerkats."

Charlie went pale and stumbled backwards as if the other man had just slapped him with a chair.

"Good, well now that we've established I am indeed you without having to do the whole bloody David Copperfield thing maybe we can get on. This evening was the last straw. You remember the woman from the conference? Pretty, dark hair, laughed at our stupid jokes about Jaffa cakes? Maria, her name wasn't it?"

"What the fuck has she got to do with anything?"

"Fuck yes, ha-ha, very clever but too late. No. Again, without wishing to put it crudely, I was in there my son. She would have let me fuck her no question about it; she made it very clear, and I knew it too – but I walked away. Just like I've walked away from everything remotely exciting or spontaneous or difficult my entire life."

"Are you crazy? I wasn't going to have an affair! I'm a happily married man!"

Charles shrugged. "Well I'm married, I'll give you that."

"Stop saying I! And me! You're not me!"

Charles continued as if he hadn't said anything. "But in answer to your original question, your car is being dealt with as what it is: the detritus of a failed life. Just crumbs. Most of them have already been swept away. Most, I say." His hand strayed to the knife with which he'd used to cut up his brownie. Now that he looked at it properly Charlie saw that it wasn't the kind of blunt-ended knife you were given for cutting up a cake. This had a wooden handle and a sharper point and was much larger. More like a steak knife.

"What?" Charlie scoffed just a little too loudly. "You're going to kill me and take over my life, is that it?"

"You're half-right except that strictly speaking there's nothing to take over. It's already mine." He stood, the knife gleaming in his hand. "I *am* going to kill you though, you're absolutely fucking spot on there. A straight swap would be no good at all would it?"

"Wait!" Charlie backed away, hands in the air. "No you're not, not if you're me. I could never actually hurt anybody. Least of all myself."

"Oh, very good. Nice. Clever. But no, sorry. I know too much about what does on in here, remember?" Charles tapped his temple again and shook his head tutting. "The things I've fantasised about doing to Ruth, for example. We are a very sick puppy my friend."

Charlie ran.

Out into the cold and the drizzle, skidding, spinning around to find someone, *anyone*, who might see this and raise the alarm, call the police. Seeing no one, running, small whimpering noises of denial escaping him, past the fuel pumps and the big parking bays for trucks and caravans, all empty, the world a gleaming chiaroscuro of floodlit tarmac and black shadow, past the picnic area, the swings, the kiddies' climbing frame.

He hid in a wooden fort, surrounded by cigarette butts and candy wrappers. *Detritus. Trading up. Stop me if you've heard this one before.* Freezing cold water was dripping inside the collar of his hoodie.

Through a crack in the timbers he watched Charles appear around a corner of the building and stop, scanning the area. Even at this distance Charlie could tell the difference in him. His suit was more sharply tailored, his shoes shone, cufflinks glittered, and he moved with an assured lack of haste which spoke of athletic power. Even the knife looked longer and sharper – something for carving long slabs of flesh.

"Charlie!" the other called into the darkness. "This really isn't doing any good you know! You're only making things better for me!"

Charlie felt in his pockets for anything he could use as a weapon and came up with only his car keys. He could grip them between his fingers, he supposed, like in those female self-defence classes Ruth went to. It was laughable. Before he could stop himself a half-hysterical snort escaped his nose.

Charles stepped off the concrete and onto the grass towards the playground.

Charlie broke cover and ran, sobbing.

If he was thinking anything at all it was of escaping, not fighting. It was true – he'd never been in a fight, never confronted anybody over anything until tonight. He didn't deserve to live. It was only dumb animal survival which kept him moving.

Behind him: the rapid patter of expensive Italian soles in pursuit.

He skidded around the corner and found himself in the car park again; he'd run right around the building and found no refuge, no help. The car had changed too. It was no longer just a slightly flashier version of his old Golf – no more than Charles' suit resembled his original jacket and brogues. It was low-slung and streamlined, like an oil slick on wheels. But if it belonged to Charles didn't that mean it was his too? That was the question because the keys were still in his hand. He fumbled with the fob as he ran, begging it to unlock.

He must have hit the wrong button because instead of the lights flashing to tell him it was unlocked, the boot started to open. He moaned – a tiny desperate noise of defeat – and fetched up against the side with both hands, cringing, waiting for unimaginable pain to find him between the shoulder blades, unable to summon up even the minimal courage to turn and face his killer. Better not to see. Better not to know.

There was a skidding noise, a *whoa!* followed by a sharp *thock!* like a cricket bat hitting a ball for six, a heavier meatier thud, and then silence.

Nothing stabbed him in the back.

He turned and looked.

The problem with expensive Italian soles, it seemed, was that they had very little traction in the wet. Charles had come on too fast to avoid the suddenly opening boot, slid, and cracked his skull on its metal edge. He lay on the ground, groaning, bright red splashed across his forehead. The knife lay a few inches from his slowly uncurling fingers. It took most of what bravery Charlie had left to kick it away into the night.

Then he slammed the boot, jumped into the car, and locked all the doors. Time to get the fuck out of here.

He'd never been in something so expensive before; everything either smelled of leather or gleamed mirror-clean. There didn't seem to be actual buttons to operate anything. He touched the steering wheel and without any transition it was the steering wheel of his Golf, as out of place as a rotten tooth in a Hollywood grin. He snatched his hands back. He gingerly toed the brake pedal and recoiled when the plush carpeted footwell was once more littered with junk-food wrappers, old carpark tickets and bits of gravel. Was this what Charles had meant when he'd said things were *in flux*? If this kept up he'd have nothing but his old wreck to drive home. Not that escaping this nightmare wouldn't be sweet enough but still – the promise of a better life was right here in front of him and it was reverting to the same old shitty normality one shuffle of his arse at a time. How had it come to Charles? What had he done to earn it?

He glanced in the wing mirror and saw Charles's lower leg sticking out from behind the car flexing slowly as he began to come around.

You're only making it better for me, he'd gloated, as if replacing Charlie wasn't enough.

Killing him, on the other hand...

And an idea bloomed like a black rose in his mind.

It took him a moment to locate the ignition; it was a thumb-pad sensor but it worked for him because of course this *was* his car, and it didn't revert to a normal key slot either, which told him that his instincts were right. The engine purred awake and he shifted into reverse. The steering wheel became smooth polished maple again as if to reward him for his wise decision.

In the end it wasn't much more dramatic than reversing

over a speed bump or a roll of carpet. The back wheels slipped on something and span a bit but he goosed the throttle and cleared it. Then the front wheels though there wasn't as much resistance for them.

"Snap," he whispered and smiled.

He got out of the car and looked at the motionless shape. One trainer had come off and lay in a puddle, its laces like entrails. Its hoodie, already wet, was blossoming with darker stains of blood from hidden injuries. Something red and glistening bulged from the mouth. It looked strangely deflated like the husk of some sort of insect – although that could have just been because of the tyre.

The rain was heavier now, threatening to ruin his nice new suit so, satisfied that Charlie was well and truly dead, he got back in the car and pulled away to the roundabout which gave access to each direction of the motorway. From here he could either go back the way he came or continue his journey home – whatever that looked like now.

He sat that way for a very long time, considering his options.

THE APPLE TREE

Marion Pitman

CHLOE LOOKED ROUND disapprovingly. "Why do you have to have it all here? Why can't you work on it in situ?"

"If you'd seen the situ," I said, "you wouldn't ask."

"Don't they mind you bringing it away?"

"I got the impression they were only too glad to see the back of it."

"I thought you were working on a valuable archive. This looks more like waste paper."

"Oh for heaven's sake. It's immeasurably valuable; that doesn't mean it's worth a lot of money. And I told you, this lot wasn't with the archive. I tracked it down. I'm rather proud of myself, actually."

She made a dismissive noise, and went out to make coffee.

I HAD A distant relative, Eleanor Gray, who collected folk songs and stories in Dorset and Somerset between the wars, and I was researching her life and work with some idea of writing a book. Among her papers was a transcript of an interview with a friend of hers, made some years after Eleanor's death, in which the friend - Alice Clark - said: "there were some songs she wouldn't publish. Mostly I think the ones that were, you know, a bit rude, a bit risqué. She kept them all in a box. She called them her black box songs. She said they weren't very good or she wasn't sure they were genuine, but when I looked at them once – she didn't often let people see them – I thought most of them were the rude ones.

"I don't know what happened to the black box. When she had to move into a home her nephew Edward took all her stuff to the Institute, but he left the black box behind. He didn't approve of it. I don't know what happened to it after that."

It seemed likely that the black box had been destroyed but I wondered if it were still where Edward had left it. It seemed worth having a look, when I took a break from the papers at the Institute, at the house where Eleanor had lived.

THE HOUSE NOW belonged to a charity, with a shop on the ground floor and offices above. The manager, a large harassed-looking man, was clearly annoyed by my presence and the absence of any really convincing argument for getting rid of me. When I persisted he resentfully led me down some badly lit stairs to a basement that contained a couple of hundred stacking chairs, a mid-Victorian cast iron range, and an ominous smell of damp.

"If there *were* anything," he said, "it would be in here. But it seems to me more likely to have been thrown away."

"I daresay it was, but I want to make sure." It seemed to *me* he had by now expended more energy telling me the papers probably weren't there than would have been necessary to bring me down here to look in the first place. The place was dank and unpleasant; I imagined the ghosts of servants toiling down here out of the daylight, and shuddered.

There was a large cupboard, perhaps originally a walk-in larder or pantry – what's the difference? I wondered – set in the wall. With some difficulty he opened it, first the handle sticking, and then the door itself grinding against grit and detritus that had built up against it. He pulled it back finally and said "I wasn't here when we moved in but I believe some stuff was put in there." He left me to it and went away muttering back to his computer.

Alone in the damp basement I looked for a light switch for the pantry but couldn't find one. I used the torch in my pocket and looked around; the walls were shelved but there were only a few empty jars and plant pots on the shelves; on the floor however were half-a-dozen large cardboard boxes. I dragged the nearest to the door, to look at it by the strip light in the passage. Stuff seemed to have been pitched into the box randomly: a blanket, roughly folded, and under that a bunch of papers – old receipts, bank statements, formal letters. I burrowed to the bottom, but there was nothing of interest.

The second box was clearly more recent than Eleanor's departure, containing stationery from the charity upstairs with their name misspelt. Why on earth didn't they throw that out? I went on. There were kitchen utensils, some damaged china, a box of newsletters from a local residents' group in the 1970s. As I opened each box my hopes rose and quickly sank. I stood up to ease my back and shone the torch round again – and there on a shelf in the corner, half hidden by a heap of rusty baking trays and Wellington boots caked in dried mud, was an old black metal deed-box. No, I said to myself, don't be silly, it wouldn't be a real black box; too easy. I picked my way around the stuff on the floor – and nearly shrieked when the light in the passage went out. I stood quite still for a moment but nothing else happened so I guessed it was on some kind of time switch. I shone my torch on the deed-box, opened the front and looked inside. There were stacks of large Manilla envelopes, just like the ones in the archive. My heart beat absurdly fast as I pulled one out, and peered inside: verses in Eleanor's handwriting. I realised I was shaking. Then I nearly screamed again as the light in the passage came back on.

With it came the manager, explaining that they were about to close.

"Oh right. Listen, I think I've found what I'm looking for. Is there somewhere I could take it where I could see it better? Perhaps come back tomorrow?"

"You may as well take it away with you – when we clear this lot out it'll all go on a skip."

I could hardly believe it. Getting it away was a bit of an issue since I'd come by train, and the box was awkward to carry, and full enough to be heavy, but in the end the manager deputed a minion – a good-looking young man with no conversation – to drive me to the station, and I persuaded someone to help me get the box on to the train. At the other end I persuaded someone else to help me off, and decided to spring for a cab – I wasn't letting the box out of my sight if I could help it.

The first thing I did when I got home was to take all the envelopes out and look to see if they all had songs in. I skimmed through one batch; some were just mildly suggestive but a couple were downright filthy, and Eleanor hadn't censored them at all.

It was at that point that Chloe came home and I felt obliged to move everything to my study. Technically I'm Chloe's landlady but, although younger than me, she's a strong-minded girl and a distant cousin; I know my place. I went through a few more envelopes before I went to bed, enough to satisfy myself that this was indeed the *black box*. I was almost too excited to sleep but I was also physically exhausted, and that won.

The next day I had to get on with some editing for a man with more money than skill, who was paying me to knock his novel into shape before he self-published it. It was dreary work but he paid, and I was behind schedule. I finished about tea time and realised with a spasm of irritation that I'd agreed to be sociable that evening – Chloe was bringing her new man back for dinner.

We don't bother each other much and we don't feel obliged to meet each other's guests. But it happened tonight that I'd agreed to share dinner with them – she was cooking – and if I went back on it now it would look unsociable, plus I'd have to get my own dinner. I hoped we'd eat early so I could go through the black box before I went to bed.

Chloe prefers older men so I wasn't surprised that Douglas looked to be in his mid-fifties; grey hair, bit of a paunch, not bad looking, but not my type. It took me entirely by surprise when he said "Hallo Julie. Been a long time."

The voice rang a bell and I looked at him again and my heart sank. "Hallo," I said, "yes, long time. Didn't recognise you at first."

"Ten years is it, since you dumped me?"

"I'd hardly say that. We only went out together once." After which I'd decided we weren't suited, and he'd been persistent and bitter for about two years before he gave up.

Chloe, not quite sure what was going on but sensibly not liking it, suggested making a cup of tea and asked if I'd mind going out for some milk. It was a bit desperate - there was a quart of milk in the fridge and Chloe never drinks tea, but I gave her full marks for initiative. I went to the corner shop and by the time I got back with another pint I presumed she'd had a go at him, since he made only one or two more references to our previous encounter. Once he said "You didn't stay with that young chap then?"

"What young chap?"

"The one you dumped me for."

I was baffled. I'd dumped him, if that's the word, because he was earnest, intense, humourless, a bit unbalanced and a terrible bore. He'd presumably seen me with another man at some point.

"Clearly not," I said, "since I'm not with him now."

"Was that it though? Was I too old for you?"

"Well I do tend to go for younger men. But really—"

Chloe glared at both of us, poured some more wine, and started to talk about government plans to abolish the BBC - another sign of desperation since she never watches television and couldn't care less.

I escaped as soon as I could to my study - really a box room, it's not a big flat - and went on with examining the contents of the black box. One envelope was marked "Baker" and when I looked inside there were just two sheets. I'd found what I'd hoped for.

ONE OF THE first things that had excited me in the archive was a short recording and a photograph of a man named Frederick Baker. I presumed he was a farm labourer since many of the sources were, and Eleanor didn't specify anything else. It was right at the end of my first session with the archive - I'd had a long day - but I kept thinking *one more envelope.* The archive contained a few recordings which had at some point been transferred on to a tape cassette. I had borrowed an old player. The sound of the voice, as I looked at the picture of the long-dead singer, had a weird effect on me – I suppose it was because I was so tired I suddenly felt displaced, as if I were seeing through Eleanor's eyes as she listened to Frederick Baker.

She looked at his hands, twice the size of her own, sinewy and sun-burnt dark, covered with scars and callouses. He wasn't a tall man but broad in the shoulder, with a square face, burnt as brown as his hands, and dark blue eyes. His hands lay immensely still on the arms of the chair as he sang.

It was only a moment and then I was back behind my own eyes, realising I needed to get some sleep. I picked up the photo of Frederick Baker and gazed at him again. He looked to have been in his sixties, which of course was older then than it is now. Eleanor described him as "a handsome old man" – Eleanor was in her late twenties and gay; I'm in my late thirties and straight. He was very handsome; his eyes had that trick of seeming to look out of the photograph straight at you, and his voice, even on the scratchy scrap of recording, had a power and beauty that blew me away. I felt I was half in love with him by the time I found the letter next day.

The handwriting was quite clear but had the quality of writing that has been learned at school and remembered for many years, but seldom called upon.

Dear Miss Gray, I take the liberty of writing to ask you again to be careful about "The Apple Tree". I was not sure that I explained well enough that you should not allow anyone to sing it to that tune. It is very bad to do so. I ask you please to believe this. You are a good person and I would not wish evil to overcome you. Your obedient servant, Frederick Baker.

It was a while longer before I found a reference to "The Apple Tree" in Eleanor's journal.

Mr Baker gave me a ballad called "The Apple Tree". There is a tune also called "The Apple Tree" that his cousin played on the fiddle, and I remarked that the ballad would go well to that tune; he was alarmed and said that song should never be sung to the fiddle tune. When I asked why, he said that the song had been made to that tune and when it was sung bad things happened, but the words or the tune on their own are safe. The tune to which he sang the words is well enough, but undistinguished.

There was no song called "The Apple Tree" in the archive and I wondered if Eleanor had decided to discard it, perhaps because of its undistinguished tune, though that would have been unlike her; but now here it was with the smut and the music hall songs, in the black box.

I saw why she called it a ballad: it had the form of an old ballad but the language was quite different, as though someone had written it perhaps in the late nineteenth century, modelled on the old form but in their own everyday language. Its story was very like a ballad: two men are rivals for a beautiful woman except that rather than brothers or friends they are father and son. The father takes a shine to the son's lady friend. She prefers the older man, either because of his maturity and sophistication or because of his wealth and position - both views being suggested, one from the father's point of view and the other from the son's. The son inveigles the father into a fight (under an apple tree, where the lovers used to meet, hence the title) and kills him with a concealed dagger, then rounds on the young lady, blaming it all on her, and says that both he and his father will haunt her. It's not quite clear whether he intends suicide or flight or giving himself up to be hanged. If flight, presumably his haunting would begin a little later. The woman, rather than repudiating the whole distressing mess and dissociating herself from the family, becomes distraught and attempts to stab herself with the dagger, but the son prevents her and stands over her predicting a great deal more grief for everyone left alive. And there it ends. Very ballad-like, as I say, but not convincingly antique. It had rough edges and some lines were very awkward, but it did have a certain power - not that of the universal but of the very specific, as if someone on a train were telling you all about a gruesome murder and you suddenly realised they'd done it themselves.

It was a great satisfaction to have found the words of "The Apple Tree", but now I wanted to hear the fiddle tune. Eleanor didn't collect tunes without words - maddening when she mentions something as "a really beautiful tune, not like anything I have heard before". Perhaps I could find it somewhere else.

I was just reading the song again when there was a knock on the study door. It was opened by Douglas who said "Good night, Julie. I'm going now. See you again I hope."

I said "Good night" and he went away. *Not if I see you first*, I thought. I waited till Chloe had washed up and gone to bed before I came out of the room. No doubt we would have to talk about Douglas, but not yet.

I managed to put it off for a couple of days, till Chloe had calmed down a bit. She wasn't prepared to think ill of Douglas; she was quite enamoured of his earnestness and intensity and she thought he'd had a raw deal from other women – including me obviously – and felt a mad urge to make it up to him. She's always disapproved of my attitude to men anyway; she's worryingly old-fashioned and wants to be cherished. Cherishing just irritates me – I want to be entertained. However she agreed not to bring him to the flat for a bit and I agreed to be polite when she did.

The next thing I did was call up a fiddle player of my acquaintance and tell him about "The Apple Tree". He was fascinated and promised to look into it; I said I would scan the lyrics and email him.

I didn't find anything more in the black box except slightly or very rude songs, and some popular songs that were obviously quite new at the time and not of interest from the folklore point of view. Eleanor was very thorough in her collecting. I went carefully through the archive looking purely for anything about "The Apple Tree" or Frederick Baker; he had given Eleanor twenty-three songs (all clean), most of which were slightly variant versions of common songs; none of the others was entirely unique. The cousin who played the fiddle didn't turn up again. There were a few details of Frederick Baker's life and his conversations with Eleanor, over which I pored rather obsessively but really there was nothing out of the ordinary. He was a widower, he lived in a small and immaculate cottage with one of his three daughters, who was hugely amused that this strange woman was so interested in her father. I didn't get the flashback effect again – except that when I was reading Eleanor's account of the conversation about "The Apple Tree" I heard a voice in my head saying "Don't sing it to that tune. Very unlucky. Don't sing that." The voice could easily have been the voice on the tape, that of Frederick Baker; but then again my mind could have created it. I wondered if I was brooding too much; maybe I should get out more.

Douglas turned up around the house occasionally and made a rather sketchy apology for not letting bygones be bygones. Life would have been impossible if I hadn't accepted it politely. He asked me questions about Eleanor and borrowed a copy of the words of "The Apple Tree" and we managed to have the occasional civilised conversation.

After a few weeks the fiddle player emailed and said he'd found a couple of candidates, and if I could give him dinner and beer the following week he'd come and play them to me.

The first tune he played was from Derbyshire and although it fitted the words it wasn't especially memorable. The second, though, had been collected in Dorset, in roughly the right area, and had a slightly eerie quality that sent a shiver down the spine. Douglas had the words in his hand and began to sing them as Gerry played. They fitted perfectly. The effect was electrifying and I cried out "Stop!" before I quite knew I meant to. I heard the voice in my head again, urgently "Very unlucky. Don't do that."

Gerry stopped playing. Douglas sang another line, then Chloe said "Stop it Doug. Julie, what's up? I thought that was the idea, to put the words and the tune back together. You don't surely believe that about it being unlucky, do you?"

I shook my head. "I didn't think I did but he— I don't like it, the sound of it." I realised they were all looking at me, Chloe baffled, Gerry startled, Douglas (I thought) with contempt. "Sorry," I said, "but not now. Really. Let's have another drink."

Gerry was happy to let me be superstitious; he privately thinks that singing just gets in the way of good music anyhow. He played and drank beer, and Douglas and Chloe sang a bit, and I had a couple of beers and thought about things. Frederick Baker seemed to have got under my skin and inside my head. I wondered what he had to do with the song – and why did no one else sing it? How did he come to know it? Was it something passed down in his family? Or was it just coincidence that everyone else had stopped singing it? If it was so dangerous why did he sing it at all...? Dammit, I really needed to get out more.

In the next couple of months I almost abandoned Eleanor – and looked for other versions of "The Apple Tree". I did discover a few references over the years, always, so far as I could tell, to the version Eleanor had transcribed from Frederick's singing, which it turned out had been recorded in the seventies by a fairly obscure band from Gloucestershire. So the song was out there, if only flitting by in the distance. I couldn't find out anything about Frederick Baker. The family had died out or moved away; I tried births, marriages and deaths, but Baker isn't an uncommon name, and nor were the names of his sons-in-law. I simply didn't have the time or resources – I had to earn a living and I couldn't even say the projected book justified it. I still knew nothing more than that he was a handsome man with a beautiful voice and three daughters.

A couple of months later I got a phone call from the manager of the charity shop in Eleanor's old house. I was surprised and pleased he remembered me and hadn't lost my phone number. He said they were planning to turn the basement into a café and all the stuff in the cupboard was going in a skip the next week; if I wanted I could come and go through it and take away anything I liked. I saw, of course, that that would mean less for them to lug out to the skip; but anyway it was nice of him. I said I would be there and tried to think of someone with a big car I could ask to drive me. There might be nothing worth keeping but I hadn't looked at everything, and you never know...

I told Chloe about it and I was surprised, not altogether pleasantly, when she said she and Douglas would take me – he had a large estate car, which would admittedly be very useful. I couldn't find anyone else available in the time so I accepted.

The handsome young man with no conversation was in the shop and took us downstairs; Douglas gave him a dirty look and was most ungracious. In the basement the young man explained that the light in the passage was operated by a motion sensor and if it went out we just had to go into the passage and move about.

There was still no light in the larder but I had brought a biggish portable lamp and a couple of LED torches, and with the light from the passage we managed quite well, separating the definite rubbish from the possibly interesting. Getting it upstairs was going to be a pain. Chloe went up to ask if they had a sack trolley or anything we could use to transport stuff out to the car, which was parked in the nearest car park. While she was gone Douglas started singing "The Apple Tree". I had no idea he could pick up a tune that well from one hearing. Fear gripped me like a fluttering claw. I said "Please don't sing that." He went on singing, and the passage light went out. I gasped - not loud enough to be a scream - and he turned the lamp out and came towards me, still singing. He was between me and the door. In the dark I couldn't see where the boxes were and wherever I tried to move I caught my foot on something. I said "Please stop" but he took no notice. He caught me against the wall and put his hands round my throat.

Part of my mind was thinking *I can't believe this is happening*. He just held me there, a shelf pressing hard into my shoulder blades. It was like one of those nightmares where you can't move: the fear, and the whole unreality of it, held me paralysed. Then he bent forward and pressed his face to mine and began to kiss me - and somehow I managed to move again. I tried to push him away but he was heavy and stronger than me; I tried to kick him but couldn't get any purchase.

Then I realised that with his mouth on mine, his tongue forced between my lips, someone was still singing "The Apple Tree".

It was a woman's voice, rather thin and quavering, more as if she were uncertain of her singing than as if she were old. It was not a pleasant sound.

I tried to remember what my mother told me about self-defence. I reached up to his hand and tried to force the little finger back. He gasped and said "Bitch" and I convulsed away and head-butted him – not very hard but he let go of my throat – then he stepped back and punched me in the head. I fell sideways, since I was against the wall, on to one of the boxes of papers. I was in such a position that it was almost impossible to get up, especially with my co-ordination gone. I tried to scramble away from him but got nowhere; and all the time the woman was singing.

He picked me up and slammed me against the shelves. I felt like my body was breaking in bits – and the woman went on singing, only it seemed now someone else was singing too, a man's voice. Douglas grabbed my throat again and just before I lost consciousness I thought I felt a hand on my shoulder, a voice saying "The woman wrote it, and cursed it. I should never have let Charlie play you the tune." Then there seemed to be a flash of light and I passed out.

I WOKE UP in hospital and was pretty much out of it for several days. I didn't ask what happened. I assume Chloe and the good-looking young man had come back. The police took a statement and Douglas was charged with assault. I think he was put on probation; I seem to recall something about anger management. He had a good lawyer. I just hope I never see him again. Chloe went to stay with her sister; she said she was having a nervous breakdown. I thought about getting another lodger but did nothing about it. After three months Chloe got fed up with her sister and came back. We didn't talk about it. We don't talk much at all now. To begin with I kept seeing Douglas's face, far too close to mine, whenever I closed my eyes, but that's worn off. I'm working and even writing the book, but all of that, all of the Now, seems to be as it were behind glass. The face I see now, my eyes open or shut, awake or asleep, is Frederick Baker's; and I hear his voice, sometimes singing, sometimes saying "I'm sorry. I shouldn't have sung you the song, or let Charlie play you the tune. I'm sorry." I hear the woman's voice too. I haven't seen her face. Not yet. I don't know where it will end.

THE GARBAGE MEN

Tony Richards

FROM THE WINDOW of the attic room that he was renting, Marcus could hear children playing on the street below. He could hear them dancing around and chanting loudly.

One, two, three-four-five,
The garbage men will eat you alive.
Six, seven, eight-nine-ten,
You better stay clear of them garbage men.

He got up from the narrow bed that he'd been sitting on and went across to take a look. Before he'd even reached the glass the town of Thaxtall began spreading out before his gaze. It wasn't even all that large. You could see its outer edges from this vantage point. Beyond, the gently rolling hills of the East Midlands sprawled away toward the far horizon – not a farm in sight, no features in the slightest, nothing he could make out save for empty unused grassland.

The rooftops of the town itself were uniformly grey. The streets were not on a precise grid pattern but were close enough. Marcus had researched the history of this whole place. It had been nothing but a rural village till the early 1920s, when a pair of massive factories had been set up and thousands of new terraced homes had been constructed for the people who were going to work there.

Except the factories had both gone out of business more

than ten years back. Thaxtall was the kind of place that people who didn't live here generally called "post-industrial".

One, two, three-four-five,
The garbage men will eat you alive.
Six, seven, eight-nine-ten,
You better stay clear of them garbage men.

He stared down at the children. There were twelve of them that he could count, evenly divided between girls and boys but all dressed pretty much the same. Soccer jerseys from the famous Midlands' clubs adorned their upper bodies – likely not official ones but knock-offs from the local market. Below that they were wearing polyester jogging pants or even shorts, in this wintery weather. On their feet were the thick-soled training shoes that nearly everyone in Thaxtall seemed to wear. Marcus had driven into Coventry and bought himself a pair before arriving here.

You better stay CLEAR of them garbage men!

The children yelled it for a final time and then broke up like shooting stars and went their separate ways. Marcus watched them curiously as they disappeared. "Garbage men" wasn't part of any local dialect. It was – so far as he had ever been aware – an Americanism, so he supposed they'd picked it up from TV shows. What precisely had that chant been all about?

To say he didn't come from this place was to put it mildly. Marcus Stuart Hale had been born and lived for most of his life in the pleasant market town of Upper Sloham, thirty-four miles south of here. He had been educated at a private school and he was currently on a short break from his studies of Ancient and Modern History at Balliol College. What he really wanted to be was an author. No, correct that... What he *really* wanted to be was the next George Orwell, whose work he admired beyond measure. That was why he had decided to move here for a little while. This was his own *Road to Wigan Pier*, living among and studying people who were far less fortunate than himself.

When he went down to the living room, his landlady – Sally Church – was in her usual place at this time of the day, sprawled out on her threadbare sofa with the TV on. She was dressed in one of her habitual bright orange tracksuits, was absurdly overweight, and had dyed the foremost fringes of her hair an iridescent purple. She noticed him standing in the doorway and smiled cheerfully enough when she shifted her face toward him.

"Settlin' in okay up there, are you Marky?"

Here, he wasn't Marcus Stuart Hale. Here in Thaxtall, he was simply "Mark". *Room to let*, the sign in the newsagent's window had said, when he'd first caught a train into the centre of this town to give the place a look. *£40 per week. Cash ONLY.*

"Yeah thank you."

He couldn't replicate the local accent but had learned to tone his own one down.

"Everything is fine, only... Those kids out there?"

"Noisy little sods, aren't they? I must have been the same at their age, though."

"They were chanting something. Garbage men?"

Sally's eyes were still fixed on his face, only that the gleam of life in them seemed to have been temporarily extinguished. Her mouth had stopped half open so that he could see her tongue and teeth. She looked like her whole body was about to twitch.

Then she simply blinked and shrugged.

"I dunno. Some kind of game that they've been making up?"

"I'm not sure."

"Just the stupid nonsense little kids come up with."

With that Sal turned her attention back to the quietly murmuring television set.

"If you want something from the fridge then help yourself," she added – but wouldn't look at him again.

IT WAS PRACTICALLY eleven in the evening when the hammering started on the front door of the house. Both of Sally's daughters were back home by then, chubby jolly teenaged girls who mostly only showed up when they needed a change of clothes or wanted a bed for the night. Neither of them seemed to take the slightest notice of the loud insistent banging.

Marcus wandered out onto the landing and then bent over the railings, listening.

"Who the hell is that at this time of the night?" Sal was shouting from the downstairs hallway.

"Sal? It's Iris! Open up, for heaven's sake!"

Marcus recognised the voice of Iris Wheeler, one of Sally's friends, five houses down. Chains and latch were rattling in another instant.

"Iris? Christ, what is it, love?"

"It's Frankie!"

Who was Iris Wheeler's ten-year-old son, possibly one of the kids who had been playing on the street this afternoon.

"He's *gone*! I were fast asleep in front a the telly! An' when I woke up the kitchen door were open!"

"No Iris, that can't be right."

"He must a wandered out into the back! An' I've told 'im a thousand times not to go out there when it gets dark!"

"Iris, wait a minute, listen to me love. He's just gone running off, all right? Kids that age, they do it all the time. We'll get together, the whole street, and we will find him."

A lost child at this time of the night – it was a very serious business. Marcus went hurrying down the stairs to help.

Both women had already moved off by the time he reached street level. Sal was pounding on her neighbours' doors, imploring them to "move their arses". Poor Iris Wheeler... She was shuffling along in her friend's wake, a painfully thin woman, old before her time, with tangled curls of hair that matched the dangling grey cardigan she wore. She looked like she was shaking and in tears.

It took a while but the residents of Western Street finally started coming out – well, *some* of them at least. A few opened their doors to Sally but then shook their heads and went back in. In some houses lights were showing, only no one answered.

Plenty of the people who had ventured out had obviously been asleep. Some of those were quite unsteady on their feet, alcohol affecting their co-ordination. No one round here had a job. They'd all scraped by on benefits for years. The thought of actually achieving something was an alien concept to them. He could see it in the numbness on their faces.

"You four!" Sally kept on shouting at them nonetheless. "Get on down to Gladstone Park and see if he's gone there! The rest of you spread out and keep calling his name as loud as possible!"

The group split up. Yells went up against a sky the colour of dark slate. *Is no one going to bother calling the police?* was Marcus' first thought. Then he realised how naïve he was being. Booze and drugs and petty crime were normal around here, and so the police were not welcome.

He was alone beside the kerb after a few more moments so he set off by himself.

"*Frankie?*"

He went by a rusted lamppost.

"Frankie *Wheeler?* This isn't a *game*, kid - everyone is *worried* for you!"

Marcus fell silent as he reached the opening to one of the dark alleyways. They were a common sight around this part of town, running in between the fenced-in little backyards of the terraced houses. There was no lighting at all down this particular one and he could make out only vague dim shapes, rectangular ones for the most part. This was where people kept their rubbish bins - their "garbage".

A peculiar chill seemed to overtake him as he kept staring in and he couldn't understand precisely why that was. The dark had never bothered him before not even when he'd been a child himself. Standing at the black mouth of that alley, Marcus thought that he could sense—

He heard a noise from deep in there, something like a throaty gasp. Then another faint one like the shuffling of feet. He was certain he saw something move. He took a step in.

"Frankie? Kiddo, are you here?"

He paused a nervous moment but then stiffened his resolve. He was on the verge of pushing even further in - when a hand grabbed at his sleeve.

Marcus almost yelled out loud. He spun around sharply only to find himself staring at a figure he was certain he'd not seen before, a massive fellow, six foot eight at very least, dressed in only a T-shirt and pair of faded jeans despite the early February chill. It was the man's face that alarmed Marcus more than anything.

Thick pursed lips and cauliflower ears. Eyes that were quite tiny and extremely dark. A huge hooked nose. A cleanly shaven scalp.

Except the genuinely startling feature was the tattoo on the guy's bare forehead. Who would opt for anything like this? A third eye had been inked there centrally. It was far larger than the other two, and was so lifelike that you practically expected it to blink, as though this man might be a relative of Polyphemus.

"What you goin' there for?" he asked Marcus.

"I thought I could hear someone."

"Nah lad. Nothin' down there but for rats, some of 'em as big as spaniels."

"Surely we should take a proper look?"

That pasty dome of a head shook emphatically.

"You think I'm wrong? Well let's find out."

The giant lifted his dark gaze.

"Frankie Wheeler!" he bellowed out abruptly in a voice like thunder. "If yer there then show yerself, you dozy little imp!"

There was no slightest movement in response and not another sound came from that alley.

"See?" The giant shrugged, pursing his lips. "Any kid from round 'ere would know better than to go down there. Nothin' there at all but rats an' shadows."

Fifteen minutes later, keeping only to the open streets, Marcus had found nothing and was heading back. The others were returning too but none of them were towing any little boy along.

Iris was now bawling furiously. Sally clutched her round the shoulders, hugging her and trying to calm her. Surely they would have to involve the authorities by this stage of events? Yet nobody suggested that.

Sally peered across at Marcus with her distraught friend still in her grasp. Her big soft features had gone very stiff and every drop of colour had drained from her skin.

"I'm going to have to take her home, okay? I'll probably be gone a while."

"So—"

"Don't go worrying yourself about this, Marky. Just the way things are round here."

He was still puzzling over that last comment as he climbed back to his attic room. How could any incident like this be "just the way"? It really made no slightest sense.

Not that he genuinely understood *too much* about the denizens of this forgotten place. Take Sally herself, for instance. She was a nice sort of person in her own casual way. Only his whole time here she'd not asked him a single serious question. Where'd he come from? Why'd he even moved into a town like this? All she really seemed to care was that he paid his rent and paid in cash so that her benefits were not deducted. Most people around here were that way, not enquiring about the details of their lives but simply drifting through them.

Marcus closed the door behind him, took his A4 notepad out from underneath his mattress, wrote that observation down. Still holding it he wandered over to the room's big window. The street below was now completely empty but there were many more lit windows than there had been earlier.

This whole business, it must have left these people feeling quite uneasy. Marcus returned to his bed, sat down on its corner and then started scribbling, recording this entire episode, the sights, the sounds, the spoken words and his own thoughts and feelings.

By the time he'd finished, it was gone one in the morning. He had no idea if Sally had returned but a number of the lights in the small houses were still on. He flicked approvingly through the pages he had filled but then started feeling slightly guilty, since a missing child... That was an awful thing. A mother's grief was very stark and raw. These were human beings he was dealing with not merely the subject matter for a book. Perhaps he'd only be a proper writer when he learned to balance those two concepts.

Surely somebody should call a social worker, at the very least? But Thaxtall seemed to exist in a hard transparent casing that let almost nothing in. There was no way he could think to change that, though. Marcus simply closed his pad, hiding it beneath the mattress once again. He flopped down on the bed and pulled his knees up to his chest and lay like that until sleep claimed him.

HE WOKE UP bleary the next morning. Last night's cloud had cleared away, and with the winter sunlight streaming through his window and some birdsong in the eaves he could have been back inside his parents' home, even in his rooms at Oxford. Reality then set in, the compass in his mind swinging around to *true*.

Marcus sat up, rubbing at his face. The events of last night seemed like a dream by now, only he knew they were not that and wondered what the outcome had been. Surely Frankie had returned home and was safely in his bed? What other ending could there be?

The street below him was still empty and the house around him was entirely quiet. Sally's daughters both drank heavily most evenings and would not be up until the afternoon. Sally didn't usually appear until midday. Put plainly, she had nothing to wake up for.

Moving softly around the place he fixed himself some breakfast, washed himself down rather than switching on the noisy shower, shaved and changed his clothes and then spent at least an hour in the living room watching the news channels. He had never once watched TV in the daytime since he'd been a little kid, but hey when in Rome...

Finally - sometime round ten o'clock - noises started reaching him from out on Western Street. A few of its inhabitants had started to emerge. Marcus went into the hallway, pulled on the cheap padded overcoat he'd bought and headed out.

A cold wind was blowing hard despite the brightness of the day. When he turned around to shut the door Marcus noticed something from the corner of his eye - a compact shape, a human one.

A skinny little boy was sitting on the next stoop down. He was smaller than the other kids he'd seen, his jet-black hair quite badly cut and spectacles perched on his brief stub of a nose. His head was tucked down and it didn't even come up when the door slammed shut. The kid looked miserable and lost in thought.

"Hey, little man?"

His face finally lifted, twisting to a scowl.

"I'm not a little man. My name is Eric."

"What're you doing there, though?" Marcus smiled. "And why so sad?"

"I was friends with Frankie Wheeler and he's never coming back."

So Iris's son was still missing? It was not the kind of news that Marcus had been hoping for but he did his best to put a brave face on it

"How can you be sure of that? He could turn up at any second, couldn't he?"

"No 'course not. The garbage men have got him."

Marcus felt his pulse bump over.

"Garbage men? Like in that song?"

"They hide behind the bins at night, in the shadows where they can't be seen. And anyone who goes into them alleys – that's the last you'll ever hear of 'em."

An urban legend that the children of this district had created, then? Or else...?

"You don't mean bad people, do you? Violent types or the kinds of people that go after little kids?"

The boy just squinted at him.

"Garbage men ain't any kind of person. No. They grow out of the shadows at the start of night and in the mornin' they just disappear. But they come back as soon as the sun's gone. They always do. They're there forever."

Marcus could only think to pull a face and shrug. What need was there for any Brothers Grimm when children were so adept at inventing their own fairy tales? Still, his interest had been piqued. He retraced his steps of last night stopping at the entrance to the same dim narrow alley.

It looked different in the daytime, although not

completely. Not a single ray of sunlight seemed to get into this place and shadows clung to it like moss. This was a colourless environment that he was gazing at, standing almost separate from the world around it. And markedly colder when he stepped inside.

Underfoot were strands of grass mixed up with gravel so his shoes made gentle crunching noises every time he moved. There were puddles everywhere despite the fact it had not rained in days. The smell was like a mattress that someone had left outdoors for the entire winter.

The bins were considerably more visible than they had been last night, hefty plastic things on wheels. Some of them were filled to overflowing so their lids would not shut properly. Debris was scattered around every single one. Marcus kicked away a tattered ball of cardboard and then moved along.

"One, two, three-four-five," he'd started muttering beneath his breath

He wasn't quite sure why; the rhyme had simply sprung up in his head like some sort of strange mantra.

"The dum-dee-dum will eat you alive."

Why could he not even bring himself to murmur those words out loud? It made him feel slightly foolish. Had an urban legend got to him?

"Six, seven, eight-nine-ten. You'd better stay clear of those—"

Something moved behind the bin nearest to him and Marcus went jumping back, the breath freezing in his throat.

A tail and part of a grey flank appeared for a brief moment. It was nothing but a rat and a small example of the species too, nowhere near the size of any dog. Which meant that he had managed to deflate *two* urban myths.

Marcus let out a short bark of a laugh and wiped some sweat from beside his nostrils before heading off.

BY ALMOST MIDDAY he was standing on the edge of Gladstone Park. He'd spent more than an hour wandering the high street, which was nothing at all like the one in Sloham. Pound shops, pawn shops, discount supermarkets, fried chicken outlets, small liquor stores and closed-down pubs. Sally didn't buy her tracksuits from any shop, she bought them from the local market. The same thing went for vacuum cleaners, kitchen wear, bed linen and towels and even cigarettes.

The park was as bleak and deserted as it had been the first time he'd seen it. There were trees across the whole rear area but without their leaves they just looked deathly grey and skeletal. Over to the left there was a massive patch of nettles which had grown as tall as a man's waist. That ought to be bad news with little kids around, only that no one seemed to play here.

He still had Frankie Wheeler's disappearance in his thoughts though, and so Marcus made up his mind he would give this place a proper search. Some residents of Western Street had set off here last night for sure, but that was in the dark and they had not been gone for very long.

He started with the nettles, keeping his hands clear of their broad leaves. Except, why would a small boy come here? He gave up that idea and started hunting through the trees instead. He was forced to stop after about ten minutes, short of breath from scrambling among the tangled roots. His head went down. He clutched his knees.

By the time that he had straightened the gang had already moved in around him. He had been unaware that they were there. They had slipped out from between the trees like phantoms.

Six of them, all white, all pallid. All about his age, the same slim build. Each of them wore a different-coloured baseball cap; the peak of every cap was tilted backward.

"'oo the hell are you?" one of them sneered.

"I know oo 'e is," broke in another voice.

Marcus' gaze swung nervously around and fastened on the person who'd just spoken.

"'e's that bloke what's moved in with Fat Sally."

The one who had identified him edged in closer. He was slightly taller than the rest, with short blond hair beneath his baseball cap. Marcus thought that he had never in his life seen eyes such an intensely ice-bright blue but wholly devoid of emotion. This young man was fairly handsome yet had no expression.

"Moved in just a few days back. Only thing is..." and he closed right in until his face was mere inches from Marcus' "...why would anyone do that? Hoping to further your career by moving 'ere, are you? Or perhaps you like the scenery, the brilliant social life, the better class of people? No? So what the flying frig-all *are* you doing here you ponce?"

"I'm ... not sure what you're talking about," was all that Marcus could manage to get out.

That bright blue gaze bored into him a good deal deeper.

"Posh boy, ain't ya. Trying to hide it but I can still hear. An' what's a posh boy doin' in a dump like this?"

"Reckon 'e's a benefits snoop Jezza?" asked another of the gang.

"Nah mate. That's not it but I can't quite figure this one out."

This "Jezza" looked Marcus slowly up and down, those eyes of his practically glazed over.

"Some kid vanished on your street last night. An' you got anything to do with that?"

Marcus found himself taking another sharp step back, his chest going rigid and his pulse increasing. When he tried to answer he could hear the tremor in his voice and he was painfully aware that they could hear it too.

"I was home all evening I swear it. When that boy went missing I came to help. Ask anybody if you don't believe me."

"Okay then mate." Jezza grinned. "I'll have to take your word on it now won't I?"

The next thing Marcus knew there was a darkened flash inside his head. His eyes were somehow closed. When he tried to open them again his eyelids barely came apart a slit. He could tell that he was lying curled up on the ground.

Pain started to kick in beneath his nose, around his lips, and he finally took in what had happened. Jezza had just punched him squarely in the face, very fast and very hard. The pain was growing worse with every passing second - he couldn't move, could barely breathe. Directly above him his attacker's voice was going on like nothing had happened.

"So you're not a paedo. So, what *are* you then? You make no sense to me at all. Tell you what, I don't like that. So you'd better shove off outta here, find somewhere else to plant your arse because I see you on these streets again I'll do a whole lot more than I just did."

A swift kick to Marcus' ribs followed. After that there was nothing else. The gang had wandered off as silently as it had first appeared.

Marcus managed to sit up after a while, his fingers going to his mouth. They pulled back very sharply; his upper lip was split and they were stained with blood which was now running down his padded coat. He found some tissues in a pocket, wadding them beneath his nose.

Back at Sally's house he hurried up the stairs hoping he could make it to the bathroom and clean himself up before she saw the state that he was in. But she was on the landing, still in her night clothes. The contours of her big wide face re-arranged with shock.

"Marky, what in Christ's name happened?"

She was heading off into the bathroom before he could even answer, re-emerging with some antiseptic fluid, cotton wool and Band Aids. She made him bend down so she could reach his face. Cleaned away the dried-up blood and then applied the antiseptic, making gentle clucking noises the whole while she did so.

A kind-hearted person really. Marcus had already heard a little of her story. A teenaged pregnancy had forced her out of school. There'd been a marriage but that hadn't lasted very long. By the time a second daughter had been on the way "Mr. Church" was well and truly gone. She'd been left with no choice but to fend for herself. She'd even had an admin job at one of the big factories but that had been more than a decade back.

She was unpeeling a Band Aid, still clucking and shaking her head wearily.

"Who did this?" she finally asked him.

"Nobody. I fell."

"Oh balls. When people fall they get scuffed up. Can't see no scuffs so who exactly hit you?"

When Marcus described the culprit her whole face went stiff again.

"Hell's bells Marky, that was Jezza Danes, whose dad has been in Belmarsh for the past eight years. Lucky that he only punched you love. He's been known to carry a straight razor – not for shaving if you get my drift."

Beyond which point she took over his life and started making his decisions for him. He was going to stay indoors for the remainder of this day.

"Know Gin Rummy? I've got a deck of cards somewhere I'm sure, an' it's been ages since I played." She even got some beers out of the fridge and the pair of them settled down quietly at the kitchen table. But it couldn't last forever. After little more than half an hour Sally's youngest daughter leant out of her room and started screeching something down the stairs. Sal went up to find out what the fuss was all about. Some kind of furious row broke out which ended up with doors being slammed and then the upper storeys going very quiet.

Marcus waited for a long while before accepting the fact that Sally wasn't coming back. These people lived chaotic lives, he decided, their plans discarded from one instant to the next. He finally stood up, grabbed both the cans of beer and went through to the living room. Switched on the TV again. An old Western was showing; he left it playing with the sound turned off. He swigged more of the beer but wasn't used to drinking too much at this time of day. His face was still sore and his head had begun throbbing. The cowboys on the TV screen started blurring to a pastel-coloured murk.

When he re-awoke it was pitch dark outside. He glanced at his wristwatch – it was almost seven. The house seemed even quieter than it had been in the morning. He was still alone down stairs, which was rather odd. Sally should be sitting here by now watching her favourite soaps.

For himself, he felt like an old dishrag, his clothes crumpled and still stained with blood. The least that he could do was change them so he wandered back up to his room. Its door was wide open. Sally was sitting on his bed, her head tucked down so that he could not see her face.

His big notebook was lying open on her lap.

A cold sick feeling seeped through Marcus, the pain around his mouth suddenly forgotten. For how long had she been sitting there and how much had she read? A fat tear dropped from Sally's face and plopped down on an open page. Marcus twitched with shock.

"Thought I'd give your room a little tidy-up." She mumbled that without even trying to look at him. "Wasn't meaning to snoop, I really wasn't, but that doesn't make the two of us, now does it?"

Marcus felt his whole mind starting to go numb, except the numbness had a steely edge to it, like the bars of a cage.

"That thing, Sal ... it's just a diary really. Something that I like to keep, a record of–" Only he was lying and he knew that for a fact. And so did she.

"Do you think I'm so stupid that I cannot even read?" Sally started flipping through the notebook's pages. "All these smart remarks and witty observations? You've been studying us like bugs under a microscope. And me particularly."

Her fingers stopped at a random page then curled tightly.

"I accepted you into my home, shared my food with you, tried to be your friend. All the while ... the whole while I was doing that..."

Then words appeared to fail her and she snapped the notebook shut and held it out for him to take. Her face had still not lifted. There was no way he could figure to retrieve this situation. Not the slightest possibility that he could smooth over the damage and make everything all right again. There seemed to be a strong vibration running through his whole frame and he realised his hands were shaking.

"Sal, I..."

Her head finally lifted. Her entire face was wet, the eyelids red and puffy. Her gaze had gone hard with contempt. "I hear so much as one more lie out of your mouth," she said, "I'll go for you I swear I will. I want you out of here in no more than a minute. Simply take your stuff and leave."

She kept watching him closely as he moved around the little room, studying him the way he'd studied her, seeing him for what he really was. He gathered up the few belongings he'd brought with and shoved them into a backpack. He could feel her staring but did not look back. Couldn't bear to meet her eyes. Only a few hours ago she'd tended to his injuries, then tried to keep him company and cheer him up. He had paid her back by hurting her. He hadn't *meant* to but was beginning to see that his intentions didn't count. It wasn't what you thought that mattered, it was what you did.

The click of the latch sounded as loud as a gunshot when he pulled the front door shut behind him. He had never been made to feel so bad about himself. Had always been the good guy, the golden boy, never once a liar or betrayer. That peculiar vibration was still running through him, was making him feel rather sick.

The wind was blowing hard again; lone clouds scudding across the dark sky so that the moon and stars kept peeking through. He was alone on this street again. What he needed was a train to carry him away from here. What he *really* needed was his parents' home, where no one ever cried or shouted, nothing was chaotic. He started heading for the station with his head tucked down.

It was a functional grey concrete block approached by way of a broad concourse. Marcus rummaged through his pockets for the cash he'd need with which to buy a ticket. Couldn't find his money. Stopped. The angle of his vision shifted. Half -a-dozen men his age were sitting to one side of the steps that led up to the station's entrance. Each of them had on a backward-tilted baseball cap.

Marcus started pulling back hoping they'd not noticed him. But heads began bobbing around, then lifting. He spun away so quickly that he dropped his backpack. Tried to reach down for it, missed. Someone shouted something – and he ran.

Only when he'd reached India Avenue did he dare slow down a little and look back again. He knew that he was a good runner – except Jezza Danes and his gang appeared to have matched him stride for stride. Now he'd eased off they were catching up. His lungs felt like they were sucking in fire but Marcus forced a deep breath down and then continued round the corner.

The opening to an alleyway was coming up in front of him. His pursuers had not rounded that last corner yet so if he disappeared from sight...?

This place smelled exactly like the one from yesterday. Again, there were puddles underfoot. It was so dark in here he could barely see but maybe if he followed the fences along he would emerge into another street. Only he could make out no other exit even when his eyes adjusted. He'd gone down a dead-end lane.

The rubber soles of training shoes came clattering to a halt out on road. He could hear hurried voices, like the gang was urgently discussing something. Marcus hid behind a bin and hunkered down trying to stop wheezing, sweat leaking into his eyes. Something chilly brushed against his neck making him freeze rigid. It could have been an ice-cold breeze but he had noticed not the slightest touch of wind since coming into this tight space.

It brushed against his neck again and then a third time, rhythmically. Marcus' blood was running cold. It was difficult as all hell yet he managed to turn his head a couple of inches. Just enough to see.

The shapes crouching behind him were not human. The same general shape, yes, but stockier and larger-limbed, with heads like crudely squared-off blocks. With eyes that were glowing emerald green from lid to lid. There were no other features he could make out - these were the darkest things he'd ever seen.

He wanted to let out a scream - and struggled to remain completely still. There were three pairs of those shining eyes studying him closely. The creature nearest to him leaned in even closer and then sniffed, as though it were a massive dog. One of its companions followed suit. The creatures stared at each other and then - carefully - their huge heads shook.

All three of the things were melting off into the darkness a bare second later. A tight strangled noise pushed its way up Marcus' throat, exploding from between his lips. His body was seized by a spasmodic jerk, made him stand the whole way up.

Jezza Danes had entered into the alley and was grinning at him coldly. Almost stumbling over his own feet Marcus stepped out from behind the bins. He was vaguely aware of his hands moving - and that he was trying to speak.

"Nuh - uh - nuh," was the only thing coming from his mouth though.

Which only broadened Jezza's grin. He thought that Marcus was afraid of *him*.

"Told yer what would 'appen if I saw yer on these streets again."

"Jezza lis— Just *listen*."

"Warned yer proper I did - 'cept that posh boys like you always think that they know better."

Jezza was reaching calmly into the back pocket of his jogging pants. A straight razor came into view, lifted - and the blade displayed.

"No Jezza, you don't understand. We—"

There'd been an ochre glow outlining his assailant just a second back, the street lighting from India Avenue. But right now it was gone. In its place was nothing but a depthless patch of shadow. A thick black arm came reaching out of it. A huge hand clamped itself round Jezza's mouth. He screamed into its palm, his eyes growing completely round.

Another hand came shooting out and fastened round one of his wrists. More grabbed the edges of his clothes. He was being hauled backwards. One of those massive squared-off heads came into view though it was hard to see against that pitch-black background. Its jaws stretched open very wide before sinking into Jezza's shoulder. The young man's wails became even more frantic, muffled but intense.

That depthless patch of shadow - it closed over him completely.

He was never going to be seen again.

HOW MARCUS MADE it to the edge of town he couldn't properly recall. There were a few vague images inside his head - stumbling over an abandoned building site, splashing through a narrow brook. His shoes were soaked. His feet felt bruised. Nobody had tried to stop him.

When he finally stopped running he was halfway up one of those gently rolling hills he'd stared at from his attic window. He turned unsteadily - the whole town spreading out in dim grey shades below him.

One, two, three-four-five.

Why had the garbage men not taken him? Why had they immediately gone for Jezza? He seemed to remember how they had sniffed at his neck and— What had they been smelling? Marcus' thoughts were churning like an ocean caught in storm. It took a while to figure anything out but at last he started to believe he'd understood it.

The garbage men had been smelling Upper Sloham. They'd been smelling a good home and a good family and Balliol College, Oxford. An impending first-class honours degree. Maybe even more than that. Studying for his Master's or his PhD. A shining bright career in academia and books. They did not take people like him, it seemed. They only preyed on people who had no real hope and no real future, people who the world in general would not miss.

His mind caved in at that point, the last of the strength draining from his body, and he was forced to sit down. He was still there come the start of the next morning, shivering and rocking gently back and forth.

After a long while a few small children from the nearest houses came outside to stare at him.

GET WORSE SOON

Stephen Laws

COLIN CONSIDERED HIMSELF a frugal man.

There were some, he knew, who accused him of being a penny-pincher. But he saw no sense in spending more money than was necessary; indeed, he remained baffled at why people complained so much about the price of living when they clearly did not take as much care as he (and his mother) did with their own household finances.

In recent years he had become a devoted advocate of a shopping phenomenon which had swept English High Streets – stores where every item costs only one pound. One sovereign pound! There were a number of such franchises and now, in a current scenario of stressed market forces, unemployment and falling wages, it was often possible to find three or four different brands of store locally – all vying for the pound in one's pocket.

Colin's favourite (indeed, also his mum's favourite) – was The Quidstore. ("Everything you could possibly need for a Quid!" declared the official logo. "Yes – you're 'Quid's In' at the Quidstore!") Colin's obsession with the "everything for a quid" initiative also stemmed, he now realised as he entered middle age, not only from an impoverished childhood but also, strangely, with an image he'd seen on an American comic book depicting an old American-store tradition – the five and dime store.

Back then, as a child, he'd pored over that image – from a story long forgotten – of a store that, much like Aladdin's cave, was filled with shelves of all manner of amazing comestibles, domestic appliances, toys, gewgaws and doodads; bright, gaudy and very, very cheap. Although there had always been "cheap" stores selling "cheap" goods – particularly in the slum neighbourhood in which he'd been brought up – these were more akin to junk shops than five and dime stores.

How wonderful then, perhaps as a direct inspiration from the US of A – and when all things American appeared to have been influencing British culture – that the "all for a pound" stores had appeared in the United Kingdom. From bathroom plungers to battery packs; from plastic Chinese dolls to dog whistles, from DVDs of obscure European horror movies to fly spray – all for a pound (sometimes less!).

Happy days!

In bright mood and expectation of interesting finds, Colin perused the aisle and shelves of his local Quidstore, a wire shopping basket dangling from one arm. He had once gone on record as saying to a drinking colleague that the Quidstore stocked goods that he didn't even realise that he wanted until he found them. His friend declared that he was *such a twat* – ending the fragile friendship there and then.

Ambling contentedly, Colin's attention was drawn to a purple box on one of the shelves. At first he might have missed it since it was shoved in alongside a garish collection of novelty items – a pink packet of fake plastic boils, scars and warts to "stick on your face for amusement". "Make your own Second World War aeroplane out of balsa wood (balsa wood not supplied)"; and cellophane-wrapped mini-dolls with fierce smiles, empty eyes and orange hair: Popsie Popstar – "She'll play with you whenever you want". It was the cartoon graphic design on the purple box that caught Colin's eye. An obese clown-like man, bending double, was clutching his middle, eyes popping in distress and with a mouth that was twice as big as his head emitting a balloon that said "*Eeeurgh.*"

Colin picked it up and looked closer. A banner across the

top of the purple box declared: *Get Worse Soon.*

Colin turned it over. There was nothing on the back and nothing on the sides. No maker's name, no source of origin, no address, nothing. Just the cartoon man who looked as if he was about to throw his guts up, and the words *Get Worse Soon.*

Colin shook the box.

Something inside shifted with a soft thump, the sound that a packet of playing cards might make if some of the cards inside were missing. *Scher-lump!* He turned and twisted the box, listening to the same sound.

"A mystery," he said aloud without thinking – and a little old lady with a plastic basket filled with laundry items looked at him as if she had just been propositioned.

Colin dropped the box into his basket with his other acquisitions and, struggling to overcome embarrassment at the possibility that the old lady had seen what he was buying, headed for the checkout with his head held high in a manner of innate superiority. Colin continued that struggle when the slack-jawed boy at the checkout began plucking his items out, roughly swiping the barcode of each with stubby fingers, sniffing loudly throughout. Was he making value judgments with those sniffs on each of his purchases? The situation was further exacerbated when the old lady with the laundry stuff stood right next to Colin in the queue and watched him hurriedly dump each item, rudely scanned by the slack-jawed fumbling sniffer, into his own shopping bag.

Three boxes of Anti-Ant-Attack pellets: "To get rid of that ant problem in the kitchen". (Colin had lived in the same house all his life and had never had an ant problem in the kitchen.) Four mini-cans of Blue-Zade: a sugar-rich carbonated drink that turned your teeth blue. Super-Hero Toothpaste with a Japanese superhero on the tube of whom even the most diehard and avid superhero devotee had never heard; three brushing sessions with which (after drinking Blue-Zade) would turn Colin's teeth back from blue to off-white but was apt to make everything he ate for the rest of the day taste of varnish; and – of course—

Get Worse Soon – whatever that might be.

Colin paid, aware of the little old lady's scrutiny. Receiving his change from clammy fingers that felt like pork sausages, he found courage to give her a haughty glare and to ask "Anything of interest to you?"

"No," she replied blankly. "But you've bought a lot of crap there."

"And I suppose *you* haven't?"

"My stuff's to clean crap out of the toilet. At least I know the difference."

"Caveat emptor," said Colin swinging the shopping bag away as if he was swirling a cloak.

"And the same to you," said the old lady.

BACK AT HOME, a two-up two-down Council house on a street that never seemed to see sunshine, Colin unpacked his shopping in the kitchen. His mum was visiting her sick sister in hospital that afternoon so he had the place to himself and wouldn't have to put up with the usual domestic fuss and bother until she got home.

The kitchen cupboards were filled with Quidstore product. Cans of soup, vegetables, curry and minced meat of various kinds were ranked in military and colour-coded precision. Dry packets of food had their own section; jars and bottles of various sauces also had their special place. Kitchen utensils, cutlery, pots and pans - all from the Quidstore; and many of them (Colin's mum was proud to announce to anyone who would listen) were discontinued lines and therefore, probably, collector's items. Colin's mum was even more addicted to the Quidstore than himself - if such a thing was possible.

Colin sat at the kitchen table - glad to be alone - and strangely excited by the Get Worse Soon box. There was no plastic covering (which was strange) and the edges weren't sealed with those little plastic lugs that you would sometimes have to break off with a kitchen knife to get into the box. When he examined more closely he saw that it did indeed open up at one end like a new pack of cards. He pulled it open - upended it on the table - and three purple envelopes (the same colour as the box) slid out. When he looked back in the box he could see that there was something else inside there. After a little teasing with a forefinger he was able to extricate three sheets of purple paper.

Each sheet had the same cartoon character as the one depicted on the box, centred at the top of the page. And Colin was puzzled to see that each sheet was laid out like one of those official Certificates in big bold lettering (with occasional smaller text) like something you'd see in a glass frame on the wall of a doctor's surgery or a chemist's shop. A quick glance showed that they were all the same. Before he read what it said on one of the certificates he could see that he had overlooked another piece of paper, the edge of which could just be seen sticking out of the box.

He pulled it out. It read:

Congratulations! You now have the chance you've always been looking for! Not just one chance – but FOUR chances! (My, thought Colin, what a lot of exclamation points!) *Yes – FOUR chances to really get your own back on those who have terribly wronged you. When you're ill, when you're unwell, when you're down in the dumps, what's better than a "Get Well Soon" card? We've all sent them, we've all received them. What? You haven't? Well, boo hoo! We say: "BOO HOO!"* (That's a bit rude, thought Colin.) *But that makes you even luckier, doesn't it? Because that makes the cards you've got* (Well – letters really) *even more powerful than ever – for reasons that are much too complicated to go into here.*

This is getting a bit odd, thought Colin.

No it isn't... continued the piece of paper and Colin dropped it with a start as if it had suddenly spoken to him. Aware that his heart was bumping for no good reason Colin picked up the paper again, ran a tongue over suddenly dry lips and continued.

No it isn't wrong to be fed up when no one sends you "Get Well Soon" wishes, but what about when someone does the dirty on you? That's where the "Get Worse Soon" card comes in. Isn't there someone in your life who deserves a "Get Worse Soon" card? Believe it – this card WORKS! Just fill in the blanks, fold up the card, and put it in the envelope...

Colin looked at the four purple envelopes. The centred over-elaborate text on each read *To Whom It Concerns.*
...*put the address on, post it, and–*
VOILA!
For some reason Colin was startled by the sudden *loud* text.
The person to whom you have sent the card will – wait for it– GET WORSE SOON!
Don't delay!
Get posting today!
Someone, somewhere, needs to hear from you!
Someone needs – the big BOO-HOO!
"The Big Boo-Hoo," said Colin turning the piece of paper over in his hands looking for a Made in China label in little writing, or some evidence of its origin and manufacture. Like the box, there was none.
"I'm not sure this is legal," continued Colin to himself. "This is just a poison pen letter!" And then, after a little while, he said "What a waste of a quid" (not for the first time). "I should report this."
The purple paper felt coarse; somehow unpleasantly *hairy.*
He read what was there:
DEAR– (with a blank space for a name, and then the cartoon of a vulture):
A little birdie said today
That I should send a note your way
Because your life is good and fine
And getting better, not like mine!

You were not kind with me, you fool
You were bad, and you were cruel
And so I send this card to you
It guarantees a Big Boo-Hoo.

On the day this card arrives
You will have one day to survive
Count those hours – until noon
'Cause then you'll die – so Get Worse Soon!

"This is just sick," muttered Colin gathering up the

certificates, the paper and the envelope.
No, it's not.
"Who said that?"
Startled, Colin sat up straight and looked around the kitchen. He was sure that someone had spoken. But then the refrigerator made a clicking noise, a car horn sounded in the distance and the moment was gone. The Get Worse Soon material was swept up and put on a side table.

Mum came home at the usual time. And yet again Colin listened to the detailed description of her latest visit to her sister – his Aunt Rhoda – with the usual teeth-gritted lack of patience that his mother always mistook as patience.

That night in bed, with purple light shining through the curtains of his bedroom window, Colin realised just how much he disliked his Aunt Rhoda. Selfish, opinionated, arrogant, over-bearing, selfish, greedy and boring.

The purple light through the curtains reminded Colin of the purple box that the Get Worse Soon card had come in. When he put the bedroom light off all he could see was that big cartoon face with its cartoon mouth going: "*Eeeurgh.*" Which is why – unable to sleep, just for the hell of it – he found himself going downstairs to find the box, pulling out one of those garish certificates (just to look at), and then filling in Aunt Rhoda's name on it (just for something to do).

On the following morning Colin collected his disability allowance and his mother's pension from the post office. It was enough to keep them both, provided that they were frugal (the Quidstore supply was a pivotal factor in their household finances). Colin's disability, although recognised by the state (hence the financial allowance) had a tendency to vary in its symptoms, dependent upon who had the temerity to question the specifics of the ailment – another reason why Colin had ceased to visit Aunt Rhoda since she had a tendency to indulge in such penetrating questions when it came to Colin's health, and his ability (or otherwise) to look after her ailing sister, his mother.

It was these thoughts that were in his head when he diverted from the post office to the Quidstore for a loaf of bread (ten pence cheaper than the supermarket) and a litre of milk (twenty pence cheaper than the local store) together with a box of teabags (the same price as elsewhere, but he felt that this was a question of customer loyalty. He had in fact asked the girl on the Quidstore checkout if they'd ever considered the possibility of a Loyalty Club with membership cards that included discount privileges for long-standing customers. But the way the girl had said "Whaa...?" with her slack jaw and glassy uncomprehending eyes had restrained Colin from further enquiry.

The health inquisition from an Aunt who had his mother running around after her when she was absolutely *loaded* with cash, and the memory of the failed Loyalty Card enquiry, brought Colin's attention back to the Get Worse Soon pack. Curiously, although he remembered filling in his Aunt's name on one of the certificates, he could not remember putting it in one of the purple envelopes. But when there were only three certificates left in the pack, he checked – and sure enough there was the filled-in certificate in the envelope, addressed to Aunt Rhoda.

The envelope was still in his hand when he went downstairs to make a mug of tea for Mum and himself. He put it on the kitchen bench, gummy side of the envelope up, and boiled a kettle.

My, but his lips were dry this morning. The sight of that gummy strip made them water, somehow.

Colin took a mug of tea into the living room where his mother was watching people on a television studio stage screaming insults at each other over a paternity test. He wondered if it was possible to buy a paternity test at the Quidstore. He put the mug down next to his mother. "Tea-for-Two-Minus-One" it said on the side of the Quidstore mug.

"Little bastard," said Colin's mum.

"I beg your pardon."

"I don't reckon that test is going to show her husband's the father. Poor little bastard."

"Who, the baby?"

"No, the father." Colin's mum looked at him impatiently, shooed him away and sipped her tea.

Colin returned to the kitchen and sipped from his own Quidstore mug. ("TNT" read the slogan on its side, depicting a teapot exploding). It tasted of glue. Colin smacked his lips in disgust.

And saw that the Get Worse Soon envelope on the bench was sealed. He picked it up, examined it; could not for the life of him remember licking it and sealing it. But he could still taste the glue. He sipped more tea to get rid of the taste.

"Send something nasty like that in the post," he said quietly to himself. "She'd call in the police. Wily old bird. They'd probably check the postage stamp on the envelope. Start house to house enquiries." The old bat only lived fifteen minutes away. He had watched all the re-runs of *Columbo* on the telly. They could track it down, no problem.

No, they couldn't.

Colin spun around.

The letter box flapped and the post pattered onto the Welcome mat (plastic, heavy-duty, £1.99 from the Indian corner shop. Not available at Quidstore although enquiries had been made.) It was nothing but junk mail. Pizza discount offers, driveway work done to your specification ("We don't even *have* a driveway!" said Colin, with exasperation), friendly plumbing work undertaken ("As if I'd *want* an unfriendly plumber!"), low cost funeral arrangements and—

The Get Worse Soon envelope with Aunt Rhoda's address on it was also somehow in his hand. Colin looked back from the hallway to the kitchen. He was sure that he hadn't picked it up when he went to collect the post. But he must have done.

Colin finished his mug of tea and when he went to collect Mum's empty mug he asked "Bastard?"

"Yes," replied his mum without taking her eyes from the television. "And so's the baby."

"Going out for a bit."

"Where to?"

"Thought I'd take the bus to Thermingdale."

"It's got a Quidstore, hasn't it?"

"Yes."

"That's nice."

Get Worse Soon

And Thermingdale was a good fifty minutes away on the bus. Which meant that the envelope would be postmarked Thermingdale and no one in Colin's family came from or had any association with that town.

"See you later."

"All right, son."

AUNT RHODA DIED two days later, apparently tripping on her dressing gown belt and falling down the stairs.

"It seems as if," Colin's mum tearfully explained on return from his Aunt's house, "her neck had been broken."

Now it looked as if all those other... (and his mum struggled with the word) ...*bloody* relatives would descend to claim whatever inheritance was available despite the fact that none of them had shown any interest beforehand, leaving all the day-to-day support to Colin's mum. The next-door neighbours listened sympathetically to Colin's mum over the back-garden fence.

"Colin is just so *quiet* now," she confided. "I'm really worried. I never realised that he loved his Aunt so much."

IN THE WEEKS that followed, an inquest into Aunt Rhoda's death arrived at a finding of death by misadventure. Although Colin's mum had been the only relative to have visited, waited on and looked after her sister, there were three other sisters in the family, all older than she – together with a nephew of the eldest, who had remained invisible for decades, but now suddenly emerged in all his professional glory as a solicitor – best placed "to represent the interests of the family". As such, all matters related to the funeral arrangements, reading of the will, disposal of assets and property, proceeded with the exclusion of Colin's mum and (of course) Colin.

After the funeral service, the nephew – Arthur Ginniver – (of Ginniver and MacPherson) – attempted to shake hands with Colin.

Colin – aware that his mother had received only £500 of a "sizeable" estate (bare recompense for running around after her sister in the twilight years of her life, and in the complete

absence of the others sisters' support) - refused to take his hand and said:
"There was an old woman called Rhoda
Who lived in a Chinese pagoda.
And the walls of the halls were adorned by the balls
Of the tools of the fools who had rode her."
"Well," declared Ginniver, "I think that is in *really* bad taste."
"So is this," replied Colin, farting loudly and walking away.

His mother, weeping quietly into a handkerchief on the other side of the cemetery, saw that an exchange had taken place but could not hear the words. She did, however (like Mrs Bradley, the next-door neighbour who was comforting her) - see that he had declined Ginniver's handshake.

"Oh dear," said Mrs Bradley.

"Poor Colin," snuffled Colin's mum. "I'm afraid he's taken Rhoda's death so very, very badly. He's become so ... so *quiet*."

AUNT RHODA'S HOUSE had been cleared and sold, the scandalous dissemination of her earthly goods had been completed and her ashes had been laid to rest.

Life had returned to normal.

And the Get Worse Soon card had never reappeared.

No mention of it.

No police investigation.

It had probably gone into the bin with all the other rubbish.

And quite without conscious decision - or so he thought - Colin found himself sitting late one night at the kitchen table after his mum had gone to bed, with a second certificate.

This time, with great ease and a flourish of his pen (in a surprisingly easy disguised hand-style) he filled in the name on the envelope: Arthur Ginniver.

He procured the address of Ginniver and MacPherson from the telephone directory but this time - instead of licking the glue-flap on the envelope (and he still couldn't remember doing that the first time) – he took a dab of water from the kitchen sink tap with a sponge and rubbed it on the glue.

Then *slap!* With the heel of his hand to avoid fingerprints. Job done.

On the following morning Colin told his mum that he was taking another bus trip to Thermingdale.

BUT ON THE day after next, when Colin listened to the local television and radio news in the afternoon and evening, there was no mention of any – activity – at Ginniver and Mac-Pherson.

Nor the day after.

Or the day after that.

Which meant that the business with Aunt Rhoda had been nothing but a fluke. On the following day, with still no news, Colin's mum told him that she was becoming worried.

"At first you were just so quiet, Colin. I know how much Aunt Rhoda's death affected you. It affected me too. But now, in the last few days, you just seem *irritated* all the time. It can't be good for your health, son."

My health, thought Colin. Maybe I need a Get *Well* Soon card.

"Aunt Rhoda isn't coming back."

No, she isn't, the old bat!

The morning, afternoon and evening news were no news at all. Not for Colin. At last, against his better instinct, he could take no more. In the town centre he found a public telephone box and rang Ginniver and MacPherson.

"Hello?" said a woman's voice. "Ginniver and Mac-Pherson. How can I help?"

"Have you got a Mr Arthur Ginniver working for you?" asked Colin in an affected basso profondo voice. He added a bronchial cough for verisimilitude.

"Yes," replied the woman (a secretary perhaps). "Arthur Ginniver is the senior partner."

Is! Colin's free hand clenched and unclenched unconsciously. His teeth gritted. *Is!* The present tense. Arthur Ginniver was still alive! How could Colin have come to believe in a ridiculous Quidstore set of joke cards? How could he have made such a fool of himself?

"Unfortunately," continued the secretary, "Mr Ginniver is on holiday for a week and won't be back until the day after tomorrow. Perhaps our other partner, Mr MacPherson, can be of assistance?"

Colin could not help spluttering into the telephone receiver. Ginniver had been on *holiday!* That meant the card hadn't been delivered yet. It was probably in an office in-tray right at this moment awaiting his return. Of course!

"No ... no thank you," said Colin clearing his throat. "My business can wait."

TWO DAYS LATER Arthur Ginniver arrived back from holiday and was back in his office at 9:00 a.m. promptly.

On the local television news at noon it was reported that a window cleaners' cradle on the roof of solicitors Ginniver and MacPherson had fallen over the edge of their office building, still attached to its ropes, its pulley like a tangled pendulum. The plummeting platform had not only jerked to a halt immediately outside the plate glass windows of Arthur Ginniver's office but - like a pendulum - had exploded *through* those windows in a crashing of glass that was heard four blocks away. Not only was Arthur Ginniver speared to death instantly by multiple jagged shards of plate glass, but the pendulum/platform had scooped him up from his desk and on its outward swing flung him back out through the shattered windows, where he tumbled - a bloody scarecrow in a once-expensive business suit - six storeys to the street below and straight under the front wheels of a double-decker bus bound for Thermingdale.

Colin missed the first announcement on the lunch time news. But he was sipping tea in the kitchen when the news announcer told the story again in a summing-up at the end of the lunchtime broadcast.

When Colin's mum returned from (Quidstore) shopping there was a broken teacup on the kitchen floor in a puddle of tea. Colin remained in bed for the rest of the day with an unexpected migraine.

*

"I WANT TO speak to the Manager," demanded Colin.

The man at the checkout counter wore a Quidstore jacket with the logo on his top pocket. Bearded and bespectacled, the thick lenses magnified his eyes to an alarming degree. Colin supposed that he was a few years younger than he; and therefore his social inferior.

"That's me," said the man.

"Pardon?" queried Colin, doubly confused since (a) the man's upper moustache covered his mouth so completely that none of his facial muscles moved when he spoke and (b) he was serving at the checkout and didn't have a "Manager" badge on his lapel.

"Me," repeated the man. "I'm the Manager."

"*You're* the Manager?"

"Yeah. Me. How can I help?"

"I wondered who was responsible for your Get Worse Soon packs."

"You what?"

"Your Get Worse Soon packs?"

Sweat had instantly squeezed through the skin pores on Colin's brow and neck and it felt like it was spreading quickly over his entire body.

"Human blotting paper," said Colin and flinched, not understanding how that had suddenly slipped out.

"Blotting paper? No, we don't sell blotting paper."

"No!" Colin instantly corrected. "Those packs that you sell. You know - *Get Worse Soon* - with the letters, I mean certificates, inside."

This was going even worse than he'd feared. All night long he had fretted and gnawed and worried about what he should do. Go to the police and come clean about the fact that he'd sent those letters to people and they had died? They weren't poison pen letters in the accepted meaning of the term after all, were they? They were - well - *joke* letters. The opposite of Get Well Soon cards and the kind of thing that you could buy legitimately from joke shops, surely? He hadn't meant any harm and if there was any real danger in them - then they shouldn't be on sale, should they? But he *had* bought them and he *had* sent them. Moreover, how on *earth* had they worked so well that they had caused these terrible things to happen?

But you did want something bad to happen. That's why you sent them.

"What?" exclaimed Colin in disbelief.

The Manager shifted position impatiently. "I *said* – we don't sell Get Worse Soon cards."

Colin wriggled in his clothes, felt a rivulet of sweat trickle and tickle down his spine.

"Yes you do."

"No we don't."

"I bought a pack here. Last month."

"Not from here you didn't."

"Yes I did. Look – I know what you're doing – and it's not going to work."

"We don't stock or sell the item you're referring to, sir."

"You want me to get the blame for what happened. Well that won't *wash!* No way! You shouldn't be selling things like that and then getting people into trouble."

"If you have a legitimate complaint, sir, maybe you would like to put it in writing or email it to the Complaints Department at our central office?"

"Aha! There! You see – you accept that there are legitimate grounds for complaint!"

"If you don't leave the premises, I'll be forced to call the police."

"*A-Ha!*" Colin straightened in righteous indignation, convinced that the reference to police had confirmed his conspiracy theory. The rivulet of sweat from his spine found the crack in his buttocks, causing a squirm and shuffle of discomfort and such a potential for the perception of lack of control on his part that he quickly transformed it into a brief and controlled war dance of victory. "Well I'm not having it, I tell you! I won't be held accountable for your selling goods that are flagrantly in contretemps with the Trades Description Act. They are *enticements*. It's ... it's ... entrapment! That's what it is!"

Colin charged off into the store heading for the stationary

section where he had first discovered the offending article, intent on finding another and waving it under the Manager's nose, denouncing Quidstore and its management for such irresponsible trading. The Manager was not far behind him, lunging around the checkout counter and colliding with a carefully arranged tower of Quidzstore pea soup cans ("Pound for pound more peas to be found!"). They tumbled and scattered in a clattering avalanche.

"Not my fault!" yelled Colin as he found the stationary shelf and began scattering items in his search for that familiar purple package. "*That* was *not* my *fault!*"

Somewhere, a customer screamed.

Alarm bells began to ring.

"ALL RIGHT COLIN," said the female police constable.

The Quidstore storeroom was cramped and full of branded Quidstore boxes so that Colin had to keep his hands and elbows down between his legs as he sat on the wooden stool, feeling like a small boy being castigated and in detention at school.

"I can call you 'Colin', can't I?"

"Well that's my name," said Colin peevishly, "so I suppose you can if you want to." He looked up at the burly male police constable standing over him, with his arms crossed in condemnation. Unlike the female constable he hadn't even taken off his PC cap, and Colin knew what that meant.

"The Manager has said that he doesn't want to press charges..."

"He slipped on a soup tin," declared Colin. "It was his own fault."

"He has decided *not* to press charges," continued the female police constable with great patience, "even though he would be within his rights to do so."

What about *my* rights? Colin almost said aloud but managed to clench his teeth and keep his mouth shut.

"You didn't steal anything. And it seems that there must have been a misunderstanding about an item that you say was for sale here, but which the Manager assures us has *never* been sale here *at any time*."

Colin resisted the urge to lose his temper again and said quietly "They are called Get Worse Soon cards, and they are in very bad taste indeed. Very offensive."

"They don't exist, Colin. Never have done. And they're most definitely *not* on sale here. The Manager has shown us the stock records and paperwork."

"I suppose I could not have…" began Colin and then thought Wait a minute! He began again. "Then I couldn't be held accountable for sending out cards that don't exist – and result in any 'unfortunate' incidents that might befall anyone who receives them? I mean – they can't receive them, can they? If they don't exist?"

The female police constable looked up at her male colleague. His expression remained fixed as if he was trying to ignore a nasty smell.

"No Colin. You're not accountable."

"And I'm not 'wanted' in connection with any police enquiries about sending Get Worse Soon cards?"

"No. There are no ongoing enquiries about cards that you say you have purchased here since they don't exist. Unless you've been making cards of your own and sending out poison pen letters…?"

"No! Of course not!"

"Because if you *have* been sending out your own threatening letters then it's in your own interest to tell us…"

"Absolutely not! I mean – no, of course I haven't been sending out my own letters!"

"Very well then."

"So Quidstore don't sell Get Worse Soon cards?"

"No. No one does."

"And I can't be in trouble for sending cards that aren't on sale here because they don't exist?"

"No."

"I'm free to go then?"

"Yes Colin. If you promise to behave…"

"It's my Aunt, you see. She died suddenly and I've been very upset…"

COLIN'S SENSE OF relief was short lived when he returned

home.

He had been assured that there would be no police action against him on the basis that the so-called Get Worse Soon cards did not exist, which was patently absurd. And there, when he got back, was the purple packet on the kitchen sideboard – a purple packet that shouldn't be there.

Anger flaring, Colin's first reaction was to reach for the telephone, ring the police and the Quidstore management in righteous indignation. But where would that get him? Proof that the cards *did* exist, that for some reason the Quidstore people were lying? And bringing his own role in sending those cards out to people who had died back into the equation? Colin replaced the telephone receiver into its cradle.

It was a good thing that his mother was out of the house (shopping) so that she wouldn't become alarmed at the seething and alternate displays of relief and frustration that saw him stomping around the lounge, throwing sofa cushions, kicking chairs, and punching the air. Just before his mother returned the sofa cushions had been carefully replaced, the chairs rearranged back into their original positions.

And Colin had a plan.

THE MANAGER OF the Quidstore stood back with his electronic tag and watched as the security mesh finally rattled into place, protecting the facade of the store front.

He was a happy man.

The way he'd dealt with the weird guy and his obsession with birthday cards (or something) – cards that the Quidstore did most definitely *not* sell – had made a significant impression on Storeroom Suzanne, who he had been trying, so far unsuccessfully, to chat up for months.

But now the ice had been well and truly broken, when she had come to the mistaken belief (based on the dozens of tinned-pea cans rolling around on the floor) that he had engaged in hand-to-hand combat with a dangerous lunatic – an encounter that had necessitated the presence of the police. (No one had actually seen what had happened, and when the

Manager realised that Suzanne was allowing herself to become overly impressed with his bravery he had allowed the situation to develop on its fantasy course, and she had agreed to spend the weekend with him at his parents' caravan at Spitting Point; said parents being conveniently fifty miles away at that time, staying with friends.)

The Manager whistled all the way home to his downstairs flat - six streets away. And Colin, having waited in his hidden vantage point in a shop doorway on the other side of the High Street, watched him do so, followed him home without being seen - and also whistled all the way to his own home thereafter.

The fates were with him. The Manager didn't live miles away, hadn't used a car or public transport, and had made the discovery of his home address much easier than Colin would have expected. He didn't need the Manager's name. "The Manager, Quidstore" and then the address was all he needed. And there was one purple certificate and envelope left in the Get Worse Soon box at home, waiting to be filled in.

ONE DAY LATER.

"Look what I got from the Quidstore," said Colin's mum pointing at the kitchen table (Ikea £14.99).

"The mirror?" asked Colin, checking the newspaper for stories of bizarre death that might suggest someone else had discovered a Get Worse Soon kit and was putting it to some good use.

"No, not that," replied Colin's mum. "That!"

"You mean the Quidstore kettle? I've seen that already." The tea it made tasted crap, unless it was the Quidstore's own "Fifty Teabags for a Quid" brand, so he reckoned that something strange and complicated was going on there.

"No!" Colin's mum came back with sufficient impatience to elucidate an equally impatient explosion of air; combined with hunched shoulders suddenly expanding with widened arms - to give the effect of projecting it out with an even greater degree of impatient force.

"What then?" hissed Colin copying his mother's gesture.

"*That!*" And this time Colin's mum moved huffily into the kitchen, rapping sharply on the kitchen bench with a blood red thumb nail that looked like a small vulture's beak.

Now Colin could see that there was something new on the kitchen bench after all – next to the Quidstore kettle. It was an oblong piece of blue plastic (two shades of blue plastic, actually) with what looked like a red plastic miniature doorknob attached to the top of it, resting on a sheaf of white paper. Someone had been drawing blue patterned circles on the paper around it – apparently at random. The sight of it drew Colin into the kitchen too and, still holding the newspaper open, he idled in, seeing now that the blue circles on the paper contained not patterns but letters and words. Craning his neck to read what each one said, semi-curved in the centre of each circle, he exclaimed in pain as he cricked his neck and knew he'd have to use that deep-heat rheumatoid cream in the medicine cabinet (Boots the Chemist £2.99). As he turned to ease the kink in his neck, he read: The Dowells, 25 Misteria Crescent, The Hovells, Bacram BLU 321.

"Mumm..." began Colin, a dreadful *something* now squirming in his stomach. "What's *this*...?"

And before Colin's mum could answer he began to read what was printed on the side of the blue plastic box, so that his reading and her response was correspondent.

"Quidstore Stationery Kit."

Colin turned to look at her, his jaw slack.

"It only cost a pound," she beamed at him.

"And you bought it so that you could...?"

Was that really the sound of Colin's voice? He hadn't intended to say anything and it certainly didn't sound like him – to him.

"So that you can stamp our name and address on the back of the envelopes we post. Just like the olden days, when my Auntie Betty used to send her letters to us with that same sort of stamp on and we'd feel all tingly 'cause she always used to put some money in, as well. Not that we're putting any money in ours of course – but it's still nice, isn't it? Only cost a pound."

"Mum?"

"Yes love?"

"Where's that envelope that I felt on the hall stand this morning?"

That small anxious wiggling thing in Colin's stomach was beginning to claw a hole in his stomach wall.

"Don't worry. I posted it for you so it would catch the first delivery."

"And did you...?"

"Yes love. I put our new Quidstore stamp on the back of the envelope. First time we've used it."

ANOTHER DAY LATER.

Colin's fingernails were bitten to the quick as he stood in the shop doorway opposite the Manager of the Quidstore's home, on the other side of the road. It was the same shop doorway he'd stood in two days ago when he'd followed him home and discovered the address.

His heart lurched when that door opened and the Manager stepped out.

He was whistling. That was good.

He didn't look upset or troubled. That was even better.

When he closed the door he turned with a secret smile on his face. Colin could not suppress a deep sigh of relief. The Manager looked untroubled and - an extra bonus - he hadn't used a key to lock the front door.

It was eight in the morning and although the postman didn't make his rounds in the area until sometime after nine, Colin had been standing in the doorway since six a.m. He did not want to take any chances.

That Get Worse Soon card must be intercepted at any cost. After the incident in the Quidstore, the fact that the Manager and the police knew his name, the arrival of that card (despite the insistence that it did not exist!) could open up all kinds of questions.

Overhead, thunder grumbled in the sky - and to Colin it sounded like the closing of a huge prison door.

The Manager strode off, still whistling and smiling. Colin waited until he'd reached the end of the street, and then hurried over the road. Trying not to look suspicious he quickly scanned the living room through the windows. He was convinced that the Manager lived alone but was bedevilled by the possibility that there might be an elderly relative in there. Maybe someone bedridden. That couldn't be helped. He would just have to be very, very careful.

Colin headed off in the opposite direction to that taken by the Manager. Reaching the end of the street he turned into a side alley and hurried to the back lane that ran parallel to this row of terraced houses. He had already reconnoitred the area.

The Manager lived at number 63, which was twelve doors down in parallel at the back lane. Colin counted the back doors carefully as he moved and found the small wall and patch of grass that served as a back garden for number 63.

The grass had not been cut. Given the fact that Quidstore shears were on sale for a pound at the Manager's own shop, Colin found this highly offensive.

The back lane was deserted apart from a ginger cat sitting on a nearby garbage bin. Colin made a small friendly but fearful noise. The cat hissed, jumped down and ran away.

Moments later, Colin was over the small garden wall and was striding across the back garden. Fences on either side screened him from being seen by the neighbours. On his early morning vigil, he had come prepared for all eventualities. Quidstore screwdrivers of assorted types to remove locks in their entirety. Quidstore hammer, Quidstore glass cutter and Quidstore Tea towels for the removal of panes of glass in doors or windows to affect entry.

None was required. The Manager had left a small window in the downstairs lavatory, next to the back door, slightly open on a latch that could easily be unfastened and opened. This was a disgusting lapse of security.

Anyone could get in, thought Colin. People should really have more care.

Pausing a last time to check that he was not being observed, Colin soon had the latch and bar unfastened. The lavatory had no occupant.

So far, so good.

Heart hammering, Colin shunted his backside onto the window ledge and swung his left leg over and inside - bones aching and gritting his teeth to suppress the sounds of effort. There were no cluttered ledges or sills in there; nothing that he might displace or knock over.

Holding onto the window frame he dragged his other leg in and over, grazing his thigh on the sill as he did so. His teeth made a grating sound that seemed so loud that he clamped his hand over his mouth.

Slipping down from the window sill, he closed the window. He was *in*.

Socks and underpants were drying on the lavatory radiator next to the sink. He didn't recognise them as Quidstore brands.

Colin opened the door, catching the sneck to make sure that it didn't click when he opened it. There was a small corridor. From there, up ahead, was a room facing the back garden. An ironing board in the middle of that room. A pile of laundry in a basket waiting to be ironed.

Creeping into the corridor he could see the front door up ahead. To the left and right beforehand, two doors on either side of the corridor. Probably a living room and a bedroom.

Colin paused, listening. Nothing. Just a clock ticking somewhere.

He looked back at the front door. There was nothing on the mat under the letter box.

Yet.

Colin moved carefully onwards. He was right. The door on the right led to a small bedroom... The door on the left gave access to a living room, with sofa, chairs and television. Colin crept to the living room door and paused, barely breathing.

Still nothing but the beating of that unseen clock.

The bedroom was empty.

Another step into the living room - but when he put his foot over the threshold there was a crack and groan from the floorboards beneath a hideous purple deep-pile carpet that stabbed icy panic in his heart. It was much louder than any such sound should be. Sweat trickling on his face and down his spine, heart racing and struggling not to make sounds as he panted for breath, Colin waited for the subsequent and inevitable sounds of alarm being raised.

Tick ... tick ... tick...

But there were no screams, no shouts, no slamming of doors, barking dogs, or clanging alarm bells.

Time was somehow stretching. He would just *have* to assume that there was no one in here, that the Manager lived alone. It certainly *looked* as if he lived alone.

Carefully, steadily, Colin moved on into the living room – step by careful step – waiting for the next crack or groan from the floorboards underneath. But there was no further sound as he avoided the macho leather sofa (bound to squeak if he sat on it) and settled carefully in the padded armchair that had a good sight-line of the corridor and the front door. With great relief he could see that his vantage point was out of sight of the living room window.

Steadying his breathing, Colin checked his watch. It was 8:25 a.m. and it had taken him twenty-five minutes to affect his entry. He wondered if he could become a professional burglar – and then decided that his heart could not take it.

His plan was basic, crude even, but borne out of panic and necessity. The postman would arrive sometime within the next hour according to his calculations. He would retrieve the envelope from the front door mat and beat a hasty but careful retreat back the way he had come.

Something hissed at the living room windows and when he looked across in alarm he could see rain sheeting at the glass. He remembered the earlier grumble of thunder. The sound of the rain still did not cover the ticking of that damned clock. He looked around, searching the room and everything within his sight, but he could see no such clock. He put his hand on his chest wondering if the sound might in some strange way be emanating from his heartbeat. Feeling ridiculous he snatched his hand away, and waited.

And waited.

Come on...

Tick ... tick ... tick...

Bloody postman...

Tick ... tick...
Come on...
Something bumped and then tinkled – from the direction of the lavatory through which Colin had entered the house. His heart lurched and he sat forward in the armchair, gripping the armrests.
Tick ... tick...
Another *bump*, another *tinkle*.
Colin swallowed hard and the sweat was on his brow and trickling down his spine again. Someone was moving back there.
Oh no! Now there was silence and Colin strained to listen. Be nothing! Go away! The rain continued to hiss at the living room window.
Bump! Tinkle!
Someone was letting themselves in through the back door. Those sounds could only be the sounds of someone fumbling to put their key into the back-door lock.
Oh my God—
It couldn't be the Manager coming back, having forgotten something. Could it? He'd left via the front door. But maybe he'd just remembered something he left at home and had taken a shortcut back through the back lane? Or perhaps it was his wife, or partner, or cleaning lady, or a relative? Or a real opportunistic bloody burglar?
Oh my *God!*
Colin stood up, moved quickly to the corridor and carefully – agonisingly – leaned forward to look back. But the angle of the corridor and his position blocked a clear view of the back door.
Bump! Tinkle!
Colin backed out of the living room, head craned sideways and keeping his eyes fixed in the direction of the back door, still unseen, while he reached for the front door handle. Thank God the Manager hadn't double-locked *that* door on his way out.
Bump! Tinkle...
Colin realised that he'd been holding his breath as his hand found the front door handle and he carefully twisted.

He hadn't been seen and he was going to get away – although what the hell he was going to do about that letter was something he was going to have to re-think when he was out and away. He exhaled as he felt the door open and rain sprayed into the hallway.

"Good morning," said a strange voice and Colin jumped back with a strangled gasp from the figure that was suddenly standing outside the front door in the rain.

"Oh sorry!" said the figure, who was obviously not the Quidstore Manager. "Didn't mean to frighten you."

The figure held out his hand.

"Not such a good morning really," continued the postman. "I'm afraid the rain has blurred the writing on the envelope a little. But I'm sure it's for you."

Colin saw his own hand outstretched, saw it take the envelope from the postman's hand.

"Thank you," said Colin in a small voice.

"You're welcome," said the postman, vanishing into the rain.

Colin looked at the familiar now rain-smeared purple envelope.

Behind him, the lavatory window catch – which had unfastened again – bumped against the window sill. The drawstring on the lavatory ceiling light swung in the resultant draught, its metal tip tinkling against the lavatory door.

"The Man..." said Colin aloud reading from the envelope in a flat and hollow voice. The "...ager" of Manager and "of the Quidstore" had been obliterated by the rain. But the address was still clearly legible.

Rain continued to splash on the purple envelope as he realised what had happened.

He didn't have to open the envelope to know that he had just delivered it to himself.

PEELERS

Ralph Robert Moore

OUTSIDE THE ICE cream shop's front window, snow falling like it used to, in childhood.

Whiteness, silence.

Hard to tell how many people passing by on the sidewalk are eel eyes. Hats, overcoats, chins tucked down, to where he couldn't see the faces.

But. Some of. Them. Are sniffing. Not. The snowflakes but. The glass. Window. Of this shop.

Irene sitting opposite him at their small wrought-iron table.

Their favourite restaurant. Where they first met. Yeah. She asked him this morning to meet her here, happy on the phone. Those large blue eyes that now always seem moist. Her bowl of vanilla ice cream untouched. He ordered French fries because the ice cream shop served them sizzling from the deep fat fryer. Crisp and salty, slicked with the reddest ketchup, burning his tongue. That was the way to eat French fries.

"So, I went to Dr Oster again? Guess what he told me!"

Hard to understand her since she's jumbling up her words, putting the verb at the end of each sentence as if she were speaking Latin. But he had a general sense of her question. "He told you some good news?"

"Good news?!" Hand reaching across the table top, a lover running across a field, for his larger meaner hand. "He said he now thinks my ovaries are okay after all!" She sits back, happily re-enacting with a rise of her head how astonished she was in her doctor's office. Where she had been sitting sad and alone, staring out the window at a tree. "Brandon, he thinks he can treat them! He thinks I'll be able to have babies!"

Once again, she's not putting her words in the right order and using far too many foreign phrases. It's confusing him. "You can have babies?"

"Yes!" All that pain showing on her face, from years of pissing on a pregnancy stick in so many bathrooms.

She's giddy. "Maybe, maybe I can finally be a mom." Head twisting to one side, face red, tears dripping. "And you can finally be a dad?"

And he sees. Out the window. Pretending to be just passing by. Quite a few eel eyes. Too many eel eyes.

A moment of sadness? Hidden of course from her and her excitement.

Big grin on her face. A kid again instead of a woman in her early forties. "Maybe we can have a baby!"

"I'm just ... overwhelmed. I have to go to the bathroom."

She laughs, looks puzzled, but spreads her right hand above her ice cream. "Sure! We'll talk when you get back." Drums her little knuckles on the white tablecloth.

She asked you once, shyly, not looking directly at you, if when you're walking away you would look back at some point, just to let her know that even though you're going somewhere else you're still thinking of her. So just before you disappear into the hall at the back of the restaurant you do turn around, see her give you a happy wave, nod back. Goodbye.

The restaurant isn't that large. The men's restroom is empty.

All employees must wash their hands after every visit.

You head into one of the two grey stalls, shut the door behind you. Peelers generally wear reversible clothes, jackets one colour on the outside, a different colour if you turn the jacket inside out. Same with shirt, trousers, even ties. You strip down. Fold your clothes, put them in a far corner of the stall where they won't be sprayed with blood.

Get down on your naked knees facing the toilet. Lift the lid.

The toilet itself is made of hard cold white porcelain. Perfect.

Start saying the words.

Raise your face above the toilet's front rim. Take a breath. Smack your forehead down against the hard porcelain rim. Raise your face, again smack your forehead down. Raise your face. Pink and red across the glossy white porcelain rim. Taste of blood in your mouth. Hands reaching up, you tap your fingertips around the split in your forehead. The split's too thin.

Smack! Raise up your face. That one really hurt. Blood in your eyes, dripping off your chin.

Fumble fingers up. Crack's much wider. Still saying the words you curl your fingertips under either side of the split in your forehead, pull both sides away from each other, cracking open a walnut.

God, that hurts!

But liberating.

Stand up, bleeding.

Peel the spilt sides of your head down to both shoulders. This next step requires some strength. Peel down with both hands, grimacing, peel all the way down to your waist, left side of your face hanging down by your left ankle, right side of your face hanging down by your right ankle.

Breathing heavy now.

The door to the restroom creaks open.

Footsteps.

Have to stop peeling because the noise is loud, and it's so unlike any other sound.

Piss hitting porcelain in the restroom's urinal.

"How's it going?"

You in the stall, unseen, half your face hanging above your left foot, half above your right foot. "Going good."

"You try the marinara sauce? *The Chronicle* said it's the best in the city but it didn't taste that fresh to me. Not that much brightness to it."

Your hands are red with your blood.

"Never tried it."

Chuckle, piss stopping. Starting up again. Stopping. Little bit more. Finished. "Well, don't. You've been warned."

Door creaking open. Closing.

Lift your left foot, pull off the left side of your body.

Lift your right foot. Peel off the right side of your body.

Peel off all that pain and sorrow and humiliation and frustration and joy and love of this body, this life.

Start at the top of your discarded left half. Using your fingers, push the scalp into your mouth, chewing, chewing. Hair, ear, left nipple, fingers, genitals, which came off on the left side, that frequently happens, all the way down to your toes, swallow. Swallow again.

Time to swallow your right side.

Afterwards, your newly emerged self drying, losing its rawness, hair sprouting along the limbs, you unravel white toilet paper from the silver dispenser screwed to the wall, lots and lots, the roll bouncing in its speedy unwinding, blot up the splotches of blood on the blue wall tiles, drop the flat paper intestines of toilet paper into the toilet, flush, watch your old self whirl down, clockwise and away.

Dress.

At the basin, wash your hands.

She's probably wondering what's keeping you. May be worrying. Anxious to talk some more about having babies.

You exit the public restroom wearing your inside-out clothes. Make your way unhurriedly down the aisles, passing tables, that's the way to do this, past hers, unrecognised, glancing down, seeing she still hasn't touched her ice cream, waiting for you. Melting in the bowl.

You feel bad for her.

But then you're outside, in the swirl, black night lowering onto the bright city streets, snow falling on your new hair.

Eel eyes everywhere. You were smart to peel. They walk right past, not recognizing you.

*

HE CAME TO on a cold sidewalk.

Realised someone was shaking his shoulder.

Cheek on the concrete, widened his eyes, trying to focus.

In front of him, a black high heel.

He looked up.

Dark-haired woman's face staring down at him, concerned. "Are you okay?"

Rain bouncing off the sidewalk. His clothes soaked.

"Yeah. No. I don't know."

She tried to hoist his height up off the cold concrete, small hands in his armpits, backing up in her high heels, but of course she couldn't. He slid one of his shoes under him, used that leverage to shakily rise, his weight falling against her raincoat.

She helped him down the city block to the glass door of an apartment building. Umbrellas passing behind them.

He leaned against the side rail of the rising elevator, shaking his head.

She in the opposite corner, petite and well-dressed, watching.

At her floor she helped him off, led him down the dark designs of the carpet to her door. Propped him against the green wall while she fingered through her keys, found the one she wanted, slid it into the keyhole's chin.

Escorted his body down the interior hallway, him careful his shoulders didn't brush any of her framed artwork off the white walls, to her bathroom. The floor was tiled, which made sense. If he's going to drip rain this was the best room for it. Easy to clean up tile.

Sat him down on her toilet.

Stark overhead light.

Threw his wet hair, contours of his face into relief.

Slid her raincoat off her dress, backwards. Laid it across the vanity. Really, she was very pretty. Dark hair, large black eyes, elegant cheekbones. "Someone has beaten you up badly. Or several people have done this. There is a lot of blood on your face and the front of your shirt."

He snapped his head to one side, eye swollen. "Is there?"

"Do you not remember?"

"I don't."

"We must get you out of your wet clothes. And you have to take a hot shower to bring your body back up to warmth. Can you undress and shower by yourself?"

He was becoming more aware of where his body hurt and what strength he still had left. "I can do that. Thank you. For taking me in."

"I will nurse you. But for now, shower. Clean yourself off. I have some clothes I think will fit you."

After she left, clicking the bathroom door closed behind her, he rose off the toilet. Removed his clothes, looking in the mirror above the vanity. At the large dark bruises on his body.

On the vanity, some oddly shaped bottles of perfume.

The hot shower felt good. He used some of her hair shampoo and conditioner. Wasn't sure if he was supposed to but...

Swiping his palm across the moisture on the mirror he saw his upper lip was split, his nose had a gash down the bridge, and his left eye was black and swollen.

Could be worse.

Ran his tongue along his top teeth. Everything intact.

Outside the bathroom door, a short square pile of folded pyjamas. He took them back in the bathroom, removed the towel wrapped around his waist. Put on the pyjama's stripes. Leaving the door open to get rid of the steam he rolled off some toilet paper, got down on his haunches to wipe up all the rain that had dripped off him. Flushed the wet bundles of white paper down the toilet.

She was sitting in the living room drinking white wine, watching TV. A comedy about mismatched people living together. The lead, wearing a chef's hat and an apron, asked the other cast members how to boil water.

She put her wine glass on the table in front of her, stood up. "You need to get some sleep, to heal." Crooked her little finger which he followed out of the living room, down a short interior hall to a small room with cardboard boxes stacked against the walls. And a bed. "You can sleep here. I've made it up. I will see you tomorrow."

He was tired. Exhausted. In a lot of pain. Thanking her, he turned down the white sheets. The smell of fresh starched linen. A woman's smell. When he looked back at the doorway she was gone.

Woke up, feeling more refreshed than he had in months. The sun streaming in from the room's window had already advanced across the carpet while he slept, shining a rectangle on the white wall.

He walked down the hallway, hearing kitchen noises.

"Ah! You're up." Turning back to her stove she clicked on the flame under a skillet. "I'm serving you scrambled eggs, because fried eggs are too much trouble."

He sat down at her kitchen table. "I really appreciate you taking me in."

Swirling a wooden spoon in the skillet she looked over her shoulder at him. "So why did these guys, whoever they were, beat you up?"

"I owe them money."

"Of course. And you don't have the money?"

"No."

"Why did you borrow the money from them?"

Big man with bruises, feeling embarrassed. "Drugs."

"Ah-ha." She brought over their plates, steam rising from the yellow curds.

He swallowed. "This is delicious."

"I use an extra yolk. My mother taught me that. Makes it more eggy. What drugs do you use?"

"Cocaine."

"Why do you do that?"

"I was trying to be happy."

"What do you do for a living?"

"I'm an emergency room physician. Mostly trauma cases."

"Well, that's good."

"What do you do?"

"I am a legal advocate for the poor. Mostly rent disputes and domestic violence cases."

He wished there were more scrambled eggs on his plate. They really were delicious. "We both help people."

"You are a peeler?"

The sideways scrape of fork tines across his plate stopped. "Why do you say that?"

"After you went to sleep I went into my bathroom, picked up your clothes from the floor to wash them. They were reversible."

WHILE HE WAS recovering at her apartment she'd get food delivered every few days and he'd prepare their meals. He actually was a good cook. Knew quite a few dishes, having lived so many lives.

One night after dinner, his bruises faded to yellow and really no reason for him to continue to stay there, he asked her to tell him about her life.

"You are interested?"

He was.

She put her fork down on her plate. Lit the one cigarette she allowed herself each evening. Her pretty profile. "I didn't know my father. He took off once my mother was pregnant. Not a guy who wants responsibilities."

"Do you hate him?"

She laughed. Which he realised just then she rarely did. "I have to know him to hate him David, and I never knew him. I don't know his story. Perhaps he had a reason? Perhaps not? It doesn't bother me. In a way, I feel kinder towards my absent father than I do towards my mother because I lived with her issues every day.

"My mother, she was a drunk. A functioning drunk. She held a job, and I don't think she ever drank on her job, but was always hung-over, which must have been noticed, and would frequently call in sick with the flu. The employed alcoholic's go-to excuse. I don't know why they didn't fire her. But I'm glad they didn't! That would have been rough for us, especially when I was a little girl. Somehow, although she always owed money to everyone, she always had some extra cash. She treated herself well. And treated me well. I would be the one who would have to walk down to the fish store and ask for two lobsters and tell the man behind the counter to put it on my mother's credit, which was ridiculous, stores don't really have open credit accounts anymore, but they'd usually nod and oblige, maybe not to embarrass this little girl, and my mother would give them some cash from time to time. And my mother and I would eat lobster that night. So it was good times.

"As I got older and met more people, girls my own age, and their parents, I came to realise my life was very different from theirs. Their parents were sober. They were responsible. They were not as close to their daughters as my mother was to me, the two of us living in this tiny apartment, fending for ourselves, but I preferred my friends' lives to mine. I studied hard in school to make my life better. Got mostly A's. When I became a teenager, I wanted to date but was too embarrassed to bring any boys back to my mother's apartment. She had gotten wide in the middle from her years of drinking, she walked around our rooms all the time in an old orange nightgown, and she would be so drunk she'd leave hamburger meat out on the counter and forget about it, to where it would have maggots by the time I discovered it, and a few times her stomach distressed from all the alcohol she put in it, she'd defecate on the kitchen floor before passing out in her bed. It was easier to clean up her mess from the linoleum than it would be from the carpet, but even so.

"I studied for the bar and passed it the first time. Got my own apartment, this one here in fact, but I only had her over once. She was drunk before she got here and got in a stupid argument in the elevator with an older couple I liked. Slurring her words, keeping her eyes closed too long, too often.

"She died two years later, my only mother, of liver complications. I saw her every day while she was in the hospital. Her last words to me were to call me an ungrateful cunt. But, you know. If someone calls you the worse thing they can, and you survive it, you lose respect for that person. They don't really know how to destroy you. They don't really know you."

Pain in her eyes, no tears.

He reached out his hand. Held hers. Palms covering her knuckles. First time he had ever touched her. She felt warm.

They decided he would stay on, renting the back room.

She offered to move the boxes out, put them in storage, but he said it was fine if the boxes stayed. Which they did. Maybe they both felt it wouldn't be that long before he moved into her bedroom, anyway.

It was different from any other relationship he had ever had. They'd wake up each morning in their separate beds, wander out to the kitchen, turn on the radio, and he'd start breakfast. During their days, spent apart, they usually phoned each other at least once, to check in. Just to talk, to hear the other's voice. The nights were special. Eating on the sofa, watching the news, a movie.

Their touches took time. Her light fingers on his forearm, his clasp on her shoulder, quickly lifted away. He was one of those men shy about touching a woman, unless it was clear she approved. Harder still with a woman whose hair was perfect, every strand in place. They both knew where they were headed and there was a peacefulness, in their quiet apartment, drifting there so unhurriedly, for a change. An aromatic raft floating down the river, flowers on both banks.

When that night did happen, and it was unplanned, they had been living together for a month. He was telling her some jokes he had found on the Internet, doing, he had to say, a great delivery, she was laughing, more wine poured, it was a Friday night, they both had the weekend free, rain started up outside their opened windows, they could smell it, and she leaned in, and up, and kissed him on his lips. Settled back down to her lower height, eyes opening, looking up at him. His arms around her thin back, drawing her up to him, her delicate hands behind his neck, stroking his nape, both of them shuffling sideways, towards her bedroom, clothes coming off, and he finally got to see her bare thighs, her small breasts, smell her hair, they were in bed, he was on top of her, big legs between her encircling legs, and after about ten minutes of fucking he came, she faked.

And he knew she faked.

And she knew he knew she faked.

"I need time."

He was so happy to have bedded her. To be this intimate with her. To be in love with her. "Take as much time as you need."

As it turned out, she never came with him. Not once. He didn't know if she had ever had an orgasm in her life. A subject she was uncomfortable discussing. "But you do enjoy it, physically, when we make love, right?" Her embarrassed readjustment on the sofa, wanting to change the subject.

"Of course I enjoy it, David! You can't tell?"

THEY MOVED UP the coast to where the higher-paying jobs were, city by the sea, long red bridge for suicides. It's good to start over.

Because this was a much larger city it held more eel eyes.

He first spotted them on street corners.

From a distance they looked fairly normal. But as you got closer you started to notice things. Clothes didn't fit quite right. Blank expressions. Hair that looked ... odd. And those eyes. Eyes that were too dark, pupils, irises and whites blurred together. As if it must be difficult for them to see. Like eels.

None of them appeared to speak. They moved funny. Walked, but never seemed to be going anywhere special. Sometimes, if his business took him back and forth across the city, he'd see one downtown in the morning, what looked like the same one judging by the clothes, uptown hours later, then back downtown as it was getting dark.

He tried to never be in close proximity to any of them because they frightened him.

Like walking around in a zoo where the animals have been let out of their cages.

One time, eating lunch in a restaurant between shifts at the hospital, he looked up from his table, soup and sandwich finished, noticed someone had seated themselves at one of the tables up front. After leaving the cash for his bill at the table he walked past the chairs towards the wide front windows. But as he got closer, something about the man sitting there, even though he could only see his back from this angle, and his silence, his not moving at all, made him slow his steps. He took a detour to the right, to another row of tables, so he could walk to the front of the diner from one row away, a little distance between them.

From this angle he could see the face in profile. Staring straight ahead. Skin pale, moist. Too moist.

Crowds passed by on the sidewalk just ten feet away on the other side of the front windows, which was somewhat reassuring, but of course no one in the crowd was looking inside the restaurant or paying any attention.

A lot of them were missing something. Eyebrows, or Adams apples. Or had too many fingers on one hand. One of them was accidently hit by a car. When it was brought to the emergency room for an assessment the physician, who found the accident victim to be alive but non-responsive, had the man stripped. Looking its body over for injuries he saw the man had no anus. On another occasion, a physician examining one found that man had no urethral slit for its penis. A third had no pores. The skin was smooth as milk. But each of these were treated by the different physicians as isolated cases. An oddity. No one ever made the connection.

HE AND YVETTE had a good life together.

She didn't want to have children, fine with him.

Always that emotional distance with her, the fact she would never have an orgasm with him, or even allow him to try, but over the years he got used to it. They still slept in the same bed.

He won some awards for his work in the emergency ward. She was named in different legal journals for some of the landmark cases she handled.

About the time they started thinking they should begin preparing for retirement, making sure they saved enough money each month, and invested it wisely, she woke up next to him one morning, smile on her face, finger raised as she cleared her throat, to indicate she wanted to say something, just give her a moment, and then she coughed up blood. Onto her lower lip, her chin. She wasn't aware of the blood at first, starting to talk about what food they should have for their upcoming wedding anniversary, but he stopped her, told her she had coughed up blood. She wiped the fingers of her right hand across her chin, looked at their under-pads. Puzzled.

"Do you feel okay?"

"Yes. I mean, I feel fine. You know?"

It was a Saturday. He kept an eye on her during the day, while they tended to their orchids, but she seemed okay. Both had forgotten about it when just as they settled in their chairs at the rear of their property, ready for some cold beer after planting seven lilac bushes, she leaned forward in her chair, threw up blood on her lap.

He made an appointment for her with their doctor. He went with her, reading magazines in the waiting room. Articles about people who had been clawed to death while they slept. Or found in elevators, large chunks of their bodies bitten, missing. Why would the physician's office not screen its reading material more carefully? When she came out, looking frail, she said their doctor had referred her to a specialist.

EACH DAY THERE were more and more eel eyes in the city and he could tell they were starting to become aware of him. Whereas before he could walk down a sidewalk and just pass by them, none of them noticing, now they lifted their heads at his approach, sniffing the air.

Before too long...

Time for the test.

Friday night. He found a spider during lunch at one of the pocket parks, tore off one of its legs so it was A Spider With Seven Legs. Put it in an empty orange plastic vial that the local pharmacy had used for his blood pressure pills.

When she got home he asked if she had heard from her oncologist. They were waiting to see if a biopsy came back positive or negative. She hadn't. And probably wouldn't over the weekend. Three more days of them worrying.

He poured her a whiskey. He already had one. Her face looked tired. From worrying, or from the cancer that might be inside her? Her face had changed over the decades. No pertness left. But of course, the same for him. He was developing arthritis in his right hand. Just had to flex his fingers, or try to pick up a penny, to see what it was doing to his dexterity. Hadn't mentioned it at the hospital because that would mean losing his position. But he knew Ian was already observing him more closely while he performed trauma surgery. Gretchen, too.

She took a long swallow. Sitting in her favourite living room chair overlooking the bay. "I know I'm drinking more than usual. More than I probably should. But once we know one way or the other I'll get back to normal. I will."

From behind her chair he massaged her shoulders. "I know you will."

Looking out at the bay, as his hands rhythmically rolled her head forward. "I'm not going to turn into my mother."

"Of course not."

"HEY, YVETTE, WOULD you help me, please?"

She got out of her chair, came into the kitchen, working on her third drink.

"They've got me on hold at the Thai place. Would you kill that spider, please?"

His spider. Shaken out of the vial onto their white counter.

He actually wasn't on hold; he hadn't called yet, just held the phone to his right ear as if he had.

The spider was motionless on the counter, looking around.

"David, could you kill it?"

"I'm on hold."

"I'll take the phone."

"Come on! Just kill the fucking thing. Use that magazine." Which he had placed on the counter a moment earlier.

"Oh..."

"Come on! Before it crawls away somewhere and we're uneasy every time we turn the lights on in the kitchen."

She took another long swallow of her drink. Picked up the magazine. "I really hate doing this."

"It's going to escape and hide somewhere. It could bite us in our sleep. Just kill it."

Her slap of the magazine down on the white counter missed the spider by an inch. It crawled darkly to one side, not as fast as if it had all its legs, but it was getting too close to where the counter met the wall, where it could crawl up, live on the ceiling.

"Yvette, kill it!"

Slapped the magazine down again, missed. The spider crawled its seven legs up off the counter onto the wall. Scurrying up. Slap. Almost out of reach, Slap!

She lifted the folded-over magazine away from the wall. No spider. Turned the magazine around. Flattened starfish image, black and yellow.

She threw the magazine into the trash can. "I didn't even get a chance to read it yet."

He felt bad. But he had to do the test.

And surprise, it didn't work. The eel eyes were still there, on the streets. The one person in this life he thought was most likely to love him had killed The Spider With Seven Legs, but the eel eyes were still moving along the streets, which meant she didn't really love him. Enough. No one he had ever met, fleeing across lives, had. Quite the doughnut to have with his morning coffee at the hospital.

So how much time did he have left in this life? No idea but not a lot.

Yvette didn't have cancer. The blood was a false alarm. They decided to celebrate at the first restaurant they went to when they arrived in the city, decades ago. While he was dipping his spoon into his crab diablo someone bumped the back of his chair pushing his head forward. As he tried turning around in his chair, he felt cold clammy hands in his hair, searching for ears, nose.

He got out of his chair, knocking over one of the lit candles onto the white tablecloth.

That waxy complexion, those eel eyes.

Tony raced over, pushed the eel eyes back, disconnecting its fingers from David's lips. "Dr Aronton, I'm so sorry! What's the matter with you?" Shoving the eel eyes back. "Who let you in here?"

Back at their home. Pouring herself a fresh whiskey. Taking that deep breath we all take at different points in our lives. "I lied."

His own fresh whiskey. "About what?"

The wide window in their living room was black since it was late night. The bay beyond unseeable. "The test came back positive."

"The...?"

"I do have cancer." Her small shrug. "I wanted us to have one more happy night before I told you. What is that noise?" Ears moving around.

He looked helpless.

"It is coming from the air conditioning vent, isn't it?"

He stared at the large grill above the hall leading to their bedroom.

"David, is it a rat? A huge rat?"

Echoing through the metal horizontal lines of the vent, bottomless clings and clangs of metal being heavily treaded. Getting closer.

"I'm going to get us some ice cream."

"You are doing what?"

He was getting confused again. She was using so many Latin phrases he couldn't parse what she was saying.

"We need to hang on to what was happy tonight. To make it last as long as possible. I'll get some ice cream."

"At this hour?"

"Frankie's is still open. They stay open until midnight. It'll be okay."

She used to complain, in their early years together, that he never looked back once he left her. So he made a point, this time, holding the front door open, to look back.

His wife of thirty-three years, standing alone in the middle of their white living room, already a little tipsy, like her mother. "Will you be long?"

His sadness. Which he hid quite well. Plenty of practice. Shook his head.

OUT ON THE darkening sidewalks, moving through the late-night crowds, some of those in the crowds swivelling around as he passed, sniffing.

He had nowhere to go so he did in fact wind up at Frankie's.

Bright lights inside, not too many customers, most of the

long aisles empty.

He wasn't going back to their home, wouldn't be ever again, so he didn't buy ice cream. Really wasn't in the mood to eat ice cream.

Music playing overhead. What was it? Took him a minute, passing the bins of green produce, displays of blue plastic-wrapped cartons of mushrooms.

Beethoven. The Waldstein sonata. Listening to the logic of the notes, their joy, created in an era when the world was different.

Swam down a random aisle.

An eel eyes, staggering down the aisle from the opposite end, towards him, boiled eyes blind, groping forward, hands knocking cans off the shelf. Nostrils lifted, sniffing.

And more behind him.

He retreated to the back end of the aisle, by the. Meat. Displays. Eel eyes on. Either side. Smelling. The air, fumbling. Forward.

He pushed through the Employees Only double doors.

No one back there.

Stacked cardboard trays. Mostly produce. Cantaloupes, bananas, avocados. Wouldn't do. Too soft.

But at the rear of the Employee Only area. Eel eyes feeling their way through the double doors. A stack of institutional-sized cans of plum tomatoes, imported from Italy.

Working quickly, you take off your reversible clothes.

Toss them in a corner, away from the stack of canned tomatoes.

Eel eyes sliming closer. Never before, in any life, had they gotten so close.

You raise your head up high. Bring it down against the hard metal circle of the institutional can's edge.

Raise your head, smack your forehead down again.

The words! You had to say the words.

Heart beating, trying to remember.

An eel eye drops his cold wet hand on your shoulder.

Whiteness the whiteness of white fish bellies.

What were the words?

More hands. Throat, back, crotch.

Not like this. Not this way.

Our fatter hue, heart in heaving, hollowed...

You bang your head down, but you can't peel. Bang your head down against the edge of the large can but you can't peel, you Bang! can't peel, your face bleeding, your blue eyes glistening with fright, strong fingers around your throat, dozens, white as the white of white bellies but you Clang! Clang! Clang! Clang! can't peel this time.

AN EYE FOR A PLASTIC EYE-BALL

Gail-Nina Anderson

THERE ARE FASHIONS in all things – Scott certainly knew that. One generation's cutting edge soon looks dusty and tired, then laughably outmoded and then, if it hasn't already been junked, comes that wonderful transformation into vintage, kitsch, collectable, suddenly worth looking at again.

That the principle might also apply to ideas hadn't really occurred to him. Since he had become, as he liked to put it, gainfully unemployed, he had happily scavenged the recent past for distinctive objects, the saleable discards of life. He had an eye, he thought, for anything teetering between the council tip and a profitable sale on eBay. But that ideas might follow the same pattern, emerging from the shadows, revived and transformed by the passage of time, wasn't on his agenda.

And he really should have guessed that something was going wrong, that there had been a subtle shift in the nature of reality, when he let himself into his sister's flat. Hearing his key in the door Sheila sang out rather too emphatically "We're here in the kitchen, Scott, having tea."

Tea at past 5:00 p.m.? Twenty years as an overworked school secretary ("Head's assistant, thank you") had left Sheila an unwavering wine-at-five kinda gal, except when the day had been particularly annoying and she had no recourse but to reach for the gin. Anything less alcoholic tended to be industrial-strength coffee, but tea? At least it was as near as dammit *teatime?*

A step to the kitchen showed him why. Perched precariously at the breakfast bar was a very small old lady, apparently wrapped in several layers of porridgy knitwear, including a high-necked jumper that almost swallowed her chin and descended to her knees.

"You remember Miss Stonecraft, don't you? She was at the school when we were both pupils there." The woman held out a hand that Scott was sure must be bird-like, except that it was encased in a woolly glove.

"Apologies for the wrappings but I do feel the cold so terribly these days. Age, you know – and I'm sure you're far too young to remember me."

It was a question disguised as a statement but Scott thought she could well be right. For a start she looked at least a hundred, and he certainly didn't recognise her from forty-something years back. Perhaps she'd taught one of those girly subjects that never came his way, like needlework or home economy or religious studies?

Sheila helped him out. "Miss Stonecraft had *my* job before she retired."

"Ever so many years ago, dear – but I've always kept in touch with the school. I like to think I might be a conduit between the happy past and the progressive present."

"There's some very sad news. Miss Fish has been taken ill and probably won't recover."

"*Certainly* not, I'm afraid," cut in their visitor. "Poor dear has been taken off into care and really isn't going to come back to her home. And as I'm her executor and have sole claim on everything she's left ... well, I thought best to get it sorted as soon as possible. There'll be more than enough to do with funeral arrangements and so on – but I've explained it all to your sister, and I've already stayed so much longer than intended in her lovely warm kitchen."

When she had left, after an excess of politeness and a seemingly impossible additional layering of woolly garments, Sheila paused only to open a bottle of wine before jingling a set of keys in front of her brother's bewildered face.

"*Goodies!*" she said, "well worth a pot of tea, though it was a bit of a shock seeing old Stoneyface on the doorstep like that. I was absolutely convinced she'd died several years back."

"Well *I'm* pretty astounded to hear that Miss Fish is still alive, even if only just. She was getting on when she taught us biology, and that was forty years ago."

He sipped his Cab Sav - it hadn't had time to chambre properly, but at the moment, instant gratification felt more urgent than taste. He called up the memory of their teacher, tall and flat, always wearing her white lab coat, ginger hair coiled up at the back of her head, pale eyes bright and bulging, as she tried to convey her enthusiasm for the inner workings of the formaldehyded frog. With an inrush of hindsight, it occurred to him she couldn't have been much more than forty back then, so yes, potentially still around.

Sheila echoed his thoughts. "Very much still around. She taught on beyond retirement age and the school had a devil of a job getting rid of her. Sat on every board she could, offered extra-mural biology courses, home tuition, organised charity events - and always with that mad certainty that science was *the way of the future*. Trouble was, *her* future never progressed much beyond the Festival of Britain."

"No later than the sixties, that's for sure. I can remember all those big colourful wall charts she put up, and the instructive glass and plastic things she used to produce with a flourish - 3D model of the alimentary canal, huge replica of the human eyeball..."

Once again Sheila jangled the keys in front of his face.

"And *that*, dear brother, is where you come in, thanks to Miss Stonecraft's over-anxiety to fulfil her dying friend's dearest desire. When she was finally booted out of the school lab she took absolutely all of that stuff with her. *We* were glad to see it go - nowadays we just sit the little sods in front of computer screens and pretend not to notice when they spend the session playing *World of Warfare*. But she apparently had a little lab set up in her house and wanted to go on working. I can remember her packing it all up, saying something like

'Well Rosalind Franklin didn't need computers to unravel the structure of DNA and I'm sure I can still manage something useful, even if the school regards me as a fossil'. I suspect she was thoroughly stuck in the past by then and never did catch up with the modern world, because her greatest anxiety in recent days had been that all her equipment should be left to the school where it might once again be of maximum use."

"But the school wouldn't even give it storage room?" Scott speculated, as the implications started to dawn on him.

"No, my poppet, and it would be silly to trouble it with an unwanted bequest when the keys to Miss Fish's house have been given directly to *me* with the heartfelt request that I arrange for everything relevant to be taken out straightaway."

"Before she's even dead?"

"She might well be dead already. She's not coming back and Stonecraft got so dithery about wills and distant relatives and solicitors and things that might be legitimately gifted when the owner was still alive, but could just end up on the tip once she was dead. In short, you've got a free hand."

She tossed the keys towards him. "Scavenge away. Just regard this as an early birthday present from your loving sister."

The next morning approaching Fish House, as they had irreverently begun to call it, Scott went over a familiar mantra in his mind. He wasn't without a conscience but since he had lost his job and come to rely on ad hoc second-hand trading to see him through, his ethics had become accommodatingly elastic. It was, he assured himself, really an act of charity to rescue anything of value from the house of the dead. And on this occasion, he'd been *invited* to do so even if the original owner's intention might have been slightly at variance to his own. No school would want Miss Fish's outmoded teaching aids but somewhere they would find a buyer – find a home. Curiosities always did – a museum of education or science, fun tat for a themed pub, post-modern chic for a shop window or a hipster's sitting room. He'd look through likely direct contacts first, then perhaps put items up on eBay, or maybe have a stall on Tynemouth Market. And in term time there might be vintage fairs on campus; students loved this sort of rubbish. He thought fondly of the day they had cleared out the old dental department of the medical school. He'd got there early, even before the art students who had come looking for arcane oddments to add character to their dreary installations. As the workmen had carried stuff to the tip, all the best things just went directly into his van. Amazing the allure of vintage false teeth; and the dentist's chair had made him a mint. It wouldn't be stealing he thought. Should he happen to find any cash or jewellery (though she'd hardly been the jewellery type) he'd leave it where it was - or better still, note it down and tell Miss Stonecraft it had better be removed for safekeeping. That would safeguard his own reputation for honesty, just as he was snapping up the unconsidered trifles of laboratory equipment. He appreciated how neatly things might be managed.

Fish House was Victorian in the most stolid and suburban manner, and apart from its comfortable size seemed remarkably undesirable. Ugly coloured bricks and a cracked stone porch, a neglected garden behind an overgrown hedge, small front windows with dull heavy drapes closely drawn. A potential doer-upper, though. He'd perhaps keep an eye open when it came on the market. You wouldn't get anything this size on a teacher's salary these days, but Sheila had told him that the place belonged to Miss Fish's grandparents, then to the elderly mother she'd nursed there until surprisingly recently, when the old woman had finally died at an absurdly advanced age. What with that and the scientific obsession, it stood to reason that the place was hardly resembled an advert from *House and Garden*.

Unlocking the front door, he waited for that surge of excitement familiar to all bargain hunters on the verge of a fresh opportunity. It didn't come. The door was damp and had to be pushed hard to open - he had a sinking feeling that the same damp might have seeped unnoticed into everything and destroyed his spoils before he even saw them. The narrow hallway was so darkly panelled that even switching on the light didn't cheer it up much. Doors to either side, a stairway up to, he thought, two more substantial floors, a kitchen at the back. He tried this first – some possibly antique Tupperware and some certainly collectable vintage Pyrex. China an undistinguished mixture, but some nice old sherry glasses that must have been handed down virtually unused. It was clearly a tea-and-biscuits place, with a microwave that spoke of quick ready meals and two – three – fridges that suggested an elderly owner stocking up on the same. Could he possibly appropriate the glasses and casserole dishes on the grounds that they looked a bit like lab equipment? Best not to try it. Not yet, at least.

He stepped back to the front rooms: looked like mother's bedroom and parlour. Big bed, portable TV on a trolley, dark furniture, overstuffed or spindly, knick knacks and doilies and deeply uninteresting lamps. No sign of jewellery; cavernous wardrobe, bare, except for some dusty furs. By the time Mrs Fish senior had died her daughter probably couldn't even give these away. Scott sighed. Funny how ethics had affected the market. He'd had some very nice ivory gaming pieces recently but had to sell them as "bone", which surely reduced the value.

The sitting room was a better bet, with ornaments that must have come from the previous generation. Lovely – some Staffordshire figures, a couple of ugly little Parian vases, a wooden tray with, under glass, a selection of bright-winged butterflies laid out in their deathly glory. The Victorians certainly didn't share mealy mouthed modern ethics, he thought. Perhaps grandfather had travelled, for there was an umbrella stand made from an elephant's foot and – joy of joy – two glass domes in which iridescent humming birds were eternally fixed in artfully constructed spirals of avian energy, as though fluttering around felt flowers and wax fruit. Now surely he might claim that these constituted biological specimens, hmm?

At that moment a noise interrupted his train of thought – something outside the room, a series of little thumps. Bloody hell, had there been any pets? No, surely those would have been taken care of. It came again – a scurrying? Mice or even rats in the kitchen, he thought, but the idea of any sort of company jolted him into a slightly queasy sensitivity concerning the legality of his own presence in the house. Better move on quickly.

There was no sign of movement as he mounted the stairs but he was suddenly aware of a school-room smell. Faint damp, yes, but surely that was formaldehyde, the pervasive aroma of long-ago biology classes? And – stronger now – chalk, that blackboard smell. Appropriate, he guessed, but unpleasantly ... retrospective.

The first-floor bedroom was small and undistinguished. A couple of lab coats among a tweedy wardrobe designated it as belonging to Miss Fish herself, a woman clearly without vanity. But the second door opened onto a space so large it must represent two rooms knocked together. Bingo. Miss Fish had effectively recreated her school lab, complete with all the charts and models and scientific glassware, in amazingly saleable wooden cupboards and display cases. Oh yes, there was the giant eye encased in plastic of a morbid fleshy pink, surely never manufactured since the fifties. The transparent torso, the cunningly levered model limbs, the charts of amoebae and dinosaurs and animal tracks. Even the rubbery uterus from which the coiled foetus could be removed to further illuminate the wonders of reproduction, though never via the birth canal as that might have deflected entire classes from the prospect of parenthood. All treasure – and even a skeleton hanging in the corner. He didn't remember that from school, but surely he could take it. The best replica he had ever seen. He reached out and took one bony hand. The wires that held it together cold to the touch but the bones surprisingly warm as he raised it for closer examination.

A noise, definitely more than a rat scuttling, a step, then some scratching and puffing, as though someone was bending down or getting up. Then a foot on the stairs.

"Is that you, Miss Anderson?"

"Er no. It's Scott, her brother. Sheila asked me..."

The tiny muffled face of Miss Stonecraft peered happily round the door. "Oh, what a good idea to get you to do all the work. I should have suggested it to Sheila myself. That will be your van outside, won't it? You'll be able to collect all the stuff from the lab in one go and take it away directly. I do so hate fuss."

Scott breathed out at the sheer luxury of being cast as the good guy. He caught the smell of chalk again, stronger this time, and noticed the powdery marks on the old woman's sweater – and fingers. She mistook his distraction and said reassuringly "Did you hear a little noise just then? I'm awfully afraid there might be rats"

"Lab rats?" he queried, aware that as jokes go this didn't, but it earned a smile anyway.

"Not these days, dear. I think she got past that stage years ago. But I'll leave you to your work. You'll know what to take won't you?"

Scott could only nod in complete agreement.

"I don't know if there's anything of interest upstairs. The second floor was a bit of a no-go zone, if you know what I mean."

"Lumber?"

"Probably. Anyway, I just popped in to check that it was all going to plan. I mean, to see if you needed anything but you're obviously more than adequate so I'll let you get on. I'm off to the nursing home. This morning she was still hanging on but only by a thread. It's the waiting that makes one so anxious."

After she had let herself out, locking the door behind her with the unnecessary caution that Scott unsympathetically associated with age, he took stock. It was okay – surprisingly so. He could load all this stuff into the van and Miss Stonecraft would be glad to see it go, the school would be grateful never to receive it, and he would profit from some well-placed sales. But was it worth investigating the upper floor? Would it be broken bedsteads and piles of old paper or might there be treasures? He took two steps upwards before something struck him about the décor. The carpeted pine stairs of the lower floors were replaced here by metal treads with what looked like a black rubber covering. The banister was metal too, and peering upwards he could see that the whole floor was closed off by a dark door.

His mouth went suddenly dry. Right, perhaps not. He had

the keys, he could always come back if he felt so inclined. Take what he'd found so far but now he felt too jangled to make a good job of it. There was no rush so first he'd help himself to a cup of instant coffee in the kitchen to set himself up for the task ahead. It was a relief to remember that the lower stairs were carpeted but as he descended there was a definitely a noise, as though something small was moving round and round.

Rats. He could take them in his stride. Indeed, if he saw one in the kitchen he'd throw it a biscuit. He had stepped down into the hall before he took in the changes. Since he had first arrived the rugs that had covered the floor had been roughly pulled back and on the wooden boards an elaborate and oddly unsettling design looked freshly chalked. A star in a circle, a disturbing confluence of angles and curves highlighted with abstract sigils that certainly didn't look scientific. So much for the lab equipment, he thought. He'd seen enough horror films to know that someone was dabbling not in experimental biology, but in the occult.

Out, now.

He fumbled for the keys he'd been given and turned them furiously but when Miss Stonecraft left it must have been a different lock she was operating and the door wouldn't budge. He'd call - he'd call Sheila - but the sudden crescendo of noise caused the phone to drop from his hand. From behind the doors on either side came not just the rat-like skittering but a series of ominous thumps, a dragging noise, a swishing falling sound and soft slitherings, the sharp explosion of breaking glass and the whirr of little wings. Instinctively he put his back to one door, trying to defend the safety of his territory, but from behind the other one he heard growls and screeches and the sound of claws scratching at the wood. He flung himself across the hall to keep it closed, but that left the first one under a more furious assault from inside. There was an ominous thump that got heavier and more complex, as though some heavy creature was flexing its growing weight, but worse was the furious fluttering and incessant barrage of soft bodies throwing themselves against the panels with an unnatural and terrifying force. Scott stood between the doors and watched the design chalked on the floor begin to *glow* in an unhealthy way. A rat in a maze, he turned desperately, but a clattering from the stairs froze him where he stood, his heart lurching painfully into his mouth. Then the noises, each one horrible in its own way, seemed to find a rhythm that brought them together. The effect was a pulsing chant from lipless voiceless things that should long ago have gone beyond death. Whatever was channelling their energy from dark places and abysmal depths, Scott knew then that the world of secondary school science had never even begun to cover it.

MISS STONECRAFT WAS well-known at the nursing home. It always warmed her heart to see how many former pupils had taken dear Miss Fish's teachings to heart and remained loyal. Of course, there remained two different camps, hers and Victoria's, but she supposed that if you'd taught biology for a lifetime you were bound to explain everything scientifically. And there was no doubt that the surgical experiments had been hugely useful, if sometimes a little inelegant. That wasn't *her* way but still, if the outcome was achieved... She ran her hand round her throat, sliding it inside the high neck of her sweater.

The receptionist smiled sympathetically. "Are those scars still causing you irritation, Miss S? You must let us find you some suitable lotion – after all, modern medicine is good for *something*."

They exchanged a smile as the young woman led her down a corridor and into a room where an elderly wasted figure lay on a neat bed. "She's been hovering near the threshold, but I think we have to classify her as clinically dead now. Are you quite sure..."

"Oh yes dear, you know that with *my* methods that won't be a problem – and I was having such fun with that stupid boy Scott. It should all be pretty much over by now. Unlike Victoria's science my murkier methods don't require precise timing. But I should quite like to be alone with her when..."

"Of course." She withdrew tactfully and closed the door. Miss Stonecraft sat by the bed and tenderly took her friend's cold hand. Miss Fish lay quite still for several minutes, then suddenly took a convulsive breath. Her hand began to feel warm and a blush of colour was apparent under the bluish white skin. Miss Stonecraft leant forward and whispered.

"I can't wait for you to wake up properly, Victoria dear. This time even *you* will have to admit that it was magic rather than science. One day I'm sure we'll find that exact border where they meet and overlap but meanwhile—" she smiled a secret little smile just for the woman in the bed "—it's the debate that keeps us going."

REMEMBER

Keris McDonald

I'VE HATED BONFIRE Night ever since I got this job. Well, not just the fifth of November to be honest. Bankside Rescue Centre is sited in Bradford, so that means the fireworks actually start with Diwali in October and go on right the way through November, then die off in December until it all goes mad again at New Year. It's like a bad night in the trenches sometimes - you wouldn't believe the noise unless you heard it for yourself. It's worst around Bonfire Night though, and every year I cross my fingers and hope for a wet autumn that'll keep everyone indoors. I hope it pisses it down for weeks.

It's the dogs, you see: they're terrified of fireworks. And it churns my guts to watch them cowering in the kennels, some panting so hard that they've almost gone into a trance, others flinching at every new burst and running around in tight helpless circles. They try and hide under the bedding. The worst cases just mess themselves. And there's nothing you can do about it because the poor bloody things are too scared to even notice your existence so you just end up in a knot of helpless resentment, wanting to go out and shove a maroon right up that idiot who's sending the barrage up three streets away.

It wouldn't be so bad if it *was* just one night, but that's a joke. Kids run riot in the streets for weeks, throwing air bombs under cars and into other people's gardens. My brother was on a bus when some dickhead teenager hopped on and set a lit rocket off down the aisle; he said there were little kids and pensioners in tears after that, they were so scared. I have no idea why the damn things aren't banned, I really don't. If it were up to me of course, there'd be a lot more than fireworks I'd crack down on, and teenagers themselves would be high on the list. Okay, I freely admit I'm not very tolerant of humans in general - that's why I ended up working with animals. Now *them* I never get tired of. Pat says that for an impatient bloke I'm an angel when it comes to doing the things no one can cope with - like cleaning out the kennels every day.

Pat is great. She's the one who set up Bankside Rescue Centre in the first place, and she works eighteen hours a day to keep it going. Most of that is spent trying to raise money of course, because we don't get any funding from the City Council or anyone. Me and Shell are the two who have to feed and muck out the dogs, then walk them all in turn, though we do get help from volunteers. We walk them down by the canal; that's the best bit of the day to my mind. Pat does the paperwork and the worrying about where the cheques are going to come from.

You see, unlike a lot of dog homes we don't put our dogs down just because they've been here more than a few weeks. That's why Pat set up her own place, she says - she just got so angry about the waste of lives in some of the big rescue centres. There, it's a month's reprieve and then if no one wants you you're for the chop. All very humanely done of course. But here every dog gets to stay for as long as is necessary to find it a new owner. I suppose that's why the place is so expensive to run - it makes for a lot of vet's bills. And it means we're always full despite having thirty kennels, all of which will take two dogs. It's a lot of work but I wouldn't want to do anything else, and believe me I've tried some right jobs in my time. I've cleaned Portaloos and patrolled carparks and done a bit of building work. Driven a forklift for a supermarket. Delivered scaffolding up and down the A1. It's all crap. This job at Bankside pays the worst of the lot but I get to do something I like, so it suits me. Of course, I'd love a dog of my own for a bit of company at nights, but my landlord won't allow one in the flat.

Pat knows just about everything there is to know about dogs, I reckon, but even she couldn't explain about the fireworks when I brought it up over our pre-start brew-up in the office one day. It was a wet foggy October, not yet turned frosty so we all had head colds. And it had been a bad night all over town.

"Why is it that dogs are so scared of fireworks?" I asked.

Pat has grey hair that always looks a mess because she runs her hands through it. She looked up from her desk where she was reading the local paper, her head propped up on her arm. "It's the loud noise I suppose," she said. "They've got such sensitive hearing."

I shook my head. "I thought that but I was walking Deefer down to the bridge today and this bloody big lorry came roaring up behind us, engine gunning, all stinking of diesel, and he didn't turn a hair. Just looked at it. But I know he freaks when he hears fireworks."

"He's scared of thunder too," Shell said from where she was sat against the radiator reading *Dogs Today*.

"Isn't that weird, don't you think?" I asked. "Thunder never hurt any dog. I mean lightning might, but if you got hit by lightning you'd never hear the thunder. But they're just about all scared of it."

"And what about Andy?" Shell agreed. Andy was a lurcher and an ex-poacher's dog, as we'd had confirmed when we'd got a bloke around with an air-pistol to shoot the rats that summer. "He likes the sound of gunshots – he goes all doo-lally for it. But he hates fireworks."

Pat sat up straighter, frowning. "Maybe it's something we can't hear. Maybe the thunder has the same resonance as a dog growling."

I twisted my chipped RSPCA coffee mug. "And the fireworks? I've noticed it's not the ones that just go bang that are the worst – it's the whiz-bang of the rockets. The ones that go *skreeeeee!* before they explode."

"Well, most dog instincts are carried over from wolves," Pat said. "Perhaps it reminds them of something they feared back before domestication. Some predator, though I admit I can't imagine what sort of animal could make that noise. Owls?"

"Wild boar," I suggested. I'd worked in a sow unit one winter and the noise you get off an angry pig beggars belief.

"Nazgûl," said Shell with relish. "Or velociraptors." She watches far too many films, does that girl and it messes with her head. I don't like fiction myself though I've got lots of books in my flat. You can find all sorts of stuff in charity stores.

"Now Shell," I told her, "there wouldn't be any dinosaurs around when dogs evolved." She stuck her tongue out at me. "'cept maybe plesiosaurs in the lakes," I added, thinking about a paperback I'd read recently. *Alien Animals*. It had been quite good. "Scientists think that perhaps the Loch Ness monster is a prehistoric marine reptile, you know."

Shell shook her head and stuck it back in the magazine.

"Well I doubt we have to worry about dinosaurs roaming the streets of Bradford," Pat said with sigh. "A good job too or we'd end up having to re-home them as well."

I went out to open up the outdoor runs and give the dogs their feed then. They get fed twice a day, mostly on a basic biscuit meal though there are some that need special diets if they're nursing pups or whatever. I like feeding times; dogs are always so grateful for food. *Same old biscuit again*, I tell them but they dance about and wolf it down like it was steak.

I have my favourites naturally. It's impossible not to. Sometime I'm quite sorry when a dog gets adopted by a new owner though I know it's the right thing. Doesn't stop me feeling blue when I see them drive off in the back of a car though. Then I go back and there's always another one needing a ball throwing for it in the wire run and I feel a bit better.

This time though things were not normal. I opened the door to the inner corridor and was greeted by what I took for the usual chorus of canine bellows but when I looked into the first cubicle, where Buttons and Bella - one piebald elderly Staffie, one brindled ex-racing greyhound - should have been waiting eagerly, I was surprised to see only Buttons, who was pressed against the door and whining softly. There was a strong stink of piss in the cubicle, and the hatchway to the outer run was open. My first reaction was to be annoyed; I knew I hadn't left the hatch open last night so I assumed that Shell had. Then I started to feel worried - even if Bella had strayed out into the cold she should have come back in to greet me. And Buttons was acting strange. I hurried round to the outside.

Each of our kennels has an inner and an outer half connected by a hatchway. The inner stays warm so they're locked in there for the night, and the outer is where - hopefully - they go to dump. Out there they can see each other through the heavy wire mesh walls between the kennels, but the roof keeps the rain off. When I went out that morning it was immediately obvious something was wrong. The outer door to Buttons' run was solid up to waist height, mesh above, so that visitors could look in at the dogs. The mesh half had now been peeled back to leave a gaping triangular hole - and there was no sign of Bella.

I swore and grabbed at the mesh, wiggling it back and forward like a loose tooth trying to work out how it had come free. My first fear, that it had been clipped with heavy-duty cutters, was proved wrong. It turned out the ends of the wire were still intact and had been pulled loose from their staples. For a moment I thought that Bella had pushed the wire loose herself and made a bid for freedom, and that fear was still bad but a different sort than before. Then the fear flipped over again to expose its first face, as I realised that it was the top corner of the wire that was loose. Either Bella had stood up on her hind legs and pushed at a height of about seven feet from the ground, or she'd taken a flying leap and gone through the fence like a cannon ball.

Then I saw that the connecting hatchway had been ripped off its splintered runners.

I went back to Pat with a feeling in my guts like I'd eaten a very bad vindaloo. "I think we've had a break-in," I said. My voice sounded strange to me. "Bella's gone."

Every animal home has the occasional break-in, I reckon. Thieves are usually after expensive purebred types that can be resold on the pet market, and at least then you've got some hope that the animals will end up in a decent place. More sinister is when it's the mastiffs or bull terriers that go, then you really feel that cold pain in your guts because you know they're headed for an illegal dogfight somewhere and there's no hope at all. That just makes you feel sick. Why someone should steal a greyhound though, I didn't know. They're ten a penny round here. Poaching maybe? Or I suppose Bella was still young enough to be a possible goer on the flapper tracks. I didn't want to think about the other possibilities.

Pat rang the police once she'd confirmed my suspicions. She has a sympathetic contact at the copshop; PC Warren is a dog-handler and teaches obedience classes in the evening, plus he's taken a couple of Alsatians off our hands in the past. He promised to put the word out and told us that if we saw anyone suspicious on site he'd come straight away, but he didn't send anyone down. It's not like in the movies where they come out and fingerprint at the drop of a hat. Shell snuffled into her hanky and petted Buttons, who leaned against her and shivered. I wondered what he'd seen.

I spent most of that day hammering extra staples into all the kennel frames, though without much hope that it would act as more than a deterrent to future attempts at theft. To make the place actually secure would take a hell of a lot more money than we have. When night fell I arranged to stay on late and sat up in the office where I could keep an eye on the dark bulk of the kennel building, well enough to spot any movement anyway. I assumed that the dogs would start up their usual racket if anyone did approach but it was quiet all evening except for the sporadic ack-ack fire of rockets shooting into the drizzle. At nine I did a round of inspection, found everything undisturbed and set off home on my bike leaving the office light on.

The next morning was much, much worse. I got in early and went straight to the kennels without pausing to put the kettle on but I found Shell had beaten me to it. I wish she hadn't; the girl was in tears as she leaned against the mesh.

This time whoever it was had come in through the roof of the run ripping back the tar-paper and prising up the wooden boards to leave a gaping hole. There should have been two dogs in that kennel: a Rottweiler bitch called Zoë, who had a face like Mike Tyson and the character of Little Orphan Annie, and a trim Jack Russell called Jamie, who was convinced that he was really a twelve-stone warhound that everyone else in the kennel feared. Neither dog was there – but there was blood spilt on the concrete and hair matted into the blood.

I stared at the dark splashes on the floor and the thick clots clinging to the jagged edge of the roof, and I felt my throat fill with helpless fury rising up like vomit. I was still swearing a blue streak when Pat arrived but I shut up when I saw her ashen face and her mouth worked into a little twisted line. I just wanted to crawl into a hole then. I'd tried to protect her from this and my vigil had failed.

"I'm staying overnight," I told her at lunchtime as we sat and picked at our sandwiches. No one had much appetite.

"They won't be back a third night in a row," Shell mumbled.

"How do you know?" I demanded. "You willing to risk that again?"

She didn't reply.

"You could be right," Pat agreed listlessly. "We should take it in turns to keep watch."

"No," I said flatly. "Don't be stupid. You might get hurt. I'll do it."

She frowned at me then and asked slowly "What are you planning to do, Mike, if someone does turn up?"

"Oh, I'll call the police," I said looking her straight in the eye.

She blinked first. I'm sure she didn't believe a word I'd said but she just looked away and murmured "Okay. Be careful, Mike."

Call the police? Fat chance. If PC Warren was on duty okay, *then* there was a faint possibility of getting a response, but not in time to stop anyone escaping the site. And the reality was that there wouldn't be anyone available to help, that they were stretched too thin on a Friday night, that the theft of a dog was low priority, that the police didn't really give a shit. No, there was no point in relying on the boys in blue. I didn't have a very detailed plan and any notion of what the consequences might be were deliberately pushed aside, but I did know that it involved beating the living crap out of anyone I caught that night.

There were some pieces of battered scaffolding behind the big dog run that I'd scrounged off a skip when we were painting the office exterior. I chose a piece and took a hacksaw to it, cutting myself a length about as long as my leg. All I had to do was bind one end with cloth to make a good double-handed grip and then I was ready.

When night fell I waved the others off, locked up and eventually went into the interior kennel corridor. I was wearing my coat but it was warm enough anyway since all the wall-heaters were on for the dogs, and they lit the building with an eerie red glow. I sat myself down upon a pile of newspapers and waited for the tumult to die down. The dogs will bark at any human just to get attention but as I sat quietly they eventually grew bored and settled, all except Maisie at the far end who was crying softly to herself like a grieving mother. The noises from outside grew more distinct: the muted hum of traffic, the patter of drops from the overhanging trees, and of course the pop and fizz of distant fireworks.

After some time – my arse was getting numb by then – the fireworks suddenly started up much closer and louder. I bit my lip trying to listen to the noises between the explosions, trying to ignore the dogs who instantly started to whine and pant. I had no idea what time it was and the light was too dim to read my watch face, so I pulled the torch out of my pocket and played it across my wrist. It was only eight, though it would be midnight dark outside – or as dark as it could get in the city at this time of year. Under the sodium glow of the clouds great blossoms of golden sparks would be opening and falling as little rockets from domestic gardens went whizzing their pathetic few metres into the haze to cough out magenta lightning balls and the expensive cluster bombs from organised displays stuttered across the sky with gunpowder crashes that shook your teeth. My torch flicked briefly down the length of the corridor reflecting in the eyes of the dogs; sixty pairs of green lamps staring at me, frantic and beseeching and wordless. The smell of dog-breath from their concerted panic was bitter in the warm air.

So chaotic was the sound all around that I nearly didn't hear the crack of breaking wood. It was the sudden breath of cold air that drew my attention. One cubicle up from where I sat, Deefer suddenly leapt to his feet growling. I staggered up from my uncomfortable couch as quietly as I could and in the submarine glow approached the barred door. The hatchway to the outer run was gaping open – and something black clung to one edge. Deefer and his kennel-mate Lucy were flattened against the side of the pen, hackles bristling, staring at the opening.

Something dipped into view through the hatch and there was a noise.

I read once that tigers are supposed to be able to roar at a frequency so low that the subsonic vibrations scramble the nerves of their prey, who are temporarily paralysed. Maybe that's what happened with the noise in that kennel because I've got no other explanation. It was loud all right but I've heard louder – a descending plane makes more racket. It was the way it went *through* me that I can't compare to anything else; I felt it hit my guts like a blow and for a moment I just stood, stunned as a rabbit in the headlights, and watched as a hand slid in through that hatch groping toward Deefer. It looked, in the gloom, like a human hand but it was much larger and the arm that followed it was impossibly long for a man. Just as the hand closed around Deefer's neck the shoulder and head of the thief came into view too. I think it was that – or maybe the sight of Deefer flopping to the floor with spasming legs – that shook me out of my stupor just enough for me to flick the torch back on and shine it straight into its face.

It wasn't human. It looked a bit like a man but it wasn't. Its skin was shiny and dark, and its face— I didn't see any eyes or nose, just folds of skin like wet leather, leather that's been left out in rain till it gets that film of slippery mould. It looked – I tell you – like those bog-men they've got in museums, the ones where the bones of the corpse have dissolved to mush and all that's left is the folded wrinkled peat-stained skin. But it did have a mouth because as the light hit it, it opened a hole like a wound and screamed at me.

I screamed back – the dogs screamed too – because the pain in my head was like a bloody explosion going off. But it broke my fear wide open and I was already reaching for the door-bolt before I'd opened my eyes again. I dived for that vacated hatchway, my scaffold-pipe and torch both thrust in front of me. I'm a biggish man and it was no easy exit but if you can squeeze something the size of a retriever like Deefer through that hole you can fit my shoulders too. I scrambled out into the wet darkness, caught the glisten of slick leather in the flashing beam and brought the pipe down on it as hard as I could.

I don't think it did have any bones, not from the soggy way it folded up around the rigid pipe, like sacking soaked in tar. No bones or joints maybe, but it had rawhide arms that whiplashed around and bony nails that laid my face open. I staggered back then rushed in again, so high on fear and rage that I wasn't even feeling any pain. But it was way faster than me and had hooked itself up through the top of the broken outer door before I could swing. The pipe bounced off the wire and I dropped it as the vibration jarred through my arms. Then the sky lit up in a blaze of green rain and for a moment I saw it silhouetted there. Just for a moment. Then it leapt into the tree branches, screamed again, and was gone.

As I sat down hard – that hissing *skreeee!* still ringing in my ears – my hand fell onto Deefer's broken body.

I'VE THOUGHT ABOUT it a lot since but I still don't know what that thing was. I have to assume there's no scientific name for a thing like that – it's a forgotten beast. But I reckon it's old; it's a survivor. It must have been around for a long time, back thirty thousand years ago I should think when men were just tempting wolves to come and sit near the fire. There can't be that many of them left but there must be a few. I think I can work out some things about them, having seen it with my own eyes even if only for a few seconds. It wasn't much bigger than a man and most of that height was in its spidery legs and arms. So I'd say it's nocturnal and it lives up off ground level, probably on the tops of buildings now. It's a climber and a leaper. What does it live off? Mostly cats I should guess – thousands of them vanish every month across the country, many more than ever get handed in to rescue centres or end up squashed on the roads.

Why hasn't it been discovered? Well, my thought is that unless you see it moving it doesn't look like anything you'd recognise as a living creature. If you found the corpse of one of them bundled up by a factory chimney, picked at by the seagulls, you'd assume it was just some piece of unidentifiable industrial rubbish.

It – the bogeyman, Grendal, whatever you want to call it – it's a scavenger and an opportunist. It uses its voice as a weapon. It isn't brave. That one's never been back to the kennels since I smacked it one. But it's best not to be too cocksure. There are supposed to be thousands of people missing in this little country alone, at any time. They must have gone somewhere.

I know I sleep with the windows shut these days.

BROKEN BILLY

Adrian Cole

TRETHEWY, A BIG man even for a farmer, listened at the bedroom door. The voice of his nine-year-old son Bran came clearly, the multiple conversations rapid, uncannily natural. Trethewy never mocked the boy; Bran was a mite odd, locked up in his fantasy world. He eased the door open. Bran had several of his toy playmates around him, sitting astride their plastic farm vehicles or herding a bizarre mixture of animals – cows, pigs and sheep to dinosaurs and lions. Their incongruity was irrelevant to the boy.

"Tea's up."

Bran nodded, gathering the inhabitants of his manufactured farm landscape and putting them carefully into the battered trunk he kept under his bed. Satisfied they were secure he went out to the kitchen.

Bran ate well. If Beth, his mother, could have seen him she'd have approved his healthy glow. The boy would need plenty of meat on him when he was older. Farm work was getting more demanding. Trethewy just wished Beth were alive. He shied from the thought and the darkness it always brought.

"Ivor Stricker's coming tomorrow. Doing some planning with me. Tracey's coming too."

Bran made a face. Tracey was a girl.

"You be civil to her, mind. After school I'll get you a new toy."

Bran's expression was a mixture of pleasure and annoyance.

"Okay, I know they're not *toys*, Bran. So ... deal?"

"Deal." Bran smiled, content.

TRACEY STRICKER WAS a pale gangly creature, eight-years old, her oddly wide eyes staring like she was always apprehensive, expecting the worst. She'd met Bran a number of times and they'd exchanged a few muttered words, but no more than they had to. Bran avoided looking directly at the girl, gesturing for her to follow him out on to the porch. It was a bright day in late September, warm enough to play outdoors. Bran slouched uncomfortably. "What do you want to do?" he said.

She shrugged. "Don't mind." She was clutching a doll. It looked pretty old, its dress threadbare in places. One arm was barely attached, sure to come loose before long.

"You got more dolls at home?" he asked.

"Yes but this is Mary. She's always with me. She's special."

Bran looked around and kicked the grass before saying "You got corn dollies?"

"Oh yes, quite a lot. I've made some but I'm not very good."

"Want to see mine?"

Her eyes grew even wider. "You've ... made some too?"

He nodded. "These are my best ones yet." He pointed to a barn.

She followed him, her doll clutched to her chest, its button eyes as wide as hers as though equally as excited. In the barn he ushered her to a space between stacked bales of straw rising up to the high roof. Sitting on the bottom one in a neat and tidy row were several small dolls, all fashioned from corn stalks, dressed in simple material with bright hats and woollen shoes.

Tracey gasped. "They're beautiful!"

Bran was mildly embarrassed though pleased.

"You made them yourself?"

He nodded. They stood together looking at the dollies, not needing to speak. Eventually Bran pointed to Tracey's doll. "Mary's arm's damaged."

Tracey hugged the doll tighter. "Mm. She needs extra care."

Bran seemed to be struggling to say something. He looked away and back again a couple of times. Finally he got up the nerve to speak his mind. "I could mend her."

At first Tracey drew back as though the idea of letting anyone else touch the doll was unthinkable.

"I won't hurt her," said Bran. "I promise."

It seemed as if she would run off but after a few moments she gently handed the doll over. He took it carefully and spoke to it, his words so low that Tracey didn't hear. But she smiled. It was to be the day when everything changed.

FOR THE NEXT few years Tracey visited the Trethewy farm with her father as often as she could. Bran never completely overcame his shyness, but he opened up a little to her. After he'd repaired her doll that first day he'd gone on to show her more of his corn dollies and as he grew more confident over time he showed her the scarecrows he'd made for his father's maize fields. Bran was gifted at the art and most of the farms in the county had examples of his creations.

"They're scary," she told him.

He gave her a rare grunt of laughter. "They're supposed to be! Crows and gulls and the like need to be chased off."

"It's the way they move. Creepy," she persisted. Something he did to the joints made them react to the slightest breeze, their heads nodding, their arms rising and falling like unfolded wings.

"Wouldn't scare the birds otherwise."

One day he'd taken her to the barn and showed her one of his trunks. He had a number and she knew they were very private. It was a rare honour to be allowed to see what was in any of them. He dragged it out and unfastened its leather straps. She peered inside uneasily, expecting there to be some terrible secret here.

"Broken ones," said Bran. "I never threw any of my toys

away. I've outgrown them now but I still try to mend them when I get time."

"Then what do you do with them?"

"There's always kids who'll have them."

She saw the mixture of figures and animals, some missing limbs or with damaged heads, some partially repaired. She wasn't surprised he'd kept them. His love of animals and the way he tended them extended to this odd collection. She'd seen him nurse an injured fox back to health once, amazed that he could have any sympathy for an animal that could be a scourge to local farmers.

"You could start a business up one day," she said. "You're magic." She looked embarrassed for a moment, then giggled.

He smiled. "Maybe. But my life will be spent on the farm. My dad won't last much longer. He's never been right since mother died. He takes pills for his heart." Although he spoke pragmatically she sensed it was with an effort, his face masking deeper bruised emotions. Bran rarely spoke about his mother or the cancer that had killed her. Something that no one had been able to fix.

He straightened, forcing a smile. "I do have a bit of magic though. Want to see some?"

She nodded, her hand to her mouth as though she couldn't trust herself to speak.

"Come with me then. Mind you this is secret stuff. No one knows about it, not even father."

She followed him out of the barn and up a sloping field into the sunlight. Above them was a long hedgerow, its bushes higher than most obscuring the field beyond. Tracey knew those fields were usually fallow, overgrown with meadow grass. Not even the sheep were sent out to graze there. Another barn, less well tended and partially derelict, formed a kind of gateway. As they reached it Tracey drew back, suddenly cold. She trusted Bran and knew he'd never do anything to hurt or disturb her but something wasn't right about this place.

"Feel it?" he said, grinning.

"It's not nice. I don't want to go any further."

"It's okay. I put it there. It's a barrier. No one goes near this barn, not even the animals."

"What's inside?"

"It's empty. It's what's on the *other* side. It's a big field. You can only get into it through the barn, but my spell puts everyone off. The field is private."

She frowned at him. "What kind of spell?"

"Earth magic I call it. Just using what's natural. Wicca. Oldest medicine in the world."

"You're spooking me. I want to go back."

For the first time ever, he reached out and held her hand. "No, it's okay. Really. It's not evil. It heals and protects and stuff."

She gripped his hand tightly. It was the only thing that prevented her from running.

"Trust me Tracey," he said although the words were an effort. He'd never pushed himself this far emotionally before. Her answer meant so much to him.

"Okay," she said, the word almost lost.

They entered the barn through a narrow door and stood for a long moment in its enveloping shadows. It was uniquely still and silent, and colder than it should have been, she thought. She still held Bran's hand. It was warm and she could feel a current of energy transferring into her, his determination to reassure her. On the other side of the barn, visible through an open large doorway, they could see the lower slopes of the field. It rose up steeply on all sides like a huge amphitheatre, its thick tall grasses shifting restlessly in a breeze that had sprung up. Tracey stood very still, like a mouse looking for the safest way through the grass, watching the skies for swooping danger.

Bran was in no hurry, letting her study the view. "I call it Secret Hill."

"It is magic isn't it?" she said. "I can feel something. It's like ... a window. Somewhere else."

"I knew you'd understand. Look, there's one of my friends."

She stared up to where he was pointing and drew closer to him, her chest tightening with unease. It was one of his scarecrows.

"Sometimes they don't quite work," he said. "And others get damaged. That one up there is called Jazzle. He was attacked by crows. Don't know why. It was after a storm and his arms got bashed and broken by the wind. He reckons the crows knew and took advantage. Their revenge."

Tracey nodded seriously. Somehow coming from Bran the words made perfect sense.

"You saw my box of broken toys. Well this is like that. It's where I bring the scarecrows that aren't right or have got broke. Some are old and have been chucked away. I rescue them."

"How many are there?"

"Come up the hill and I'll show you."

Although she couldn't quite rid herself of the feeling of unease, she let him lead her up to the higher meadow and from its crest they could look around them at the silent valley. There was no sign of a bird, even high up. Tracey studied the scarecrow Bran had called Jazzle, some dozen yards away. It had been hung up, its arms draped over a cross-piece of wood, its head lolling on one side, bizarrely like a man with a broken neck. Its face was made from sack-cloth and Bran had meticulously shaped it in such a way that it had clear features. For eyes it had two shining coins or discs. In a swirl of the breeze the head swung gently round and Tracey jumped.

"It's watching me!" she gasped.

"He," corrected Bran. "And he's okay. You probably frightened him more than he scared you. He saves the really scary stuff for the birds."

"But ... you don't grow anything here," she said looking around her at the meadow grass and lush patches of weed.

"Jazzy isn't ready to go back yet. And you're wrong. Look at the flowers. Up here we don't think of them as weeds."

She realised as he said it that the whole meadow was peppered with wild flowers, their bright colours showing through the grass. She laughed softly. He took her to meet other scarecrows: Megg and Mara, the twin girls who'd been caught in a fire and rescued barely in time; Verdun, the soldier who some loutish kids had used for catapult practice;

and Oddwick, the clown who'd been stolen by a circus hand and stripped of his clothes and buried.

"The roustabout wanted to be a clown and with Oddwick's clothes, he saw his chance."

"What happened to him? The roustabout?"

"Didn't work out," said Bran glancing up at the dangling shape of the clown. Bran grinned as though there was a private mystery attached to this. "I cleaned Oddwick up and repaired him and gave him some new clothes."

Tracey nodded. Oddwick's shirt and jacket were a blur of colours, all checks and big dots, sewn together randomly. His trousers were striped, his thick hair lavishly bunched behind grotesque ears and his face painted in a typically exaggerated clown's grin. He winked at her and a bubble of laughter broke from her lips.

"I like him," she said.

"He's a bit nervous of people after what happened. He wants to make them laugh. It's why he was created even though he's a scarecrow. It took me a while to teach him to frighten the crows but I told him they're friends of the kids with catapults who hurt Verdun. Oddwick and Verdun are good mates."

"Will they go back to their original owners?"

Bran guided her down the hill away from the standing shapes where they couldn't be overheard. "I think they'll probably all stay here now. For the first time they're happy. They have each other – and me. And you if you want," he added hesitantly.

"Oh yes. I'd like that Bran. They're like real people."

BRAN'S FATHER DIED a year later. There was a brief service at the local church before he was buried in the small cemetery next to the grave of his wife. Bran said it was for the best, it was what his dad wanted, to be back with her. Bran inherited the farm and everything attached to it. He flung himself into working it, determined to do as much of the labour himself until Tracey persuaded him to hire two other men to help him temporarily. They were energetic young men, labourers from the town, and they set to with a will and by the time they left a few months later the farm was paying its way. Bran saw little of Tracey. She'd sensed his withdrawal and wasn't sure how to break back into his world.

Eventually the decision was pushed on her. She came to Bran's farm one spring morning, driving the battered old car her father had bought her for her eighteenth birthday. Bran hadn't seen her for over a month and as he stepped down from the farmhouse porch to meet her he smiled, something of his former self restored to his face. "You look very..." The words tailed off.

She was used to it even now and smiled back at him. "You seem more like your old self."

"Yeah, I'd been a wreck. Got to get on though."

You mend things, she thought. Now you need someone to mend you. She blushed at the idea.

He noticed her left arm was bandaged from the wrist upwards, the dressing partly hidden by her sleeve. "Have you had an accident?" He went to her instantly concerned.

"Sort of."

He stood close to her, hugely embarrassed, unsure what to do.

"It was Billy," she said as though the name would explain everything. She could see Bran was bemused though. "You remember? You made me a scarecrow for father's farm."

He nodded slowly. "Yes ... a while ago. Wasn't he the one I got at the County Fair? I called him Broken Billy. His back was rotted out and half the straw was gone and he only had part of his face. I didn't think he could be mended but you insisted. Has he been okay?"

"He was until recently. He's been sitting in his field since you put him there, waving his arms about, but he's never stood up."

"Sure. I could have pulled him apart and put a new spine in but I always thought it would have taken something more away from him. You know?"

"Yes, I do." She knew that he believed the scarecrows had a soul or something equivalent to it. It was a bit spooky but also kind of sweet.

"What happened?" he said.

She looked around her as if to be sure no one was listening. She knew people would think them both mad if they heard how they spoke about the private part of their world and the things that lived in it. "He's been trying to stand up ... to impress me. I could see it hurt him too much and made him stay put. He's frustrated and angry."

Bran looked again at the bandaged arm. "Did he do that?" His own anger was curdling - she could sense it.

"He bit me."

Bran drew in his breath, startled. "That's not right—"

"I was making him sit and he swore at me and grabbed me. He was stronger than I thought, Bran. I was frightened. There's something about him. It's not just his body that's broken."

"Okay," he said after a moment's reflection. "I'll have to fetch him. He'll have to go up in Secret Hill until I can sort him out."

"Do you mind?" He put his hand on her shoulder and she leaned her head on it, her eyes again filling with tears.

"Thank you. You always understand."

He pulled her to him and she gripped him tightly, her head against his chest. He put his head down to hers and whispered something. She couldn't make out the words but she felt herself thrumming like a wire. "I brought him," she said pointing to the boot of the car. "He's in there. Mother and Father hate him and have always told me to get rid of him. They don't know he bit me or they'd have burned him."

"That's not the answer," said Bran. He went to the boot and lifted it. There was a small tarpaulin inside. Carefully he unrolled part of it. Broken Billy was lying face down, his wormy spine displayed like something diseased. Very gently Brad lifted the scarecrow, carrying it like a child to the nearby barn where he set it down in some loose straw.

"Leave him with me for a few days," he told Tracey.

She nodded, leaning forward, hoping he would ... and he did. He actually bent his head and kissed her gently on the lips as if it was the most natural thing in the world.

TWO DAYS LATER Bran took the repaired Billy to Secret Hill.

He made a place for him near the boundary where the darkness of the forest eagerly crowded in and set him up on a knoll that had a good view of the valley and several of the other scarecrows. Bran had made a special harness for Billy, a strengthened jacket that supported the weak spine. He attached this to the upright of the cross he had embedded in the soil. Bran tightened the harness and stepped back. Billy was in a sitting position, legs spread out on the grass, but from here his view was unimpaired.

"That was a bad thing you did, Billy: biting Tracey. We want no more of that you hear me? Otherwise you'll be punished severely. This is going to be your home now. She'll come and see you." Billy's face, restored but criss-crossed with stitches in its sack fabric, mooned, the big button eyes reflecting sunlight. The creases in the fabric gave him an expression of acute anguish that filled Bran with pity.

"You're with friends here – and remember, Tracey is your friend too. But for her you'd have been taken away and burned so don't upset her. In fact she's important to me. I'll tell you a secret if you keep it to yourself. When I get back I'm going to ask her to be my wife. If she says okay she'll move into the farm with me. So – you just watch the skies. Keep the birds off this hill. Okay?"

AFTER THE WEDDING and the excitement it generated in their tiny community, Bran and Tracey settled in the farm and their universe, already a small one, shrank down even smaller – though it burned like the brightest star. They honeymooned on the farm. Neither of them wanted to share their new life with anyone or anything else, not yet.

For a long time they didn't go near Secret Hill, concentrating on the daily round of chores, most of which they did together, from the first light of dawn until sunset.

"I ought to go and see to the scarecrows," Bran said one day.

She knew what he meant. "Yes. They'll wonder what's happened. I hope they're okay." He kissed her and set off whistling as he went. Tracey watched him until he disappeared. She never tired of looking at him. There was plenty to do to keep her occupied until he returned, which would probably be in the evening.

During the day, tidying their bedroom, she went through an old chest of drawers. Bran had said it was okay to sort things out. He said he was not a very tidy person, as if she hadn't known that for years, so he didn't mind her sprucing things up. There were old papers and bills and stuff in the drawers, most of which she thought could be tossed away. There was also a battered old envelope. She knew as soon as she found it there was something special about it. The envelope wasn't sealed so she opened it but not before looking nervously through the window at the yard and beyond. Nothing stirred there.

The picture was faded, a black-and-white shot of a woman, her arms hugging a small boy to her chest – so obviously Bran as a toddler – her hair trailing over him like a protective scarf. Tracey had never met Bran's mother but knew this must be her. She was smiling softly at the camera, her love for the boy a soft glow on her features. For a moment the expression seemed vaguely familiar and Tracey put it down to a family resemblance.

She slid the photo back into the envelope and secreted it in the drawer. No doubt Bran would share it with her when he was ready. In all the years she had known him his mother was the one thing he very rarely spoke about. *Father and I were helpless*, he'd said once. *Nothing we did could heal her.* Tracey thought of her own parents. She couldn't imagine what it would have been like to have lost either of them.

"You've got me now, Bran," she said to the window imaging him standing there. "I'll give you everything you need."

BRAN, MEANWHILE, HAD been visiting the scarecrows, spending time with all of them, telling them about his good fortune. They were all pleased as he'd known they would be although for some reason there was an odd atmosphere surrounding their hill. He couldn't figure it out until he came to Broken Billy.

There was a strange grin on his face; his lips were darker

than Bran remembered, smudged with - what? Lipstick? Paint? What was that? Bran leaned closer, his foot catching on something in the grass as he bent down to where Billy was sitting, splay-legged. Bran parted the grass and drew back in alarm. There was a dead crow, its wings spread, both broken and its eyes dull and lifeless. Blood had coagulated on its head and neck and some of it coated the grass immediately around the corpse. An unusual amount of it. Carefully Bran lifted it as if even at this stage he could repair it. He looked across at Broken Billy. The moon face somehow mocked him as if to say *I did that. You want me to scare crows. I scared the shit out of that one.* Bran knew now what the smeared mouth meant. Billy had *bitten* the bird just like he'd bitten Tracey - but this time it had been fatal.

That evening, sitting down to supper, Bran's slightly sullen mood was easy to read. Tracey set his food down and put an arm on his shoulder. "What is it lover? You've hardly said a word since you came in."

He reached up and squeezed her hand. "I'm just a bit worried about Billy. He's not right. I don't just mean his spine. You know what I found today? A crow. He killed it - bit its neck and broke its wings. I buried the poor little bugger. We want them chased off but not killed. That's not right."

She knew how distressed Bran got when anything died. He would have been deeply disturbed at having to bury the bird.

"Billy has to be punished this time," he said trying to sound resolute.

She fought back her alarm. "How?"

"I'll sort it out tomorrow. There's a spot way back at the top of Secret Hill, out of sight of the others. I'll move him there. For a while anyway. He has to learn."

She was about to speak when something behind her made her turn. It was as though a door had opened and a cold draught had breathed on her neck. She went to the window, shuddering. Outside everything was still.

"What is it?" said Bran.

"I thought for a minute we were being watched." She

secured the window and pulled the curtains.

BRAN WAS UP early to see to the cows and for once Tracey didn't accompany him. She knew he was wrestling with the problem of Billy. Better to leave him to it. And to be honest with herself, she'd no wish to see the scarecrow. She knew it didn't like her. There was a particular bitterness in it. Maybe that was due to its condition. Whatever, Bran would sort it.

The day wore on, clouds piling up in the west preparing to overrun the fields and hills. A rainstorm had been forecast. Tracey fetched in the washing before the first spots fell. The afternoon was waning. Still no sign of Bran. That was odd - he usually came in for a bite to eat around midday. She didn't like the silence, the stillness of the air before the storm. She slipped on a spare coat of Bran's; she loved being immersed in it and its smell. She went outside deciding to go and meet him.

As she approached the barn, the gate to Secret Hill, the rain began, big leaden droplets that presaged a deluge. Quickly she entered the barn. Through the door to the hill she watched the cloudburst, visibility immediately reduced to a vague blur. No sign of Bran. She waited, pulling up the hood and clutching the coat tighter. Eventually she chose a moment when the rain had eased but she knew it was set in for the rest of the day, a steady swirling drizzle with the promise of more heavy showers. She went out and climbed Secret Hill. The world had shrunk around to her immediate surroundings, rain muffling sounds and blotting the usual view. Even so she couldn't see any of the sentinels on the ridges. Had Bran moved all the scarecrows?

She came to the place where Broken Billy had first been set up. The supporting pole was gone leaving just a scuffed pit and scattered soil. Bran had obviously done what he'd threatened. Tracey looked around - breaks in the swirling clouds confirming that none of the scarecrows were in their usual positions although she could see their posts, stark crucifixes against the skyline. Bran must have decided to move them all.

She reached the last long rise up to the far end of the

meadow to the high woods. That was where Bran must be. She held to the knowledge as she trudged through the thick wet grass. It clung to her, dragging her back. It was deceptively further than she'd thought. By the time she came under the shadow of the trees she was exhausted. She gazed around her. Where was he? For a while she studied the meadow to her left and right until she saw where the grass and plants had been flattened along a rough trail. She followed it and up another knoll – and gasped when she saw him.

He was sitting in the grass, his arms spread on either side of him, resting on the cross-piece of the wooden construction – Broken Billy's. His head hung down limply, his hair sodden. For a moment he looked like one of his own creations. Tracey rushed to him and his head jerked up as though he'd been asleep. "What's happened!" she cried. Only then she realised his arms were tied to the wooden cross.

"They're all scared of Billy. They do what he tells them. I was getting ready to set him up when they crowded in on me. All of them. I couldn't get them off."

She plucked at his bonds.

"Careful," he said. He didn't seem able to move. "The ties are leather. Tight. Going to get worse in the wet. Shrink."

She was on her knees in front of him. As he spoke the rain intensified, compounding his warning. "Have you got your knife? I'll soon cut you free."

"Oddwick took it. He threw it over there. You need it, Trace. You'll never undo me otherwise."

She made a brief effort to prove him wrong but it was hopeless. Turning, she went to the edge of the flattened grass and started searching. The daylight wouldn't last. Her efforts to find the knife became more frantic. There were so many questions she wanted to ask Bran but they'd keep. The rain lashed her mercilessly. Something rose beyond her, a hunched figure, its clothes ridiculously bright – sodden now – its head bulbous, hair tufted round its ears. The painted face with the garish mouth fixed her with a smile that was both mirthless and malign.

"Oddwick!" She leaned back, still on her knees.

The scarecrow lifted one of its jointed arms like a giant marionette responding to its operator. It had bleached white gloves and in the raised hand it held the knife. "Looking for this?" The voice was little more than a croak, taunting.

"Why are you doing this?" she said angrily. "Bran never harmed you. Give me that knife at once!"

Oddwick snatched his hand back and shook his head, spraying drops of rain like a dog. "Billy says no."

"Where is he?" she snapped, getting to her feet. There were other shapes out in the rain-mist: Verdun the soldier, Megg and Mara the twins, and at least another four. Something shifted in the grass like a huge coiled serpent, and Tracey was sure Billy must be there orchestrating this rebellion. The thought of him fuelled her anger – and with it a memory. This coat, Bran's – something in the inside pocket. She reached into it. It was there. An old lighter. She pulled it out and held it up for Oddwick to see. "You know what this is." She tried to control her shaking, praying he wouldn't be aware of it.

Oddwick's horrible mouth sagged. Oh yes, he knew what it was. There was nothing that terrified the scarecrows more than fire.

"Give me the knife, Oddwick or I'll set you alight. God help me I will."

Immediately the shapes around them melted backwards and the slithering monster in the grass shifted away as well. Oddwick stood transfixed, painted eyes gazing at the lighter in abject terror. His painted face was melting. Slowly he opened his hand and displayed the knife, inching it forward. Tracey went to him equally cautiously. One flick of her thumb and the lighter would ignite. Or not. In this rain it could so easily fail. Was Oddwick prepared to take that chance?

She snatched the knife almost dropping it in her haste. Oddwick drew back and as she watched retreated after his companions. The weather closed in. Tracey opened a blade of the knife. Bran kept it very sharp. It didn't take her long to part his leather bonds and help him to his knees, but he staggered. It was going to take a while for him to restore circulation to his arms and legs. He couldn't move quickly, but with an arm around Tracey's waist he hobbled away.

"Can you make it back to the house?" she said as they began the long descent.

"I'm exhausted. Been tied up for too long. I didn't think Billy could be so cruel. I thought up here away from them he'd have time to reflect on what he'd done, maybe repent. He's corrupted them, Trace. He's far worse than I imagined. He wants to lead them out of the sanctuary."

"To do what?"

"Revenge I guess. Hunt down everyone that slighted them."

"That's mad!"

"It stems from Billy. I tried to tell him I was his friend but he said I already had a friend. It was all right for me. I didn't need fixing. I said I couldn't fix him. If I tried I might finish him off. He said I didn't care about him. Only you. You have to be careful, Trace. He'll hurt you if he can."

Tracey did her best to hurry them on down the slope but Bran moved awkwardly. The rain was incessant now, a blanket over the land obscuring any sign of Billy or his companions.

"They'll be in the barn," said Bran. "I have to find Billy. The others will stop this if I stop him."

At the bottom of the slope the barn loomed, its door gaping like the maw of a huge beast eager to feed. As Bran and Tracey approached figures emerged from it, plodding laboriously through the pooling mud, spreading out on either side of the door where they waited in the downpour, careless of being drenched. Oddwick lifted an arm jerkily and pointed at Tracey. Water dripped steadily from the sodden shape. "You won't set fire to anything out here now," he growled.

Bran straightened up, the strength slowly oozing back into his limbs. "You don't want to be doing any of this," he called raising his voice against the deluge. "No good will come of it."

The scarecrows had formed a half-circle and were inching forward in a coordinated movement obviously designed to snare their victims. Bran looked to one side of them to where a broken-down wagon leaned against the side of the barn, one wheel collapsed. Several feet above it was an opening to the hay loft. Bran nudged Tracey, who saw what he was looking at.

"Up there," he whispered. "Can you climb?"

She nodded and they shifted sideways edging towards the neglected wagon.

"You can't go beyond the barn," Bran called to the advancing figures. "Is that what Billy wants? Revenge?"

"We won't kill them," said Verdun, his mock-medals gleaming through the mud that spattered him. He looked bizarrely as though he'd just clambered from a trench. "We'll take them into us. Make us stronger. You showed us how."

"What does he mean?" said Tracey, shivering with the cold and something more.

"I suppose part of me always goes into them when I repair them. A spark maybe. If they kill—"

A new shape appeared in the barn doorway, crouched down on all fours, a predator weighing up a kill. Slowly and awkwardly it crawled forward and lifted its head, its eyes partially hidden in the folds of its sack face. Strands of thin hair, slick with rain, dangled over its features only partially hiding the stitched mouth and its cruel smile.

"Hello Tracey," said Billy. "I've been waiting to see you."

Bran gave his wife a final push and she bolted for the wagon, almost slithering into a fall, bumping up against its wet slippery wood. She turned, face ashen. She wanted to call to Bran to hurry but for all the rain her mouth had dried up. She felt the creep of paralysis.

"You can't go outside," Bran repeated to the closing shapes.

"You'll do what you're told!" snarled Billy leaning on his arms with spider-like patience. "You don't want to see Tracey harmed. You wouldn't want to see her up on the hill mouthing at the birds."

Bran glanced at her, willing her to scramble up on to the wagon but she was transfixed, waiting for him. "I can handle this," he told her. "Go on!"

She slumped in the rain, knowing Bran had few reserves left. Billy laughed, a dry cackle, a promise of pain and worse. Bran felt his arms gripped and tried to shake off the scarecrows but they had closed in on him like a pack of dogs. He couldn't bring himself to strike them, instead pushing and shoving. It wasn't enough and they held him firm. They forced him towards the barn where Billy waited.

"Open the way for us," Billy demanded. "Undo the spell."

Bran shook his head using his last dregs of energy to try and break free but the hands holding him were the elements of a machine.

"Okay," said Billy his voice rasping with effort in the teeming rain. His own strength seemed to be failing and every movement executed at a price. "Have it your way. Tie him!"

Bran winced as the scarecrows brought more leather straps and prepared to bind his hands a second time. He struggled making it difficult for them to tie his arms. Billy pointed to Tracey. She looked like a squashed doll propped against the wagon. "And her too. His little darling. We'll see how he feels once she starts to scream."

Jazzle and two of his shambling companions trudged through the viscous mud towards Tracey. They had become automatons, their expressions blank. Their clothes blended with their constituent parts, animate but inarticulate, almost mindless. Nothing more now than Billy's puppets. Tracey's right arm groped about in the wagon and found something metal – a rusty old pitchfork, half of its haft gone. She pulled it out and swung its prongs in the faces of the scarecrows. They leaned back momentarily, stumbling out of reach.

Bran watched in horror, his fury mounting until with a last desperate effort he yanked two of the scarecrows holding him off their feet. They toppled into the muck. Billy scuttled back towards the barn mouthing crude commands.

Tracey broke free of the encircling Jazzy and his companions and ran towards Bran, the pitchfork aimed at his tormentors like a short lance. At the last moment she swerved aside and charged towards Billy. He backed off instinctively, bumping up against the wooden cladding of the barn wall behind him. Tracey couldn't halt her mad rush, sliding into Billy and jabbing the pitchfork into his lower chest. It tore through the weak fabric of his torso, up under where his heart - if he had one - should be. The points of the prongs sunk deep into the wood behind him, pinning him to it by his faulty spine. He jerked, a drab butterfly presented for display.

Billy's mouth opened in a silent shriek of agony. His body writhed briefly, the dripping sleeves of his coat spraying corn stalks as though leaking vital fluids. Tracey drew back aghast. Billy sagged down, no more now than a bundle of rags and straw dangling from a peg like an empty set of clothes.

Immediately the other scarecrows staggered, barely able to stand. They stared vacantly at Billy's crumpled shape until the light went out of their eyes. Bran felt the grip on him easing and broke free of them. Tracey ran to him. He hugged her briefly before turning towards Billy, as though facing him took a huge effort. "This wasn't meant to happen," he murmured. He crouched next to Billy, put his arms about the diminutive form.

Tracey stepped closer and heard Billy's last strangled words "...just wanted you to mend me..."

Tracey saw tears on Bran's cheeks, mingled with the rain. Huddled here like this with Billy he reminded her of something. That hidden photograph she uncovered in the house. Yes, the mother and child. And the face. Billy's face - Tracey realised where she'd seen it before. In that picture. The resemblance was undeniable. Bran's mother smiling through her hair. Just as Billy smiled now.

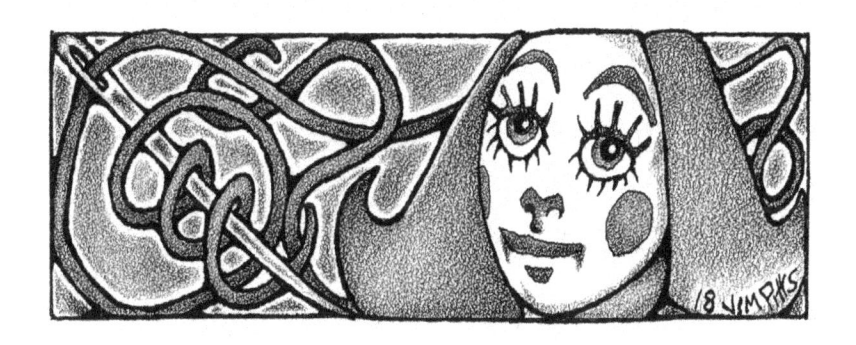

THE FULLNESS OF HER BELLY

Cate Gardner

ELLA'S NEEDLES PUNCHED through plastic. Thick black thread looped around the knee joint to secure the doll's leg to the cushion – the head bobbed forward, eyelids closing over painted blue eyes – then, she secured a further thinner cushion over the doll, pulling the inner thread tight so that she could externally work the right fist and leg. Velcro straps secured the cushion to her belly and the flowered maternity dress concealed its construction. Ella pressed her hand to the small of her back to ease phantom pain. She knew how to play pregnant; she'd been practicing since she was eleven.

She climbed the stairs, heart heavier than her belly, and threw the remains of her previous pregnancy into the spare room. Cushions with doll parts sewn into them littered the floor, many buried beneath the weight of their siblings.

"THIS HAS TO stop," her mother said, clutching Father's hand until her knuckles burned white. "People are laughing. Oh, Derek."

Mother buried her face in Father's worn tweed jacket. Ella didn't understand why they took *her condition* upon themselves. She lived on the other side of town; they didn't know the same people. Apart from group, Ella didn't know anyone.

"You said she'd grow out of it," Father said. "You should have grown out of it. What's wrong with you?"

"Emptiness."

Emptiness, a word that didn't fully describe the gnawing ache within that her obsession only stuffed a tenth of. To carry a constant ache, to spend each waking hour resisting cutting her belly open, reaching into her womb and stuffing it with cotton wool and mechanical parts. Why did they bother to visit? Each time they threatened she'd never see them again. As a child they had regulated her behaviour, consigning it to the house. They didn't own her anymore and they never noticed that they left her emptier.

Her father slammed his fists into her belly.

What if there was a real child there?

"I AM A desert," Ella said to group. "I plant seeds but none of them take."

She stroked her belly. No one at group asked to touch her stomach or to feel the baby kick when she winced, thus she dispensed with using the strings here. Geoff stared at her belly, occasionally leaning down as if to look up her skirt.

"You'd be able to get a better look if you were a toad," Ann Marie said.

Ann Marie was Ella's group buddy; they were assigned to look after each other. Ann Marie wore a white dress and shoes, her hair and eyebrows bleached white, her teeth shone, and she always protected her skin from the sun. For Ann Marie, her phobia had started after seeing a photograph in which a red splotch spread across the dress she wore.

She thought it an omen.

"We don't ridicule." Their group leader, Doctor Tom Sanders, rocked back in his chair, arching his sculpted eyebrows. The jab was aimed at both Ann Marie and Geoff but only Geoff reddened.

Geoff believed his long-missing parents were toads and that if someone kissed him he'd become a toad. *We all share madness here.* Ella shifted. If not for her cumbersome belly she could dart forward and kiss Geoff, end his phobia. Unless he did turn into a toad. She giggled to herself drawing a reproachful look from Doctor Tom.

At tea break Geoff apologised.

"I welcome your curiosity," Ella said, "but would rather the illusion wasn't shattered. Do you ever doubt my pregnancies aren't fake? Do you ever think what if her waters break and we have to deliver her baby?"

"No," he said, and moved away.

ON THE BUS home Ella snatched at the squawk that escaped a baby in his pram. She pressed her belly closer to him, trying to encourage her own cushion-baby to learn its cry. Seeing her totter forward, and mistaking it for a fall, an elderly man stood and offered her a seat. Ella wiped sweat from her forehead and thanked him. There were tuts at some of the younger people who hadn't stood up for her. She tried to gobble up the memory of the cry but a cartoon playing on his mother's mobile phone now appeased the child.

At home, the child's mewling formed in her chest. She allowed it to roar across the living room and, for a moment, thought the baby attached to her belly kicked - tiny foot against a 1970's patterned dress - but she must have caught the string. The sob grew into her own, not to be settled by a gentle hand of a mother or the technicolour spectacle on a small screen. She cried until dark settled over the house and then she crawled to bed with the cushion-baby still attached. The illusion always maintained.

Ella woke drenched, heat surged from her belly up to her forehead. *Menopause.* Too early for her body to betray her; she hoped. Fresh cries emanated from the other side of the room. Ella switched on the lamp and swung her legs over the edge of the bed. She was long-practiced at getting out of bed with the cushion-baby attached. The crying seemed to come from the wardrobe. If it were day she would dismiss it as nonsense but the night filled the old-wood with promise. Fingers shook as she turned the metal knob. Although the crying intensified, the inside of the wardrobe offered only clothes and tired handbags. On her hands and knees, she dragged the bags out but, even once the wardrobe was emptied, the crying continued. It came from the next room.

The spare room. The nursery.

The sensible thing would be to investigate in the morning, but sometimes magic only exists in the night time. In the hallway outside her rooms the cries intensified until it seemed a hundred babies cried for their mother. How many cushion-babies were in there now? She couldn't calculate. Mother had thrown away her earlier babies, burning them in the back yard and covering the neighbours washing with soot. Her parents' embarrassment had started then. She opened the door.

Despite the cacophony there was stillness to the room. A waiting. To lie amongst them would send her mad. *Madder.* When she closed the door, the cries dulled to a single wail.

"I'M NOT LYING, Mum."

The phone cord wound around Ella's wrist, threatening to cut off her circulation. Her hand would turn a purple-blue that would disturb Ann Marie.

"The cushion-babies want to live. I don't know what to do."

At three in the morning the crying had started again. That time she'd not investigated. Ella tugged harder on the cord, waiting for the silence at the other end to pass. Eventually the line went dead, while upstairs the cushion-babies began to cry again, and that at her belly squirmed without her pulling its threads.

"IT WANTS TO live," Ella said to group.

Only she could hear its cry. It rang within her mind, shooting up from invisible attachments in her womb.

"Your problems are off the scale," said Geoff, the man who believed himself a toad.

"I could kiss you," Ella said.

A giggle reverberated around the room ending at Doctor Tom, who Ella suspected wasn't a doctor at all. He tapped his finger to his chin.

Doctor Tom asked "Would you like to tell Ella how her worsening condition makes you feel?" He looked about the group. "Does it impact your own conditions?"

Why would it? Madness wasn't a disease that spread or caught, except perhaps in volatile situations and here was calm if edgy. A few nervous coughs echoed across the room. Ella shuffled on the seat, pressing her hand to her back to ease actual pain. Her belly felt burdensome today.

"It moved," Rachel said, pointing at Ella's fake belly. "It squirmed. It kicked."

Rachel, a nervous octogenarian, believed everyone wanted to kill her. She kept a knife taped to her ankle. The knife plastic and decorated with cowboys. A child's toy.

"Do you believe it's alive, Ella?"

"To want to live must mean there is life and yet it could also mean that there isn't."

"Perhaps a mechanical reaction. You do employ mechanics?"

She shook her head. "Just string."

A baby's cry burped from her throat. Ella pressed fingers to her lips.

"Now she's a ventriloquist," Geoff said.

"That was the toad caught in her throat," Ann Marie said.

No one laughed.

WINDOWS RATTLED, PLASTER dust rained from the ceiling and cracks formed in the walls. The strength of the cushion-babies' cries enough to cause a fissure to run from the house and down into the town centre. She waited for the neighbours or the police to knock, for someone to complain about the noise and the shifting of the house's foundations. She stumbled to the front door and stood outside. Here there was no crying. Here, the house appeared undisturbed. Her neighbour nodded then she rushed back into her house. They all thought her odd here.

Back inside her home the crying had stopped but there was fresh nightmare. The cushion-babies had crawled onto the landing and onto the stairs. They watched her. Blue, green, and purple eyes all focused on her. Somewhere within them the word *Mama*.

"I'm sorry," she said, pulling out her mobile phone.

At group they each had a buddy so Ella phoned hers.

*

ANN MARIE HAD scuffed her shoes on her way to Ella's, and because of the black streak against patent leather she'd thrown the shoe into a gutter and hobbled to the house. Now her tights were black on the pads of her feet and Ann Marie almost inconsolable. In the hallway Ann Marie dropped onto the bottom step, amidst the cushions, and began to take off her tights. The cushion-babies watched her, eyelids opening, teeth bared.

This is just my madness. They do not see. They do not hear.

"Throwing these cushions away would be a start," Ann Marie said as she pulled on a fresh pair of tights, failing to see the irony.

The cushion-babies pressed against her legs. She didn't seem to notice. Ella grabbed her hand and pulled her up.

"Easy," Ann Marie said.

The discarded tights lay amongst the cushion-babies and one of them sniffed them and turned to another. Ella couldn't name them; their only distinguishing features that one was a light blue cushion and the other grey. She didn't know nor understand her creations. Ann Marie tottered into the kitchen. She looked drunk. Ella would offer her fresh shoes but she didn't have any in white and for Ann Marie even cream wouldn't do.

"They're alive," Ella said, although it was clear that Ann Marie hadn't noticed.

"Who? Oh no sweetheart, you just spread them out about the house as if they have a purpose."

"I didn't." Voice quiet.

"Do you mind if I use your loo?" Ann Marie asked, kicking off her spare shoe.

Ella nodded without considering that Ann Marie would have to make her way through the cushion-babies to get to the upstairs bathroom.

Her *no* died at a jammed door. Ella pushed against it, shoulder, knees, foot, but it wouldn't budge. A scream cut off by something thudding against the floor. Something made of bone. She considered going out the back door and running along the alleyway to the front but she'd left her key in the door and, besides, they would jam that door instead.

"Leave her alone," Ella said, hammering her fists against the door until they bled.

BLOOD SPREAD ACROSS Ann Marie's white dress and belly, visible where teeth had bitten through fabric and then skin. One had tried to climb into Ann-Marie's stomach, eager to gnaw through to the womb. This should be Ella, not Ann Marie. She had *birthed* them.

"What have you done? What have you done?"

What have I done?

She knocked the cushion-babies aside but there was nothing to be done for Ann Marie. Her eyes blank, more animation in the blue and purple paint of the dolls. The doll at her belly began to squirm, to press against its cushion. Ella almost tripped over Ann Marie in her haste to get to the front door. The cushion-babies did not hinder or follow her. She carried one of them attached to her. In the street she tried to undo the Velcro straps but they dug into skin and she was a little afraid of revealing the doll to her neighbours.

That's it – doll. It's just a doll. It does not kick, punch or bite.

Ella phoned Doctor Tom. He'd gather some of the group to advise, to help. The bus caught every traffic light and stop and no one had the right change. Ella rubbed her back against the velour seat. The Velcro straps itched against her skin. The walk from the bus stop to the community centre proved lonely, and Ella jumped at every shadow when in truth she carried the monster with her. She arrived before the others, which proved to be the Octogenarian, the Toad, and the Fake Doctor.

"My illusion became reality."

Ella held up her hands. Dried blood covered them from where she'd banged her fists against the door; possibly traces of Ann Marie's too. No one would believe her story, not in this room or without. They'd think her a murderer, a woman with a history of mental problems; even her parents would admit to that.

"Ann Marie is dead and before you assume I'm the culprit, I didn't do it and this is my blood. We were attacked."

"Have you called the police?" Rachel asked, reaching for her cowboy knife.

"And there is the problem," she said, tugging at the Velcro straps through the thin material of her dress. "There is the part that sees me committed. Damn and blast, someone help me get this thing off."

Without a second's hesitation Geoff was out of his chair. "I in no way mean this as a pervert, toad or otherwise, but you're going to have to lift your dress. Eyes closed. Promise."

For the first time the weight of the cushion-baby falling to the floor proved relief. Evidence presented itself in the bite marks on her stomach and the torn innards of the cushion, at the doll parts that thrashed and gnashed and, if it could turn itself over, would scurry across the floor to choose a victim.

"I could kiss you," she said to Greg. The humour didn't reach further than her lips. "Sorry."

"So what exactly happened?" Doctor Tom asked.

"Either I lost my mind and hallucinated or those *things* attacked Ann Marie, one of them burrowing to her womb and in doing so ... murdering her. Sounds mad. Is mad. I really hope this is a hallucination but if you can all see..."

The cushion baby continued to squirm.

Rachel crouched over it.

"Careful," Ella said.

Rachel stabbed the doll in its biting mouth, jamming it in what, Ella surmised, was its throat. The doll stopped moving. They all stood over it, half expecting it to move again.

"Well, that's that," Geoff said.

"Not quite. There's at least another forty back home."

"Next time reign in your obsession," Geoff said.

"Geoffrey," Doctor Tom said. "We'll go to the house with you. If your cushion-babies are still moving we'll film them and then phone the police."

"Show them all the videos you want they'll still arrest Ella, they'll still try her for murder, and us as her accomplices."

"Maybe they'll have eaten all the evidence. Ann Marie that is," Rachel said, retrieving her knife from the mouth of the doll. "Did she have any family?"

"That isn't ethical," Doctor Tom said.

"Phoning the police now would be the expected thing," Geoff said, "but then none of us has ever done what is expected of us. Look at me: I remain a man despite my genes."

DESPITE RACHEL'S ADEPTNESS with the knife, it was decided only Geoff and Doctor Tom would accompany Ella home. How she wanted to be proved mad. For Ann Marie to be in the kitchen drinking a cup of tea or to have left a note saying she'd gone home. For Ann Marie never to have visited at all.

They couldn't open the front door. When Ella looked through the letterbox she saw the cushion-babies had barricaded themselves against it, purple eyes blinking into hers. With a yelp Ella dropped the letterbox. When Doctor Tom checked he too saw the same purple eyes.

"They hate you," he said.

"Gee, thanks for that doc," Geoff said. "I'm sure that helps ease the situation."

"I doubt they like me or you either."

Ella pressed her hand to her belly. Although not exactly flat, it was certainly the flattest it had appeared in her adult life. The dress hung off her frame. They would gather attention standing on her doorstep. One nosy neighbour and she'd be in a police cell under interrogation with no reasonable answers to save her. They'd have to try the back door.

Looking in the kitchen window all seemed normal. Remembering that they'd found a way out of the spare bedroom she knew they could work a door handle. This had to be done. Door open, she rushed to the cutlery drawer to remove knives. Now they could defend themselves.

The kitchen door opened.

They toddled, they crawled, they advanced. The sight of them was enough to disarm. Ella gripped tight to the base of the knife. There were too many of them. She stabbed forward but her actions and those of her colleagues did nothing to dissuade them. Using his mobile phone Greg filmed them.

"It'll look fake," Doctor Tom said. "You sure you didn't mechanise them?"

"I'm not some evil genius," Ella said.

Ella backed up towards the door but Geoff kept filming. She tried the handle, pulling at the door to open it. If they could lure them out then the chances were others would see them and this would all help in her defence or at least a conviction for insanity rather than calculated murder. Too busy filming Geoff hadn't noticed that Doctor Tom and Ella were heading into the back garden. The cushion-babies circled his ankles and before Ella could cry out an alarm they bit.

Geoff fell. His phone somersaulted towards the back door cracking the glass pane. They'd tear him apart. Throwing the knife aside, Ella dragged at Geoff's shoulders. The weight of them crawling across his body was too much, so to free him Ella did the unthinkable.

She kissed him.

No one ever expects a man to turn into a toad, at least not of the small scaly variety, but that's what Geoff did. The air emptied and Ella smacked her nose on the tiled floor, on emptied clothing. Somewhere within the mass of cushions Geoff scrambled. Now she was the object of their bites, of their hate, and it did not matter that she had created them. Ella dragged herself and several of them out into the garden. Where was the knife? They tore into her arms. She was afraid to look, certain they exposed bone. Something hopped from amidst them to land on her back. *Geoff.* He couldn't help her.

"Doctor Tom."

"In a minute, in a minute," he said. "I have to do this. It's the only way. The only way."

Ella flapped her arms, slammed them against the doorway, but she couldn't shake them off. She fell back. Hard to fight with your arms pinned, when every part of you is gnawed and smothered. From her new position she saw that Doctor Tom was gathering wood and building a pyre. He thought to burn them. Did he think to burn her? They were burrowing into her belly now, just as they had done Ann Marie.

They were burrowing into her belly. They wouldn't all fit. Those remaining outside of her freed her arms. Neck ached as she tried to lift her head. They were trying to close her belly to keep the others safe within her. How many had crawled inside? She couldn't survive this. Everything hurt, even crying. As Doctor Tom continued to gather wood – he'd have to burn her now – Geoff hopped across the garden, disappearing at times in the long grass. Then he emerged at her eye, hopping onto her face.

He kissed her.

Ella didn't turn into a toad but he did return to human form. Naked.

"I'm not so afraid now," he said as he began to tear the cushion-babies from her body.

She wanted to tell him it was too late but only blood slipped between her lips. She was pregnant with them, and pregnant with them she would die. She nodded as Doctor Tom pulled her towards the pyre, with no thought to save her. If his mind had not fragmented he would think to call the police, to somehow exonerate and not incriminate himself. Geoff and Doctor Tom pulled her between them. Into the fire, out of the fire. The fire that was still only a pile of dry wood. A scream from a neighbouring house broke their fight.

Self-preservation returning, Doctor Tom ran out into the alley and away from the scene. The cushion-babies crawled after him. The scream continued but Geoff stayed, and Geoff helped. All that remained now was her, Geoff and those in her belly. The others had chased or escaped, couldn't make it far. Ella pulled her dress across her belly. Her skin was ragged and torn and she shouldn't be able to stand. Sirens screamed.

"Trust me," Ella said and kissed Geoff.

Staggering into the house, she placed Greg on the counter and filled the sink with water. As the front door to her house caved in beneath the weight of a police officer's boot, Ella collapsed onto the floor. They'd think both her and Ann Marie attacked. They wouldn't be fully wrong.

The babies in her belly kicked.

She'd have to protect them.

IN THE ROUGH

Suzanne Barbieri

FIRST I WAS a goddess.

A small cult grew up around me, the miracle child who cried diamonds. Real tears, real diamonds, not palmed crystals slipped into my eyes like the pennies a stage magician retrieves from behind children's ears. There was a myth in my culture of a snake goddess who carried a diamond in her forehead. I was seen as her incarnation, returned to see why she had been forgotten for so long, why she and her sisters had been replaced by a new male god.

I was carried on velvet cushions: the ground deemed unworthy of my sacred feet. Or perhaps there was concern that tiny beads of diamond sweat might mingle with the earth and fall into the hands of undeserving villagers. I was too young to understand that this would have been a good thing, that distributing wealth among the poor would lift them out of the prison whose bars they couldn't see. My family was poor. Poor, god-fearing, and honest. I suppose that's why they gave me and my diamonds to the priests rather than sell them and live in comfort.

There were those who thought I was a fake. The irony is that it would have been better - safer - if I had been. All the while no one was sure if I was genuine, the hopeful believers could claim I was a miracle from God; my diamond tears the glittering stigmata, the sign that their piety had been rewarded. It wasn't enough that they had their own miracle, however, they wanted to share it with the world.

People came from everywhere. Scientists, doctors, film crews. At first the priests wouldn't let any of them touch me, but eventually the opportunity to have their miracle proven became too much to resist. I was taken to a hospital on the main land, tested, and brought back again to await the results. It was the first time I had left the temple in more than a decade, and I became curious about the world outside. For the first time in my life I began to view my life of opulence as a prison.

The tests were deemed inconclusive and someone came to the temple to collect me. He said he was one of the doctors who had observed the testing. I didn't recognise him but there had been so many, it could have been true. The high priest would have none of it.

"No more tests," he said. "You come to take our miracle away. Go."

But this doctor wouldn't leave. He sat outside the temple and waited. Villagers brought him food. They knew why he stayed and so did I. He stayed because he believed; and because I willed him to. I willed him to take me away from here and show me the world.

One night when everyone was asleep I crept outside to where the doctor was sleeping and gently shook him awake. He woke slowly, groggy after smoking with the locals. All of my followers smoke opium; they believe it offers protection against snake venom. I've never smoked. None of the temple snakes have ever tried to bite me.

Upon seeing me he bowed his head. Then I knew: the tests were not inclusive – they had proved me genuine. So why did they want me to go back?

"You're not safe," he said. "One of our team made a chance remark ... there's a verse in the Bible, Ezekiel 28:13. Do you know it?"

I didn't. Their Bible is not ours. Our path is ancient and pre-dates theirs by millennia.

He continued, "It's about the fallen angel Lucifer. They

equate him with Satan, the Devil."

"You came here to convert me to your religion?" I almost laughed. I was a goddess and he wanted me to bow to his god? But that wasn't what he meant.

"The verse states that when Lucifer was created he was set with precious stones..."

I also learned that this Satan had taken the form of a serpent to make the first people disobey God, and that this god had lied to them. The serpent had told them the truth and given them great knowledge. Surely the truth-teller, the educator, should be the god they chose?

"You must never speak like that!" the doctor said. "You could be killed for it."

Jack, for that was my doctor's name, was not a believer of their religion. He had seen the dangers of it too often, so he risked his life to liberate me. With nothing but the clothes on my back, we left that very night. We didn't go to the hospital. We went to Jack's house. It was modest but it would do.

We had planned to stay there for a while before deciding what to do, but our hand was forced. Word spread that the once-holy child had grown into a she-demon, the living embodiment of Lucifer. Within days I was on the television news and my temple was ablaze.

FIRST I WAS a goddess; then I became a devil.

The moment it was proven beyond all doubt that not only were the diamonds real, they were manufactured by my body, those who saw me as a holy creature changed their views. Suddenly I was a devil girl. The most damning indictment being that Lucifer himself was set with precious stones, therefore I must be his living embodiment. Fortunately, there were still some who believed and they helped us leave the mainland and head to the western world.

And what a world it was. Filled with wonders of a very different kind. I saw cars up close for the first time, and buildings made of glass that reached up into the sky, and inside those buildings were small groups of people rising up and sinking down. Jack explained they were riding in elevators. I wanted to be there. Encased in glass as though floating in a solidified sea. Ah, but I should be careful for what I wish.

In the beginning, I missed home so much I wept constantly. I tried not to cry in public but sometimes the tears just came, tumbling down my cheeks and skittering over the paved ground. Jack would scoop them quickly up before anyone saw what they were. Dear Jack, whom I came to love, despite everything. He left his old life behind to walk unfamiliar streets with his pockets full of my tears.

Eventually we made a home here; a secluded house was found, and money was no problem once we made contact with Mr K. We never discovered his real name. All we knew about him was that he laundered blood diamonds. If only he'd known how literal my blood diamonds were.

I had cried so much for the loss of my island, my family, I could cry no more. No tears, no diamonds; no diamonds, no money. And it took a surprising amount of money for people like us to remain safely hidden, to cover our tracks, to buy silences. We called it our work. It made it easier somehow. Jack hated doing it, especially without any local anaesthetic, but I made him.

He'd take my arm, kiss it, then look at me with such sadness in those fathomless dark eyes.

"Do it, Doctor Jack." I'd say. "The sooner you do it, the sooner it will be done."

Then I'd place the scalpel in his hand, position it over my vein and push against it until he complied and cut me open.

The blood diamonds were different from the tears. With the tears, the diamonds formed deep within me in response to my mood. Those from the blood we extracted formed before our eyes, like an alchemical process.

We leant over the crucible and watched breathlessly as the transformation took place. First, the essence separated from the blood, leaving two distinct liquids: the blood, red, unremarkable; and the essence, pale, shimmering, opalescent. Then, in seconds, the essence congealed, floated on the surface of the blood like the moon reflected on a crimson sea. Finally, as the congealed essence hardened, the diamond began to form. Even in its raw uncut state we could see it would be beautiful. And valuable. We stared at each other: I the White Queen, Jack my Red King, and our stone, the offspring of our Chemical Wedding.

    The temptation to create many more was immense. But it would have been foolish. Questions would be asked – and we couldn't know if it would damage me. We waited a month before undertaking the process again, and our second stone was every bit as beautiful as our first, as was our third. For now Mr K seemed content to know nothing of the diamonds' origins, as long as we let him get away with paying us far less than they were worth.

WE COULD HAVE been happy there, just us two. We didn't need anyone else, and I'd seen enough of the outside world to know that its wonders were all shallow trickery. For a while all was bliss but such is the curse of my kind, I knew it couldn't last. Perhaps it was the cutting that made it happen; perhaps knowing that we were outcasts in a hostile world caused unease within me; I began to change. I barely noticed it myself until the physical manifestations.

    First came a lump in my forearm at the site of the incision. I asked Jack to cut it out but he refused, said he couldn't bear to hurt me again. I took the scalpel myself and tried to force the blade into my skin, but I was afraid. I gripped the instrument harder, my fingernail pressed against the blade. A sound, a sharp metallic scratch, and the tip of the blade broke off and fell to the floor ringing like a tiny bell.

    Jack brought my hand up to his mouth and gently bit down on one of my nails. He winced as his teeth grazed against it and almost chipped. I ran my nails across the granite counter top. Deep lines followed in their wake. I scratched at my skin. It opened to reveal the tip of the rock beneath. I pulled. There was no pain, just a satisfying release, like the removal of a scab that frees the soft new skin beneath.

    I dropped the crystal on the counter. It was long, perhaps six inches. It would be worth a fortune.

    "We can't sell this," Jack said. "It will bring unwanted

attention."

"Not if we cut it." I said.

"It's too beautiful to cut."

"Then let's save it. For a rainy day."

Little did we know what the rains would bring.

THE CHANGE CAME slowly. A stirring deep within me, like bubbling magma readying itself to explode to the surface. My blood itched. At times I wanted to scratch my skin off and be done with it, flay myself down to the bone. I wondered what my bones would look like. Would they be opaque white like human bones, or clear as crystal, transparent yet unbreakable? The heat inside me was almost unbearable, a liquid fire I could hardly contain; yet still it bubbled, still it burned, until at last it was ready to erupt.

The line of crystals that grew out of my spine meant I couldn't sit down or lie on my back. I had to stand, all day, all night. The crystals were joined by others all over my body and soon I wore a coat of iridescent quills. Even my hair hardened into one hundred thousand glittering rods.

"Listen," I told Jack, "while I can still speak, listen carefully. If you sell the stones we still have there'll be enough to keep you for a very long time."

"To keep *us*," he said. "We stay or move on together."

"I have to stay. Soon I'll be too heavy for you to carry."

"Then we'll stay. Forever if need be."

AND SO WE stayed, and I became a prisoner in my own body.

By now I could no longer move or speak, though I could still see and hear. I'm sure Jack could tell because he filled the void of my existence with his beautiful words. I learned more about him in those weeks than I might otherwise have done in a lifetime. How much was bare-naked truth and how much embellishment for my entertainment, I may never know. And I didn't care. He kept me going and gave me hope for the future. When he went out at night to obtain supplies I counted the minutes until he returned.

Little wonder that my heartbeat quickened when I heard movement outside less than an hour after he'd left that night.

But it wasn't Jack. There were voices, some I didn't recognise but one belonged to Mr K.

"You'd think the fool would've kept it hidden," he said. "But it's just there in plain sight. I guess crazy people don't think straight. Heard him talking to it too. Though if I was sitting on such a fortune maybe I'd talk to it. Maybe that's what made him a crazy junkie."

How dare they? How dare they speak of him like that? It takes a great toll on a person to pretend to be a doctor, to weave a false life so that you might kidnap your goddess and make her fall in love with you.

"Who cares?" said another. "The stuff he took will keep him quiet for a very long time."

There was laughter.

A different voice said "Don't speak ill of the dead."

My Jack is dead? They poisoned him with their impure supply? I would cry a river if I could but draw breath. In the end, though, he loved his addiction more than he loved me. All my followers smoke opium. It eases the burden of my presence.

I heard the door unlock and open. Many feet, four maybe five pairs. I couldn't turn, I couldn't see them until they circled me and each was eventually in my line of vision. Four men accompanied Mr K. They were all dressed in black from head to foot; including gloves.

"It's beautiful," one said. "Who could have made such a thing? The detail..."

He thinks I am a man-made thing. I made me. No one else.

"It's a *Trompe l'Oeil*," said another. "You can only see the figure when you look at it straight on. Catch the wrong angle and it's just a mass of crystals."

A third spoke, the one who chastised them for speaking ill of Jack. "It's like there's a real woman inside. Like she's trapped in a diamond cave."

The others laughed at him. He shuddered. Whether at losing status in their eyes or at the thought of me imprisoned I don't know, but he turned it into a shrug, to make out as if he didn't care. Though I could see that he did. A small part of him was more concerned that there might be a woman inside this "sculpture" than about how much money could be made from cutting me into smaller more manageable pieces.

Then he put voice to his concerns.

"It's too good to break down. It'd be a sin to destroy something like this."

"Stoker's in love," one said and sniggered.

"Relax, no one's going to smash it up." This was Mr K. "It's going to take pride of place in someone's private collection."

FIRST I WAS a goddess; then a devil; now I am a work of art.

That's how I came to be here in a room so perfectly lit for me that light reflected off my every facet and cast rainbows all around. Though for all its beauty it was still a prison. I belonged to one of the wealthiest men in the world. He introduced himself as Adam although that wasn't his real name. He said, even if he told me, it wouldn't mean anything to most people. The truly rich and powerful shy away from the spotlight.

He liked to talk about himself even though I could not answer and he had no way of knowing if I could even hear him. He was, he said, one of the world's few multi-trillionaires. He had made every penny himself; he was not born into money. That much was obvious. No one who was used to riches would feel the need to boast about what they had.

I was part of his most secret collection. Reserved for those pieces that were not only priceless but whose very existence was the stuff of legend.

"You see, I just had to have you, Diamanda," Adam said. Diamanda wasn't my name. It was what the people outside of my island had dubbed me all those years ago in an attempt to co-opt me for their faith. Saint Diamanda. The girl who cried diamonds. He didn't know me, but he knew enough to suspect I might be more than legend and that the figure he now possessed might be more than a sculptor's tribute.

"Even though we've had such little time together it seems we must part, albeit for a short while. I have to go away on business. I will return in a week. Two at the most." He inclined his head in a small bow and left the room.

Everything about him was an affectation: how he spoke, how he dressed, the ostentatious displays. It was clear that having this level of wealth was not natural to him. He either felt undeserving or else feared it would be snatched away, thus fuelling his desire to become ever richer. Perhaps one day he would acquire enough that he could rest easy. Somehow I doubted it.

With Adam gone I was alone for the first time in years. Whether the calm I felt caused this or it would have happened anyway, I cannot say, but I felt myself changing again.

It began with a fizzing in my veins. My blood – congealed for so long – was finally on the move. There was a shattering sensation in my chest as warm blood filled my heart and set it beating again. Air rushed into my lungs, inflating them, pushing at my ribcage which had not the room to expand. I feared my first breath in so long would be my last and I would suffocate within my own hard shell. Then came a tearing sensation. A seam opened along my spine and my skin, my frozen glinting skin, began to shed.

My bare feet hurt as I stepped through the discarded coat of diamonds. My flesh was as soft as a newborn's. Is this how it would be? Would my skin harden and shed again, snake that I am? Or was this a once in a lifetime occurrence?

FIRST I WAS a goddess; then a devil; a work of art; now a two-legged snake, new and raw, rising from my cast-off skin.

The house was locked and bolted so I couldn't escape. Besides, I didn't know where I was. All I could do was look around and maybe find some clothes, some food. Please, let there be some food, I hoped. I had never felt so hungry.

There were women's clothes in the closet of one of the bedrooms. Had there been a wife who'd either left or died, or had Adam selected these for me in preparation for my thaw? If so then perhaps he knew more about me than I knew myself. None of the clothes were practical. If I did get out of the house how far could I run in an evening gown and heels?

Instead, I searched the other rooms until I found some of Adam's clothes. Most of those were evening wear too, but hidden amongst them I found a thick black sweater, jodhpurs and riding boots. The sweater came to mid-thigh so I just took that and the boots, which were too large – though with three pairs of socks I could just about keep them on even though the rough wool of the socks rubbed my delicate feet.

I was keen to see what other curiosities this private collection contained. There were paintings and sculptures here and there. I guessed the secret things were contained within their own special rooms, as I had been. I could find only one such room. It was in the basement.

The door was closed but it swung open as I approached. I stepped through into the darkness. A subtle glow began to emanate from the centre of the room. It brightened as I approached, as though it had been asleep waiting for me to wake it.

It was a tree. A tree made of many coloured gems. I reached out and laid my hands on it. An explosion of images and sounds in my head. And knowledge. Knowledge of things good and evil. How histories and mythologies are all one but become scrambled by word of mouth and mistranslations, how at the centre of everything is always a tree: a tree of life, a tree of knowledge, a tree connecting the heavens and the Earth. A tree on which to hang a god, a tree whose branches grow in everyone. Not a tree: The Tree. This whirlwind of information spun in my head and pulsed through my veins. It was all I ever wanted, and all too much. I felt my self becoming lost. Everything went black.

GODDESS; DEVIL; ART; snake; wisdom.

I don't know how long I lay there beneath The Tree but when I came to The Tree's light had gone out – and mine was brighter than the sun. I stood slowly, then left the basement and went to sit amongst the diamonds I had shed and wait for Adam's return.

HE WAS SURPRISED to find me dressed in his clothes, but not that I had shed my skin.

"You've explored the house, I see," Adam said.
"I had no clothes. I'm hungry. You left me no food."
"And you found The Tree."
"Perhaps The Tree found me," I said.
"Perhaps, indeed. I wasn't expecting you to ... transform quite so soon."
"Neither was I."
"It is true then."
"Yes," I said.
We were both strangely calm.
"I expect you'll want to leave," he said.
"I expect I will, some day," I answered.

I WASN'T SURE whether Adam was afraid of me or simply in awe but he managed to fire questions at me as I ate.
"How often do you change like this?"
"This is the first time."
"How did it happen?"
"The crystals came out of my body. I became frozen. Then I shed my skin and was back to how I was."
"Do you still cry diamonds?"
"I don't know. I haven't cried in a long time."
"Because you are happy?"
"I suppose so."
I wasn't. But it was safer to lie.

HIS QUESTIONS KEPT coming well into the evening. I soon grew tired but he pressed on, his tone becoming almost confrontational.
"So you're alive. Really alive, like ... me?"
He was going to say "like a human" but stopped himself in time. He didn't know what to consider me. To him I was both mythical and sub-human, goddess and animal. And that meant I would never be safe here.
"Can you ... breed? With us, I mean."
My senses sharpened but I didn't show it. I glanced at the door. Could I make it before he blocked my exit? Could I overpower him if need be?
"And if you did," Adam said, "would the child make

diamonds too?"

Imagine that. So fearful of losing his wealth he would make a diamond mine of his own child.

"I don't know," I said.

"Sweet Diamanda." He laughed mirthlessly. "Together we could rule the world."

It was then that the pieces of the puzzle slotted into place and I realised who or what Adam was. He shared the common trait of all those who have ultimate wealth, power or success: a complete lack of empathy that enables them to climb over others to reach their goals. Psychopaths, narcissists, sociopaths. That Adam thought he could own me, force me to have his child, and use us both in his bid for world domination, marked him out as one.

The killer move was so fast even I did not see it coming. I was guided by The Tree's knowledge that sometimes one small act of evil serves the greater good. I'd hidden several diamond shards about me and I held them between my fingers like claws. My two fists thrust into Adam's chest and pierced his rotten heart with ease.

I am death.

Adam looked surprised as his lifeblood ebbed away. Surprised that his first night questioning his treasure turned out to be his last; surprised that I had the gall to do it; surprised that he couldn't second guess me. But why would he have expected to? The Tree had given up its knowledge to me, not to him. To the woman. As it should be.

PERHAPS I SHOULD have moved on but I didn't want to leave The Tree just yet. I left Adam's body at its roots and by morning his remains were gone. This house was a good place now. I would remain as the Keeper of Knowledge and when the time was right I would spread it out across the world.

FIRST I WAS a goddess; then a devil; next a work of art; and then a snake.

I am knowledge. I am death. I am self-made. I am whole. I am the woman who will walk on the bones of men who would use and destroy me. And I bring with me a new world.

BLUEY

Ray Cluley

"Come on everyone, chapter four. Karl, Demi, books please." Half of them hadn't even sat down yet. Or they had but on the tables.

"Mike, stop throwing paper. Put it in the bin if it's rubbish."

Shaun only noticed Philip when he picked a ball of crumpled paper from his lap and set it on the table, just as another joined it, sending both to the floor. Little Philip Scott - precisely the afterthought his initials suggested - transferred into Shaun's class because of "an inability to fully integrate". As if putting him with a different group of kids was going to save him.

"Demi? Book."

Demi tutted, looked to the ceiling, and reached into her bag for a book Shaun knew wouldn't be there. Karl sniggered, saw Shaun was watching and rummaged around for his own book as well. "Got it, Mr Stevens," he said. He even pretended to put his phone away.

"Sir, I don't have my book."

Of course you don't, Demi. But I bet you have your lipstick and your mobile phone and a copy of some shite celebrity magazine. "You'll have to share."

She acted like that was absolutely the worst suggestion *ever* but moved closer to Jemma or Emma or whoever it was beside her. He could never remember. Blonde clones with forgettable faces.

"Okay. Now, last lesson we—"

A hand went up.

"Yes, Philip?"

"I need a book."

"Here." Shaun gave away his own copy to speed things along. He knew the bloody thing by heart anyway. "I'll need it back at the end."

"That's not fair, I have to share."

Yes, but who would Philip share with, Demi?

"I really like this book," said Philip.

Oh, Philip. You idiot.

The class filled with choruses of Sir, Sir, I *love* this book, I *love* school, Sir, I'd love to suck your—

"That's enough! As you've so much energy we'll read aloud, shall we? Tom, nicely volunteered."

Phillip sat with his shoulders hunched, eyes down, only now realising he'd been thrown in with the lions. Different lions to his last class, maybe, but lions all the same. It was always tough for new kids joining mid-year, but when you moved between classes, and when you were so small, with ill-fitting clothes and a permanent damp smell...

"Philip!"

The boy jumped, startled, and everyone else smirked, sniggered, or laughed. Shaun had meant to prompt Tom to read, only the wrong name had come out because he was focussing on Philip but, *man*, the kid needed to pull himself together.

Philip began to read, his voice soft and quiet. Shaun glanced up at the clock, wishing already that the lesson would hurry up and end.

IN THE STAFF room he went straight to the coffee pot.

"You look like you had my weekend," Amanda said. She was on one of the sofas, plink-plinking a couple of pills into a plastic cup of water.

"Not had one of those for years," Shaun said, thinking it

was more like ten, *twenty* maybe, and admiring the view as the young woman leaned to put the pill packet back in her bag. Amanda was new. She still loved the job, thought she could make a difference – *Dead Poets Society* was probably her favourite film – but she'd soon learn.

"A class is a wild animal," Shaun had warned her once. "Our job is to tame it."

"Don't smile until Christmas, isn't that it?"

"Exactly. If you're too nice then you're a pushover for the next five years."

"Crack the whip?" Amanda had raised an eyebrow and smiled. She'd mimed the action, with an added "wha-*kish!*"

"You've got to or they'll tear you to pieces."

"What's the matter?" she asked him now, grimacing around the taste of her medicinal fizz. For a moment Shaun thought he'd been caught staring, but she continued with "Bad class? Bad student?"

"Philip Scott," he said and she nodded.

"Oh yeah. Him," she said and somehow they both knew what each other meant.

Not that Philip was a bad student, it was just...

Filling his cup at the water cooler nearby, Glen Hemming said in a meek voice "Mr Hemming, I really *love* PE."

The three of them laughed.

"WHAT THE FUCK?"

Shaun chose to ignore the comment as he entered the classroom. Someone else asked if they were making revision posters – they'd only seen the cardboard in his hands, not the shape – but he ignored that too. They didn't make posters in his class unless he was far too ill and even on those days he'd usually give them a FO-FO, sending them away to the library to Fuck Off and Find Out so he could catch up with marking. But not today. Today he had something else planned.

"Sir, who's the new kid?" Raj asked, thinking he had a good joke going.

"This," said Shaun, holding up the cardboard, "is Bluey."

During his lunch "break" (ha!) he'd cut a sexless human

shape from blue cardboard, a simple silhouette of head, body, arms and legs. He'd used average dimensions for the height and weight and he'd carefully chosen a colour that was racially neutral, though they'd probably assume a gender. That was okay though. He would address that as part of the lesson.

"Bluey is new to the class. How do you think Bluey might feel, facing you lot?"

"Gutted to be in this tutor group?"

People laughed but that was okay. It was an appropriate answer.

"Suzanne?"

"Scared?" she said. "Nervous?"

"Amazed by our three-dimensional forms?"

Nice one, Luke. You're too cool for school.

"How about different?" Shaun prompted them.

"Well yeah," Luke said, "he's blue."

Again, that earned him a laugh.

"Who said Bluey's a he?" said Shaun.

"Is it a girl then, Sir?"

"Maybe."

Someone muttered something about tits.

"What was that, Karl?"

"Nothing, Mr Stevens." (Never *Sir*, not from Karl.) "I just said, doesn't look like it."

Shaun turned his attention back to the class.

"Bluey feels different," he said, "and yeah, Luke, maybe colour is part of that. And gender, too, Karl." (He would address the "tits" comment indirectly later). "What else might make someone feel different?"

He made them go through everything. They covered race, religion, sexuality, behaviour, interests, family background, class, hair colour, *everything*. And they were *engaged* for once. Probably because there was nothing to read or write. Even Shaun was having a good lesson.

"Okay. Good. Excellent. Lots of things can make a person feel different. But sometimes people use those things against someone. Why?"

This was tougher, but they surprised him with their

insight. It *shouldn't* have surprised him considering bullying was part of their everyday existence, but it did. They spoke in depth (if not very eloquently) about pack behaviour and bullying as a way of forming an alliance, as well as addressing the way it deflected attention away from themselves and towards someone else. If Ofsted had been observing they'd have loved it. Student involvement: tick. Evidence of learning taking place: tick. Equality and diversity (more important than anything else these days): tick that box, baby. Jump through that hoop.

Philip raised his hand but Shaun pretended not to see. He was running out of time and there was more to do. Plus, he didn't want the others to remember "oh yeah, we like to bully this one". Most of all, he didn't want some soppy comment about how effective this personification of a cardboard cut-out was, Sir.

"All right, now I want you all to line up."

There were groans at this because they had to move from wherever they slouched and there was danger now that he'd split them into groups without their friends (oh dear God, isn't life *terrible*) but they fidgeted, at least.

"Come on."

"Do we have to?"

"Yes Macey. Come on, everybody up."

Eventually, slowly, they did as they were told. He knew it wasn't only laziness that kept them seated; there was nervousness too. Because this wasn't normal and what if it was embarrassing and, like, ohmyGod, what if it was *embarrassing?*

"That's it, line up against the wall."

Shaun held Bluey in front of them as if he was presenting someone for a firing squad. Which, in a way, he was.

"Okay. Good. Now, in turns come up here and insult Bluey."

He let them exchange looks and grins. Let them swap comments back and forth for a moment.

"Insult Bluey," he told them. "I mean it. And rip off a piece."

"Rip off a piece? Is that, like, old person slang?"

Shaun held up his hand to quiet the laughter. "No, I mean literally. Rip off a piece of Bluey when you say whatever you say as your insult. Lisa?"

"What?"

She knew what, she just didn't want to be first. But Shaun knew she'd do as she was told and he needed to get the ball rolling.

"Come on," he said.

Lisa approached Bluey, hesitated, and looked at Shaun instead. Shaun nodded. She faced the cardboard, said "You're too skinny" (something she'd certainly never heard herself), and Shaun nodded again. He gestured to Bluey held up between them.

"Go on."

She tore off the left hand.

It was easier for the rest of them after that, and their enthusiasm grew as Bluey diminished in size. Shaun could tell some of the boys wanted to swear, but mostly everything was based on the previous discussion. Bluey was a Gaylord, Paki, and Slag. Two-Faced, Fatty, Four-Eyes, and Spaz. Shaun allowed Paki because it came from Raj. Was that racist, too?

Maybe it was good Ofsted wasn't here after all.

When Philip stepped up Bluey was little more than a head and a ragged neck.

"Go on Phil," Shaun urged, "go to your dark side."

The boy hesitated. You're ruining it, Shaun thought. You're part of the group right now so come on. Stay in the group. They'll leave you alone if you stay in the group.

"Sir—"

"Come on, Phil."

Some of the class took up the call: "Come on, Phil", "Go on, Phil", "Do it, Philip".

"Can I just—"

The boy was clutching at himself as if in physical pain.

"Just do it, Philip. Let it all out."

For fuck sake you little shit, this is for you.

"You little shit," Philip said, and Shaun was startled. The rest of the class hushed, the kind of hush Shaun recognised as the quiet vacuum before an explosion. But Philip hadn't finished. Had only just begun, in fact.

"Tiny little motherfucker, always in the way, saying stupid things, wearing shitty clothes, cheap clothes, singing gay songs. Philip Snot, Philip Scott-no-dad, Philip Scott-no-friends, mummy's boy faggot waste of space just fucking *die!*"

Philip tore the head in two down the middle, dropped the pieces – and released a stream of piss into his trousers.

Then he ran.

The rest of the class, stunned for only a moment, erupted into thunderous laughter and cheering, jeering, noise.

"WHAT THE HELL were you *thinking?*"

Shaun assumed the question was rhetorical and waited. This was the first he'd seen of the Principal's office since the new one began her reign of terror. She'd gone for a minimalist look which, considering the cuts she was making around the school, seemed an apt representation of her character. Desk, a few chairs, qualifications on the wall. No knickknacks, no plants, certainly no art. Nothing without practical function.

"And you *asked* them to do this? You *asked* them to say Paki and spaz? *Jesus.*"

No, not Jesus. Then we'd have to include Allah, Krishna, Jehovah, Bu—

"Explain to me the point of this exercise," Cassandra said but paused too briefly for him to do so. "He says you wouldn't let him go to the toilet."

"He didn't ask."

He'd tried, though, Shaun remembered. He'd raised his hand. He'd clutched at himself. Shit, Shaun had even told the boy to "let it all out".

"You know, his mum is demanding we pay for new trousers."

Shaun almost laughed. Philip had probably been wearing the same trousers for years, or somebody else had. They were shiny with frequent wear and far too short at the ankles. Shaun doubted it was the first time they'd been pissed in, either. But he answered the question Cassandra seemed to have forgotten asking.

Bluey — 353 —

"It was a tutorial about inclusivity."

"How does shouting politically incorrect insults do that, exactly?"

They were hardly shouting. Well, not until Philip.

Shaun, twenty years older than the woman across the desk from him, wanted to shrug and slouch in his chair. Dunno, Miss. Fuck you, Miss.

"It was meant to show them how words can hurt," he said. "They'd say ... well, whatever they wanted to say—"

"Paki, spaz—"

"Yeah that, or something else, and then they'd tear off a piece of Bluey. The cardboard student."

The firm line of her mouth softened a little and she leaned back in her chair. Either she was warming to the idea or she recognised it from the school's tutorial website. Maybe she even saw how it could have helped a student like Philip.

"So they hurt Bluey, verbally," Shaun went on, pressing his advantage, "which is reflected in the physical damage, and then—"

"Okay."

Cassandra waved the rest away. It took him a moment to realise she was waving him away as well, but it came as something of a relief.

BLUEY WAS PINNED to the wall as a reminder to the rest of the class. Shaun had put two pins in the face where eyes would be and others in the hands and feet. It was a mess now, a criss-cross chaos of Sellotape where he'd repaired it. A ridge split the middle of the body like a front spine. One foot was on the wrong way around. One arm was shorter than the other because a piece was somehow lost in the short time between ripping up Bluey and putting Bluey back together again. But as with that clumsy fuck Humpty Dumpty, putting Bluey back together again could not be done, not properly. Not with all the king's horses or all the king's men, and certainly not with Year 10. That was the point. An insult or an offensive action changed a person, regardless of attempts to repair the damage. That was the full aim of the lesson. That's what all the Sellotape was meant to show.

Bluey's bisected head was angled as if curious. "What did I do wrong?" Bluey seemed to ask. "Why did you do this to me?"

To teach someone a lesson.

Shaun turned back to his marking with a sigh. The caretaker had mopped the floor hours ago but the faint odour of piss seemed to linger behind the disinfectant.

"Staying all night?"

Shaun flinched, startled, but it was only Glen. He was standing in the doorway, a whistle on a loop of cord spinning this way and that way around in his hand, gathering into his fist each time.

"Yeah," said Shaun, "looks like it." He eyed the whistle (around again, stop, around again, stop) and felt envy. Fucking PE. Playing games and calling it a lesson. Shaun didn't have a whistle. He had a great thick file of half-sentences and doodles that would take hours to mark.

"I hear you were torn off a strip by our new lustrous leader."

Torn off a strip. Brilliant, Glen. And it's illustrious, you moron.

Shaun nodded. "A bit."

"Fuck her," Glen said. His tone was so casual it sounded like a solution rather than a dismissal.

"Not really my type," Shaun said hoping for a laugh and hating that he hoped. Hating even more how happy he was when he got one.

"What about that new girl? Amanda?" Glen squeezed at make believe breasts. "You getting any of that?"

Shaun told him no, he wasn't "getting any of that", and he said it with such indignation that Glen shrugged an apology and left him to it.

"What?" Shaun asked at the wall. His tone of indignation had been replaced by something more defensive.

Bluey said nothing.

SHAUN NEEDED TO move quickly if he was to beat the kids to class. They were already clogging the halls in dawdling gangs, spread like trawler nets across the corridors. Travelling in packs and managing to wander with their heads down, scrolling through mobile phones. He dodged his way around a group of Year 7s—

"...you can just copy mine..."

—and pushed his way through a group of untucked Year 11 girls—

"...so I was, like, only with a condom..."

—and eventually managed to get into his room. Year 8s, still pretty docile and easily sedated with a dose of "Death by PowerPoint". Perhaps not the most effective method for introducing a new topic but it got him an IT tick for his lesson plan. Sit 'n' click was the new talk 'n' chalk.

"Hey!"

The call came from the corridor as Shaun reached to activate the projector on the ceiling (someone had stolen the remote long ago for reasons that eluded him).

"Hey, watch it!"

Shaun began writing his aims and objectives on the whiteboard. There came another "Hey!" from the hall, louder this time. He recognised the voice.

Shaun sighed and went out to see Philip being shoved back and forth by a group of laughing lads. Shaun took a turn at saying "Hey!" as well and the gathered boys dispersed to whatever class they were supposed to be in, though one made a point of lingering, looking Shaun up and down before he went. Practising his man stuff.

Philip watched them leave. A primal instinct maybe, ensuring the predators were gone before he dared move. When Philip finally turned Shaun saw the papers stuck to his back. There was a "Kick Me" of course. And a "Piss Pants". And one wonderfully detailed piss-streaming penis.

Shaun opted for subtlety, tugging each of the papers quickly upwards for minimal pull on the Sellotape before crumpling them in his hand just as the boy turned to face him. Did Shaun imagine the look? The silent reprimand for not being there sooner, for not doing more?

"Thanks Sir."

Philip hurried away before Shaun could say anything. He felt like he'd written the fucking notes himself.

He marched back into his classroom— "Settle down, come on, quiet." —and yanked the projection screen into position, but it flew back up again with a bang. It silenced the class more effectively than anything he could have said and they remained that way throughout the entire PowerPoint.

Bluey's eyes sparkled in the computer light.

It wasn't until the end of the lesson that Shaun realised he was still gripping a fistful of insults. He dropped them in the bin while Bluey stared - drawing-pin eyes still bright with reflected light - and he sighed at the ink on his hands.

SHAUN REMAINED AT his desk long after the last lesson, determined to finish his marking before going home, but every time he tried to read an essay his eyes went to the display board.

Bluey seemed different, somehow.

Perhaps it was the position on the notice board? No. It was the head. The head was tilted differently. No not that either, not quite. It *had* been tilted but now it was straight. And the arms. Once held out low at the sides, now they seemed a little wider, a little higher, more distant from the torso. Surrendering. Or welcoming. The thing had been unseamed from the nave to the chops and yet here it still was.

"I got into a lot of trouble because of you."

Actually he hadn't. He'd had his wrist slapped, that was all, only it had come from a woman who was younger than him who'd been in the job for all of five minutes. The first two points shouldn't have bothered him but they did.

He turned away from Bluey and tried to focus again on the class work. Twenty-five essays on the role of the supernatural in *Macbeth*. He'd hoped the focus would generate some enthusiasm for the play but those he commanded moved only in command, not in love, to paraphrase the bard. Their work was littered with misquoted lines, some from entirely different plays; Gloucester from *King Lear* made a curious appearance. Philip, however, made several good points and presented a strong argument about how the supernatural was merely a device to emphasise human qualities and frailties. Shaun put an X through his work. He'd Google it later and no doubt find it online. The kid was saying things Shaun hadn't even taught them yet.

After the Scottish play, twenty-six essays on the relationship between George and Lennie, all regurgitating his own words back at him or retelling the story as if he hadn't read *Of Mice and Men* a dozen fucking times already.

"I before E," he muttered circling another spelling error, "except when you want to spell it however the fuck you want." He read on for a few moments and then "Oh, you do it *now*. Now that it's Steinbeck. E, I, *Jesus Christ* how many times? E I, E I, oh, you fucking *retard*."

The *tink!* of metal on metal punctuated his sentence, followed by the sound of something rolling on the floor.

It was a drawing pin. It turned a circle upon itself and settled flat, point upward. Shaun's first instinct was to ask "who threw that?" before remembering he was alone in the classroom.

A rustle behind him drew his attention to Bluey. He couldn't remember if the feet had ever been pinned but they weren't pinned now. He'd only heard the one pin though, so it couldn't have—

Couldn't have what?

Bluey stood open-armed ("come at me bro") and Shaun stood up so abruptly that he knocked over his chair. He marched to the board and yanked Bluey down, blinking away from any pins he might pluck from the board with it. He tore off each arm, the legs, the head, gathered them together and tore them down to a smaller size, throwing the whole lot towards the bin. Limbs scattered and span and landed all over the place.

"There."

One of the pieces had been written on. "Sack", it said, in the thick blue lines of a board marker. Dark blue pen on light blue card.

"What?"

He picked up the fragment to look closer. The handwriting was familiar. He picked up another piece and found "of shit" on the back. "Sack of shit."

Charming.

He turned the other pieces, all of them, and found a "dumbfuck" and a "waste of time", but that was all. Someone having a laugh, knowing something Shaun didn't know.

He went to the drawer for more Sellotape and stuck the pieces of Bluey back together again for the second time. He returned the repaired mutant shape to the board.

"We'll sort this out tomorrow," he said, pushing pins into Bluey's hands. The feet. When he pressed one into place for an eye the point pushed through the circle of the pin cap and into Shaun's thumb. He snatched his hand away with a "Fuck!" and thought, *Dumbfuck* and then he laughed, despite himself. He sucked his thumb like a child. By the pricking of my thumbs, he thought. Something wicked...

"Sod it."

He'd go home. Leave the fucking marking. It would still be there tomorrow.

Tomorrow, and tomorrow, and tomorrow.

He showed Bluey his injury as he passed. "Thanks," he said, offering a blood-spotted thumbs up as he left.

THE STAFF ROOM was lively with conversation by the time Shaun arrived. He wasn't late exactly (and still time for a quick coffee) but he had missed the morning meeting.

Oh well.

"What's the newest grief?" he asked, thinking each minute teems a new one.

"Inspections," said Amanda, glancing at the clock.

"When?"

"All the rest of this week, beginning of next," said Larry, counting calculators into a box.

"They can't just drop in," Shaun said, mentally checking his day's lesson plans.

"It's not Ofsted, it's in-house," Glen said. He was remarkably calm. But then he would be, wouldn't he?

In-house. That was worse. As if rearranging the staff room and classrooms and altering the timetables and increasing the number of meetings wasn't enough this year. Now, mock inspections.

"Looks like the rumours about downsizing might be true,"

said Trish. She drained the last of her coffee and grabbed her stack of science papers. "Evolution," she said. "Survival of the fittest."

"Shaun?"

The others hushed, stifling their complaints; Cassandra was standing in the doorway.

"Good, you *are* here. Quick word, please."

"I've got a lesson."

"This won't take long."

She didn't give him a chance to say anything else, walking away so he'd have to follow. Amanda winced at him in sympathy but then Glen said something that made her laugh.

Shaun went to the coffee pot but it was empty.

"Great."

So he went to the principal's office without coffee, thinking, wow twice in one week. I must be going up in the world.

"DESCRIBE FOR ME what makes good feedback?"

Shaun glanced again at the papers on Cassandra's desk. He recognised the top one as Samuel's, the boy's thin scrawl more like a rapid heartbeat than handwriting, and judging by the title - what makes a *trajic* hero? - it was from Shaun's own class.

Shaun had missed the j.

"Where did you get those?"

"They were on your desk. I had a look this morning, doing my rounds before the briefing."

A pause to show his absence had been noted.

"And it's just as well that I did. How do you tend to mark them?"

Bleary eyed and half-asleep, he felt like saying. He wanted to know what she'd meant by "just as well that I did" but knew he wouldn't find out until he'd answered her questions.

"Usual way," he said, and described the process. Green pen (because red was too aggressive, apparently), circle the spelling errors, underline the grammatical ones, tick as often as was humanly possible, and write a summative comment at the end that couched negative comments in a "compliment sandwich". Not that they ever read it.

"Compliment sandwich," Cassandra said.

"Yeah. Praise, constructive criticism, praise."

She picked up the top paper and turned to the summative comment. "Sort your fucking handwriting out," she read to him, "because I can't read this Etch-A-Sketch bullshit."

"*What?*"

She picked up the next. "I before E, you fucking retard," she quoted and cast it down before him so he could see for himself.

"I didn't write this," he said.

"If you focussed as much on the play as you do on Demi's tits you'd get a fucking A star."

"I didn't *write* this."

"*Jesus*, Shaun."

"I swear, this isn't me. It's not even my writing."

But it was. A bit clumsy, as if he'd written it drunk (which was sometimes the only way) but certainly his.

"Is it stress?" Cassandra asked.

"No it isn't fucking stress."

She leant back in her chair and crossed her arms, giving him the *stare* every teacher had to master.

"Sorry," Shaun said.

"Don't you see—"

"I didn't mark them. I left them here - overnight."

Cassandra sighed. She'd probably already compared the writing to something he had on file. "Maybe you should take some time off."

"Is that a suggestion or..."

"Just think about it," Cassandra said. "We could manage." She gathered the papers together and shuffled them straight. "I'll take care of these."

Shaun left the office to the sound of tearing paper.

ONCE THE CLASS had calmed down as much as they were ever going to (lively because of his lateness, thank you oh *lustrous* leader), Shaun went to Bluey and began removing the pins. He took his time, taking care not to prick himself again but also taking the opportunity to assess the reactions of each student, looking for signs of guilt.

"Bluey and I had a little chat yesterday," he said.

A few in the class laughed. Most ignored him, too involved in their own conversations.

"Seems someone wasn't content with verbal insults."

He had more attention now but they were only mildly intrigued.

"What Bluey couldn't tell me though, was—" he took the cut-out down from the board and turned it to the class "— who's responsible for this?"

Suddenly everyone in the class was *very* interested. Very surprised too. More than he thought it deserved, actually, their eyes wide and mouths open, some of them. And then all of them were laughing. An eruption of shrieks and braying and pointing, looking around the room to share their laughter as a class.

"It's not funny. This—"

But when he looked at Bluey he didn't see the writing from yesterday. Or rather he did but it was only a secondary observation. What he saw first was a gigantic penis drawn up from between Bluey's legs. An erection of wishful proportions, with the inevitable and equally disproportionate drops of semen spurting from its tip. These were shooting their way up to a new huge set of breasts, giant circles with spotted nipples the size of saucers.

Shaun cried out, dropping Bluey, and the class laughed again and laughed harder. What had shocked him most was the face someone had added. A massive crescent smile, wide and toothy, and eyes that had been drawn looking sideways at Shaun.

The class were laughing so hard it was difficult to judge who was to blame. Even the quiet ones were amused. Tina smirking with her never-ever-speak-ever friend, Harriet. Toby brushing his greasy fringe aside to stare and smile. Even Philip. Philip was looking around the class with delight, turning in his chair to share his pleasure with the others. It made his smile difficult to assess.

"Philip, do you know anything about this?"

"*No* Sir."

But did the little shit look smug?

Shaun retrieved Bluey from the floor and presented the cut-out to the class again, shaking the figure as he shouted "What the hell *is* this?"

"Puberty?"

The laughter had been dying down but here it all was again. Someone even clapped. Shaun crushed the blue body into a buckled twist of card and Sellotape and shoved Bluey into the bin, glaring around the room.

At that moment the door opened and Cassandra, clipboard in hand, entered the room with a stern "*Quiet*" that immediately silenced the class.

The screwed up corpse of Bluey expanded, not liking the new shape it had been forced into, and emerged from the bin like a slow motion Jack-(and Jill-)in-the-box. The principal saw Bluey's cock, saw Bluey's tits, and widened her eyes at Shaun who tried to stuff the offending cut-out deeper into the rubbish.

"Everything's under control," he said.

Cassandra made a note on her clipboard. "I think I'll stick around for a while," she said. "Maybe learn a few things."

She took a seat at the back of the class.

"Right..." Shaun began.

Cassandra made more notes in the lesson than any of the students.

FINALLY, THE LAST lesson.

"Okay everybody, time to be quiet, lots to do. Come on."

It had been a long day and he still had a meeting with the principal to get through. He didn't think there'd be any compliment sandwiches.

"Your coursework is due in less than three weeks and we've still got *lots* to get through. *Karl. Be quiet.*"

"Sorry Mr Stevens. I didn't mean to wake anybody."

"*I* don't care that it's less than three weeks," Shaun went on. "*I* don't have to write it. I've got my grades and I get paid whatever happens."

Although maybe not next year.

Nobody was listening. Not that the "I don't care" speech ever worked anyway, because they didn't care either. They just carried on about their business as if he wasn't there. As if the classroom was a meeting place for some kind of youth club. Did they even have youth clubs anymore? James and Ross were having a loud conversation between themselves at the back while they each had separate conversations with others via text message. Demi and her bleached-blonde doppelgangers were leaning around a magazine, pointing and giggling at something. Philip was sitting with his book open at least, but he was singing quietly to himself instead of looking at it. No, not to himself. To Bluey, up on the wall. Who the fuck had put that back up?

Shaun put the heels of his hands to his eyes and rubbed them, then massaged his forehead for a moment. He had a meeting with Cassandra after this and a shitload of marking to do over the weekend and only three weeks left to drag some coursework out of them and—

"Be QUIET!"

There was a sharp moment of hush. Shaun opened his eyes. He was about to thank them for it, albeit sarcastically, when there was a *tink!* of metal ricocheting off metal. He'd heard it before. A drawing pin striking a chair or table leg. He looked at Bluey as another pin *pinged!* from the wall. Bluey's leg lifted away from the display board.

What horrible imaginings is this?

One arm pulled free.

Is this what a stroke feels like?

The other arm.

Am I having a heart attack?

Bluey bent at the Sellotaped waist as if taking a bow. The pins in the head fell from the face and rolled on the floor.

The room was silent, so silent you could hear pins drop (ha!) and the crumple-rustle-crease of cardboard as Bluey dropped down from the wall. Shaun watched it happen.

How...?

Saw the way Bluey filled out, expanding into solid form. Saw him stretch and bend from flat to fat, the writing on Bluey's back – "be quiet", "I don't care", "shut the fuck up!"

– curling into new shapes as Bluey solidified. Board marker tattoos: "fuck her", "bossy bitch", "nasty Nazi cunt". Then, as the chest expanded, ballooning to fuller size, the writing stretched into lines no longer recognisable as words, simple sentences becoming a complex thread of arteries and veins. Angry ink pumped from something heartless.

Bluey's head turned, pin-prick eyes looking at Shaun. He felt himself thinning. Folding. Sliding flat from his chair into a crumpled concertina at the front of the class. He tried to tell Bluey to leave but managed only "Out... out..."

Bluey looked down at him, bigger now as Shaun downsized, and when a mouth tore open in that featureless face Shaun decided he didn't want to see any more. He reached for fallen drawing pins with flattening hands, folding his fingers around one, then another, and before he could think too much about what he was doing he pressed them firmly to his eyes.

The pain of it tore his own mouth open but no scream came. His mouth was a flat and soundless circle. The voice that ripped through the classroom was not his.

"Things are going to change around here."

And with that, Shaun was cast aside.

Discarded.

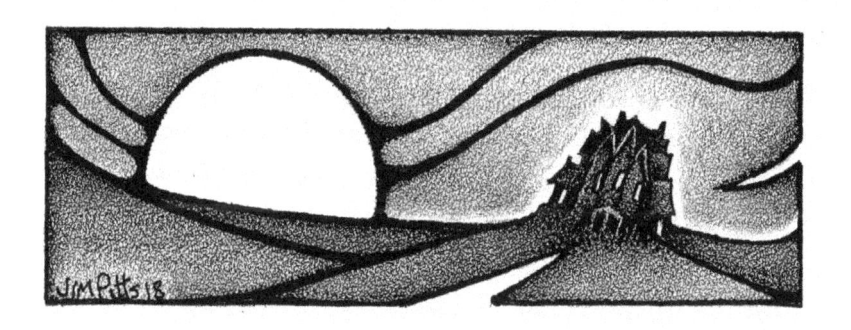

TOO LATE

John Grant

"Nap time?" He gave her a Vincent Price leer.

"You and your naps," said Heidi, looking bored.

They were out on the sun-drenched veranda at the front of the house. Pedro, the burly young local who cycled the five or six kilometres from the village every morning to bring groceries and do some housecleaning and some gardening for a few hours until they paid him and told him to go away, had left for the day. Heidi was on the lounger. She was wearing a quite modest pale-blue bikini. She stretched her long body luxuriantly in the heat. Her flesh was covered all over with very fine, almost invisible hairs that darkened to a more golden blonde on her head and, Griff knew, at her armpits and crotch. She'd been reading a paperback with a lurid cover but had cast it to one side; unlike Griff, for whom it was a matter of honour to finish a novel if he'd started it, Heidi was quite content to discard any book the moment it began to weary her. On the little rusty wrought-iron table at her elbow sat a bright-red drink and a packet of Gauloises.

"You go upstairs, darling," she said, once again stretching like a cat – at least, like a cat with purple wraparound sunglasses. "I'll nap out here. There's no one for miles around."

A couple of weeks ago, on impulse, she'd painted her toenails scarlet. The polish had partly chipped away so it looked, in Griff's eyes, as if her feet bore bloodied talons.

He picked up his tall glass of iced tea, now lukewarm.

"Okay, honey."

Trudging up the stairs alone he wondered what had gone wrong. They'd been married just four years, three of which they'd spent slowly but inexorably drifting apart. So they'd booked themselves a fortnight here, in the middle of nowhere in the countryside of northern Spain, in the hopes they'd rediscover each other. Instead what they'd discovered was how wide the divide had become. They'd made love just once since arrival several days ago, and then it had had an air of obligation about it.

The bedroom was the most glorious space in the house. It filled much of the upper storey and, with a large bay window facing southward, to the house's rear, was habitually flooded with light. Through the window could be seen grasslands stretching all the way to the horizon, a brownish-green sea with a few isolated islands of trees.

Griff sat down on the bed and gazed idly out of the window. The binoculars Heidi had given him at Christmas, and which he therefore now had to use for his birdwatching even though his old pair had better optics, lay on the basketwork table in the middle of the bay. That was the other problem with this holiday. He'd seen hardly a bird. Perhaps it was something to do with climate change driving the habitats northward.

He took a glum sip of his tea.

Maybe he should find himself a mistress. Except he didn't *want* a mistress. It wasn't just intimacy he was yearning for; it was intimacy *with Heidi*. Why had she changed? It was the old cliché, multiplied tenfold. Before they'd got married she was insatiable, inventive, experimental, wild; barely was the honeymoon over than her ardour had started to cool. She was hardly even his friend any more. Now it seemed she regarded sharing physical affection of any kind with him as a chore, a connubial duty. Each time his desperation had grown to such a pitch that he'd taken her on that basis, he'd been racked with guilt afterward, as if he'd committed some sort of rape.

Although the air was hot and sticky outside, here in the bedroom it was cooler. He no longer felt ready for sleep. He debated with himself going back down the stairs and begging Heidi to come up here with him – or just tug her pale-blue swimsuit aside and make whoopee on the veranda, who cared? – but he wasn't in the mood for self-abasement, or for the kind of shame he'd feel later.

He picked up the book by the bedside. He'd read late into the night and could now only dimly remember what the last twenty pages or so had been about.

Putting the book down again, he flipped open his laptop and began booting it up. The stupid little Windows chord disturbed the air. Before flying across here he'd loaded half a dozen Langgaard and Rautavaara symphonies onto the disk, thinking it'd be fun to lie awake during the Spanish night with Heidi by his side listening to music neither of them knew. A fantasy. Even at the time he'd known she would become impatient within minutes. Now, he felt a small but welcome flush of triumph as he double-clicked Rautavaara's *Angel of Light* symphony and the first portentous chords lurched out of the laptop's squeaky little speakers.

Griff got up and went to stand in the window's bay.

There was a wind kicking up so that waves ran through the muddy-looking grass.

Something caught his attention.

Squinting, he raised a hand to his forehead to shield against the glare of the sun. How strange he should never have noticed this before. There was another house out there, almost at the limits of visibility – perhaps a couple of kilometres away, perhaps more: it was so difficult to tell distances when gazing across the plain.

He frowned. The rental agency had told them they'd be very much on their own, that the nearest human beings would be in the village, which was in the opposite direction...

Griff turned away, shrugging. What difference did it make?

He lay down on the bed, facing away from the window's brightness, and tried to forget how unhappy he was. As he did increasingly often, he attempted to conjure up the faces of old girlfriends.

It must have worked, because before long he was asleep.

THE NEXT MORNING, he realised he'd already started counting the days until the vacation would end and they could fly home to Stevenage. He'd be every bit as depressed at home, of course, but at least it would be a depression he was familiar with.

He suggested to Heidi they take a drive into Santander to see the cathedral there, find somewhere quiet for a spot of lunch; but even before he'd finished speaking he could see she wasn't really interested. Although it was still breakfast time the air was becoming muggily hot, and the day's lassitude was clearly infecting her.

"You go if you'd like to," she said. "I'll be all right on my own."

Griff's instant reaction was to refuse. Outings were surely supposed to be for two. People enjoyed them because they were doing things together – the sights and the activities were secondary. Going on his own would be to defeat the whole point of the exercise.

But then he bit back the words. Getting out of this house might be the best thing for him. Being apart from Heidi for a few hours might make him feel less remote from her, paradoxically less lonely.

"It'd be a shame to go back home not having seen the country we're staying in," he said, trying to make a half-joke of it.

Heidi sniffed as if the idea of there being anything to see in Spain was ludicrous.

Griff dug out the battered road atlas some previous tenant had bought and left in the house and plotted his route, making a little itinerary for himself in pencil on the back endpaper of his diary. Someday soon he must get himself one of those electronic gadgets everyone else used for this sort of thing.

"You sure you'll be all right?" he said as he prepared to leave.

Heidi waved dismissively. She was already out on the sun lounger, although this morning, in deference to the fact that Pedro would soon be arriving for his daily routine, she was wearing a red-and-orange checked dress rather than just a bikini.

"Have a good time, darling," she said lazily. "Bring back a bottle or six of wine if you see anything that looks drinkable."

Only once had they let Pedro bring some of village's vintage. It had been the colour of earth, and of roughly the same taste and texture.

Driving off down the dusty road, Griff watched the house receding in his rear-view mirror. The featurelessness of its surroundings made the building look like one of those perfectly scaled models people buy so they can construct miniature villages in their living rooms. And Heidi, lolling with her book and her big straw sombrero in front of it, was becoming a plastic figurine. The house and the woman looked as if they'd just been freshly unpacked from the box.

And then he rounded a bend and the fancy evaporated.

The cathedral in Santander had fewer saints and angels and Christs dying in agony than he'd expected. There was modern stained glass being inspected by strangely quiet children holding their parents' hands. It was marvellously cool inside the place, and Griff enjoyed the way people's footsteps echoed and shafts of coloured light played with the dust motes in the air.

Afterward he strolled through busy streets, not wanting to stray too far from the main thoroughfares because the quieter alleys and side streets abroad are always much more frightening than those at home. The place he found for his lunch was hardly the quiet little family café he'd imagined, but his grilled herring was good and he enjoyed watching the young Spanish secretaries flocking by on the pavement. The glass of wine that came with his meal tasted fine to him, so he negotiated purchasing a case of the stuff; for a couple of euros, one of the kitchen staff carried it to where Griff had parked the rental car.

When he got home it was the middle of the afternoon but as he approached the house it was as if no time had passed at all. The sky overhead was still painfully blue. Heidi was still lazing with her hat and her shades and her book.

He pulled to a halt on the gravel and climbed out.

"I got us some wine."

She tilted the brim of her straw hat up and smiled at him. "Good boy. We can try it out at dinner."

"Let me get it inside," he said. "Then I need a siesta." He rubbed one eye with the ball of his hand wearily. "Driving's hard work when the sun's this bright."

"What do you want for dinner?"

"Your company," he said.

She gave him a thin smile. "Food, I meant."

"Whatever's on the table."

Still puffing from the effort of bringing the case of wine in from the car and stowing it at the bottom of the larder, he decided to have a quick shower before sleeping. The intentionally lukewarm water of the shower woke him up a little and, sitting on the bed, he found himself in two minds as to whether to have that siesta after all.

Naked, he stood in the bedroom's bay window.

Far in the distance he could see the other house. I suppose this could be classified as indecent exposure, he thought with a grin. But from that far away they'd have to be using something like the Hubble to see anything incriminating.

Absentmindedly he picked up his Christmas binoculars and trained them on the distant building. As he pulled the lenses into focus he was surprised by the clarity and magnification. Maybe he'd misjudged the quality of the apparatus, deceived into thinking the binoculars were crap by the glossiness of the packaging they'd come in.

The other house had been designed very much along the same lines as this one – in fact, if you'd put the two of them side by side, Griff mused, you'd have been hard pressed to tell them apart. The front door was even painted the same colour, a sort of ochrous, drying-blood brown. And yet there was something subtly different, something Griff couldn't quite as yet put his finger on. He shrugged and the scene in the binoculars' field of view lurched crazily.

Once he had it steadied again, he found he was looking at an area to the right of that half-open red-brown door. There was a lounger with a woman lying on it. He couldn't make out many details except that she seemed to be fair-haired and that, if she were wearing anything, it was significantly less modest than Heidi's pale-blue bikini. He felt a small stir of arousal as well as a pleasurable sensation of peeping-tom guilt. With an effort he shifted his view away from the reclining woman to look once more at the house's facade.

Then something, some half-detected motion, made him look back at the woman.

She was rising from the lounger and, yes, he'd been right in his guess that she was as naked as he himself was. Tall, slender, bronzed, she turned away from him toward the house's door, grabbing up a flimsy silvery-green robe as she went. On the threshold she stood for a moment, rocking slightly on the balls of her feet, before stepping into the shadow within.

Despite the heat of the afternoon, Griff felt a cold sweat on his forehead and upper lip as he slowly put the binoculars down on the rattan table.

It wasn't just the robe – lots of people had silvery-green robes – it was the way she had paused in the doorway, swaying slightly, enjoying the ease of her limbs.

He'd seen that movement a thousand times before.

Griff sat down heavily on the bed, brow furrowing. The more he thought about it, conjuring back up in his mind's eye what he'd just witnessed, the more he became convinced it was Heidi he'd seen.

But how could that be possible? He'd left her just a few minutes ago. Even if for some reason she'd wanted to sprint through a kilometre or more of grassland, stripping off her clothes as she ran, to throw herself naked onto someone else's lounger, she wouldn't have had the time.

He pinched himself, aware of the cliché, pinched himself again, then grabbed the binoculars once more.

The woman hadn't reappeared. The front door was now shut. The lounger had gone. But Griff was at last able to identify what it was that he'd noticed earlier as different between the two cottages.

When he'd left Heidi lazing outside *this* house the whole veranda had been baking in the fierce raw heat of the Spanish afternoon. But the light bathing the front of the distant house was of a different quality - the cooler light of morning, or perhaps of early evening.

Which wasn't possible.

He shook his head, and resolutely put the binoculars down again. It must be the stress getting to him - the stress of living with someone he adored in every way but who so casually rebuffed his adoration. Perhaps he should see someone when they got home. Or perhaps he should pluck up his courage and face the fact that a clean break from her would be the best solution.

Or perhaps it was his fault, and he should try harder.

THE NEXT MORNING, to his surprise, dawned misty and grey with the threat of rain in the air. He'd been hoping to lure Heidi out for a drive in the countryside, just to see the sights, but obviously that wasn't much of an attraction under the circumstances. They lit a log fire to expel the chill from the house - no such thing as central heating here, of course - and settled down with books. Griff plugged headphones into his laptop and, despite a slight hangover, listened to the Rautavaara again while he read. In the middle of the second movement he was startled when he suddenly realised Pedro had arrived, clearly some minutes ago, and was talking to Heidi. I wish, thought Griff, I could still make her face light up like that, the way it does for other people.

He pulled off the headphones, leaving the music running, and smiled at the Spaniard. Pedro wasn't very good at what he did, in either the house or the garden, and dealings with him were complicated by the fact that his English was barely rudimentary, but he was so eager to please it was hard not to like him. He'd brought fresh bread, cheese, milk, and was telling Heidi how much the groceries had cost.

An hour and a half later Pedro was wobbling off down the road on his bicycle. By then the sky was beginning to clear, with sunlight creating slantwise pillars where it poked through the clouds. According to the weather service Griff was able to access on his laptop, the afternoon was going to be fine. He broached his notion of going out for a country drive, and after a moment's hesitation Heidi agreed. They had an early lunch of the bread and cheese Pedro had brought, poring over the tourist map as they ate.

And all this while Griff had not thought once of the other house.

AS EVENING FELL they found a small roadside café with an extraordinarily lovely waitress, lacking entirely in English, where the food was excellent – great big greasy sardines, a different fish entirely from the brisling that comes in cans. Nervously, in light of their experience with the village vintage, they tried the house plonk, and it proved sturdy and pleasant, even if still rough around the edges. They drank far too much of it and left the café far later than they should have. Griff drove home with the sort of exaggerated care drivers display when they know that, back home in Stevenage, they'd never dare be on the road with as much alcohol in their bloodstream as this. Heidi, giggly, pointed out that even half-smashed he still couldn't drive as madly as most of the other motorists.

She was still giggly when they got home. They showered together – which was something they hadn't done in a long time – fell into bed together, made love together with joyous clumsiness, and Griff thought that at last, just maybe, everything between them had been repaired.

In the middle of the night he woke, bladder full and mouth parched. Beside him Heidi lay snoring softly, her sleeping face as always looking almost childlike. He climbed out of bed as quietly as possible so as not to disturb her, and crept to the bathroom. After peeing and drinking about a litre of the bottled water they kept there, he came back into the bedroom. He wondered about waking Heidi up, wondered if she'd want him to, but then went to look out the bay window.

The night sky was full of a million stars but that wasn't

what immediately held his attention. Away in the distance across the dark invisible plain, the house he'd seen before was so bathed in moonlight as to seem almost spot-lit. He groped in the darkness for the binoculars, and then paused.

The moon had been setting while he and Heidi were driving drunkenly home. Where was the moonlight coming from?

He trained the glasses on the house's front. The windows were dark. Surely everyone there must be fast asleep, the way Heidi was, the way he should be.

But then a light came on in an upper window. Griff calculated. If the two cottages were as similar inside as out, someone had just switched on the light in the small spare bedroom.

No, not switched on the light; drawn back the curtains.

He strained to see the figure standing in the window more clearly. It was the woman who had reminded him so much of his wife.

Behind him, Heidi snuffled softly as if to reassure him that she was still here with him in the bedroom.

The other woman seemed to be looking directly at him. He knew that must be an illusion - standing here in the darkness he couldn't be seen from outside - but he was unable to shake himself free of it. She was wearing a colourful loose peasant dress, rather like the one Heidi had worn today, Griff decided.

As he watched, the distant woman very slowly undressed, as if putting on a show for him ... or perhaps for some unseen lover closer to the cottage, hidden by the night.

Once naked, she stood in the window a few moments longer, rocking slightly forward and back before grabbing the curtain and pulling it closed.

Griff, mouth dry once more, slowly put the glasses down and got back into bed.

Heidi rolled over.

"Ooh, look what I've found," she said drowsily. "Is this for me?"

THE NEXT MORNING, though, Griff's hopes were dashed. His

honeymoon girl, as he'd called Heidi more than once during the night, had disappeared. The first bad sign was that she dressed for breakfast. Griff looked across the kitchen's pine table at the woman opposite him sipping orange juice and playing with a croissant and realised he might as well be breakfasting with a stranger, as sometimes one does at hotels. She was very quiet this morning, like somebody trying to escape with as little commotion as possible after an unwise one-night stand. By the time they'd cleared the plates away he was more depressed than if yesterday had never happened. Even so, he asked if she were in the mood for another drive.

"It looks as if it's going to be a scorcher again," she said airily, straightening a cushion that didn't need to be straightened. "It'll be hot and stuffy in the car. I came here to soak up all the sun I can, so that's what I'm planning to do. I'll not mind if you go find another cathedral to play in."

Sensing he could only make himself more unhappy by hanging around in the house or insisting she come with him, he said his goodbyes. A couple of hours later he found himself in a coastal town called Castro Urdiales, whose bay was overseen by a huge church. The streets were full of too many tourists but he did his best to ignore them – them and the shops selling the kind of *faux*-traditional artefacts that tourists attract like magnets. He skipped the church, as if to frustrate Heidi, and instead took a tour around the castle, which looked like something designed several centuries too early to be a Disneyland feature.

He was home by mid-afternoon. Heidi, once more in her pale-blue swimsuit, seemed almost flustered to see him.

"What's the matter?" he said.

"Nothing. Nothing at all. For some reason I'd thought you'd be home later. You just surprised me, that's all."

"I bought you an ocarina," he said. He hadn't been able entirely to ignore the tourist shops after all.

She looked at the porcelain object with interest, her shades almost sliding off her nose. "How do you play it?"

"Much the same as you would a penny whistle, I imagine. If you like I'll go online and find out."

"I can do that myself," she said. "Later."

"Wine?"

She pursed her lips. "Not yet, I think."

"I need a shower."

"I told you it'd be stuffy in the car."

Inside, the living room was a billow of sunlight – to think that only yesterday they'd had to light a fire! – but the kitchen, with its two small windows, offered a comfortable gloom. Through the small window he could hear Heidi playing a few experimental tootles on the new toy he'd given her. He got some chilled water from the fridge and drank it greedily, then headed upstairs.

At the landing, he looked toward the door of the spare bedroom. Since arriving, he and Heidi had opened it just once, during the first half-hour when they were exploring their new territory. The single bed had been stripped and spartan. The drab tiled floor had thrown up the colours of the bright rag rug beside the bed. It looked like a room a child could love. Griff and Heidi had had no reason to go in there again. Now he found himself wondering illogically if, behind that closed door, he might not find the blonde woman he'd seen from afar last night, if only he summoned the courage to look.

He snorted, shook his head impatiently. Stupid fancies. He wasn't thinking right. The stress. Or maybe just too long out today in the blistering heat.

Griff spent his time in the shower, first bathing himself in hot water and then turning the temperature and the pressure down so he could luxuriate in a cooling lukewarm patter. Stepping out, he didn't bother with a towel but padded through to the bedroom, waiting for the warmth of the afternoon to dry him off.

Besides, he wanted to see if the strange woman – the other Heidi, as he'd come to think of her – was there.

Waiting for him.

He stopped that thought. Even if she really existed, even if she wasn't just a figment spirited up by his loneliness, she couldn't ever have seen him, not at this distance, couldn't even know he existed. He was like a dirty old man spying through a keyhole or dreaming of long-ago glories.

But he still wanted to see if she was there.

It was as if the binoculars leapt into his grasp. Surprisingly, they were still in the right focus – why is it that binoculars and telescopes slip out of focus even when they haven't been touched? – and the house's front door sprang into clarity. He panned a little to the right and there, sure enough, was the blonde woman, sitting astride the lounger, wearing a straw sombrero and very little else, and reading a paperback in the morning sun.

Griff relished the sight of her. A great yearning built up inside him, not entirely a sexual yearning, just a desire for closeness.

He lowered the binoculars to his chest. Who was she? Was she just a stupid dream of his? Should he cut short this vacation, using whatever excuses he could, and get home to Stevenage and sanity? Or, at least, some faceless counsellor who could talk him back *into* sanity?

There was a flicker of movement out on the plain, something new.

He put the glasses back to his eyes and, with difficulty, found its source. He began to grin.

Clearly Pedro had two jobs, catered for two houses, not just the one. What had drawn Griff's attention was Pedro's head and shoulders, leaning over unseen handlebars as he pedalled along a track Griff couldn't see because of the swaying grass. Obviously the track was bumpy – nothing unusual about that around here.

When Pedro got to the house he jumped off his bicycle, letting it fall where it would – just as he did every morning when he arrived at the villa Heidi and Griff had rented. He paused for a few words with the woman on the lounger, then made his way indoors carrying what Griff assumed would be cabbage, cheese, bread, cold cuts...

The woman sitting on the lounger had made no move to cover herself during all this. Perhaps it was simply that, at this extreme range of the binoculars, Griff couldn't see what she was wearing.

As Pedro came back out of the house he was pulling off his blue denim shirt, throwing it away from him. The woman on the lounger put her shades and book on the table beside her, picked up the glass that was there and drained it, turned and held out her arms to the handyman. Griff could almost but not quite see the smile he was sure she was giving him.

Well, *damn*, he thought. Pedro, you horny young bugger.

One of the many fantasies he'd been constructing was that the other woman might be sort of a redesigned version of Heidi, one who might welcome him where Heidi rejected. He was confused about whether or not he ever wanted to meet this other Heidi in person; just the fact that she was there, or potentially there, or merely there in his imagination, was enough. Yet clearly the "other Heidi" had no idea of his thoughts. Rather, she was beckoning Pedro toward her, pulling down his pants, doing something to Pedro which Heidi had always been deeply reluctant to do to Griff...

Griff wished he could pull his gaze away. But then he was forced to. Moving the binoculars, he saw that coming out through the red-brown door was a man holding over his shoulder, like a golfer with a golf club, what looked to Griff like one of the andirons from an open fireplace.

The man stalked forward, looking instinctively from right to left, until he was within a pace or two of the couple. At this very last moment Pedro obviously caught sight of him, because the handyman broke away and began to lope toward the grassland.

The man with the andiron paid him no attention. Griff could see the consternation on the woman's face as she looked up, could see her raise her arm in self-defence, could see the heavy metal implement come swinging down.

And he could see enough of the man's rage-contorted face to recognise it.

The next he knew he'd torn away the binoculars, thrown them who knows where, and was lumbering nakedly down the stairs, scraping the skin off his elbow against the wall. With luck he could stop this before it happened.

Out into the insane brilliance of the afternoon. At first, he was blinded by the merciless blaze of the sun.

Out onto the veranda where Heidi sprawled. Next to her, the andiron. For a long moment he could see nothing but

the blood pumping from the ghastly wound on the back of her head.
 Too late.
 So much blood.
 Too damned late to save her.
 So very, very much blood.
 Spreading all the way across the overheated land to the horizon, and then soaking up into the shredded sky.

CONTRIBUTOR NOTES

Gail-Nina Anderson is a cultural historian of a Gothic bent living in Newcastle, where she delivers courses on art history, literature and film. An active member of the Folklore Society, in 2013 she gave the Katharine Briggs Lecture on "Artlore", examining the way art history creates its own myths. A member of the Dracula Society and a contributor to Fortean Times, she has written and lectured on the links between the Pre-Raphaelites and Dracula. She writes ghost stories for Phantoms at the Phil, a twice-yearly evening of spooky tales delivered in Newcastle's wonderful (and possibly haunted) Literary and Philosophical Society Library.
http://gail-nina.com/

Jenny Barber is a writer of weird things, short fiction fan and co-editor of anthologies including *Wicked Women* (Fox Spirit Books) and *The Alchemy Press Book of Urban Mythic* (volumes 1 and 2, The Alchemy Press). Her non-fiction books *Let's Try Tarot* and *Let's Try Cartomancy* are due out in late 2018. www.jennybarber.co.uk

Suzanne Barbieri is a musician and writer whose first published work, *Clive Barker: Mythmaker for the Millennium*, was published by the British Fantasy Society. Her other works include "Its Secret Diary", which was nominated for a BSFA award, and "Half Light", from the drama *The Daemons of Devil's End*, and the tie-in novelisation *Olive Hawthorne and The Daemons of Devil's End*. As a singer and musician she has provided vocals for many artists and companies, and also produces solo work under the project name of Beloved Aunt. https://suzannebarbieri.wordpress.com

Debbie Bennett tells lies and makes things up. Sometimes people pay her for it. Writing both fantasy (as Debbie Bennett) and dark crime/thrillers (as DJ Bennett), Debbie has also branched out into script-writing with an IMDb credit for a Dr Who spin-off DVD. She claims to get her inspiration from the day job – but if she told you about that she'd have to kill you afterwards... www.debbiebennett.co.uk

James Brogden is a writer of horror and dark fantasy. A part-time Australian who grew up in Tasmania and the Cumbrian Borders, he has since escaped to suburbia and now lives with his wife and two daughters in Bromsgrove, Worcestershire, where he teaches English. His short stories have appeared in various anthologies and periodicals ranging from *The Big Issue* to the BFS award-winning Alchemy Press. His most recent novel *The Hollow Tree* was published by Titan Books in March 2018, and his new book *The Plague Stones* is due in 2019. http://jamesbrogden.blogspot.co.uk

The Oxford Companion to English Literature describes **Ramsey Campbell** as "Britain's most respected living horror writer". He has been given more awards than any other writer in the field, including the Grand Master Award of the World Horror Convention, the Lifetime Achievement Award of the Horror Writers Association, the Living Legend Award of the International Horror Guild and the World Fantasy Lifetime Achievement Award. In 2015 he was made an Honorary Fellow of Liverpool John Moores University for outstanding services to literature. *The Way of the Worm* completes his Brichester Mythos trilogy, and *By the Light of My Skull* is his latest collection. www.ramseycampbell.com

Mike Chinn is from Birmingham, UK. He edited three volumes of *The Alchemy Press Book of Pulp Heroes* as well as *Swords Against the Millennium* for The Alchemy Press. His Damian Paladin collection *The Paladin Mandates* was shortlisted for the British Fantasy Award in 1999; a second collection, *Walkers in Shadow*, was published by Pro Se Productions in 2017. He sent Sherlock Holmes to the Moon in *Vallis Timoris* and has two short story collections in print: *Give Me These Moments Back* and *Radix Omnium Malum*. http://saladoth.blogspot.co.uk

Ray Cluley's work has appeared in a various magazines and anthologies and has been reprinted in Ellen Datlow's *Best Horror of the Year* series, *Wilde Stories 2013: The Year's Best Gay Speculative Fiction*, and in Benoît Domis's *Ténèbres* series. He has been translated into French, Polish, Hungarian, and Chinese. He won a British Fantasy Award for Best Short Story and has since been nominated for Best Novella and Best Collection, *Probably Monsters*, available from ChiZine Press. https://probablymonsters.wordpress.com

Adrian Cole, a native of north Devon, England, was first published in IPC magazines in 1972; this was quickly followed by *The Dream Lords* trilogy. He has published more than two dozen novels and numerous short stories, many translated into foreign editions. He writes science fiction, heroic fantasy, sword & sorcery, sword & planet, horror, pulp fiction, and Mythos as well as young adult novels. He appears in numerous publications, making regular appearances in *Weirdbook*. Adrian's most recent book is *Nick Nightmare Investigates* (Alchemy Press), which won the 2015 British Fantasy Award for Best Collection. www.adrianscole.com

Storm Constantine is the author of over thirty books, both fiction and non-fiction, including the Wraeththu series and the science fiction novel *Hermetech*. She's also had over 100 short stories published, and is the founder of the independent publishing house Immanion Press. She lives in the Midlands of the UK with her husband and four cats. www.stormconstantine.co.uk

Cate Gardner is a British horror author who lives in the concrete wilds of The Wirral with her husband, horror author Simon Bestwick. Her work has appeared in *The Dark, Black Static, Shimmer* and *Postscripts*. Her novella "In the Broken Birdcage of Kathleen Fair" was published by Alchemy Press in 2013. Forthcoming for 2018 are stories in Paula Guran's *Year's Best Dark Fantasy & Horror 2017* and Stephen Jones' *The Mammoth Book of Halloween Stories*. www.categardner.net

John Grant is the author of some 75 books, not all of them under that name, and the recipient of two Hugos, a World Fantasy Award and various other awards. Among his more recent books are the story collection *Tell No Lies* (Alchemy Press) and *Corrupted Science (Revised & Expanded)*. http://www.johngrantpaulbarnett.com

Stephen Laws is a British horror author whose award-winning novels include *Ghost Train, Spectre, The Wyrm, The Frighteners, Darkfall, Gideon, Macabre, Daemonic, Somewhere South of Midnight, Chasm* and *Ferocity*. His short stories can be found in the collection *The Midnight Man*. He is co-founder (with Neil Snowdon) of the horror society, Novostria Macabre. www.stephenlaws.com

Samantha Lee is a graduate of the Central School of Speech and Drama and began writing while she was still a professional performer. Her output is as diverse as it is prolific, covering both fact and fiction and including novels

in the horror and dark fantasy genres, self-development and exercise books, short stories and articles, Children's TV series, movie screenplays, literary criticism and poetry. She hosts creative writing workshops at libraries and Literary. Her work has been translated into French, Dutch, Spanish, Swedish, Italian, German, Croatian, Greek and Chinese.
http://samanthaleehorror.com

Keris McDonald is one of the three contributors to the Alchemy Press Lovecraftian collection *The Private Life of Elder Things*. Her short stories have appeared in *Weird Tales*, *Supernatural Tales*, *All Hallows*, and *Terror Tales of Yorkshire* amongst other publications. Her story "The Coat Off his Back" was reprinted in Ellen Datlow's *Best Horror of the Year Volume 7*. However, she spends most of her writing time focused on dark paranormal erotica under the name "Janine Ashbless". www.janineashbless.com

Gary McMahon is the author of nine novels and several short story collections and novellas. His latest book release is the award-nominated novella *The Grieving Stones*. His acclaimed short fiction has been reprinted in various "Year's Best" volumes. Gary lives with his family in West Yorkshire, where he trains in Shotokan karate and obsesses over the minutiae of life in search of stories to tell.
www.garymcmahon.com

Ralph Robert Moore has been nominated twice for Best Story of the Year by The British Fantasy Society, in 2013, and 2016. He writes a column, "Into the Woods", for each issue of *Black Static*. His fiction has appeared in America, Canada, England, Ireland, France, India and Australia in a wide variety of genre and literary magazines and anthologies. Moore's books include the novels *Father Figure*, *As Dead as Me*, and *Ghosters*, and the story collections *Remove the Eyes, I Smell Blood, You Can Never Spit It All Out*, and *Behind You*.
www.ralphrobertmoore.com

Stan Nicholls is the author of more than thirty books, mostly in the fantasy and SF genres, for both adult and young readers. His books have been published in more than twenty countries, and his Orcs series is a worldwide bestseller, with over a million copies sold to date. Before taking up authorship and journalism full-time in 1981, Stan co-owned and managed Notting Hill bookstore Bookends, and was manager of specialist SF bookshop Dark They Were and Golden Eyed. He was the first manager of Forbidden Planet's original London store. He's Chair of The David Gemmell Awards for Fantasy. www.stannicholls.com

Marie O'Regan's fiction has appeared in many magazines and anthologies, including *Best British Horror 2014* and *Great British Horror: Dark Satanic Mill*, and her two collections *Mirror Mere* and *In Times of Want*. She has been shortlisted for the British Fantasy Society Award for Best Short Story and Best Anthology. She is co-editor of *Hellbound Hearts*, *Mammoth Book of Body Horror* and *A Carnivàle of Horror: Dark Tales from the Fairground*, and editor of *The Mammoth Book of Ghost Stories by Women* and the forthcoming *Phantoms*. She is co-chair of the UK Chapter of the Horror Writers Association. www.marieoregan.net

Marion Pitman read M R James at an impressionable age. She lives outside London though she would rather live inside it, or better still in New Zealand. She has written poetry and fiction most of her life and published it since the 1970s. She sells second-hand books, and has worked as an artists' model. She has no car, no television, no cats and no money. Her hobbies include folk-singing, watching cricket, and theological argument. Her short story collection *Music in the Bone* is available from Alchemy Press. www.marionpitman.co.uk

Jim Pitts started submitting artwork to fanzines back in the early 1970s. David Sutton was the first to accept his work for Shadow Press, closely followed by Jon Harvey for *Balthus*. He has since worked extensively in the UK, European and American fan and professional fantasy and horror fields. Jim has long been involved with the British Fantasy Society and won the BFS award for Best Artist in 1992 and 1993. He retired four years ago and now uses his time to illustrate work in horror and fantasy publications.

Madhvi Ramani writes articles and essays as well as children's books, short stories, plays and screenplays. She has been published by *The New York Times, Washington Post, Asia Literary Review* and others. She grew up in London and now lives a thoroughly bohemian lifestyle in Berlin.
www.madhviramani.com

Tina Rath lives in London with her husband and several cats. She has published around 60 short stories, some of which have appeared in *Killing It Softly 1&2, Best Horror Stories by Women, Year's Best Horror Stories 15, Year's Best Fantasy & Horror 18,* and *The Mammoth Book of Best New Horror 16.* She has also published a collection of fantasy stories: *A Chimaera in My Wardrobe.* She is an actress, Queen Victoria Look-Alike, a story-teller and performs her own poetry. She is currently the Resident Poet with the Dracula Society.
www.christinarath.wordpress.com

Tony Richards is never quite sure what he's going to write next. Principally known for supernatural horror – with two major nominations in that field and enough short fiction to fill eight collections – he also writes detective novels, short crime fiction, SF, fusion fiction, and even the occasional tale of paranormal romance. His twenty-some novels include the Raine's Landing series of supernatural thrillers. And, heading off on yet another tangent, his latest book is *The Astonishing Adventures of Sherlock Holmes in the 21st Century,* due from Endeavour Media in November. www.richardsreality.com

Phil Sloman is a writer of dark fiction. He was shortlisted for a British Fantasy Society Best Newcomer award in 2017. He likes to look at the darker side of life and sometimes writes down what he sees. His short stories can be found throughout various anthologies. In the humdrum of everyday life, Phil lives with an understanding wife and a trio of vagrant cats who tolerate their human slaves. There are no bodies buried beneath the patio as far as he is aware. http://insearchofperdition.blogspot.co.uk

Peter Sutton has a not-so secret lair in the wilds of Fishponds, Bristol, and dreams up stories, many of which are about magpies. He's had stuff published online and in book form, including a short story collection called *A Tiding of Magpies* (shortlisted for the British Fantasy Award 2017) and the novel *Sick City Syndrome*. His new novel *Seven Deadly Swords* is from Grimbold Books. Peter is a member of the North Bristol Writers. https://petewsutton.com

THE EDITORS

Peter Coleborn created the award-winning Alchemy Press in the late 1990s and has since (co)-published a range of anthologies and collections. He has edited various publications for the British Fantasy Society (including *Winter Chills/Chills* and *Dark Horizons*) and co-edited with Pauline E Dungate the Joel Lane tribute anthology *Something Remains* in 2016. Besides editing and publishing he mucks around with Photoshop a lot. www.alchemypress.co.uk

Jan Edwards is an editor of anthologies for The Alchemy Press, the British Fantasy Society, Fox Spirit and others. Her short fiction has appeared in many crime, horror and fantasy anthologies. Some of those tales have been collected in

Leinster Gardens and Other Subtleties and *Fables and Fabrications*. Her novels include *Sussex Tales* and *Winter Downs* (Bunch Courtney book one, and winner of the Arnold Bennett Book Prize). She is also a recipient of the BFS Karl Edward Wagner Award.
http://janedwardsblog.wordpress.com

NEW FROM THE ALCHEMY PRESS

COMPROMISING THE TRUTH

By

Bryn Fortey

"We, well, Izzy Abelman and I, long ago decided that this place must probably be a hotel; a large one mind, the size of a small planet, with guests coming and going at a fair old rate of knots. Izzy and I, however, seem to be permanent fixtures, not having moved on from the day we arrived. Some only stay a day or two, and we don't even learn their names, while others hang around for up to a month or so, or sometimes even longer."

Here are eighteen stories and several poems showcasing the amazing talents of this Welsh Wizard.

With an introduction by Adrian Cole.

Available 2018 from The Alchemy Press
in print and eBook editions.